DAUGHTER OF THE GODS

A NOVEL OF THE PICTS

BRYAN E CANTER

TELIKOS PUBLISING, LLC
STORIES THAT CHANGE THE WORLD

Daughter of the Gods: A Novel of the Picts

Published by Telikos Publishing, LLC.
Cheyenne, WY

Paperback ISBN: 978-1-7343710-5-5
Hardcover ISBN: 978–1734371-0-6-4

FICTION / Historical / Medieval

This is a work of fiction. All of the characters, organizations, and events portrayed in this novel are either products of the author's imagination or are used fictitiously.

flora's world

THE HIGHLANDS OF CALEDONIA
367 A.D.

PIT CLOICHAIRE

SCHIEHALLION

BUNRANNOCH

LOCH RANNOCH

AN DUN GAEL

FEART CHOILLE

DUN DRUMAINN

MORAIG STONE CIRCLE

FLORA'S CAVE

CRIDHMATHAIRNAOMH THE SACRED YEW

INCHESKADYNE

FEARNAN

OAK-BANK GRANNOG

LOCHTATHA

AN TOISEACH THE PLACE OF BEGINNINGS

THE PRAYING HANDS

TIGH NAM BODACH SHRINE OF THE CAILLEACH

LOCH LINNE

BLACK GLEN OF THE CROOKED STONES

KILLIN

LOCH TOILBHE

CRIDHALBANE
THE HEART OF ALBAN
367 A.D.

RIVER LINNE

DUN DRUMAINN

MORAIG STONE CIRCLE

RIVER TATHA

INCHESKADYNE

FEART CHOILLE

CRIDHMATHAIRNAOMH
THE SACRED YEW

DRUMAINN HILL

DRUID ISLAND

BLACK GLEN OF THE CROOKED STONES

AN DUN GAEL

GATEWAY STONES

LOCH TATHA

MILL HOUSE

MILLPOND

OAK-BANK CRANNOG

FLORA'S CAVE

FEARNAN

CHAPTER ONE

Scottish Highlands—367 A.D. Flora gazed across the pond at the mill house as if she were in a trance. The steady turning water wheel was the only moving thing in her view. The clear blue sky, the lush green trees, and even the mill itself reflected off the surface of the pond, giving her two different pictures of the world around her. The sun shone down, not in the intense, oppressive strength of mid-summer, but with a gentler warmth that soothed her soul. A slight breeze in the air caused small ripples on the surface of the pond, transforming the reflected image in subtle ways that made the whole scene less surreal, less abstract—more tangible and present for her.

The setting filled Flora with an uneasy sense of peace. Thinking back over the past several days threatened to push her over the edge into panic. It was a struggle to distinguish between what was real and what was... what? Fantasy? Vision? Imagination? Hallucination? Some things seemed like waking dreams—vague, cloudy, and just beyond her ability to recollect clearly. Others seemed almost perfect, perhaps even too perfect. Were they real? Did they actually happen? Even now, the memories taunted her, luring her into madness.

She focused on the scene before her. Although the mill, the grass, the trees, and the sun seemed almost too idealistic, the rippled reflection in the pond filled her with assurance that it wasn't just a fantasy of her imagination, or a vision induced by the "others" she felt stalking her just outside the periphery of her awareness. The slight distortion on the water's glassy surface confirmed that the scene above was true, and it gave Flora a small sliver of certainty to cling to. That certainty brought the first tenuous sense of calm she had experienced in the nightmare of the previous several days.

But the questions nagging at the back of her mind wouldn't leave her alone. They taunted her with unveiled malice, dragging her back toward the precipice. Where was this place? How had she gotten here? Was the memory of her village and her family true? Or were the gods playing cruel tricks on her psyche? She pressed her palms against her eyes, trying to squeeze the horrific images from her head. After several long moments, she wiped the wetness from the corners of her eyes and forced her attention back to her present situation.

Flora focused on the turning water wheel. Its steady, rhythmic chant helped buoy her spirits ever so slightly. Inside, the millstone turned just as steadily to grind kernels of grain into the fine powder she had so often used to make oatcakes or bread or chowder broth. There was certainty in the connection between the turning wheel and the stone and the grain that nourished. They were real, tangible things that linked together in a real, tangible world. She clung to that surety, like a drowning man clings to a piece of debris from a wrecked boat. She gazed at the water wheel. Swoosh. Swoosh. Lap. Lap. Steady. Certain. Real.

Then a subtle uneasiness crept up Flora's spine. She felt the sense of peace begin to sink away into a pit of growing blackness. Something was wrong. Something wasn't right with... with what? With the sky? With the sunshine? With the breeze? With the ripples on the pond? No. The water wheel lapped steadily onward. The water wheel. The water. The churn. The splash.

There was no splash!

The water made no splash when it dropped from the wheel into the pond. There was no splash. There was no wake. There were no waves to disturb the ripples in the pond or to distort the reflected image of the sky.

Panic and dread engulfed her in a torrent of fear, and her certainty was dashed upon the rocks, like waves crashing against the *Yesnabi* cliffs. It was too perfect. It was not perfect enough. It wasn't real after all.

She felt their presence closing in on her—the "others." What were they doing to her? Why was this happening? She buried her face in her hands and began to weep.

Amid the tears of desperation, a voice rang out in her head. It was a strong, powerful voice—one unlike the gentle breeze—a voice filled with the authority to command. "Run!"

The voice broke through her sobs. It broke through her hysteria. It compelled her to action. She leapt to her feet, turned her back to the pond, and ran. She didn't know where she would go. She just ran.

FLORA INSTINCTIVELY BEGAN to kick the deerskin *brogan* from her feet as she raced across the soft grass of the glen, but changed her mind as she neared the heath row at the edge of the forest. She would need her shoes if she was going to escape into the woods. Frantically, she searched for a path through the thick brush, but could find none. Compelled by fear and by echoes of the potent command to flee, she forced her way into the briars and brambles that clawed at her thin woolen *leine* and threatened to drag her to the ground.

Hastily, she glanced back to see if she could locate either her pursuers or the source of the voice that had shocked her into motion. She longed to see him there, imposing himself between her and her stalkers, but no form emerged to claim the voice. She desperately wanted help. She needed someone to intercede for her. She needed a rescuer.

Flora pushed her way through the hedges until a blockade of

branches forced her to a standstill. She yanked at the leather thong around her neck, pulling out the small flint knife she always carried, and hacked at the brush with the little blade in a desperate effort to break through. Scrapes and cuts emerged on her wrists and forearms, trickling small trails of blood across her otherwise smooth, olive skin. The gorse of the highland countryside was beautiful to behold on a bright spring day, but it hid a menace of barbs and thorns that came to bear if you ever chose to cross its path.

Bit by bit she fought her way through the matted mass of gnarled limbs, while the menace behind her drew steadily nearer. With a final scream of frustration, Flora tore upward with the knife and heaved her shoulder through the last layer of underbrush, stumbling into the forest beyond.

At last she was free to run, to separate herself from the nightmare behind. Under the canopy of trees, the briars and brambles of the heath gave way to a carpet of moss that was soft under her feet. Again she thought of shedding her *brogan* shoes, but despaired of the time she had already lost tearing her way through the thicket.

She ran and ran, deeper into the forest, deeper into the protective shelter that concealed her from the piercing eyes watching her from the shadows and the whispering winds that planted illusions in her mind. Shafts of flickering light danced across her path, making the woods before her shift and sway. She stumbled on a loose rock, then regained her footing and continued to run.

Her lungs burned. Her steps faltered. Her head swam. She wasn't a fighter like the women who drilled for battle alongside the warriors of her clan. Nor was she a hunter who scouted in the forests and the glens. She was a healer. She hadn't trained to fight and run and flee.

Though panic pushed her forward, exhaustion dragged her down. Instead of leaping deftly across a soft carpet of ferns, she felt like her feet were mired in the mud of the Imleach Bog.

Sunshine broke through the dim forest at a broad clearing ahead, creating an oasis of grass and small flowers that beckoned her to lie down and rest. But she couldn't stop. She couldn't quit now. She couldn't give in. She diverted to the left and skirted the edge of the meadow. As she rounded the far end, she glanced back across the open field to see if she could catch a glimpse of her pursuers. All she saw was the warm sun and a cloudless sky and treetops swaying in the gentle breeze.

Flora slowed her flight and came to a stop. She bent at the waist and hugged herself tightly as she gasped for air. She trembled all over. Her vision had blurred and narrowed to a dark tunnel, and now it flashed slightly to the rhythm of her heart. She sank to her knees and wept.

Was anyone actually chasing her at all? Were the "others" even real? Had the scene at the millpond truly been an illusion?

And what about the voice? It had seemed powerful and confident and forceful. She felt like it had come from outside of her, but from somewhere nearby—not like a phantom she had heard only in her head. But where was the man who issued the command? Where was the laird of the voice? She had searched for him and had seen no one. Did it really happen? Did she actually hear anything at all?

Her head spun and her mind reeled, partly from her frenzied run, but mostly from the torrent of questions and fears that raged through her thoughts. Was she going mad? Was she mad already? Tears streamed down her face as she listened to the silence of the peaceful day that enveloped her in its stillness. There was no real threat after all.

Then she heard it again—the voice calling to her from behind, pressing, but not urgent. "Look," it instructed her.

She spun to see who was there, but the willows and oaks were all alone. Her pulse quickened. She wasn't mad. The voice was real. She felt its presence, but wasn't afraid. There was no menace in its tone, but rather something like a compassionate insistence.

It urged her to look. Look where? Look at what? She peered around and saw nothing of significance. The trees stood as still as sentinels, the gentle movements of their branches and leaves causing a shimmering glow of light to play across the forest floor. She saw nor heard nothing else at all. No little critters scurrying among the ferns. No squirrels playing in the trees. No ground hogs poking up their heads to listen and chew. No deer grazing in the meadow. No crickets chirping in the warmth of the day. She glanced up at the sky and saw no birds gliding on unseen waves of air. Everything was perfectly still.

Then she caught a glimpse of something moving in the distance. It was odd, like a dark cloud that snaked up from the ground, morphing and moving and surging forward. It wasn't smoke. It pulsed and writhed like something alive. Slowly it grew deeper and darker as it wormed its way steadily closer.

Flora sat mesmerized as she began to suspect what the cloud might be. Then, far off in the distance, she heard faint noises that came along with the strange moving fog. It sounded a bit like rain, or rather like hail that plinked instead of splashed. And a constant, low hum throbbed in the background.

As the cloud edged closer, ever churning and flowing, the noise became louder and more distinct. The crass, raspy rain fell heavier and heavier, and the hum swelled to a steady, monotonous roar that completely drowned out the normal melody of the forest.

Flora heard the voice again, and it snapped her out of her stupor with just two words, "Go. Now." Without glancing back to see where the command had come from, Flora nodded her head and rose. The momentary respite that had set her at ease was broken, and she turned to flee once again. This time, however, the menace was not the obscure, sinister "others" who lurked just beyond the edge of her sanity. This time the threat was a very tangible one which she had experienced before. The swarming cloud of locusts pulsed directly toward her, devouring everything in its path.

Breath not yet regained, legs still limp, head still swooning, Flora forced herself onward and ran.

FLORA HEADED AWAY from the clearing, away from the millpond, away from the memories and illusions and false hopes that had lured her into a deceptive sense of safety. As she ran, her mind envisioned the swarming mass of frenzied teeth, like hundreds of tiny flint knives, tearing through the hedge, just as she had done moments ago. The swarm was like her in its intensity and desperation. But it was unlike her in its purpose and its ends. She had cut a tiny wound across the heath's embracing arms in order to win her freedom—a wound that in days would leave behind an almost invisible scar. The locust swarm, on the other hand, would descend on the hedge in a vicious onslaught to consume and destroy. Every leaf, every blossom, every hidden thorn would be shredded and gnawed, until it disappeared into a misty dust beneath grasping claws and beating wings.

But they wouldn't stop at the heath row. They would march relentlessly forward like a mighty and terrible Roman army—soldiers pressed shoulder to shoulder, with armored breasts deflecting every barb and thorn, walls of shields battering down gnarled branches, swords slicing through trunks and limbs, and spears piercing to the very heart of the forest. There would be no mercy, no remorse. Not for heath or gorse or briar or thorn. Not for oak or pine or moss or fern. Not for wolf or fox or squirrel or fawn. And not for a young girl cowering in fear.

She wondered what caused the sudden, unnatural change in these tiny creatures. Alone, in normal times, they were harmless little green hoppers that blended into the leaves of the trees, as if they were just part of the foliage, nibbling bits around the edges and causing no real harm. But when they swarmed, the transformation was instant and horrifying. They morphed into savage beasts of black and bronze that massed together to terrorize and destroy. What sinister deception caused this change? What madness drove them to this frenzy?

Flora ran in panic and without direction. Where could she go? Where could she find refuge from the mindless horde that threatened to trample her down and leave her lying battered and broken in the midst of a barren land?

Water! She had to find water—a spring or a brook or a pond. Water was the only thing the horrible little beasts feared—as if it would rust their armor or drown their thirst for blood. But she didn't know where to find it. This wasn't her home forest on the shores of *Loch Rannoch*. She didn't know these woods.

The millpond? No! She had no way to double back. The army of locusts stood like an impenetrable wall between her and that pond. And her sense of dread from the vision she'd experienced there left her cold. The "others" had lured her to that pond, and she would not walk back into their trap.

Flora froze. Maybe that was it. Maybe this swarm of locusts *was* the trap. Had the villains in her mind enticed her to seek refuge in the pond's serenity so this swarming horde would ravage her? The thought caused her to shudder, but she had no time to consider what the idea implied. She had to move. She had to find water, and she had to find it now.

Flora paused in her flight to survey her surroundings. Where could she find the safe haven of water she so desperately needed? A steep hill rose to her left. The forest wrapped around that hill and sloped gently downward to her right. Water had to be down there somewhere. There had to be a stream that fed into the millpond behind her. She prayed to the gods for the stream to be on this side of the glen and not the far side across the pond. She tried to listen for the roaring of a falls, or the raging of rapids, or even the gurgling of a brook. But the pounding in her head and the menacing thunder of the swarm drowned out every other noise. With only instinct to guide her she turned to flee down the gentle slope.

Then she heard it again—the voice in her head that had urged her onward each time. Again, it uttered only a single word. "Up."

Flora stopped running. There couldn't be water up there. It wasn't possible. And even if there was a small creek or stream, it couldn't be deep enough to protect her from the swarm. If there was a river, surely she would hear the rushing water as it plunged down the steep rocky incline.

Indecision tore at her mind. She didn't have time for this. She needed to move, now! She looked up the steep slope to her left. It loomed tall and rocky and menacing. She couldn't do it. She didn't have the strength in her muscles or the breath in her lungs to climb that hill.

How could she place her very life in the hands of a disembodied voice that echoed in the recesses of her mind—a mind that stood at the precipice of a chaotic abyss and groped in the darkness for a hold on sanity? She couldn't do it. She had to trust her instincts. She had to find the water at the bottom of the draw.

She turned back to her right and began to take a step.

"Trust me."

She hesitated, then stopped. She didn't even bother looking for the source of the sound. She knew she wouldn't see anyone there. Running her hands through her hair and gripping her temples with her palms, she tried to squeeze away the pain and frustration in her head.

Overwhelmed, she turned her tears to the sky and cried out, "Why?" Her voice trailed off to a sob. "Why should I trust you?" It was barely a whisper.

Even more than the terror of being ravaged by the swarm, even deeper than the dread of losing her grip on reason, Flora feared being forever alone. She needed someone, anyone, whom she could call a friend. And right now, that voice in the wind was the only friend she had. She turned toward the hill and started to climb.

FLORA TRIED DESPERATELY to scramble up the slope. Within just a few steps it became so steep she had to use her hands, grabbing for trees, or roots, or rocks—anything to help pull her way upward. She was reaching the point of exhaustion, with only desperation and panic driving her forward.

The hillside was carpeted with dead leaves and pine needles that formed a deceptive foundation for her feet, at once acting like soft steps which would support her weight, but then giving way suddenly, dropping her to her knees. For every five steps she moved forward, she would slide back two or three.

She reached out, clutching at a small tree to hoist herself up, but the trunk, rotten and mushy in her grasp, gave way. She plunged, clawing and grasping at dirt and rocks and anything else within reach of her arms, until she slid down at least half the length of the distance she had climbed. She buried her face in the pine straw and whimpered. She couldn't do it. She could not force her way up the hill. She simply had nothing left.

Flora felt a small thump on the back of her leg. She looked around and stared at the evil iron mask glaring back at her. The bug's eyes shimmered in the light, like gems with a thousand tiny facets. Its mandibles worked back and forth as it gnawed on the last remnants of a leafy stem, taunting her with the menace of what was yet to come. It sank its claws into the soft wool of her *leine*, and began climbing up her leg, its spindly, segmented limbs lifting and reaching and pushing with a facility that mocked her own awkward struggle up the hill.

Flora snarled. Her hand lashed out, and she smashed her open palm down on top of the locust, squashing its life into a smear on the back of her dress. She would not quit! She would not lie here and be eaten alive by a frenzied horde of little demonic fiends that would ravage the countryside, killing every living thing, just to die, themselves, within a month. Their only purpose was to destroy, but she would not become part of the desolation left behind.

Flora forced herself to get up and start climbing again. The dead locust that fell from her shift in a jumbled mass of broken wings and mangled legs was just part of the foremost ranks of the vanguard. The rest of the army was coming fast, and she had to press on up the hill.

Between repeated bouts of reaching, grasping, sliding, and

falling, Flora constantly agonized about whether she had made the right decision to climb the daunting crag. Instinctively, she knew that finding water was her best chance to survive, and the best possibility of water was most definitely down, not up.

Why had she listened to that voice? Had she, indeed, actually even heard it at all? Or was it just a phantom conjured up by her desperate imagination? Even worse, was the voice, itself, another sinister strand in the devious web woven by the "others?" Had they calculated her reactions and created the voice to give her a false hope that would be dashed against the rocks of this hill or swallowed up by a torrent of voracious insects? Was the swarm even real? Or was that menace also just part of a grand delusion?

No. She had felt the little demon locust fall on her leg and climb up her dress. She had felt its body crush beneath her terrified blow. She glanced down to see its remains, now a brownish-red stain on the wool of her *leine*. She didn't have time for this! Whatever had prompted her to trust the voice and to scale the hill didn't matter any more. It was too late to turn back. The moment she began to climb, her fate was set. She couldn't do anything now except follow it through. And that meant she had to press forward, ignoring the pounding in her head, the burning in her lungs, the aching in her legs, and the gnawing in her gut.

Flora broke out of the trees onto a rocky knoll where she could see the devastating progress of the swarm. The leading edge of the army marked a distinct wavy line across the vegetation of the forest. The land behind it was completely barren. It wasn't brown, like dormant grass in the winter. It wasn't black, like a woodland scorched by fire. It was a mixture of deep ochres, dark grays, and light tans, like the shaving ground back home where archers stripped leaves and bark from branches to shape their shafts. Only in this case, the land itself was being stripped to its very bones, and the line of advance was moving steadily upward.

Her whole clan, with their stone axes and bronze blades, would have taken many days to do what this horde of insects had done in the time it took to bake a loaf of bread. Even the Roman armies, with their iron swords, flaming arrows, and massive war machines did not so completely ravish the land. The line kept advancing steadily across the forest and up the hill, seemingly unencumbered by the slope as she had been.

Flora looked down the hill and across the valley to the millpond. The locusts had stripped away the carpet of grass from the glen and the rich green leaves of the trees she had been gazing at such a short time ago. The mass of the swarm formed a black, writhing cloud that blotted out the sun and cast a haze over the once blue sky.

The mill house still stood, with the waterwheel tuning endlessly, as if oblivious to the horror occurring all around it. Of course, it was that very same waterwheel which had so recently shattered her moment of peace and sent her fleeing from the glen. Perhaps its illusion persisted even amidst this storm. Every vestige of serenity from the scene at the millpond had fled with her in the wake of the coming siege.

Across the valley, on the adjacent hillside, Flora could barely make out a solitary patch of green amid the destruction. It was too far away for her to see clearly. She could not even discern its nature. How anything could have survived the onslaught of the swarm was beyond her imagination. Perhaps it wasn't real either. But it gave her a momentary sense of hope she could survive as well.

All these thoughts swept through her mind in the moment between two breaths as the waves of panic ebbed and crashed. She turned and left the rocky knoll behind. She scrambled around the edge of the hill to put more distance between herself and the swarm and to find the watery refuge she so desperately needed.

FLORA SKIRTED the edge of another rocky outcropping and came to an abrupt halt. The back side of the hill was a steep cliff. A jagged

CHAPTER TWO

Tiny raindrops fell on Flora's face and roused her from sleep. She propped herself up on one arm and stretched, struggling to remember where she was. She had that groggy, but somehow refreshing feeling she'd get when waking up in a grassy meadow on a cool spring day with a slight breeze ruffling her *leine* and causing wisps of hair to dance across her face.

She looked down, seeing the bag of herbs she had been collecting for Nandag, her *bean-teagaisg*—her mentor—who was teaching her the art of healing back in her village. Nandag had sent her to gather wild garlic, ivy, cowslip, harts tongue, and marjoram from the spring growth in the forests and glens. She had been successful in her quest and her sack was full of the leaves, flowers, roots, and berries they would use to prepare all manner of tonics, poultices, and other soothing balms.

Flora glanced up at the sky to see thunderclouds darkening the horizon. Rain was a perpetual part of the highlands' landscape. It was the lifeblood of the land. It caused her healing herbs to grow. It filled the sacred pools and springs with water from the heavens that mingled with waters from the earth to form a holy union. Flora liked to think of raindrops as the tears of the goddess Brigid when she sang a keening song to a tune her father, the Dagda, strummed on *Uaithne*, his enchanted oaken harp. But, for now, she would be drowned in those tears if she didn't get back to her village soon.

Flora never dreamed she would be out this long or wander so far in her search to fill the flaxen sack with herbs. She had been lured steadily onward by the abundant produce of nature and spring—a patch of harts tongue blossoming in the glen, sprigs of garlic hiding among the grass, and fresh ivy leaves creeping up the trunks of trees. Time had flittered by like a meadow pipit dancing in the wind.

And then there was that little nap in the meadow. How long had she slept there, anyway, basking in the rare afternoon sunshine? For that matter, how exactly had she fallen asleep to begin with? That bit was somewhat of a blur. But then again, she was still halfway immersed in the hazy fog that lingered at the edge of wakefulness.

She remembered bending down to pull up a yellow clump of cowslip near the edge of the forest. And then, oh yes, she'd been stung or bitten by some kind of little pest. Her hand unconsciously reached for the spot on the back of her neck where the recent bite was still tender. That was no big problem. Her arms and legs had provided a satisfying meal to more little vermin than she could count, and she had the welts to prove it. No matter, a garlic poultice would soothe away the itches and sores as soon as she got home. But the moments between harvesting the cowslip and waking in the meadow seemed to have slipped into the deep waters of nearby Loch Rannoch.

She would consider it more later. Right now, she needed to get home. Judging from the angry skies, she would pay for her afternoon slumber with a good drenching. Her village was a fair pace away and the heavy rains would certainly not hold off until the sun set. She grabbed up her sack, gathered her *leine* about her waist, and began the long walk home.

Flora headed down the hillside and picked up the pathway that followed the shore of the loch. She was making good progress and the storm seemed to be moving slowly. Perhaps she could make it back before the downpour began. She had neglected to bring a cloak when she left home that morning under sunny spring skies. She should have known better. Rain was never far away in the highlands, and the spring rains brought a chill that often had a fever trailing in its wake.

She had seen the fever kill more than once during her apprenticeship as a healer. It was a slow, painful, agonizing process. Sometimes Nandag could turn the fever with a complex combination of herbs and bleeding and sacred rituals. But there were far too many times when her arts and incantations could not prevail against the powerful spirits that burned like fire from the inside and consumed the soul.

Flora wondered why the gods would so often wrap blessings and curses together in the same package. The rains that caused the herbs and crops to grow could also bring sickness and death, and the potions and balms that Nandag used to heal could also be mixed to kill.

She kept her eyes on the rocky path, being careful not to take a misstep and turn an ankle in her haste to get home. As she continued her musings about the vagaries of the gods, she began to sense that something wasn't quite right. She stopped to check her progress and looked off in the direction of her village. At first the thick black smoke was lost amid the backdrop of the darkening thunderclouds. But then its upward march to the sky swirled into focus with horrifying portents. Flora felt the dread churn and gnaw within her gut as it morphed into full-fledged panic. The bag of herbs slipped from her grasp and she began to run.

Flora raced through a hazy tunnel, her mind fixed on the rising column of smoke. Her vision was blurred, not by Brigid's tears falling from the sky as drops of rain, but from a stinging wetness that that welled up from within her own eyes.

The column of smoke was definitely coming from her village. Though it was still too far away to see any flames, she knew the truth with a crushing certainty that bore down upon her with the weight of a millstone, grinding her like a kernel of wheat.

The storm was too far away for lightning to have ignited the blaze. Only a human enemy could have started so large a fire. But who could it be? And how had they made it past the warriors of her clan to set the huts ablaze? Her father had told stories of long ago when her people had warred almost constantly with the *Maetae*, the *Selgovae*, and the *Votadini*. But there had been no fighting between the tribes for almost as long as anyone could remember. They had long since banded together against their one common enemy.

Then the horrifying truth slammed into her like a blow from the mighty hand of Jhebbal Sag, the god of darkness and fear. It was the Romans. It couldn't be anything else. A desperate prayer escaped from her lips, "Oh Dagda, mighty protector, rescue my family."

Endless stories of Roman slaughter leapt to her mind. She had never seen them herself, but the tales were rampant among the people of the highlands and lowlands alike. Roman armies very seldom marched north of the wall. But when they did come, they left a wake of devastation and carnage across the land, destroying everything in their path.

Horrific visions overpowered her mind—images of countless rows of brutal, faceless men with iron helmets and leather breastplates battering mothers and children with enormous shields and ripping through men with gleaming swords. She imagined the evil soldiers ravaging her people, slaughtering the animals, and hurling torches onto the thatched roofs of the huts. A strangled cry erupted from her throat, only to be swept away in the wind.

"*Mamaidh! Dadaidh!*" Flora screamed for her mother and father, as she stumbled her way up the hill toward her village and toward the menacing plume of smoke. "Oh, Dagda, please! Please let my family be safe."

Surely her older sister, Searlaid, would have carried young Catriona into the woods to hide. Her instincts and training as a hunter would keep them both safe. Catriona, so young and so innocent, should never be forced to see such horror, to hear such wails, to experience such fear, or to feel such pain. Flora imagined what would happen if they failed to escape, and she fell to her knees, retching. Her stomach heaved and spittle dripped from her mouth, mingling with her tears.

She drew in another breath and gasped as her mind spun with implications of the attack. Domhnull! Her *suirgheach*, her betrothed, would not have run in fear. The memory of his strong arms carrying her through the rain-soaked forest filled Flora with a certainty that those same powerful arms, buoyed by a fierce, stubborn pride, would stand like a mighty stone against any invaders, even if he stood alone.

But how could anyone prevail against such a menace? She could see him facing them down, stout and fierce as a highland bull with its red mane fluttering in the breeze, flanked by a score of blue-painted warriors on either side, axes and spears raised in stern defiance. But the men of a single village, no matter how bold, could not withstand the iron beast of Rome.

She envisioned her soul mate raked with claws, impaled on horns, and trodden under the iron-shod sandals of a hundred feet. "Nooo!" Her agonized cry floated up to mingle with the rising smoke and to disappear in a hazy amalgamation of dismay and remorse.

A deep ache throbbed in her chest, fueled by anguish and fear—all from the dread of things she had yet to see. She shook her head to clear her mind of the devastating images. Lightning from the storm flashed across the sky, and a glimmer of hope sparked in Flora's mind.

She had a habit of always imagining the worst. Perhaps it was something else entirely. Perhaps there was no enemy assault after all. Maybe her kinsmen were clearing another section of trees to create a new pasture for more of the village's cattle and sheep.

Daring to believe for just a moment, Flora pushed herself up and stood. She took a few tentative steps up the hill and then broke into a run. It was going to be okay! It was going to be alright after all!

As she crested the hill, the scene before her slammed into her gut like a caber, wrenching her breath away and driving her to her knees.

The flames licking up from every roof and the mass of bodies lying in tangled heaps across the ground told her that the horrible truth was far worse than her darkest fears. A scream erupted from deep within her soul.

Flora awoke with a start and cracked her head on something very hard. She winced in pain and her hand shot up to rub her throbbing head. Her knuckles banged against rough stone.

She groped about, frantically trying to remember where she was. A little light trickled in from an opening just a few paces away. A cavern! She was in a cavern. Her breath came in shallow gasps and she shuddered with every movement. The panic and terror from her dream overflowed into the waking world as she linked the recent tragedy to her present plight.

They were gone! Her family was gone. Her friends were slaughtered. Her village was destroyed. She was completely alone. Their faces cried out to her from the nightmare, hands reaching out to her as if groping for salvation. What could she have done? Flora physically drew away from the grasping hands in her mind and banged her head on the stone ceiling once again. "*Mac an donais!*" This time she felt a sticky wetness when she rubbed the sore spot with her hand.

The flames from the burning huts raged across her mind, devouring everything she held dear. She could still hear the fire's roar and smell the acrid smoke, as if yesterday's horror continued to smolder. Was it yesterday, or a full moon ago? How long had she been running? A day? Two days? A whole turn of the moon? Smoke filled her lungs and she began to cough.

Suddenly Flora's attention snapped into sharp focus. The sound of the fire, the smell of the smoke—it wasn't just from her nightmares. All at once she remembered where she was. She recalled the millpond, the "others," the locust swarm, and the mysterious voice that had guided her to safety. Though she had just relived the horror of fire destroying her village, the memory had been a dream. And yet, a hazy cloud was drifting into the cavern, and a dull roar reverberated beyond its gaping mouth.

Flora edged her way toward the cavern's opening, crawling on hands and knees, wincing with the sharp pain in her right leg. Peering out, she half expected to see the locust swarm snaking its way back up the hill to finish the job it had left undone. What she saw was worse, much worse. The forest was an inferno. The land was ablaze in every direction as far as she could see.

Flora froze at the sight. For several moments, the flaming trees mingled with the memories of her village and made that vision spring to life again, resurrecting the terror she had felt when she first peered over the hill. She stood and ran into the village. She had to see if anyone was alive. She had to help the wounded and dying. She was a healer, and the instinct to offer aid was powerful within her, drowning her own personal fears in a compelling need to save her injured people.

Flora stumbled forward, tripped over a stone, and fell to the ground. Sharp pain screamed through her right knee from where she had banged it during her flight from the locusts. She rolled to her back and hugged her shin to her chest, willing her knee to quit throbbing. The fall jerked her mind out of her nightmare and back to the present. She found herself lying at the far edge of the rocky crag with flames licking up from short, scrubby pine trees a dozen paces away.

Flora's head spun. What was happening to her? Why was she having such trouble separating past from present, fantasy from reality, vision from sight? Had she actually run into the village at all? Had anyone been alive? Or was everyone dead, lying in the tangled mass of bodies she saw from the top of the hill? Were the faces calling out to her and the hands reaching for help a genuine memory, or merely a figment of her imagination? Where had the Roman soldiers been? Who had set the village ablaze? Flora pressed her palms against her closed eyes, trying to squeeze the visions from her mind and to make sense out of the chaos.

She coughed again and remembered the fire burning all around her. She had to run. She had to find somewhere safe. But as she looked around, she realized there was nowhere to go.

Then, as a new surge of panic broke against her mind, like the waves of Loch Rannoch crashing against the Raven's Beak in a storm, she realized the blaze had stopped climbing up her little hill. For a spear throw in every direction, there was nothing to burn. The fire, like the locust swarm, found nothing to consume on her rocky crag, so it checked its upward advance and spread around her refuge to form a blazing wall.

Though the flames could not progress across the bare rock, searing heat clawed at her from every side, and smoke billowed thick across the ground, shrouding the hilltop in a dense, noxious cloud. Flora coughed with a deep, raspy wheeze that swelled and grew into a continuous stream of uncontrollable spasms.

She couldn't stay here. She had to go somewhere. But where? There was no place to flee. The conflagration surrounded her in every direction.

As Flora staggered and turned, peering to find a way through the haze, something shot through the smoke and raked across her arm, ripping three parallel tears in her sleeve that immediately began to seep with red ooze. Flora screamed and dropped to the ground. She turned to face a menacing scowl, with spiked fur rising above folded ears behind a gaping spread of gleaming white teeth. She stared, unblinking, into the golden eyes of the highland wildcat for a dozen raging heartbeats, and neither moved. They lingered in a tense, frozen dance of determination and fear, willing the other to yield. A deep ominous growl rumbled from somewhere deep within the beast. Then it hissed angrily and shot away into the smoke.

Flora flinched and tried to take a deep breath to settle her nerves, but just ended up coughing again. The terrified cat was simply fleeing from the fire, just like she was. How many other helpless

animals had been trapped by the inferno without any way of escape?
Her heart sank as unbidden images leapt to her mind of terrified deer
bounding across one wall of flame to land in the midst of another, and
of baby meadow pipits screaming for their mother as the blaze
consumed the nest beneath them. She wondered how she, herself,
would ever survive.

As she stared after the wildcat's retreating form, she noticed a
plume of smoke billowing up in a strange column. That was odd.
What would cause that kind of stir in the smoke? Perhaps it was a
signal from the gods that would lead her to safety. Then again, maybe
it was a powerful gout of flame that Arawn had hurled from the
underworld to feed the raging firestorm. She wasn't sure how wise it
would be to chase after a panicked highland wildcat, but then she
recalled that animals often had a keen sense of self-preservation
which ran contrary to her own intuition.

She had been totally disoriented ever since she woke from the
nightmare, and she was now thoroughly lost amid the thickening
haze. As she cautiously scrambled over rocks, wincing in pain with
every movement of her knee, she gradually approached the odd
plume of smoke. Her eyes stung and she coughed almost
continuously.

Then, suddenly, she realized she was back at the mouth of the
small cavern where she had recently sought shelter from the swarm.
A fresh, cool, almost imperceptible breeze blew out of the cave,
causing the smoke to ripple against its natural tide. Warily, she
crept into the cleft in the rock, expecting to be ravished by the
wildcat. But it was nowhere to be seen. Perhaps it had run deeper
into the bowels of the protective lair. In any case, Flora had no
viable alternatives, so she crawled farther in and collapsed onto the
floor.

She was finally able to take a few full breaths. The smoke still
swirled around the interior of the cave, but was considerably less
dense than the noxious haze outside. And the cool dampness of the
cave helped to hold the fire's intense heat at bay. Flora felt like she

was encased inside a fragile bubble that could burst at any moment, dumping her back into the midst of the tumult.

When she had first entered the cavern last night, she didn't think it was very large. But now, she could vaguely perceive a room tall enough for her to stand up in just beyond the narrow neck that led outside. She couldn't see well enough to go any father, but was thankful for the comparatively fresh air, and was not inclined to even think about what other creatures or menacing dangers lay hidden within its depths. For now, she would sit just within the narrow opening where she found her only refuge from the heat of the flames and their noxious fumes.

FLORA LEANED back against the stone wall with her knees curled close into her chest. She pressed her palms hard against her temples and wept. She was alive, but everything else had been ripped away from her. Her village was destroyed. Her family had been killed. Everyone in her clan was gone. Locusts had stripped the countryside of every green leaf. And now a raging fire was reducing everything else to ash. Her whole tribe would surely perish in this blaze.

She cringed and shrunk back within herself. What was she thinking? This wasn't even her home forest. She wasn't in the hills around Loch Rannoch. She didn't really know where she was or even how she had gotten here. So maybe the rest of her clan was safe. Then again, something about this area seemed vaguely familiar, as if from an early childhood memory or a distant dream. From her vantage point on the hillside it had seemed as if the whole countryside was ablaze. How could anyone from her tribe survive? Could anyone from any tribe survive this horror? Flora's hopes were consumed by the raging flames and disappeared like wisps of mist in the rising smoke. She was all alone.

She thought about the "others" who had stalked her as she fled from the carnage at her village. Had they survived this conflagration?

Or was the blaze, itself, part of their grand design? Were they deep inside the cave watching her every move and manipulating every step?

Images flashed briefly in her mind of owl feathers, bear claws, bald heads, and blue painted faces—and of flames from torches, licking and dancing. Those flames! Were those torches used to ignite the very fires of the underworld in a final, terrible tribute to Biel? Was this some gross, demented aberration of the feast of Beltane that had set the whole land ablaze? Something inside her rejected the notion. She felt a powerful menace from the "others," but it seemed like it was personal and focused on her. She knew they were stalking her, hunting her, deluding her thoughts, and deceiving her mind. But she sensed, somehow, that they had not destroyed her village or started this fire. Yet if not them, then who?

The Romans! She hated the Romans! The fire burning outside was like a smoldering torch compared to the inferno that seared through her mind at the thought of the detestable monster of Rome. Their armies tore through the countryside, killing men, raping women, desecrating shrines, destroying homes, and devastating the forests. To what end? What purpose could possibly drive them to commit such atrocities? Did it satisfy some savage instinct to destroy? Was it all just some primal lust for power—power to annihilate people and to ruin the land? Over what could they exercise their power and control if everyone was killed and all the villages were obliterated? Their empire would consist of a barren desert, bereft of people and devoid of crops and herds.

Why did the gods allow this atrocity? Why didn't they intervene on behalf of the clans? Where was the Dagda with his mighty club to smite the invaders and protect his people? Why hadn't Teutates roused the clans to victory in war? Hadn't Flora's tribe been faithful in their sacrifices? Had they not honored the gods with their feasts and festivals? Or were the Roman gods more powerful than the gods of the highlands? No! That couldn't be! Yes, the Romans *were* as numerous as the gnats that filled the glens in the summertime, and yes, they had powerful war machines and great iron weapons. But no people in the world were more fierce or courageous than the highland warriors, and no gods were mightier than the highland gods.

Flora's thoughts returned to the mysterious voice that had called to her at the millpond, and a chill rippled across her arms and back. The voice had prompted her to flee even before any danger had appeared. It had impelled her onward when she thought she had nothing left to give. It had invited her to trust when all her instincts screamed at her to run in fear. And the voice had led her here, to this cavern, which had turned out to be both a sanctuary from the locust swarm and a safe haven from the raging fire.

But where did the voice come from? Who could it belong to? Was it all just in her imagination? No. If she was making up a voice in her head, it would undoubtedly have told her what she wanted to hear. But this voice had urged her—had compelled her—to forsake her instincts and to eschew her best judgment. It told her to climb *up* when every fiber of her being cried out for her to run *down*. It seemed to have come from outside of her. She heard it like she heard any other sound. But every time she had turned to see who had spoken, there was no one there.

Flora pulled at her hair in exasperation. "Who are you?" she cried, and was suddenly startled at the sound of her own voice. But only the roar of the fire and the silence of the cavern replied.

The voice had seemed to be friendly, as if it wanted to help her. But if it wanted to help, then where was it now? Had the owner of the voice also perished in the blaze? Somehow, she thought not. Well, if that was true, then he—it was a male voice—must also be hidden in the cave. There was nowhere else to escape from the fire. If he was, indeed, a friend, why didn't he reveal himself? Why didn't he come to her now?

"Aaahhh!" Flora again wailed in frustration. She was alone in a tiny cave in the middle of a desolate land. Even the voice had left her now. No one would come to her rescue.

Flora sat staring mindlessly at the cavern wall. Through the dense haze of smoke, she vaguely sensed the sun arc across the sky and fade behind the rising mountains. She reached within a fold of her *leine* and took out a small leather pouch. Aside from her little flint knife, the bag held her only remaining possessions. She tugged at the leather drawstring and pried open the mouth of the small sack. Inside, it held the most important things to her in all the world. She kept them hidden away in the little bag and carried them with her wherever she went. There was nothing of any real value to anyone else, but the contents were precious to her—gems in a world of fading memories.

As her fingers fumbled through the items in the pouch, they encountered a soft fuzzy lump. Then something sharp jabbed her hand, making it twitch and recoil slightly. With more care, she gently grasped the tangled knot and pulled it from the sack. It was a small gnarled mass of thorns from a gorse bush, matted with a clump of white wool.

Tears pricked at Flora's eyes as she remembered her lambkin, Caora. Even though many summers had passed, the memory was still coarse and raw. When Caora's mother was giving birth, he had gotten stuck. Normally a lamb's legs came out first, followed by its nose. But Caora's nose had emerged from his mother's opening first, and his legs were nowhere in sight.

Flora was watching the birth, and her uncle had pulled her close and told her to help get the lamb's legs oriented properly. Her arms were smaller and could fit inside the mother more easily than his big hands. If they couldn't get the lamb's feet out, then the baby and its mother would probably both die.

Her uncle covered her arms in lanolin oil and she slipped her hands into the mother's bloody poon one at a time. She had to reach her hands around the lamb's head and find his front hooves. Then she cupped a hand around each hoof and gently pulled it up under the lamb's chin. The process was painstakingly slow, but her uncle warned her that any quick or harsh movements could break the lamb's legs or tear the mother's womb.

Eventually Flora had pulled the legs forward and the mother finished giving birth to a healthy male lamb. Flora remembered holding the slimy little baby in her hands as the mother licked the fluid off its fur. She'd felt its heart beating and the breath flowing in and out of its tiny body. It wouldn't sit still for even a moment and immediately struggled to stand on its wobbly little legs.

Flora's uncle gave her the responsibility of raising the lamb. She had guided its entry into the world and was now charged to nurture it and help it grow. Flora treated the lamb like the little brother she never had. Her father thought her silly when she gave it a name, Caora, which just meant "little sheep." But she took her responsibility seriously and made sure Caora was eating regularly and moving about as he should.

When Caora was about six moons old, he wandered away from his mother and the other sheep to nibble at the fresh clover near the edge of the pasture. Flora had relived that day a thousand times over, in terrors of the night. She remembered having an uneasy feeling about her little lamb, but wasn't sure why. The village women always seemed to know when their small children were in danger or up to no good. Maybe she had that same sense for Caora.

Flora had noticed Caora was missing from the among the flock and went out to search for him. She eventually found him at the far end of the village pasture, wandering in and out of the gorse bushes. As she headed toward him to guide him home, an enormous wolf lunged out of the forest and leapt to within a few paces of her, the fur on its neck standing erect and its teeth bared in anticipation of a kill. Flora's scream echoed through her memory, drowning out the little lamb's fearful bleating.

As big as a bear and as quick as a polecat, a single highland wolf could bring down a *Bò Ghàidhealach* bull in seconds, despite its great strength and long, menacing horns. The warriors of her clan would tread warily around much smaller wolves than this. As Flora stared down its flaring nostrils, she knew she didn't have a chance.

Though she didn't hear Caora's pitiful cries, apparently the sounds of easier prey drew the wolf's attention. It lurched back toward Caora in a violent attack. The tiny lamb sought protection amid the gorse, but only became trapped and entangled. Without thinking, Flora yanked out her flint knife and sprang toward the wolf. But she was too late. The wolf had clamped its powerful jaws around Caora's throat and had broken his neck with a violent twist. Just as quickly, it dragged the lifeless body from the brush and retreated into the trees.

Flora just stood motionless, staring at the hedge with tears streaming down her face. Her heart pounded and her breath, momentarily frozen, returned in gasps. Her precious baby lamb—the one she had touched within its mother's womb and nurtured and protected—had slipped from playful innocence into the gaping jaws of death within the space of time between two beats of a raven's wing.

As her vision came back into focus, Flora's eyes lit on the only part of her little friend that was left behind—a small clump of white fur matted around the branches of the gorse bush which had offered the lamb no refuge at all. She hacked angrily at the hedge, cursing its useless barbs, until the wool came free amid a tangle of twigs and thorns. Then she sank to her knees, curled into a ball on the ground, and wept with bitter sobs, numb to the danger still lurking within the woods beyond.

Here in the cavern, the memory evoked by the little mat of wool and thorns caused tears to prick at Flora's eyes once again. Why did the gods take away everything that was dear to her? What good was all the worship in the world if it didn't move the gods to intervene when she needed them? What good were all the sacrifices her village offered if they didn't buy protection for the innocent and helpless?

It was just a lamb. One worthless little lamb. But Caora had danced to her heartbeats and frolicked with her soul. His memory left a tender place deep inside that she guarded carefully, lest it become a malignant hardness and devour every bit of compassion that remained in her heart. With a long deep sigh, she laid the wool aside and reached back into her little bag of treasures.

Flora pulled out the small amulet she had received when she completed her third full year as an apprentice healer. It was a figurine of two serpents intertwined to form a complex knot around a spiral disc, carved from a piece of jasper. She remembered Nandag's solemn charge to her in their private ceremony at the sacred spring. Nandag's words had been oddly formal and had made Flora feel uncomfortable. Nandag had addressed herself to Flora, but also seemed to be speaking past her, as if performing a soliloquy to the gods.

"You are too young for the people of our clan to accept you as a healer. And too... different. Even I do not fully understand your manner—your way of reaching into the deep caverns within body, mind, and spirit to draw out the vile things and fill them with light."

Flora dropped her gaze and fidgeted with the ends of the twine belt around her waist, feeling ashamed of the strangeness Nandag described.

Nandag continued. "Though your touch brings healing, your methods will frighten many. Some would call you *bana-bhuidseach* and claim your powers come from the darkness. I know this is not true. Some will claim your abilities are a curse and will fear you, but I believe they are a gift. I can see that you are touched by the gods, but I cannot discern your path."

Nandag placed one hand on Flora's shoulder and lifted her chin with the other, so she could look deeply into her eyes.

"We dare not conduct this holy consecration before your family and friends, as is our custom. Yet I cannot withhold from you what Brigid, herself, has bestowed. You are a healer of your clan. I charge you to bring your skill to all those in need, to deny no one out of hatred or scorn, to seek only good, and to do no harm. You hold the lives of your people in your hands, from newborn *bairne* to warrior chief. It is a sacred trust.

"Your learning is not complete, nor will it ever be. Never trust what you know, but always continue to seek deeper into the healing mysteries of the body and spirit." Nandag lifted her right hand toward the stars and guided Flora's attention upwards. "Draw out the strength of the earth, unite it with power from the heavens, and channel them together into the souls of men to drive out defilement and return harmony to the body."

Then Nandag squeezed Flora's shoulder firmly and looked her in the eye with a stern expression. "But you—you must cloak your unique ways in a guise of tradition, lest you incite fear and invite the flame."

Nandag led Flora into the sacred spring, wading out until they were waist deep in the icy water. Flora remembered a strange sensation, a tingling not caused by the chill of the water. It began in the arches of her feet and crept slowly upward through her calves and her thighs. As it reached into her gut, it transformed into an intense heat that oddly caused no pain. It seared steadily upward until it engulfed her heart in a torrent of fire and ice, like piercing daggers and a mother's warm embrace.

Suddenly, Flora was drowning, her lungs aching to take a breath but daring not to allow a flood of water to quench the flame consuming her soul. She was only vaguely aware of the invocation Nandag cried out to Brigid as she gently pushed Flora's head under the surface of the spring.

After an eternal moment—when all of time, past and future, was forced through a single instant, like twine slipping through the eye of a fish hook—the pressure of Nandag's hand eased, and Flora's face emerged from the water. Her aching lungs drew in a slow, deep, frightened breath, that released into a gasp.

Flora felt as if she had passed through a portal in time to stand, for just an instant, in the Otherworld of the gods. As they walked out of the water, the dew of heaven dripped from Flora's face and hair to make tiny circles on the surface of the spring that rippled out in every direction, as if Flora were Brigid, herself, standing at the center of the world, radiating life and healing to all creation.

Nandag looked down into the waters of the spring and her solemn composure broke. She gasped, and a look of awe spread across her face. Nandag bent down and lifted a small amulet out of the water and gazed at it for a long moment. Without saying a word, she held it in unsteady, outstretched fingers toward Flora.

Flora flinched and shrunk away from the talisman. She spat to ward off evil. "*Bean-teagaisg*, teacher, I can't take someone else's offering from the sacred spring. The sickness they came to heal will surely fall on me. You know this to be true. How could you even suggest such a thing? It will anger the gods for me to rob them of the gifts presented by others."

Nandag's expression changed. She pursed her lips into a thin smile. "Child, this charm was not placed here by one of our kinsmen seeking the healing power of the spring. Indeed, it was not even present mere moments ago. No, it is a gift from the goddess to you. It is Brigid's sign, the symbol of the healer fashioned from the healer's precious stone. And she has given it to you."

Flora gaped in disbelief at Nandag's words. Why would the goddess honor her with such a gift? She was nobody. How could someone as small and insignificant as she was merit the favor of the goddess?

The disbelief lingered, but the memory faded, as Flora gazed down at the amulet's twisted serpents in the dim light filtering through the smoke into the cavern. As the sun sank toward the horizon, its muted radiance mixed with the dancing glow of the fire's flames to cast eerie shadows across the stony walls, mimicking the twisted steps and flailing arms of a stalk of druids summoning the power of the gods.

The spiral disc amid the serpents' coils seemed to possess an inner luminescence, all its own. It flickered at her in mock admiration. Touched by the gods? Blessed by Brigid? Cursed by the gods, more likely! Cursed to be lost and alone in the gaping mouth of a ravenous cave in the midst of a wasted land, stalked by sinister phantoms and haunted by voices that drove her ever closer to the edge of the abyss, the precipice beyond which sanity fled.

The small pouch slipped from Flora's grasp and spilled its remaining treasures across the rocky floor. A small amber bead from her mother's wedding bracelet. A lock of Domhnull's hair. A slice of deer antler with the symbol of an oak engraved on it—a charm given by her father to protect her from harm. A small stone flecked with golden speckles that her little sister, Catriona, had given to her. And a comb she had stolen from her older sister, Searlaid, when she was acting like a selfish, conceited twit. She would give the comb back if Searlaid ever displayed an ounce of humility, so she guessed it was probably hers for keeps.

Flora stared down at her little trove of treasures strewn across the cavern floor. There was nothing so valuable she wouldn't trade it for an oatcake right now if not for the people and the memories each one represented. And now she wasn't sure she would ever see any of them again, so the trinkets became even more priceless. The collection of baubles faded to a blur as tears welled up in Flora's eyes. A deep pang of hunger twisted against the gnarled knot of emotion in her gut. As daylight was fully consumed by the fire's flickering flames, Flora's body convulsed with one last raspy cough, and she sank into a fitful, restless sleep.

CHAPTER THREE

F lora drifted in and out of consciousness like a boat being tossed on the waves of Loch Rannoch during an autumn storm. Her back and hips ached from lying on the rocky floor of the cavern, and she tossed and turned in a vain effort to relieve the kinks in her neck. Images flashed across her mind like lightning in a disturbing mixture of unconscious dream, terrifying memory, and horrific nightmare.

A roaring bonfire inside a circle of stones, with flames licking up to the stars, morphed and transformed into a blazing inferno lighting up the night sky outside a cavern mouth, disgorging a haze of smoke that choked the waxing moon. Hooded figures, stony and motionless, formed an impenetrable wall around the stone circle, surrounding a wildly gyrating group of lanky, naked men and women—all covered from head to foot in black and blue and red tattoos, that wove endless, unbroken knots across their bodies in intricate spirals around fearsome beasts from legends and lore. The golden eyes of a wildcat peered out through the darkness, reflecting the dancing flames. A lone creature mutated and transfigured as it grew up from the ground, becoming an amalgamated beast with a man's legs, a bird's feathered body, eagles' talons, and the head of a bull. The iron face of a locust, with multi-faceted orbs and knife-like mandibles, loomed larger and larger as it clawed its way up her dress and stared into her eyes. A gnarled, knotted oak branch fashioned into a staff was raised high against a blood red moon. A shield wall of Roman soldiers, stretching from horizon to horizon, advanced step by step, piercing with javelins, stabbing with swords, and crushing everything in their path under iron shod sandals. Writhing forms within the heart of a fire struggled to get free, like eels caught in a reed trap that was hurled into the flames.

Flora awoke with a start, the visions of the night still swirling and churning through her mind. She was drenched with sweat but trembled from a chill that penetrated to her bones. Her breath came in short gasps. She sensed the wildfire continuing to burn outside her stony sanctuary. A smoky haze choked off the sun's morning rays.

The night's restless sleep had done nothing to ease her exhaustion and fatigue. All she had done was wrestle through the darkness with demons that haunted her dreams. She shivered. Although her cavernous lair felt like a cauldron over a cooking fire, an icy coldness crept up from somewhere deep inside her. She wrapped her arms around herself and rubbed her hands across her skin to wipe away the goose bumps that had formed on her flesh.

Her belly growled a long and mournful wail. She couldn't even remember how long it had been since she had eaten. But the dry, sandy grit in her mouth screamed for water as an even more urgent need. At least water was something she had reasonably close access to. Although the little spring at the top of the knoll was not deep enough to hide her body from the locust swarm, it was certainly sufficient to slake her parched throat.

She crawled out of the cave's mouth and tried to stand, but her knee screamed in protest, her head spun, and her vision blurred. The air was thick with smoke from the fire that still burned all around the hillside. All she could do was crawl slowly across the rocky ground toward the beckoning spring.

When she finally saw the water gurgling up from the ground and trickling down the side of the hill, she collapsed in relief. She tentatively reached out a finger to touch the precious liquid, half expecting it to vanish the moment her living nightmare intersected with the real world. But the cool water jolted her senses, pulling her mind into focus, and giving her a surge of energy and hope.

She drew in a deep breath and reached out to scoop the refreshing liquid into her mouth, but stopped at the last moment. This sacred spring belonged to Brigid. It was the gift of the goddess that promised to quench her thirst and give her new life. She dared not greedily take her fill without first paying due homage. The last thing she needed now was to offend the gods.

Flora reached for the flint knife hanging around her neck and used it to cut a small patch of cloth from the tattered bottom of her woolen *leine*. She noticed no other swatches of cloth pressed into the rocks around this particular spring, left by petitioners who sought healing from the gods. That was odd. Such votive offerings covered virtually every other spring or well she had ever seen. But this scrap from the hem of her dress would be the first and only token of prayer at this mountaintop fount.

That thought sparked a renewed sense of dread and foreboding. Once again, she was plagued with an overwhelming feeling of aloneness, and she succumbed to a wave of grief and despair. Her tears fell like raindrops into the pool, causing ripples to dance across the water's surface. She stared blankly into the shimmering water, searching for some kind of hope.

In the flickering reflection of the wildfire's flames, Flora saw an image of the goddess staring back at her. The vision was stunning in its beauty. Brigid's face shone with the brilliance of a star and the warmth of a hearth fire. Her eyes, like deep pools reflecting moonbeams on a cloudless night, looked startlingly familiar. Flora's gaze was transfixed by the image until it finally faded and she was left staring at her own reflection in the little spring. But the eyes were still the same. The eyes hadn't changed at all.

Flora breathed a deep sigh, and the tension melted away from her clenched jaw, her knotted neck, and her aching back. She wasn't alone after all. Brigid was here. Though a wildfire raged all around her, Brigid was the goddess of the hearth fire. Though she was weak from thirst, Brigid was the goddess of the springs. She was a healer, and Brigid was the matron of healing. Brigid would protect her. Brigid would provide for her. Brigid would never leave her alone. Flora plunged her cupped hands into the cool, refreshing water and drank deeply of renewed courage and hope.

FLORA SAT by the spring and gazed at the smoldering forest all around her. The scattered brush that ringed the top of the mountain had all been consumed. The fire had burned so bright and hot that the smaller shrubs had been completely reduced to ash. Not even the skeletal bones of barren branches remained to mark the spots where hedgerows of gorse bushes had covered the hillside. Yet the embers still smoldered with a menacing red glow that disgorged endless volumes of smoke.

Farther down the hillside, the trees were still ablaze. Flames engulfed the silent sentinels from root to crown, leaving their mangled trunks and barren branches black against the grayish, brownish plumes of smoke that wove together as they reached to the sky, forming a thick blanket that threatened to smother the countryside.

The acrid stench of smoke ever promised to evoke a renewed bout of choking and coughing. Unlike the rustic aroma of hearth fires in her village that always reminded Flora of her father when he returned from his forge, this smoke smelled of fear and of death.

Flora held out her hand and watched as tiny snowflakes landed on her upturned palm. But these snowflakes didn't melt when they touched the warmth of her flesh. Instead, they piled up to create a surreal spectacle as the ash blanketed the top of the hillside like a snowcapped peak on a winter's day.

Flora's stomach twisted in a knot. There had been times in the long winter months during her childhood when she had gone several days in a row on scraps of bread and moldy cheese, so she was no stranger to hunger. But this was the longest time she had ever gone without food.

Her memories had become a muddled blur, melding thin strands of reality with horrific nightmares and waking fantasies so that she no longer had a true sense of when or where she was. And as she bleakly surveyed the burning landscape surrounding her, she had no idea where she would find her next meal. The raging fire had consumed every edible thing not already devoured by the locust swarm. Even if, by a miracle of the gods, some small patch of food had survived in the valley below, she had no way to get to it. She had no idea how long the wildfire would burn, or how long it would take for the smoldering coals to cool to the point that she could walk through the ash covered wasteland.

Flora peered back into the spring, longing to catch another glimpse of Brigid. The vision of the goddess had given her hope. What she needed now was food and guidance. She needed someone to tell her what to do and where to go. She needed her father to shelter her in his strong arms and nourish her with the fresh game he brought back from the hunt. She needed Domhnull to sweep her up in his loving embrace and carry her to the safety of her home. But they were both gone, and her home was destroyed.

She closed her eyes and whispered a silent prayer, "Brigid, please help me." It was a simple plea. It didn't include the titles and honorifics the goddess deserved, or the humble subjection expected from one seeking divine intervention. But she simply had nothing left to give. She opened her eyes and gazed back into the waters that bubbled up from deep within the earth, but the image of the goddess had vanished. Small flecks of ash floated down from the sky, landed on the surface of the pool, bobbed momentarily, and trickled away down the mountainside.

Flora wheezed, and a raspy cough shook her out of her stupor. Slowly, she crawled on her hands and knees from the little spring back to the shelter and the fresh air of the cave. She curled up in a ball on the stony floor and just stared at the wall, or rather past the wall—through the wall—into nothingness.

Flora once again slipped into sleep, and once again she dreamed. But these dreams were different. She lay on her side in an open meadow. A blade of grass tickled her nose, and she blew it aside with a puff of air from puckered lips. She rolled onto her back and smiled. The sun shone warmly on her face. She just lay there for several moments, listening to larks jabbering in the trees, feeling the breeze rustle her hair, and breathing in the freshness of spring.

She instinctively knew this must be the Otherworld. As she gazed around, everything looked the same as she had always known it to be. Fir trees rustled in the gentle breeze. Deer grazed at the edge of the glen. Black grouse strutted through the grassy fields, shrieked their raspy cries, then fluttered their wings and cooed like doves.

Yet everything was also strangely different. Underneath the natural beauty of her real world lay a hidden malevolence. Wolves attacked the deer and grouse. Fires ravaged the forests. Storms hid the sun's golden rays. Thunder shattered the tranquility of late spring days. And everywhere, men fought and strove—against the earth, against the sea, against the gods, and against each other.

But somehow, Flora sensed that here, in the Otherworld, the evil was gone. Everything good, pure, and true remained, while death was swallowed up, striving ceased, and wickedness faded away. She could not see, or hear, or smell the difference. But, somehow, she knew it, deep inside her soul.

Flora propped herself up on both hands and then teetered to one side as she reached up to catch an apple that a kindly old man had thrown to her. She didn't quite recognize him, but somehow felt the inner ease of kinship. He had creases at the corners of his eyes, partly from squinting in the sunlight, but mostly from an almost perpetual smile. He wore the silver cloak of the Otherworld, with gold bands around his waist and neck, and a circlet of jewels on his brow. His face was marked with the blue and black painted spirals of a warrior, but she sensed that his days of hefting a spear had trailed away as distant memories. She saw kindness in the soft, silver-flecked gray of his eyes. The coarse edges of a fighter had been rubbed smooth by time, and perhaps by something else. Something in his manner seemed very familiar to her.

He called to her in a deep, resonant voice that echoed with peaceful reassurance. "Flora, child, is it you?"

The voice jolted her with instant recognition. Though she had known him for only a short time as a very young girl, the memories flooded back to her now—memories of being held close in loving arms and of taking long walks in the cool forest.

She leapt to her feet and ran to embrace him. "*Shena!*" "Grandpa!"

She threw her arms around his broad chest and felt a grandfather's strength and love as he held her close. She stayed there, bound to him with relief and desperation, for what seemed like a full turning of the moon. She felt the rough scars on his hands as he gently stroked her back.

Her short gasps of breath turned to sobs, and her whole body trembled. It wasn't because her love for him was so strong. Indeed, the memories of him from her childhood were as distant as a doe bounding away in the mist. She had been so very young when her *shena* had led a small scouting party to the Great Wall and then never returned. Until this moment, she could scarcely even remember his face. It wasn't fond memories that made her cling to him like a child clinging to her mother when lightning cracks and thunder roars. It was her desperate need for anyone or anything familiar in a world that had been ripped apart at the seams.

"Hush, child. *Bà, mo leanbh.*" His rich baritone voice vibrated against her cheek. "Find your grandmother. She has the answers you seek."

Flora flinched in confusion at his words, and instantly everything was gone—her *shena*, the meadow, the sunshine, even the gentle breeze. It all vanished as suddenly as it had appeared, though the feeling of his embrace lingered on.

Flora felt a spray of water on her face and heard the echo of a distant voice. "Flora." It wasn't her grandfather's voice, but it too was oddly familiar.

"Flora. Wake up. Go. Now."

Her eyes snapped open and she started awake. For a moment she couldn't understand what she was seeing or remember where she was. But she had heard it again—that voice from the millpond—and she was instantly alert, even as her head spun from the lack of food and water. Then everything came sharply into focus as she felt her own tears mingle with the raindrops that blew into the cavern's mouth and trickled down her cheeks.

A sigh escaped her lips, and she collapsed back against the cold stone of the cavern wall. Then she began to laugh— or to cry—or maybe both. Brigid had seen her plight and answered her prayer. With a mighty stroke of his oaken club, the Dagda split the clouds and released a deluge of rain to quench the fires that ravaged the land.

As she peered tentatively out of her cleft in the rock, she saw the flames being doused and the smoke being dissipated. The inferno that had devastated the countryside was being drowned in a providential flood. Now she could go in search of food, and wet her dry, cracked lips with dew from heaven. And the voice was back. It had not abandoned her after all. It had even just called her by name.

THOUGH THE RAINFALL WAS A BLESSING, it was also a curse. It poured down in a torrent that turned the ash into a slick, gray-black muck that made her footing treacherous. Flora might have waited for the storm to abate before venturing out, but the voice had been urgent as it coaxed her out of sleep. Again she wondered why she should place so much trust in an ethereal specter she had never even seen. Yet it had served her well when she fled from the swarm.

A chill ran across the backs of her arms and caused the skin on her chest to tighten as she realized the implications of that thought. Her own instinct had been to flee into the valley to escape the locusts, but the voice had insistently urged her to climb the mountain. Indeed, she might even have escaped from the horrid little bugs if she had pursued her own course, but then she would have been consumed in the blaze. The voice had led her to safety from both threats.

How could it have possibly foreseen the wildfire so far in advance? She acknowledged that it could have plotted a path to safety from the onslaught of the frenzied locusts simply through better knowledge of the terrain. But when the little devil army was shredding its way through the vegetation of the forest, the fire was not even an imagined threat.

Could the owner of this voice see across the landscape of time as easily as she observed the hills and valleys beyond the river? Indeed, could even the gods see into the future with that kind of clarity and precision?

She had known druids and bards to spin vague prophesies about coming times of prosperity or calamity, but seldom with enough detail to guide the specific actions of those who were to live through the course of events. They painted enough of a picture to cause a sense of anticipation or dread, but rarely with enough clarity to help people prepare. They might accurately predict that the crops would fail in the season to come, but not reveal whether the cause was drought or flood or blight. They might read omens of a significant birth, without revealing which parents were to be blessed or whether the child would be a boy or a girl. But the voice had known in advance exactly where she could find refuge from both the swarm and the fire.

The thought gave her some comfort and engendered greater confidence in following the voice's instructions. But it also sparked a sense of fear. What kind of forces was she dealing with? Why were the gods responding to her pleas for help by sending rain? Who were the "others" that watched her every move and lured her deeper and deeper into danger? What kind of being was the disembodied voice that guided her through the treacherous valleys of death? And most of all, why were they all focused on her?

She was no one. She was nothing. She was just a young woman training to be a healer. That was all. She was perhaps the least important person in her clan. So why would the rulers of the Otherworld even take notice of her? Could she be the only one left?

If that was true, then why shouldn't she simply lay down, breathe her last breath, and allow her soul to cross over to her Otherbody. But then, if she were indeed the last person in the land, what druid would come to measure her with his staff? Who would wrap her body for the keening time? Who would lay her in the burial mound? Would she be able to pass over at all, without the rites of passage performed? Or would she be forced to wait in some nether realm between the Otherworld and this until Samhain, when the veil between the worlds parted so her family members could return to guide her across?

Flora slipped in the wet, sloppy ash and slide down the slope. She came to a stop and lay there covered in sludge, her heart racing and her breath coming in gasps. She didn't want to be the last one left. She didn't want to be the plaything of the gods. She didn't want Brigid to stare back at her from deep inside a mountain spring. She didn't want the "others" to stalk her and manipulate her thoughts. She didn't even want a friendly voice to give her warnings that saved her life. She wanted her family and her friends and her home. She didn't want to be alone.

Flora heard a sudden squall and lifted her head to look back up the hill. She saw a ball of tan fur dart out of the cavern and streak away across the rocks toward the spring. Apparently, the wildcat had been hiding deep within the cave after all. At least one more living soul prowled this desolate, forsaken land. If other people or animals had survived as well, she wouldn't find them laying here in the muck. She had to get up. She had to press on.

FLORA WASN'T sure exactly where to go. The rain still came down in sheets, and the wind whipped her sodden *leine* around her body like a sail flapping in a wintery gale. She couldn't see far through the storm. Her knee was tight and sore. The wet, ashen sludge was slick beneath her feet, and there was no underbrush to hold on to as she picked her way down the slope.

At this point, *down* was her only option. She paused to see if the voice would admonish her to turn and climb back up the hill, but all she heard was the howling wind mocking her temerity. It cried out for her to seek shelter in the cavern until the storm had passed, but Flora needed food, so she made her way down the mountain as carefully as she could. For all the concentration she put into every placement of her foot, still she slipped and slid a good portion of the way down the steep slope.

She didn't know which direction to go. Her main concern was to find the safest route down the mountain and avoid any sheer cliffs that would send her plunging to a pile of rocks and debris far below. She paused to get her bearings, but the pouring rain caused drips to cascade off her eyebrows and trickle onto her lashes, blurring her vision so that peering into the distance was like staring into the pitch-black darkness of the cavern she had just left. All she could see was a dull gray haze over a scorched black hillside dotted with the gnarled and charred remains of once stately oaks and elms. They reached up from earth to sky, like skeletal hands grasping for hope. The land itself groaned a deep and mournful wail at the desecration it had endured.

Flora again teetered on the edge of a morose chasm of despondency, but then physically steeled herself against the dread— stiffening her back, lifting her head, and forcing her foot to take another step. For now, her sole focus was getting down the mountain. Once she made it to the valley, she could think about where to look for food. And so she continued, step by step, climbing and crawling and sliding down the side of the mountain.

The slope eventually flattened out, and Flora was able to stand upright and walk. She was covered from head to foot in a grayish black sludge formed by the mixture of rain and ash and mud. It matted her hair, streaked her arms, and saturated her *leine*. Even the drenching showers wouldn't wash it clean.

As she wandered aimlessly through the carnage that had once been a thick forest, she stumbled across a creek. Indeed, it was probably the creek that she had originally sought when she was fleeing from the locust swarm. Now it raged as an angry torrent, its depth and power swelled by the heavy downpour. She wasn't about to try and cross it in this state, so she turned to follow its course downstream.

She really had no other choice at this point. Eventually, the raging river would empty into the millpond and lead her to one of the few potential remaining sources of food. Though the twin plagues of locust swarm and blazing fire had destroyed the herbs, berries, and roots of the forest and caused the birds and animals to either flee or be consumed in its fury, perhaps some fish had survived within the protective refuge of the water.

Flora forced back a rising surge of panic as she thought about returning to the millpond. The thought of going back to a spot she had fled just a few days ago filled her with a deep sense of foreboding. Why? What was it about the place that caused her such dread? After all, she had never actually seen anything sinister near the pond. What had shattered the peaceful tranquility she felt when she was kneeling in the sunshine on its shore? She searched through the chaotic, jumbled memories of the past few days to locate the source of her unease.

She knew the feeling came from a dread of the "others" who she sensed just beyond the edge of her awareness. But what evidence did she have that they were even real. She had never heard or seen or even smelled them. Still, she felt their presence watching her from behind, beneath, and beyond. And yet something had jolted her into fleeing from the millpond. What had it been? The voice had urged her to run, but that wasn't what struck deep into her heart like a dagger of ice. No. It had something to do with the mill house and the water wheel. Then the memory surged through her mind and flowed over her like wave of nausea. It had been when the surreal perfection of the peaceful scene was shattered as she realized the water falling from the wheel produced no splash.

Looking back now, Flora felt foolish. She panicked and fled because of a splash? Really? A splash—or rather the lack of one? Honestly? What exactly would the "others" accomplish by planting the image of a perfectly tranquil place and time in her mind? How could they even do such a thing? Even if they could, why *would* they do it? If their goal was to detain her so that she would be ravaged by the horde of bugs or scorched in the raging inferno, surely they would have better means available than to lull her with a false sense of peace. Why not just snare her in a trap or tie her to a tree? It made no sense, and Flora began to doubt whether her dread of the "others" had any source besides the vagaries of her own confused mind. Yet the voice had called out for her to flee, right? And the later threats were all too real, were they not?

Flora shrieked an angry howl, railing against the phantoms in her own dark mind. She was hungry, and she needed food. If the millpond was her best chance to find food, then the "others," and the voice, and her own paranoid delusions be damned! She would go to the millpond and face whatever horrors might confront her there. So she pressed on downstream into the stormy gale.

Flora picked her way carefully through the rocks at the river's edge. They were slick from the rain, but were thankfully free of the muddy ashen silt that blanketed the countryside. Flora removed her deerskin *brogan*. She trusted the bare soles of her feet to negotiate the stony path more than the wet animal hide.

Every ounce of her attention was focused on progressing down the hill without twisting an ankle or breaking a leg. The crash of the water against the rocks in the stream filled her ears with a steady monotonous rumble that lulled her into a trance, until the voice once again pierced through the fog and jolted her to sudden alertness.

"Jump!" it cried.

Instead, she crouched and spun. An enormous gray mountain of fur and fangs and claws sailed over her shoulder, its hind legs kicking back to scrape at her as it missed the target of its lunge. The instant it landed, it shifted its paws on the craggy rocks and whipped around to face her. With a low, ominous, savage growl it crouched down, preparing to lunge again.

"Jump in! Now!"

Without stopping to think, Flora hurled herself into the writhing torrent of water at her side. It immediately swallowed her up and began to pummel her against the jagged boulders that forced the flow from side to side and beat it into an angry froth. To Flora's horror, the great wolf adjusted its attack and launched itself into the river right behind her.

In panic, Flora clawed at rocks and limbs and any kind of debris she could use to gain control and pull herself to the other bank. She struggled to force her head up and gulped great breaths of air as wave after wave toppled over her face and hurled her from side to side. Frantically, she tried to get a footing, but with each attempt the current wrapped its tentacles around her legs and dragged her even further under. She fought to escape the tide, and the wolf fought to reach its prey. It flailed like a water wraith conjuring a storm, but it gained steadily on her, drawing closer and closer as she desperately struggled toward the shore.

She cried out with terror in her mind, for her lungs had no air to scream. She reached out, then slipped, and fell, and went under once again. She spun and toppled and gasped for air. Through the blur, she saw gaping jaws and eyes of fire and jagged claws lashing out at her.

Suddenly, her shoulder slammed against a huge boulder in the middle of the river. The impact hammered the breath from her chest and she was plunged beneath the surface. It was as if time slowed to a heartbeat. She opened her eyes and gazed about at a surreal world. She saw streams of lacy bubbles dive beneath the surface and float lazily away. She saw smooth, black, mossy stones pass by on either side, as if she were riding a canoe through a canyon of boulders. She saw the wolf's paws paddling through the water, like a horse galloping through the air. And suddenly, she was in the Otherworld, lying on her back in a grassy meadow, basking in the sunshine. She heard the voice whispering in the wind of the trees. It wasn't piqued and urgent this time. It was deep and strong and comforting.

"Relax," it said. "Just breathe. Trust me."

Flora opened her eyes. The river was still there, and so were the rocks and the waves and the wolf. But the panic was gone. Slowly and deliberately, she rolled her body over and shifted her weight. Instead of trying to brace herself against the current and fight her way toward shore, she pointed her feet downstream, let her body go limp, and allowed the current to carry her away.

She sensed, rather than saw, the wolf slip farther and farther behind. She heard its yelp as it was dashed against a stone. Then she was alone again—just her and the river. She was still being buffeted back and forth, and she bounced hard off a number of rocks. But for the most part, the river's current swept her over and around the biggest obstacles. After a seemingly endless series of shifts and turns and bumps and spills, the raging river spent its fury. It widened out, the current slowed, and she drifted safely into the millpond.

She rolled over, and with her last ounce of strength, pulled her body through the water toward the shore. One stroke. A gasp of air. Another stroke. Another gasp of air. The cycle repeated, over and over again, into forever. Then she was crawling up out of the water and collapsing on the bank, with her cheek pressed into the pebbles. And the pouring rain continued to fall.

CHAPTER FOUR

Time slipped away, swirling in currents and eddies, only to be
dashed upon the rocks in a spray that sent precious moments
hurling into the air to hang, suspended alone, as if for eternity, before
plunging back into the torrent to be drowned amid an endless sea of
memories.

Flora faded gradually back into awareness of the incessant rain
pouring over her body. She did not know how long she had lain there,
soaked and shivering —moments, days, or a *seachdain*? She blinked
away the blurriness in her eyes and pushed her head up to look
around. Small grains of sand clung to her cheek, but she was too
exhausted to wipe them away.

The torrent of rain obscured the land with a murky gray cloak,
thicker than the densest fog. Her feet still rested in the water of the
millpond behind her. She could barely discern a forest of tall, ghastly,
skeletal shapes grasping for the sky through the hazy mist. She had to
get up and find shelter from the storm, but didn't know where to go.
Slowly she staggered to her feet, and another different storm swirled
within her head causing her vision to smear around the edges and her
body to sway in the wind. So cold. So weak. So hungry.

She stumbled along the shoreline, barely conscious of where she was going. She winced as the pain in her knee caused her to trip on a large stone protruding from the pebbles on the beach. She followed the waterline because it was the only shape her mind could focus on in the haze of the downpour and the fog in her head. The rain pelted the surface of the pond, causing a thousand tiny eruptions to burst into the air and collapse again into nothingness, as if an entire Roman legion released its spears and arrows all at once into a sea of highland warriors and ground them all to dust.

Her gaze was down, tracing the shore, as tiny rivulets of water streamed off her lashes, blurring her vision. And so she nearly collided with the rough stone wall before she even noticed it looming large across her path. Her heart leapt as she realized the possibility of finding shelter from the storm. But as she glanced up and peered harder at the structure, she recoiled in an unconscious wave of panic. She was standing before the mill house.

Fear gripped her mind and she looked around in panic, suddenly expecting the "others" to be stalking her. She longed to hear the voice offering guidance. How had they cornered her again? How had they clouded her mind and lured her into their lair? She felt like a cricket snared in a spider's web. The more she struggled to free herself, the more entangled she became in their labyrinth of lies.

Flora stumbled again and fell to the ground. She lay there for several moments, sobbing tears that streamed down her cheeks and disappeared into the larger rivers of rain cascading down her face. She collapsed, melting into the wet earth, and gave up. She had fled from the sinister presence pursuing her, escaped the locust swarm, survived a blazing inferno, eluded wild beasts, and braved a raging torrent, only to end up where she had started. Now she was back within their grasp and had no will left to resist. She was frightened, hungry, cold, exhausted, and alone, and she had nothing left to give. She rolled to her back, stretched out her arms, and surrendered herself to the forces that sought to ravage her soul. "Brigid," she whispered, "I am yours. Save me." Then she closed her eyes.

The last thing Flora expected was for a fawn to nuzzle her cheek. She didn't hear the tiny animal approach and was startled when its nose nudged up against the side of her face. But the soft, pleading eyes staring back at her melted her heart. How in the world had this frail creature survived the firestorm that had scorched the land? It must have lost its mother in the blaze. Surely the gods had saved its life.

Flora's thoughts came to an abrupt halt as she realized the fawn's importance. *This animal was an omen from the gods!* She was certain of that fact in a way she didn't quite understand. Brigid must have pled for Cernunnos—the horned god, the stag—to send this sign so she would know she was not forgotten or forsaken. She collapsed in relief and lifted her gaze to the heavens in a silent praise of thanks. Brigid had heard her prayer. The gods had not abandoned her after all. She was not alone.

But what specific message was she to take from the appearance of this baby deer? Receiving an omen was one thing. Interpreting it was something else. As she gazed in wonder at her unexpected companion, the fawn nudged her once again and scampered away toward the mill house. Flora's fists clenched, and a tightness rose in her chest as she stared at the foreboding edifice. Through the pouring rain, she could faintly make out the mill-wheel turning round and round. She had no doubt the falling water was producing a splash now, in this downpour. There was no idyllic scene of peace and serenity to be shattered into a thousand pieces by such an inconsistency. Was she to follow that baby stag into a trap?

Her taut nerves urged her to flee. Her knotted gut warned her to escape. A sense of dread crushed her spirit. But her training as a healer compelled her to heed a sign from the gods. She pushed herself up from the ground where she had lain as a sacrifice and forced herself to follow the fawn toward the mill house.

How had this mill survived the fire? The stone walls were impervious to the heat of the blaze. But the thatch of the roof was one of Belanus' favorite foods, and the god would certainly have sent his flames to devour it before feasting on the wooden structures inside the walls. Yet, this mill stood as a lone survivor amid its scorched surroundings. That thought made the place seem even more eerie, and her sense of foreboding grew.

The door of the mill house stood slightly ajar. The fawn pushed its way through and disappeared inside. With a whispered prayer to Brigid, Flora took a deep breath and stepped into the murky darkness.

Expecting to be assaulted by shadowy, hooded figures or by armored Roman soldiers, Flora peered into the blackness. The tiny amount of light that followed her through the doorway only made the shadows more ominous. She threw the door wide open to illuminate more of the inner space. The mill's mechanism was still engaged, so the cogs and stones turned steadily, rhythmically—grinding nothing. What happened to the miller? Where had he gone? She wondered if the kelpies kept the water wheel turning, and the thought gave her a chill.

When no one sprang out of the darkness to accost her, Flora slowly exhaled in relief. Out of the corner of her eye, she saw the fawn nibbling hungrily at a bag of spilled oats, and a heavy sigh escaped her lips. There was food here! Raw oats and ground spelt were not exactly her meal of choice, but the pain in her gut from days of hunger left her faint and trembling.

She instantly forgot her fear and fell to her knees beside the little deer, grasping at a handful of oats. Cernunnos, the horned god, was indeed the god of bounty. Amid the devastation of the swarm and the desolation of the fire, he had led her to a treasure store of grain. Her eyes feasted on the sacks of wheat and oats and barley, and she praised the god for his goodness to her. She lifted the grains up to heaven in thanks for sending the fawn and leading her to the food she so desperately needed. Then she hungrily devoured the gift of bread from heaven.

After gorging on raw oats soaked in rain water, Flora sat on the floor and rested her back against a sack of grain. The fawn lay peacefully at her side. They were two lost souls seeking refuge from the howling wind and driving rains. With her belly full—perhaps a bit too full—Flora was overcome with a wave of exhaustion. She stripped off her soaked *leine*, wrapped herself in empty grain sacks, and allowed the rhythmic chanting of the waterwheel to lull her into a deep and dreamless sleep.

FLORA'S EYES FLICKERED OPEN, then squinted closed again. Her mind, groggy from sleep, struggled to settle itself on where she was. As memories of rain and wolves and raging rivers flooded her thoughts, she expected her body to shiver in response to the chill of soaking wetness. Instead, she felt warm all over. Her eyes flickered once again and struggled to remain open. Bright light streamed through the door and crept across the floor to bathe her in a radiant glow that soothed her soul.

Absentmindedly, she stroked the little fawn sleeping at her side. For the first time in an eternity of days, she was warm, dry, full, and in no immediate danger. She felt an odd sense of peace, but it seemed wispy and fleeting, like a candle in the wind, flickering gently with a desperate hope that the next gust would not snuff it out completely.

She stood and walked slowly toward the open door. The sight that met her gaze made her cringe. The rain had stopped. The sun shone brightly in a cloudless blue sky. The surface of the millpond glistened without the slightest hint of a ripple. It was just like when she first glimpsed that scene—how many days ago?

But that's where the similarities ended. Instead of lush green grass and fresh new leaves of spring fluttering on limbs that swayed in the gentle breeze, a forest of black, bony branches clawed at the sky from gray, muddy graves as if grasping in desperation at the last, fleeting strands of their life threads. The pall of death and devastation raged against the mock serenity of the sky. The earlier scene was, indeed, too good to be true.

As she filtered out the rhythmic turning of the mill and the soft gurgle of the flowing stream, she became aware of an absolute stillness. She heard only silence. No stirring of the hedges in the wind. No lapping of gentle waves on the shore. No animated chatter of birds that would normally greet a sunny day. It was as if the land had breathed its dying breath, and had no voice left to sing a lament or to whisper a final prayer.

She opened her eyes and withdrew her gaze from the irreconcilable contrasts of the world outside—serene beauty and devastating destruction. She looked at the mill house with different eyes and considered her plight over the last few days. As she rested in its sheltering arms, the mill seemed much less menacing now.

She reflected on the moment that initially caused her sense of fear, and began to question her feelings. She always seemed to imagine the worst and to flee from shadows. Had this all been just another case of her abandoning a refuge and running headlong into the storm? Well, no. She had just witnessed the burning of her village and the death of her family and friends, hadn't she? And she had watched as the land itself was stripped raw by locusts and scorched by a blazing inferno. Right? So if she was a bit on edge over a creepy watermill, that was completely understandable. And of course, the voice had warned her to flee.

Flora stopped suddenly and thought about the voice. She had assumed it was her friend—that it was protecting her from the "others" who pursued her just beyond the edge of awareness. But what if there were no "others?" What if no one was stalking her at all? She knew the voice was real. She was certain she'd heard it. But what if the voice was really her foe? What if the voice was constantly luring her away from her true source of help.

Could the "others" actually be trying to aid her, while the voice drove her steadily away. And who were the "others?" Could they be the gods? She felt their presence, pursuing her and watching her. But then again, didn't the gods do exactly that? Didn't they watch over her from the Otherworld, and occasionally step through the veil to put a blessing in her path? Could the voice be driving her away from those who truly were her refuge and strength?

She considered the mill, from which she had fled in terror just a short time before. The mill had stood as a stalwart sentinel through all the terrors that devastated the land. The swarm ignored it. The embers of the wildfire spared its thatch roof and timber beams. It was a true place of sanctuary. Not only did it stand as a haven against the onslaught of the locusts and the fiery inferno, but it served as a shelter from the wind and rain—and it was filled with a bounty of food and water. How much safer would she have been to have sought refuge here, inside the sturdy stone walls of the mill, than to have heeded the voice's call to climb a hill and find shelter in a barren cave?

Doubts crept across the landscape of her mind, and she began to find foes in friends and friends in foes, until her whole world was turned upside down. One thing kept nagging at the edge of her consciousness. Where was she? How had she gotten here? She had watched her village burn. She knew that. But these were not the woods and hills around her home on Loch Rannoch. How had she gotten from there to here? The answer was lost in a blur that fed a current of uneasiness flowing deep within her soul.

The question prompted Flora to step outside the door once again to survey her surroundings. Perhaps in the sunshine she could find some mountain top or flowing river she would recognize. She stood at the back of the mill and swept her gaze across the hills and the rocky crag where she had so recently taken refuge in the cavern. Nothing seemed familiar from longer ago than just a few days. Even the mountains and the glen looked very different from this vantage point, as opposed to the view she had seen when climbing the hillside in desperation, clinging to saplings and rotted trees while a cloud of hideous monsters bore down on her from above. The hill with the rocky crag looked much smaller now—less imposing, less rugged, and less stalwart. Even the larger mountains looming in the background spurred no distant memories.

Flora scanned the details of the valley floor, and her eyes settled on something odd across the glen. On a small rise, at the base of the foothills on the opposite side of the valley, a bright green spot virtually glowed in the sunshine against the charred black and gray of the surrounding wasteland. She vaguely remembered seeing a similar green patch from the hilltop during her flight from the swarm. Perhaps it was the same one.

She peered intently at the spot, and recognition slowly dawned. Though she couldn't make out the exact shape from this distance, she gradually became aware of what it must be—like a familiar figure emerging from the mist. What green thing could have withstood the onslaught of the menacing horde of locusts as it swarmed over the land and devoured every blade of grass, every leaf, every blossom, every twig? What living being could then have survived the fiery breath from Belanus' mouth that swept over the countryside, leaving only blackened trunks, gray ash, and dismal despair? It could only be one thing—something cherished by the gods and protected by their care. It had to be the sacred yew. It could be nothing else.

With that sudden realization, Flora instantly knew exactly where she was.

FLORA GAZED across the desolate glen at the only living thing within sight. The scene faded, and she remembered a green valley from six summers ago when she was twelve. She had traveled with her family and friends from their home on Loch Rannoch to the holy place, *Shiorraidh*, for a special sacrifice to honor the gods.

"*Dadaidh*," she asked her father, "is that it? Is that the sacred tree?"

"It is, my wee *fauth*." Her father had always called her a water sprite, ever since she had started swimming when she was two summers old. "The one in the middle of the clearing at the base of the hill with the big rocky crag."

"Tell me again why we traveled all this way to see it? That was a long journey, just to see a tree." Actually, it had only taken the better part of a day. But for a twelve-year-old girl, it seemed like an awfully long way.

"Do you remember when the stars fell from the sky just after we celebrated Lughnasadh? When Cerridwen hid the face of the moon as she always does?"

"I remember. There were so many, it looked like sparks jumping from a fire when you throw another log in. What caused them to fall, *Dadaidh*? Where did they land? What are the stars, anyway? What did they do when they got here?"

"That's my girl. Questions and more questions." He smiled and ruffled her hair.

Her sister, Searlaid, broke in. "It was the korrigans coming through the veil of the Otherworld to snatch away little children."

Catriona buried her face in their mother's shoulder and began to whimper. Her mother held their little sister in her arms and turned defensively away. Her angry glance at Searlaid launched shafts of arrows to accompany her verbal rebuke. "Searlaid, stop antagonizing your sister. I've warned you before. I won't tell you again."

Serlaid turned her face away, rolling her eyes in mockery of her mother's reproach and her sisters' fear.

Domhnull had walked with Flora's family to the gathering. He crouched nearby with his spear in hand. He and Searlaid had passed their ordeals together in the spring, and they had earned the right to carry spears. Searlaid was among the few girls who chose to take the challenge. All boys faced the ordeals in their fifteenth summer. Those who passed the test became men and were permitted to carry a spear, to take a wife, and eventually to move out of their father's house and build a *taigh-cruinn* for their own family. Boys who failed the ordeals lived in shame for a year and then had the chance to redeem their honor the following spring. If they failed the second time, they were forbidden to become warriors or to hunt. They were forced to take on shameful roles in the community and were scorned their entire lives. Some ran away to distant lands where their humiliation was unknown or became outlaws who scraped out a living of scavenging and theft in the forests and the hills.

For girls, like Searlaid, who faced the ordeals, it was different. If they failed, there was no shame, and they simply went back to their lives as typical women in the village. Those who passed their ordeals entered a strange sort of half-state, somewhere between a woman and a man. They could technically build their own roundhouses, but usually lived under their fathers' roofs until they married. However, they had the right to choose their own husbands, instead of marrying ones arranged by their fathers. They typically became hunters and joined with the men in war. Few girls chose this path, but the ones who did held a special position of respect in the community. Unfortunately, with Searlaid, that respect had gone to her head, and she clearly thought more highly of herself than was warranted.

The ordeals built a special bond between the ones who endured the trials together. It was a bond Flora really didn't understand. What she did understand—what would have been obvious to a highland bull—was that Serlaid wanted to choose Domhnull as her husband. That desire may have been her whole reason for facing the ordeals to begin with. But Domhnull had not chosen to take her as a wife, and it had frustrated Serlaid to no end. It made her more peevish to everyone else, and even more overtly blatant in her pursuit of Domhnull.

Domhnull leaned on his spear and stood. He was tall and broad shouldered. Even as a new man, Flora thought he looked like a chief. His long, straw-colored hair hung free in a flowing mane that gave him the appearance of a mighty stallion. For just a moment, Flora allowed herself to dream that this enchanting young man might one day ask for her hand in marriage, but then an angry glance from Serlaid pulled her back to reality. Domhnull would, no doubt, eventually be Serlaid's man. It's what everyone in the village expected.

Domhnull's expression was grave. "The falling stars are fiery arrows from Lugh's bow. They portend great battles to come. This year, there were so many stars, and they were so bright, I expect more than just battles. I suspect we will fight a great war."

Flora's father looked long and hard into the younger man's eyes. She couldn't tell what he was thinking. Was he pondering the young warrior's assessment of the omen's portents? Or was he considering Domhnull's suitability as a husband for Searlaid? After a long while he said simply, "No. The traditions are clear. The falling stars are souls of the dead, transformed into birds, flying back to the sun, back to Lugh, so the god might send them on to the Otherworld." Then he turned to Flora. "So, you see, my wee *fauth*, there's nothing to worry your head about. The streaks appear in the sky every year, because every year souls wing their way to Lugh and onward to the Otherworld. This year, there were more than usual because somewhere in the land, a great many souls were set free. Perhaps among the Brigantes down by the Great Wall. But the reason we traveled here is because of what happened next."

"That's the part I don't understand." Flora peered up at her father with a quizzical look. "If the stars fall every year, why did our whole village make this journey to the tree?"

Searlaid stepped between Flora and Domhnull. "Some healer you'll make if you can't even read the stars."

Flora glanced at Searlaid with a look of exasperation. "Herbs and poultices heal, not stars. Reading the stars is for diviners and seers, not for healers."

Flora's mother edged into view. She interjected in a flat, almost deadpan voice, "We didn't come because of the soul stars. We came because of the new star that swims against the current, just like the salmon fish do. Look. During the day, the new star is beautiful, like a young maiden with flowing hair." She pointed high into the sky.

Flora let her gaze follow the line of her mother's finger, and she could, indeed, see this new star. It was almost as large as the moon! Clouds almost always cloaked the sky in the highlands, keeping its secrets hidden from their prying eyes. But today, the skies were almost completely clear, so Flora could see the star, even in the sunlight. It did look like a beautiful maiden with long flowing hair that fluttered like a banner in the wind.

Her mother continued. "But in the darkness of night, the specter transforms into a hideous, raging old hag, with hair like serpents and eyes that shoot bursts of flame. The druid council called a gathering of the tribe to offer a special sacrifice in order to learn the significance of this omen from the gods. And since we came all this way, you will have a chance to see your grandmother once again."

The memory faded, and the green dissolved into the blacks and grays of the devastated landscape. Flora wept to think of what had just happened to this land. She recalled the star. It had appeared in the night sky over six years ago and then disappeared just as suddenly. The druid council had been very secretive about their conclusions. Usually, they were quick to inform the community about a coming disaster or great blessings. But in this case, they had remained silent about the strange star and its portents.

In retrospect, she now knew why. How do you tell a people—your own people—about their coming annihilation and the total desolation of their land? What good would it do, unless there was some sacrifice, some ritual, some sacred rite the people could perform to avert the wrath of the gods and change the course of future events? Apparently, nothing could be done to reverse the star's dreadful portents and bring salvation to the people and their land. And so now, only she remained as the sole witness of this dreadful fate.

Her gaze settled on the yew—that sacred, ancient, indomitable tree—and a tiny flicker of hope was kindled in her heart. As long as the tree survived, hope was not completely gone. The gods had protected the sacred tree. And, for some inexplicable reason, the gods had protected her. So there must still be a path ahead—a frightening, dismal, terrifying path—but a path nonetheless.

At that very moment, as these thoughts lingered in her mind, something hurled over Flora's head. Her heart jumped, and she ducked low before she realized what it was. A bird. A bird! Was there truly another living creature in this devastated land?

As her breath returned and her heart slowed, she lifted her hand to her eyes to shield the sun and then watched the bird carefully. It swooped low for just a moment and winged back up into an arc that settled into a circle above the mill. The poor thing must be hungry.

Flora ducked back inside the door to grab a handful of grain and suddenly noticed the little deer was gone. She blinked her eyes to chase away the brightness from outside and quickly scanned the interior of the mill. She couldn't see it anywhere. Hastily, she grabbed a handful of unground barley kernels and laid them in a pile outside the door where the bird could find them. Then she hurried back inside the mill to search for her providential little friend.

As her eyes once again adjusted to the gloomy interior, Flora hurriedly scanned the mill house for the fawn. She knew it could not possibly have walked out the door and past her. She certainly would have noticed. Starting to panic, she frantically pushed aside bags of grain and rushed around the grinding stone to look into dark corners and hidden crannies. She flew about the mill like a painted warrior in a berzerker rage, crying out desperately for the baby deer.

Flora had a natural affection and concern for animals woven throughout the fabric of her life. But this terror went much deeper than concern for a fellow creature's safety. Her mind spun in frenzied circles. Had it even been real? Had the deer actually nuzzled her face in the storm and led her into this sanctuary? Or was it all just an illusion—a phantom created by a desperate mind hovering on the brink? Was she being led by the gods, or stalked by the *sluagh*? A tremor rippled through her body and she glanced through the open door which did, in fact, face to the west. Was that bird one of them, one of the *sluagh*, a spirit of the wicked dead that scoured the land, searching for weak souls to plunder?

Flora pressed her palms to her temples, fell to her knees, and wailed in frustration. Her shoulders slumped, and she began to weep. Her mind groped for something certain, something solid, something tangible she could hold on to. She fumbled through the empty sacks on the floor to find her woolen *leine*. She pulled desperately at it, searching for the leather pouch that held her treasures. Those were real tokens of real memories—*her* memories of a real world. Her hands rifled through the fabric from end to end, and her panic rose to a fevered pitch. It wasn't there! The pouch wasn't there! Her treasures were gone! Her memories were gone!

She tore at the grain sacks in desperation, throwing them in every direction, grasping for a hope that slipped through her fingers. Her mind raced through the wilderness, fleeing from locusts and choking on smoke, until it settled in a dark cavern and clutched at a soft piece of wool tangled around a mass of thorns, and her heart sank. She rolled to her side, pulled her knees to her chest, and keened like a widow at a funeral pyre.

There was a pouch. It was real. Her treasures were real. Her memories were real. But they were hidden in a cavern in a rocky crag on a lonely hill across a wasteland of ash and mud. She knew she had to get them, but the thought of facing that hill again was more than she could bear. She dropped her head to the gritty dirt of the floor, closed her eyes, and shivered from exhaustion, from fear, from dismay.

A few moments passed, and she heard a scratching sound near her feet. She opened her eyes to see a bird pecking at stray kernels of barley on the floor. Stark images from stories of the *sluagh* caused her to recoil from the menacing creature. She jerked upright and began impulsively backing away. The bird straightened up, cocked its head to the left, and gazed at her with a single eye. That eye held no malice. The gaze did not pierce her soul. Rather, it pleaded gently.

Eventually Flora's heart slowed, and her frantic thoughts settled. This bird was not a raven or a crow—omens of evil that would have sent her mind over the brink and into the abyss. Flora breathed an audible sigh as she realized the bird was a robin, a sign of peace and hope. The robin dropped its head to the ground and picked up a grain of barley in its beak. It hopped in her direction and she felt an overwhelming urge to extend her hand to it. Still looking straight at her with its one eye, the bird dropped the kernel into her hand and fluttered toward the open door.

Flora stared at the grain of barley in astonishment for a long moment, then glanced up at the shaft of light piercing the darkness of the room. She assumed the robin would have flown away, but it just stood there, looking back at her expectantly. She stood and slowly moved toward the waiting creature. The bird remained perfectly still, framed by the door and illuminated by the brightness of the sun. It virtually glowed as a splash of color against the stark blacks and grays of the charred countryside in the background.

Flora stepped into the light, and the robin launched itself into the sky. It flew in a spiraling circle above the mill and then branched off across the glen. As Flora watched the bird slowly disappear in the distance, a spot of green came into view. The robin, her omen of hope, had flown directly to the ancient yew tree. A tingle ran up her spine. The bird was inviting her to follow. The gods were calling her to the sacred tree.

Flora turned her head the other way and looked at the steep hill rising up behind her. At the top of that hill lay a rocky crag with a hidden cavern. And in that cavern lay a small leather pouch surrounded by a scattered collection of treasures. Those treasures represented more than just her memories. They were her link to a world she knew was real.

She felt a dark shadow cross her mind and wondered again if these signs of hope—the fawn and the robin—had even existed. Were they truly omens sent by the gods to guide her on? Or were they fantasies from an imagination grasping desperately for some kind of hope to cling to? Or worse still, were they delusions woven by a sinister presence luring her to some nefarious end—a dreadful, ghastly purpose at which she could only guess? She had no way to tell, no way to know for sure. But she had to choose. She had to decide. She could climb the hill to recover her memories and regain her tangible link to certainty. Or she could follow the robin to the sacred tree and discover what unknown hope or horror awaited her there. Or she could just sit here, in the mill, where there was shelter from the storms and food to satisfy her gnawing hunger.

Flora thought back to the voice in the glen by the millpond, the voice that urged her to climb the hill and flee from the locusts, and the voice that helped her to escape the wolf. Where had that voice been since then? What guidance would it give her now? Was it someone or something she could trust? Or was it part of a plot to lure her deeper and deeper into the web? Flora wondered what the voice would say to her now, what advice it would give. Perhaps she could ask. If the voice belonged to a god, then surely the god would hear her request, regardless of whether that plea was eventually honored or not. Then again, she didn't even know what to call it or whom to address.

She felt silly but decided to call out, anyway. "My guide and protector, O one who has called out to me in recent days, advise me now. Which way should I go? Which path should I take?"

She grimaced at the sound of her voice. She sounded like a supplicant begging protection from a chief. Her language was more like that of the court than of a desperate girl pleading for help from a god. Still she paused, and waited, and listened. But there was no voice. No one answered. No one paid any attention.

Flora sighed and turned to go back inside the mill. Then she jerked with surprise as she heard the voice behind her, clear and distinct, and a tingle pricked her between the shoulders.

"Go. Up."

That was all.

Flora spun to see who was speaking. By now she should have known what to expect. There was no one there. But the direction had been clear. The owner of the voice had heard her request *and responded.* It was urging her back to the cave, back to the reality of her memories, and back to her past.

Flora turned and stepped hesitantly into the mill. She picked up her *leine*. It had mostly dried from the soaking rain, but was still damp to the touch. She squirmed slightly as she pulled it over her head and felt the clamminess against her skin. Then she grabbed one of the empty sacks and stuffed several handfuls of grain into its gaping mouth.

With a deep breath, she stepped out the door and strode purposefully toward the sacred yew. She glanced back at the hill and the memories she was leaving behind. That hill represented a climb to certainty, but it was the fleeting certainty of a ruined past—a past that was painful and horrible to her—a past that had been destroyed by armies and fire. She desperately wanted to hold on to those memories of the people she loved. But her family and her friends were gone now, and she couldn't bring them back. Her treasures weren't lost. They were safe in the cave. She could go back for them soon. But the gods were calling to her, and she dared not ignore their summons. The omens were clear, even to one who lacked the training of a druid.

As she stepped off the solid ground around the mill and into the muddy ash of the devastated land, she thought she heard the voice again—very faint, like a breathy whisper.

"Trust me."

She paused mid-stride for just a heartbeat, then continued on across the wasteland of the glen, toward the sacred tree and the summons of the gods.

CHAPTER FIVE

The bird was gone now, but its direction and purpose were clear. The bright green yew tree stood out against the dismal background like a beacon guiding a boat through the fog of night. Muddy ash tugged at Flora's feet, and her legs felt as if they were being slowly sucked into a bog. She leaned forward, pushing against charred stumps to force herself on.

She glanced up above the tree to see if she could see *Feart Choille*, the Forest Stronghold, a fortress of the druids. Folks said it had been carved by the winds of time from the rocky crag that rose above the glen. According to legend, the gods had built the fortress to protect the sacred yew and to guard the entrance to the great glen beyond, *Gleann Linne*, the glen of lakes and pools. It was a place of wonders and mysteries beyond the imagination. The druids had protected the secrets of the glen as diligently as they had cared for the holy tree.

Yet Flora could see no ramparts atop the rocky crag. The outcropping of stone was, in and of itself, a mighty bastion towering over the valley below. Yet it was merely a natural boulder, upon which she had expected to see the imposing walls of a mighty citadel.

From her vantage point, all she could discern beyond the sheer stone cliff was a forest of trees, scorched to cinders by the blazing inferno. Where was the fortress of legend and lore? What had become of the sacred yew's protective stronghold? Had it been annihilated like everything else in this devastated land? Had it, too, been devoured by Belanus' raging hunger?

Images from the fire that consumed her home village superimposed themselves on the scene, and she could almost see the smoke billowing from the broken ramparts of the druid's fort atop the hill. She fought back tears of desperation and shook the images from her mind. She focused her eyes, her attention, and all her awareness on the sacred tree. She could almost hear it calling to her through whispered songs dancing on the breeze.

Gradually, she emerged from the scorched remains of what had been a patch of trees and stepped out into an open field. Here, the locusts had stripped the ground bare of the grass and bracken and crops of grain that filled the open space, so there had been nothing to burn. She left the ash behind and ventured out on what appeared to be firmer ground.

Flora was coaxed, or rather compelled, to turn away from the sacred yew toward something in the field off to her right. She slowed her steps and came to a halt. She actually felt something, an energy or a force, drawing her in that direction. Somehow she knew that if she resisted its urging and continued her journey to the tree, there would be terrible consequences. It wasn't something she thought through or reasoned in her mind. Instead, she felt it deep inside her soul. And so she altered her course and moved in that direction.

As she drew closer, the objects became clearer, and a hint of recollection seeped into the back of her mind. The objects took shape, and she suddenly recalled the three great monuments that guarded the entrance to *Feart Choille*. She had seen them during her tribe's gathering six summers ago. This was where the clans had assembled to discover the secrets of the mysterious star that appeared in the heavens. This was where the druids had performed the special rites to reveal the star's meaning and to understand its awesome and terrible portents.

FLORA STOPPED and closed her eyes. She conjured the scene in her mind from the morning before the sacrifice.

She sat with Nandag, her mentor, on the grass about a bowshot away from the tribe's camp. Tents beyond number filled the valley, grouped together by villages and clans. The sky was cloudy, and a drizzling rain misted the air. It was light and wispy, like your breath on a cold winter day.

"*Bean-teagaisg*, the druids taught you how to cure sickness, right? Do you understand these rituals? What is this place? Why are we here? And what is going to happen?"

Nandag smiled at her affectionately. "You're always full of questions, little one. It's why you will become a good healer. Yes, I learned the deep mysteries of the healing arts in the oak grove of the druids, just as you will one day."

"But you are my *bean-teagaisg*. I will learn from you, not from the druids."

"There are many things I can teach you. But there are other things, other deep and ancient rituals, that you must learn from the gods. These are things you cannot learn from me. They go far beyond simply understanding which herbs and plants to gather and how to prepare them, or which poultices to apply to different kinds of wounds. These are things that you come to know through an encounter with the gods. And the druids must guide you through the experiences which cause this knowledge to become a part of your soul. Their rituals open the gateways through which we encounter the power of the gods. And those rituals protect us from that same awesome power. You will understand, when the time comes."

"Fine. It's just like everything else. I'll have to wait 'til I'm older to find out. I hear that a lot, you know."

Nandag smiled again and her eyes shone brightly. "Patience is just such a thing, as is wisdom. They aren't just there for the picking. They ripen over time. Do you remember the cherry tree we planted outside the village last year? It will take seven more summers before that tree bears any fruit. I know of some very rare plants from distant lands that flower only once in a hundred summers. That's two or three lifetimes for you and me. In just the same way, the wisdom of the druids has been cultivated from the beginning of time. It has grown and matured alongside the sacred yew. But that's a lesson for another day."

"You still haven't told me what will happen here. Tell me about the rituals."

"I learned much about the ways of healing during my time in the druid's grove, but there are many, many more things I did not learn. I know very little about the sacred rituals for divining the will of the gods, or for seeing into the future, or for reading omens. But I will tell you what I can."

Flora leaned in toward her teacher, eager to hear about the holy rites that would soon be performed in front of the assembled tribe.

"You know about the falling of the stars and of the fiery omen that appeared in the sky, yes? I heard your family discussing it on the journey here."

"Yes, teacher. I know it's a terrible and dreadful omen, and I know the druids need to make a special sacrifice to understand what it means."

"'Terrible' and 'dreadful' may not be the correct ways to describe what we don't yet understand. Perhaps 'awesome' or 'portentous' might be better terms to use. Do you understand the difference?"

"Do you mean the sign could be either good or bad, but right now we only know that it's very important?"

Nandag cocked her head and raised her left eyebrow. "Perhaps wisdom is taking root in your heart even now, little one. That is correct. The druid council will perform special rituals to attract the attention of the gods—to let them know we have recognized their sign and stand ready to receive their guidance."

"Why here, in this place?"

"There are some things I don't completely know, and other things I'm not permitted to reveal. But I can tell you this place is very sacred. It is the entrance to *Gleann Linne,* the valley of lakes and pools. You know that all bodies of water are holy. But these pools are special places where the veil between this world and the Otherworld is very thin—where the gods cross over to commune with men, and perhaps even where men can cross into the Otherworld and then return!"

Flora gasped. She knew the gods would sometimes walk among the people of this world, usually in the guise of a stranger or an animal of some sort. And she knew the gods sometimes gave visions and dreams of the Otherworld to the druid masters to help them understand the deep mysteries of life. But she had never heard of someone actually crossing into the Otherworld and then returning. She trembled at the thought such a thing was possible. She was even more astounded by the idea that someone could cross over to taste the richness, feel the textures, and drink in the fragrances of such a place, and then summon the will to return!

Nandag studied her reaction for a moment and then continued. "The gods placed the sacred yew to mark the entrance to the holy glen. The tree is very ancient. It has been standing watch over this valley since the dawn of time. They say if you walk through the gap in its trunk, you will pass through a tiny slice of the Otherworld, and it will change your soul forever."

Flora stared at the yew tree, straining to see if she could perceive even the slightest shimmer in the gap of its trunk. She thought maybe she could.

"The gods built a natural fortress on the rocky crag above the tree. Holy men have stood watch on its ramparts since the beginning of days. They protect the sacred yew, and they guard the entrance to the holy glen."

"Will we go into the valley of lakes and pools for the ritual?"

"No, child. Few people are permitted to enter the glen, and only for special purposes. You see the three stone circles across the field from the tree?"

"Well, I see them, but they aren't exactly circles. I went over close last night. They're really squares, with big boulders at the corners and small boulders in between."

Nandag scowled and knit her brow. She had a narrow face with a long nose and eyebrows that slanted in. Her upper lip was straight and thin, but the lower one arched down in a way that gave her a deep, warm smile. Laughter often sparkled in her eyes. But Flora knew her teacher's expressions. When she forced her natural smile into a tight-lipped frown and scrunched her eyebrows in so they nearly touched, then Flora was in trouble.

She quickly blurted out, "I only went close. I didn't touch anything, or take anything, or leave anything behind. I just *looked* at the stones."

Nandag's frown softened a bit, but the stern look in her eyes lingered. "Be very careful in this place, little one. There are forces here that must be handled in a particular manner—forces that must be feared and respected, and traditions that have endured for endless turnings of the moon. If you meddle with these forces in the wrong way, you could cause dreadful consequences not only for yourself, but also for our people."

Flora felt the heat rise in her face. She knew Nandag could see her shame, and she dropped her eyes to the ground. She murmured an apology under her breath.

Nandag reached out a hand and lifted her chin. "Look into my eyes, little one."

Flora obediently lifted her eyes in. She expected to see admonition and scorn. Instead, she saw a depth of love and concern she had barely even known from her own mother. Tears pricked at the back of her eyes, but Nandag's gentle gaze held her own.

"Your curiosity is a good thing, little one. But you are still naive to the many dangers this world poses to the unwary. It is okay to explore. But when you want to do that, make sure to have me at your side so I can keep you within safe boundaries." The twinkle of laughter returned to her eyes. "And so you don't step into a pile of sheep dung."

Flora smiled in a silent reply of acquiescence.

"Do you see how the tents are arrayed in an arc around the three stone circles—umm, squares?" A nod was the only signal she needed to continue. "Those stone formations are actually temples to the gods, placed there by the old folk in ancient times. One temple honors Lugh. It is oriented toward the place where the sun sets on the day of Lughnasadh. One temple is for Cerridwen. It faces to where the sun and moon meet in the sky—when Cerridwen dances with Lugh and hides his face from our eyes so they can enjoy the pleasures of a man and wife."

Flora looked up in surprise. She had never thought of the gods behaving in that way.

Nandag went on, without pausing to address Flora's unspoken question. "The third is for the Cailleach, the creator. Together, these three stone temples form a gateway to the sacred yew and to the holy glen beyond. Anyone who is chosen to approach the yew tree or to enter the glen must pass through the temple gateway and perform the sacred rituals. Anyone who neglects these rites will desecrate the holy places and incur the gravest anger of the gods.

"Do you see now why you must be very careful of where you walk? This is why our clansmen placed their tents so far away from the stone temples, and why druid guards stand watch over the area day and night. I don't know how a curious girl like you escaped their notice and was allowed to tread so close to peril."

Flora's curiosity took over again, and she rushed past the gentle admonition. "Will the tribe enter through the gates for the special ritual tonight? Will I get to go there?"

"No, child. Only the Arch Druid and the high council will enter through the gates tonight. Together, they will conduct the rituals, pass through the stone temples, and approach the sacred tree. There they will seek the meaning of the omen in the sky."

Flora's shoulders sagged, and she pursed her lips in an exasperated expression of petulance. "Then why are we here? Why did we walk all this way? Why has the whole tribe gathered together? If only the druid council is going in, why can't they perform the rituals by themselves?"

"Ahh. You have no end of questions. I'll answer this last one, and then we need to go prepare. Our tribe is tasked to protect the holy valley. This place is at the very center of our land. It is the heart that pumps the lifeblood throughout the highlands. The clans of our tribe form a shield around this most holy place, guarding it against any threat. Our clan is positioned on Loch Rannoch to the north. The Great Chief's clan at Loch Tatha protects the south side. Clan Alpin on Loch Toilbhe beyond the western mountains forms a shield in the direction of the setting sun. And clan *Mac-an-t-sagairtat* in Pit Cloich Aire guards the eastern gateway to our lands where the Sentinel Stones stand."

As she spoke, Nandag pointed in the direction of each clan's territory, showing Flora how they related to the orientation of the stone temples.

"We are all tasked to do our part to keep the sacred places safe and free from corruption. The druids stand watch as custodians and sentinels, and they can summon powerful forces to defend this place where men walk in the presence of the gods. But our tribe, the Tuath Vuin, is the shield that keeps foreign invaders at bay. Three generations ago, we halted the advance of the greatest Roman army that ever tried to conquer our land. Many tribes sent warriors to our aid, but the Tuath Vuin formed an immovable stone that broke the Roman tide and repelled them from entering the holy glen."

Flora grimaced at the mention of the Romans. Her hatred of the invaders had just recently been kindled by stories her father told around the family hearth. But grew in intensity every passing day, as tales like Nandag's revealed how much of a threat the Roman armies posed to her people.

"We also provide the crops and livestock that sustain the druid conclave which watches over this place and performs the sacred rituals. We all have a stake in the meaning of this awesome oracle, written in the stars. We must all take part in the rituals through which our spiritual leaders approach the gods and seek to know their will."

Nandag's voice faded in Flora's memory and she opened her eyes to the terrible scene of carnage which had been wrought upon the land. If only they had known back then what the course of events would bring, would they have done something different? Or had the druid council indeed learned of these things when they approached the holy tree? Did they know everything that would occur? Or did they receive other guidance and choose, instead, a path which brought the wrath of the gods down upon them all? Perhaps she would never know.

This memory did, however, help her understand the compulsions which drew her toward the stone temples. It also made her path clear. The gods were still alive in this place, even if nothing else was. If she intended to approach the sacred yew, she would have to enter through the gates, as the rituals and traditions demanded.

WITH HER FULL attention focused on the three stone temples, Flora didn't even notice the shallow embankment laying in her path until she nearly tripped over a branch protruding from its base. She assumed it was merely a low, earthen mound and absent-mindedly ignored it. But a nauseating stench wafted over her at the very moment she glanced down to see what caused her to stumble. It was an arm! A human arm, covered in pustulous yellow and purple boils.

Flora stared in horror at the dirt mound and shrunk back when she realized it was actually an immense pile of bodies covered with a thin layer of ash. Bloated faces stared blankly from a tangled mass of arms and legs and torsos, infested with ulcers that oozed a brackish puss and reeked of rotting flesh.

Flora fell to her knees and retched violently. The recent meal of oats and barley spewed out of her mouth. Her stomach heaved until the mush of grains was gone and then continued in painful bouts until putrid bile burned her throat and mucus drained from her nose in viscous strands. She whimpered as the tremors racked her body, and she gulped in great gasps of air between the violent contractions of her stomach. Slowly, the spasms subsided, and she shivered from the sweat that drenched her *leine* and dripped from her forehead. She cradled her head in her hands and wept.

With every step she took toward hope, she stumbled over a new horror. The bodies heaped up in that mound of death weren't just ordinary villagers. That would have been gruesome enough, but this was even worse. The figures in pile were clad in white robes. This wasn't a mass grave of slaughtered villagers or soldiers slain in battle. It was a mountain of druid corpses, ravaged by a malignant pestilence. These druids were masters of healing magic. They called upon the immortal power of the gods. They performed sacred rituals, received divine visions, and interpreted oracles. What kind of evil scourge could overcome this mighty coven of druids in such a devastating way?

If the druids were gone, then her people were destroyed. The druids formed the very core of their community. They were the heart and wisdom of the tribe. They kept the history and the lore. They judged disputes of law. Chiefs moved armies upon their word, and warriors halted at their command. Yet now it seemed as if every druid in the land had been cast to rot upon that festering heap.

Flora felt her determination and her strength ebb away. This last blow was more than she could bear. All along, at every turn, some new tiny spark of hope had urged her on and kept her going forward. But this pile of decaying corpses stole her last bit of courage away. If the druids were gone, then her people were gone, and she was truly alone. What could even the gods do now? Did they even have the power to restore all that was destroyed?

Why had she been spared? Why her? Was her life just a tiny strand of fate that had somehow escaped the notice of the Morrigan as they cut the remaining threads connecting her people to the world? Or was hers the most dreadful destiny of all—to survive alone in a desolate land of hopelessness and loss?

There, leaning on hands and knees over a pool of her own vomit, Flora perceived the answer to her question. She had not been spared after all. Her thread was just the last to be severed. Oh cruel the Morrigan, to make her watch everything she loved be destroyed before taking the shears to her own slender strand.

Suddenly, the boils she had seen on the decaying druid bodies sprang up in blotches on her own hands and wrists. They festered and burst in a moment of time. The secretions that oozed from the open wounds bred new ulcers on her forearms, and she gasped in horror as she watched the virulent pustules sweep up to devour her limbs.

Part of her wanted to collapse to the ground, give in to the malignant plague, and allow it to consume her soul. But somewhere, deep down inside, there was something—some innate fear of death, some primal yearning to live—that forced her to struggle on rather than give up in despair.

The sacred tree, the ancient yew, was still alive! Amid locust swarms, a blazing inferno, and a malicious pestilence, it alone remained vibrant and green. What had Nandag said about the gap in its trunk? If someone walked through that gap, they would pass through a thin slice of the Otherworld. There was no sickness in the Otherworld—no disease, no decay. If she could just make it to the tree and pass through that space, perhaps she could survive.

FLORA FORCED her gaze up and fixed her eyes on the tree. Her vision narrowed to a black tunnel where everything else faded from view. Only the tree remained. It stood shimmering and gleaming in her mind. It was her last and only hope.

She lacked the strength or the will to stand. She could feel the boils spreading up her legs and arms. Gradually, she became aware of a searing pain burning the surface of her skin. It pulsed in rhythm with her heart, and its intensity grew with every breath. Slowly and steadily she began to crawl through the standing stone gateway and toward the sacred yew.

The rituals demanded by tradition would have to be foregone, for soon she, herself, would be a living sacrifice. Would the gods accept her life in exchange for the white bull? Or would they, themselves, strike her dead before she made it a hand's breadth past the temple gate? She didn't know, and she didn't care. She focused all her attention on reaching the tree.

The distance was much greater than she had imagined. She longed to stagger to her feet and run to the tree, but the strength seeped from her limbs and drained, along with the pus, into the dirt. The tree seemed as far away as the moon. She forced herself on, but the ground tugged harder and harder with every movement of her hands and knees. She concentrated all her effort on each individual motion of her body. Lift a hand, place it down. Lift a knee and move it forward. Over and over again.

Then, suddenly, she was engulfed in a strange, penetrating stillness. It seemed as if the surrounding air was instantly sucked away, leaving no sounds, no sensations, and no feelings behind. Even the burning pain disappeared. Her vision was overwhelmed by a light so bright the sun grew pale in itspresence. Instinctively, she flinched, but her eyes snapped back open, and she stared directly into the light. In the midst of that blazing, shimmering brightness, the face of Brigid began to take form. It grew in shape and definition until Flora was gazing into the very eyes of the goddess, herself.

"Come on, little one. Come to me. Come to my sacred tree. I will give you strength. I will give you life. I will give you hope. Open your heart and trust in me."

As quickly as it had appeared, the vision faded. The air rushed back in around her, and the stillness ebbed away. Flora found herself clinging to the trunk of the tree—the sacred, ancient yew. Relief flooded her soul. She had made it! She was here! Brigid had rescued her! Now she was safe.

The world swirled around her, she collapsed in a lump to the ground, and everything went black.

CHAPTER SIX

Darkness. Stillness. A small patch of light. Just a point. Growing larger. Moving toward the light. Faster and faster. A rushing noise, like a gale-force wind. Suddenly emerging into the light, like breaking through the surface of a lake into the brightness of day.

She was flying. She saw feathers and wings at her sides. She was gliding on currents of air, spiraling higher and higher. She tried to cry out and her voice emerged as a soft, throaty whooo, like the cooing of a dove.

She broke over a peak of shadows, like a ridgeline in the air, and soared above a vast wilderness of desolation—gnarled black fingers rising out of a sea of gray ash. Climbing higher, she turned and circled in every direction. The devastation extended from horizon to horizon.

She winged silently over mountain peaks and rocky crags and long narrow glens. Everywhere the scene was the same—the charred remains of a dead land, ravaged by pestilence and fire. Her keen eyes could see every detail on the ground, even from this great height. She scanned carefully for any kind of movement, any sign of life.

The rivers and streams still flowed through the glens and into the great lochs, but her penetrating gaze could see that even those vast inland seas, once estuaries teeming with life, had been transformed into burial cairns concealing carnage and death. The fiery conflagration that devoured the forests, villages, and grassy vales somehow infiltrated even those watery sanctuaries to slaughter the fish, eels, and frogs that once took refuge there.

Can owls weep? Can wisdom shed a tear?

She glided for eons and traveled the breadth of the land, scanning the ground, seeking for any sign of hope—but hope was an elusive prey that hid itself well behind a veil of sorrow and despair. Yet she never stopped soaring and searching and praying to find an end to the death and a renewal of life.

She caught a draft and glided over a lofty peak, and a great glen came into view. For just an instant, a sudden vivid memory filled in the green grass of the meadows, the deep hues of the woodlands, and the gems of light sparkling on the surface of the loch. Then the vision faded, and she looked down again upon the bleak and dismal scene that stretched for days and months and years in every direction. But that momentary flash of color caught her attention and she peered more intently on the somehow familiar scene that rushed beneath her wings.

Then she saw it. A building that had not been devoured by flames and a water wheel that lapped and turned in an endless cycle of rhythm and rhyme. The stream beside the mill fed a small pond which was somehow different than the dull, flat gray surfaces that dotted the ashen landscape in other glens. This pond shone with light and color and life, as if it were a window into the Otherworld.

As her gaze continued to sweep across the valley floor, she spied the spot in disbelief—a green patch amidst the ashen gray—a tree that had not been ravaged or transfigured into a charred and blackened stump. And then she knew the truth. It was not just *a* tree. It was *the* tree. It was the sacred yew.

She tilted her wings and shifted her path into a great arc centered on the tree. She circled there, lingering in wonder for several moments, and then descended in a slow, steady spiral. Her path droped until she was grazing over the tops of its highest branches. Its vibrance and life lifted her like currents of air. Energy and vitality radiated from the lush foliage. Echoes of laughter and song wafted on the gentle breeze that rustled its leaves.

She alit on a limb crafted especially for her talons, and a flame ignited between her claws. She did not launch back into the air in terror or fear. Somehow, she knew this flame came from deep within her soul. It was kindled by the life and essence of the tree. It did not scorch or sear or destroy, but gently warmed and nurtured. It was not the raging fire of the inferno, but the tender radiance of the hearth. It flickered and spread throughout the branches of the tree. It burned without consuming. It sparked hope, instead of devouring dreams.

The vitalizing blaze engulfed the sacred yew and spread out from the trunk, like ripples in a pond from the drop a stone. Every place touched by its brightness burst forth in colors and fragrances and sounds. A wildfire of vivid greens, bright yellows, soft browns, and deep blues expanded in wave after wave of regeneration and life.

She launched herself into the air and flapped her wings in great and mighty strokes, flying higher and higher, so she could see the life force emanating from the tree and spreading across the land. And yet, amid the overflowing joy of hope and renewal, something was missing. *Someone* was missing. Her soulmate. Her family. Her people. From somewhere deep inside, an assurance welled up within her. She knew where to find them. She knew how to fill the void and make all things complete.

She arced high into the air and dove toward the tree. This time she did not alight in the branches. Instead, she swooped low and raced toward the gap in the trunk of the yew. The yawning breach beckoned her on, inviting her in to the great unknown. Without time to stop short or turn aside, she swept through the opening and time stood still.

Falling. Deeper and deeper. The light recedes. A window. A circle. A point. Stillness. Darkness.

Faint sounds emerged through a mist of silence—the gentle notes of a harp dancing on the breeze. They melted away into the silence once again. Nothing. Nowhere. No one. The notes came again, like the soothing whisper of sunshine melting the morning dew from the grass. The rustle of the wind in the leaves of an alder took on form and weight and dissolved into a distant melody, growing stronger, and deeper, and fuller—resonating with gentle bass tones that stirred memories from a lifetime ago. Words formed into swirling eddies in the current of a stream and drifted away. Slowly, patiently, they blended together with the tender caresses of the strings and melded into a song.

> *Down by the loch where the willow tree grows*
> *In the glen on an early spring day*
> *She is born*
> *She is here*
> *The wee bairn in my arms*
> *She has come to set my heart free*

Images formed. A father's strong arms held her close. She felt the words of the melody resonate in his chest, as his heart beat rhythmically to the tune, and warmth radiated from his body, enveloping her with peace and love.

A young sprite is she, a fair bonny lass
She bids me raise Uaithne and play
She dances
She sways
She sets right the days
In winter, fall, summer and spring

She was a young girl now, dancing in circles in the soft grass of the glen, with a spray of white heather tucked in her hair. Her daddy lifted her into the air and swept her around in a wide arc. His smile lit up her world like the radiance of the sun. She tossed back her head and giggled with delight as her feet skipped on the wind and her dress flittered in the breeze.

A daughter divine, one sister of three
As her father I see past these times
She searches
She ponders
Toward wisdom she wanders
And soon I must give her away

She walked beside her father along the shore of Loch Rannoch in the cool air of evening. She felt the strength and tenderness of his hand holding hers. They walked without talking for a long moment, comfortable with the silence, sharing thoughts without words. After reflecting quietly on the waves lapping against the shore, he slowed his pace and drew her around so he could see her face. He took both her hands and looked deeply into her eyes with a father's gentle love.

"Domhnull is a fine young man. He'll treat you well and give you a good home. If this is truly what you want, what your heart desires, then you have my blessing."

She couldn't stop the smile from breaking out across her face, or the tears from flowing down her cheeks. As she nodded her head

eagerly and jumped into his arms, she almost didn't notice the
wetness that formed in the corners of his eyes.

A maiden in white, a princess to be
With a flame set ablaze in her eyes
She weeps
And she sings
A bride of the springs
To heal the land she will rise

The music sounded rich and bold and... *real*. Images raced
through her mind of a barren, desolate land, scorched and dying. A
twisted mass of rotting corpses lay piled in a heap. Stone circles
loomed tall against a rising moon. Putrid boils erupted on her skin
and devoured her flesh. A tree—*the tree*—burned with a mystical,
radiant flame.

As the melody faded, Flora's eyes fluttered open. Blurry shapes
slowly took form. She tried to speak, but only a muffled cough broke
through her lips. She heard her father's muted gasp.

"Flora! Flora, can you hear me? Are you there?"

Then he cast aside his harp and bent low to wrap her in his arms.
"Oh, Flora. My girl. My wee *fauth*. You're awake! You've come back
to me! You're gonna be okay! Everything's gonna be okay!"

"*Dadaidh! Dadaidh*, is it you? Is it really you?" She melted into
her father's loving arms and wept.

Flora clung to her father for what seemed like an eternity—fearing
to let go lest it all fade away and turn out to be just another dream,
withering in the mist. Her body heaved with alternating sobs and

sighs as she felt her father's strong arms hold her tightly. He was her rock. He was her hope. And he was holding her now. The nightmare was over, and she was home!

Her father rocked her gently in his arms. "Shhh. Shhh. It's okay now. It's okay. You're here and you're safe, and I'll nae let any harm come to you now. Hush. Hush, now."

Slowly the shudders passed and her tears ebbed. Her father stroked her hair and continued to whisper in her ear. Still clinging to the strength and security he offered, Flora willed her eyes to open. In the faint light filtering in around the edge of the thatch, she saw an unfamiliar place. This wasn't her home. It wasn't a place she recognized at all.

A sudden chill caused her body to tense. Fear washed anew over her mind. Could this all be part of the illusion? Was she still tangled in the web? Was the spider stalking her, preparing to strike while her guard was down?

Her body tensed, and her father squeezed her gently. His reassurance helped the spasm subside a bit, but not to dissipate completely. A tinge of doubt still lingered in her mind, keeping her nerves taut and her senses on the alert.

She pulled back slightly and looked up at her father. His normally bright green eyes looked clouded and haggard, and his light sandy hair fell in loose, unkempt tangles down his shoulders. His mouth, partly hidden by his short-cropped beard, nevertheless, turned up in a light, tentative smile in a mixed expression of relief and concern.

"What is it, my wee *fauth*? You're okay now. What's your worry?"

"Where am I, *Dadaidh*? This isn't home. Where is this place?"

She glanced around the large room. No one else was there except her father. She was lying on a bed of straw, covered in a sheep skin. Smoke rose from a fire pit in the center of the room. The building was circular, much like her own home, but much smaller. There was a small copper pot near the fire, surrounded by a couple clay jars, heating stones, and a scattering of wood and bone utensils. Her father's harp lay to the side where he had discarded it, but it was the only familiar thing in the room. Bunches of herbs and wild grasses, most of which she recognized from their use in brews, poultices, and balms, hung below the lofts. A small door led to what she expected was a storage room.

Oil lamps were scattered around the space, but none of them were lit. Only the glow from the fire and the faint morning light filtering around the edges of the thatch illuminated the interior. Then Flora noticed two ram's skulls mounted on poles on either side of the main entrance, and her skin prickled. The skulls' horns curled around open, toothless jawbones, bleached white with age. The empty eye sockets glared at her with forlorn malice. She shuddered at the portent of those ominous talismans, which faced into the room and not out the door.

Her father leaned back, and he reached out to cradle her head in his massive hands.

"Flora, it's been a dreadful time. You're in a healing hut in *Incheskadyne*, the village of the Great Chief on Loch Tatha. You disappeared from our home and were missing for almost a full turn of the moon. Seven days ago, the druids at *Feart Choille* found you collapsed at the base of the sacred tree in the middle of the night. They brought you here and sent a powerful healer named Manas to tend you. Oh, my darlin', you can't imagine how we've all worried over ya."

Flora's nerves began to settle. Her father *was* real, not part of another wild fantasy. The black stains on his hands, the smoky smell of his clothes, the way he jutted his jaw when he stopped to think— all these things made her believe he was more than a dream.

But there was something else that stilled her trembling body and reassured her soul. Even in the dim light of the room she could see the little sparkle in his eyes that only happened when he was talking with her. She was his special treasure, and she could sense the particular feeling of security she had whenever he was near. She relaxed back into his embrace and her apprehension melted away.

Flora released her father and lay back on the bed, suddenly overcome with a wave of dizziness and nausea.

"I'm so tired, *Dadaidh*. I don't feel so well."

"You rest now and take your ease. I'll go and fetch the healer and your mother. She'll be so relieved to know that you've woken. She's been worried to death. And Domhnull, and your sisters. They're here as well."

Her father reached out his hand and stroked her cheek before rising to leave. "You rest now, and I'll be back straight away."

Flora closed her eyes, and the room kept spinning. She didn't have the energy to try to make sense of it all. But for the first time in as long as she could remember, she was starting to feel safe again— safe and not alone. Her family was alive. Her fiancé was here. Maybe her village hadn't been destroyed after all. Maybe her people were okay. Perhaps it had all been a dream. No, a nightmare—the most horrific nightmare anyone could imagine.

Suddenly the waves of nausea became too powerful to hold back, and she rolled over to vomit beside the bed. Her stomach heaved and wrapped itself in knots so tight she felt as if her insides would tear apart, but nothing came out except a trickle of yellow bile. She rolled back over and squeezed her eyes shut against the throbbing pain reverberating in her head. Her mouth was parched and dry, and she felt as if she had been hurled from a cliff and dashed against the rocks below. Somewhere amid the queasiness and the pain, she drifted off into blackness.

VAGUELY, Flora became aware of low murmurings somewhere nearby. As the sounds crept more distinctly into her consciousness, she suddenly bolted upright. *The others!* A strange, robed figure started toward her, and her panic surged. Grasping out for any kind of weapon she could use to defend herself, she edged frantically backward. Then across the room, she saw familiar forms rise and move quickly forward. Her father and her mother! Were they part of this conspiracy?

The robed figure slowly reached out a hand and spoke in a soft, gentle voice. "There now. I won't hurt you."

Her father called out, "Shhh. Shhh, Flora, it's okay. It's us. It's all okay."

Slowly, she began to remember where she was, and the terror subsided. She stopped her desperate scramble to retreat. She shook all over, and sweat dripped down her face. Her hair was drenched, as were her shoulders and her chest. She had no clothing on, but a thin woolen blanket covered her waist and legs.

The robed man came near and crouched down, looking intently into her eyes. She backed away, still leery of his presence. Instinctively, she pulled the blanket up to cover herself, though the protection it provided was superficial at best. The man's hair was long and white, with streaks of darker gray. A thin mustache drooped past the corners of his mouth, and merged in with his full, tangled beard. His eyes were misty gray, like the vapors coming off a hot spring on a cold winter day. He stopped muttering to her, frowned, and peered at her closely, as if he were studying a wounded animal.

With his gaze still fixed on her, he spoke over his shoulder to her mother. "Get the girl some water and a thin gruel. She's back now and will slowly come to her senses. She needs food and water more than anything else. But nothing solid for a while. I'm not concerned about her body at this point. Once she gets her energy back, I'll be able to assess her mind and her spirit. I need to consult with *Ard-Draoidh* Bhatair Rhu. I'll go to *Feart Choille* now and be back in three days."

His eyes dropped their hold on her, and he stood. Turning toward the door, he said, "She may see her family, but no one else. You may provide comfort and assurance, but do not question her about her experience. And she isn't to leave this hut until we have completed our evaluation." He crouched to duck through the low doorway and vanished from her sight.

Her mother and father approached cautiously. As her mother drew near, Flora saw the concern on her face.

"Flora, are you alright? Do you know who I am—uhh, who we are?"

That seemed odd. Why wouldn't she know her own parents?

He father pushed forward and knelt to take her in his arms. "Of course she does. She's just never seen the *lighiche*, Manas, before. I spoke with her myself just this morning, and she knew exactly who I was." He stroked her wet hair. "Good grief, girl, you're soakin'. But at least you're not burnin' up anymore. Here, let me get you somethin' dry to put on." He released her and turned away.

Flora's mother looked at her warily. "You gave us a real scare, you did. Disappearing like that with no warnin'. What happened to you, girl? Where have you been? And how did you get all the way over here?"

She tentatively reached out a hand and pushed a lock of Flora's hair back behind her ear. Flora leaned her head into the touch, which lingered a moment and then withdrew.

Her father stepped back with her *leine* in his hands. He held it out to her and glanced sideways at her mother. "We can let Manas and the druids get into all of those issues later, my dear. For now, let's just be thankful she's back with us, alive and well."

"Yes, of course, you're right. Sweetheart, we're so thankful the gods returned you to us safely, and uhh... well." She knelt down beside Flora and helped her slip the *leine* over her head. "Would you like to see your sisters, now?"

Her father interjected once again. "Perhaps, you could go get the water and gruel the *lighiche* mentioned, and let Flora get some food in her stomach. I know that Domhnull and her sisters are anxious to see her, but I'm sure she must be famished by now. There'll be time for reunions shortly."

Her mother murmured agreement and ducked to leave the hut.

After a few moments, her father sat down beside her bed. "You know she loves you, right? She just doesn't know how to show it." He grabbed a stick and poked at the fire. "She's been here since we found you. At your side the whole time. Washing you. Feeding you. Cleaning up after you."

The embers glowed brightly where he stirred the ashes, and little sparks flittered up into the air.

"She was very worried about you. We've all been very worried. We've been constantly praying to the Dagda that he would protect you and guide you home to us. We sacrificed to Brigid—"

Flora cut him off, "Oh, not a lamb, *Dadaidh*. You didn't sacrifice a lamb for me, did you?"

He reached out and ruffled her hair. "No, my wee *fauth*. No lambs died on your account. I knew if you ever came home, you'd never forgive me for that. No. But a brand new iron cauldron, straight from my forge, is now sitting at the bottom of Loch Rannoch." He winked at her and smiled. "I'm not exactly sure what a goddess needs with a cooking pot, but a whole heap of iron went into the makin' of it, along with a river of sweat and a thousand blows of the hammer." A grin broke out across his face. "And I'd've dropped a hundred of 'em in the sea, if that's what it took to get my girl back to me."

His smile warmed her heart, and she thanked the gods, Brigid *and* the Dagda, for bringing her home to her family. Well, not *home* exactly. And her thoughts threatened to veer off down the murky path from which she'd just fled, but she forced them back and returned her attention to her father's love, her mother's detached concern, and a steaming bowl of gruel.

THE DOOR OPENED, and bright light streamed in to the hut. A silhouetted figure stooped to enter and then stood up to full height. This was followed by another lithe shape, and then a much shorter one. Even against the brightness of the sunshine, Flora instantly recognized the tall muscular form of her betrothed. She dropped the nearly empty bowl and pushed herself up.

"Domhnull! Oh, Domhnull! Catriona! Searlaid!"

Domhnull quickly knelt down and took her in his arms. Flora felt tears rolling down her cheeks.

"Domhnull, I was so scared. I thought you were all dead. I thought I'd never see you again."

Searlaid looked down quizzically at her sister. "*You* thought *we* were dead? Now that's a switch, little sister. *You* were the one who disappeared without a trace for a whole turn of the moon. What happened to you, anyway? Where'd you run off to?"

Domhnull continued to hold Flora tightly without saying a word, his big hand cradling the back of her head.

Their father shot a cautionary glance at Searlaid. "The *lighiche* suggested we leave the questions aside for a while and let Flora get herself reoriented a bit." His eyes indicated it was more than a suggestion.

Searlaid gave a dismissive look and shifted her weight to the other foot. Her expression suggested otherwise, but she said simply, "Yeah, whatever."

Catriona dashed across the room and stretched her arms out to pull Domhnull and Flora into a big hug. "Flora, I missed you so much. I'm so happy you're back again."

Still wrapped in the double embrace, Flora cocked her head to the side and smiled broadly at her little sister, tears still fresh in her eyes. "I missed you too, you wee *feòrag*."

Catriona squinched her face into a petulant frown. "How many times do I have to tell you? I am *not* a squirrel!" Then she giggled, let go of the hug, and began to skip around the room. "Wow! You get this *whole house* all to yourself?" Catriona came to an abrupt halt, shrieked, and started to cry when she saw the skulls mounted inside the doorway.

Their mother rushed over to calm her down. "Now, honey, it's okay. It's okay. Those are just here to keep anything bad from getting to your sister while she's sick. They're here to protect her." Her mother cast a cautious glance back up at their father. "I think maybe

Flora's had enough excitement for while. Maybe we should let her rest for a bit."

Searlaid crouched to follow her mother and sister out the door, but Domhnull looked up to Flora's father. "*Maighstir*, could you and I stay for just a little while longer?"

Flora's father considered the request for a moment, then nodded and sat back against the wall.

Domhnull looked deeply into her eyes. She could see his relief reflected there, along with something else. Was it shame?

"I didn't know. I didn't know for almost a fortnight. I was with Chief Guaidre's scouting party in the mountains far out to the west. By the time I got back, your father and the warriors of Bunrannoch had already scoured the whole valley for signs of you and hadn't found a trace. I went out alone to search for days, but found nothing that would lead me to you—no scrap of cloth, no prints in the mud, no strand of your hair. I didn't know what to do."

"He's right, lass," her father confirmed. "Our best hunters, even Serlaid's dogs, couldn't find hide nor hair of you. It was right strange, it was. We thought maybe raiders from the Borthwicks of Fib had whisked you away, but they surely wouldn't send a raiding party into our lands without stealing cattle or sheep and take only one girl. Same would go for the *gun-dachaigh*. People with no clan wouldn't risk exposing themselves without thieving more of our livestock. We found no signs that you'd been torn up by a wolf or a bear." He shrugged, somewhat sheepishly, and continued. "So there weren't a lot of options left—other than *korrigans* or the gods. We're anxious to hear your story and find out what happened, but the druids need to talk to you first."

Flora's eyes broke contact with Domhnull's, and she looked quizzically at her father. "Why do the druids need to talk to me first?" She sighed. "I'm not even sure I *know* what happened. It's all so jumbled up in my mind."

"I guess that's why the druids want to chat. Manas should be able to help you straighten everythin' out when he gets back. For now, don't you worry your head over it. Enjoy the attentions of your man there."

Flora shifted her gaze back to Domhnull and smiled at him. "It's okay. I know you tried everything you could. I'm sure everyone did. I'm just thankful to Brigid you're alright. I'm thankful to have my family back."

Domhnull looked down at their hands clasped together. "I just needed you to know I tried. It's a sad day when a man can't keep his own woman safe. Your father trusted you to my care, and now—"

Her father broke in. "Now, son. Don't be so hard on yourself. As far as I can see, she's not actually yours quite yet. She won't be your wife until Lughnasadh, if I remember correctly. Until then, she's still in my household and is my responsibility. So all that criticism really falls on me."

Domhnull stammered, "No, *Maighstir*. That's not what I meant at all! I meant—"

Her father stood and walked over to them. He winked, smiled, and slapped the younger man on the shoulder. "Of course you didn't. And I'll still trust you with my greatest treasure in the world when the time comes. For now, we need to let our girl get some rest." He urged Domhnull to his feet. "Now, Flora, Manas asked for us to keep you inside here until he has a chance to check you out. You can relieve yourself in the back alcove, when you need to. You rest now. And if you need anythin' at all, one of us will be right outside. Okay?"

She nodded, and they turned to leave.

As he crouched to duck through the doorway, Domhnull looked back. "I *will* protect you. I *will* keep you safe. I promise." Then he disappeared into the brightness of the daylight.

As the deer-hide door cover fell closed behind them, Flora felt the overwhelming sense of aloneness return. Everyone was so concerned about her getting enough rest, but what she really needed was her family. She had been so terrified she might never again see another soul. Now she just craved the nearness of the people she loved. She didn't need them to say anything, or do anything, but just to be there with her.

Then again, maybe they were right. She didn't exactly feel so well. Her head throbbed in rhythm with the beating of her heart. She felt almost like she was moving through water, with a heaviness pushing against the motions of her arms. When she turned her neck, it took her vision several moments to catch up with the movement of her eyes. Even sounds seemed to be muted and distant.

Flora heard the wind outside begin to whisper and then to howl. Then the rush of a sudden downpour raked through the river reed bundles overhead. Flora rolled over to peer out of a small gap between the hazel wattle of the walls and the thatching of the roof. She strained for several moments, trying to glimpse the clouds or the sky, so she could gauge how long the storm might last.

For an instant, she was swept back to the deluge from her recent experience. What had it been, anyway? A dream? A nightmare? A hallucination? She still didn't know what it was or what had happened to her. She looked down at her arms and saw the deep scratches left behind as she fought her way through the gorse. So that, at least, had been real. She flexed her leg to test out her knee, and a dull ache welled up through the stiffness. Yes, that was real too.

A sudden thought occurred to her, and she began searching frantically around her bedding. She tossed her blanket aside and scanned all across the room. *Where was her pouch? Where were treasures?* She saw her small flint knife hanging on its thong from a peg on a nearby support post, but the pouch wasn't there. Her hands groped all around, and her eyes flitted across the room, alighting on perches and delving into shadows.

Then, slowly, the nagging memory clawed its way to the surface. Her shoulders slumped, and she breathed out an anguished groan. It was in the cave. She had left it in the cave when she fought her way through the rain storm that doused the fiery inferno. She hung her head in despair. They were gone now. She had little chance of ever finding that cave again. She had no idea where it was, or if it had even been real.

She wasn't sure why she was so despondent about losing her treasures. They were just things after all, and not even particularly valuable things for the most part. Their meaning to her had been wrapped up in the memories they represented—memories of her family and friends. But she had those people back now, alive and well. So maybe the tokens had served their purpose and were no longer needed. Maybe they had been there to get her through the valley of shadows. But now she was back in the light, back with the people she loved, and perhaps the symbols were no longer important. The logic made sense, but her heart still ached, deep down inside.

Flora was still exhausted. She couldn't understand why. Her father said she had been asleep for over seven days. And yet, the energy felt like it was being sucked out of her body into the ground beneath her. She was afraid to close her eyes, afraid the reality she had regained would evaporate in the mist, and afraid she would descend once more into the abyss of desolation and loneliness. The terror of falling asleep battled against her fatigue, like when the wind and the sea rage against each other, contending for which is the stronger. The sound of the rain settled to a dull, steady moan, and somewhere between the darkness and the shadows, weariness prevailed, and Flora drifted across the breach into sleep.

CHAPTER SEVEN

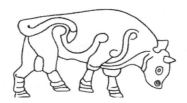

T he scream erupted from deep in Flora's throat and she bolted upright. Her eyes ravaged the darkness, grasping at specters and clawing at wraiths. Her heart raced as panic gnarled its talons around her mind. Darkness. Utter darkness. Then suddenly, a light, a lamp. Coming toward her. Coming at her! She retreated frantically, thrusting her blanket up in a desperate defense. A face emerged in the circle of light—a thin, lithe, ghoulish face that mocked and taunted her. The face of the "others." The face of malevolence and horror.

"What in the Dagda's name is wrong with you, little sister?"

The voice was familiar... close... someone she knew. Or something mimicking someone she knew to draw her deeper into the web. Her hands found something on the floor. A pot. She shrieked and hurled it at the advancing figure. It dodged her missile and leapt across the room with the speed of a wildcat. Then it was upon her, pinning her arms to the ground.

"Hey! Flora! Snap out of it! It's me, Searlaid. You know, your sister. What's gotten into you?"

Flora thrashed about, struggling to free herself. Then, as if through a heavy fog, the words took form in her mind, distantly at first, then growing nearer and clearer. Her eyes gained focus in the dim light of the lamp on the floor across the room, and the ghastly face slowly resolved into the face of her sister, finally melding together with the voice. She stopped writhing and collapsed to the ground, yielding to her sister's firm hand.

Breathing heavily, she gasped, "Searlaid, it's you. It's you." She sighed desperately and willed her heartbeat to slow.

"What is going on with you? You're wailing like the *Caoineag*. Have you lost your mind?"

With a moan of resignation, Flora whispered, "I think maybe I have. I think..." her voice trailed off.

Slowly, Searlaid released her arms and got up off her chest. Standing, she turned to make sure that the oil lamp hadn't set anything on fire. Shaking her head, she looked over her shoulder at Flora lying on the ground against the wall. "What happened to you? You're stretched tighter than a bow string."

Flora sat up and searched the hut with her eyes. "It's dark in here. Is it night?"

"Yep. Right in the middle. I got the late shift because they thought you would sleep through, but I guess not. You gonna tell me what the shrieking is all about? Do I need to call in the healer?"

"No. No, I'm alright. Just bad dreams, bad memories."

"Sounded more like a night terror to me. I'm surprised you didn't wake the whole village with that howling. So what's this all about? Where have you been? What happened to you?"

Flora dropped her gaze and fiddled with the edge of the sheepskin she had been laying on. She had always been intimidated by her older sister, and it irritated her. "I'm supposed to wait for Manas–"

"Oh, come on. Seriously? Will the story rot if you dig it up too soon?" Serlaid interrupted.

"It's just... I don't know..."

Searlaid picked up the oil lamp off the floor and walked toward

Flora. She sat down beside her and gave her a look that could almost be mistaken for sympathy. "Look, if you tell me, then I can pass it on to Domhnull. He's ashamed he didn't protect you and thinks it's his fault you went missing. You know you won't get a chance to be alone with him to tell him for yourself. So if you don't tell me while you can, it will just continue to eat at him."

Flora saw past her sister's feigned empathy. She knew Serlaid well enough to understand she was using this excuse as a ploy to gain an advantage over her. In Serlaid's mind, Flora had stolen Domhnull away from her, and she would never forgive her little sister for that betrayal. Concern for how her disappearance had affected Domhnull was the farthest thing from Serlaid's mind.

"Oh, Searlaid, come on. You know it's not his fault. There's nothing he could have done. He was away with the scouting party. He can't be with me every moment of the day. That's ridiculous."

"Yeah, well, it's not ridiculous to him. And this is the only way he's going to find out what really happened. Otherwise, it'll just continue to gnaw at him."

Flora wasn't fooled by her mock sincerity or even persuaded by her pretended concern for Domhnull's feelings, but she gave in anyway. Maybe talking about it would help her carve a pathway through the muddled tangle of thoughts that filled her mind like a thicket of gorse.

"Well, okay. Fine. But I'm really not sure what happened myself. I was hoping Manas or one of the other druids could help me understand."

Seeing the doorway of opportunity begin to crack, Searlaid pried it wide open. She urged Flora on. "Where did it start? You disappeared over a month ago. What were you doing?"

"I was out on an errand for Nandag, gathering some herbs and roots we needed to prepare some treatments. Somehow I fell asleep, and–"

Serlaid interrupted her in mid thought. "Yeah, yeah, I know all that. We all know where you were *supposed* to be. Get to the part where you ended up somewhere else."

"Look, I'm still trying to piece it all together in my own mind. It's a confused jumble right now. If you'll just calm down, maybe I can make some sense out of it. So, like I was saying, somehow I fell asleep, though I never do that while I am away from the village. It's not safe, you know. Well, anyway, when I woke up it was late and a storm was on the way, so I started back to the village as fast as I could."

"Apparently you never made it. What stopped you?"

"But that's just it. I *did* make it back. When I was just beyond Badger Hill, I saw smoke, lots of smoke, and I knew something had to be wrong. So I dropped my bag of herbs and ran to the hilltop. When I got there and could see..."

Suddenly Flora's voice caught in her throat and she stopped. She pressed her palms to her eyes, trying to squeeze the image from her mind, but the horror of that vision was seared into her memory and it wouldn't go away.

Serlaid gave an exasperated grunt. "Well, what? What did you see?"

Tears seeped from the corners of Flora's eyes, despite her efforts to be strong in front of her sister. "It was horrible..." She whispered the words. "The whole village was on fire—all the homes and barns and stables. Children were screaming over their dying parents. Our friends... our family... There were bodies everywhere, lying bloody and broken. Wounded people cried out for help. But no one came—no healers, no warriors. I looked for you and Cat, for Mother and Father. All I could see was fire and smoke and a bloodbath of twisted figures—dying people reaching out to me for help. And—"

"And you ran, didn't you? You ran away to save your hide."

Flora looked up in astonishment at Serlaid's smug expression. "Ran? No. No. I'm a healer. I needed to go to them and help them. I was the only one—"

"Yeah, well, the only problem with that whole story is *it didn't really happen*. The village is still there. Nobody burned it down. We're all here."

Flora was about to ask, "Is it? Is the village alright?" But she bit back the words. She had been confined in this tiny hovel like a caged animal ever since the nightmare ended and she woke up. She couldn't leave to eat or to relieve herself or even to see the sunshine. How did she *know* her village hadn't been destroyed? How did she know her friends hadn't been slaughtered? The only people she had talked to since she woke up were her family and Domhnull. Maybe they were the only ones who survived. She hadn't actually seen them when the village burned. Maybe they had escaped and come here for safety. Surely her father or Domhnull would have told her, wouldn't they? She pressed her palms back against her eyes and wiped the tears away.

"Hello, Flora. Are you listening to me? Did you hear what I said? Everyone is alright. No one torched the village. So, either your story is a delusional fantasy or you're lying through your teeth."

A flood of anger surged through Flora's mind. Her tears were replaced with a scornful retort. "What is wrong with you? Why do you always assume the worst about me? First you accuse me of running away. Then you accuse me of lying. What's your problem?"

Serlaid pursed her lips in a wry smile and then replied, "Aww, what's the matter with Daddy's little girl? Did I hurt your feelings?"

Flora clenched her fists so hard her nails bit into her palms. She spat out her next words. "Daddy's little girl? Really? Look who's talking. Mother dotes all over you and Catriona and treats me like an unwelcome nuisance, so I don't want to hear about it."

Serlaid smirked, "Hmm. Ever wonder why that might be?"

The two sisters glared at each other without speaking for several heartbeats.

Finally, Serlaid broke the silence. "Anyway, I don't really think you're lying. You're not stupid enough to make up a story anyone could prove wasn't true. So you must be delusional. In which case, your actions in your delusion reveal exactly what you *would* do if you were faced with a similar situation in real life. If you run in your dreams, you'll run when it really matters."

Flora wavered between anger and confusion. "Why do you hate me so much? What have I ever done to you anyway?" She resented her sister's spiteful accusations, and felt as if her sense of certainty was again slipping over the edge. Her memories were as jumbled as ever. *Was* she delusional? *Was* she going crazy?

"What have you ever done to me? Seriously? You mean like maybe stealing Domhnull away from me? My man! The one I chose at the *Cloughtie* well when I was just six summers old. The one I went through the ordeals with. He is my man, and you stole him from me! Why in the Daghda's name *should* I trust you?"

"You may have chosen him, but *he chose me."* The remark had more of a sarcastic bite to it than Flora had intended. In truth, she, herself, had always assumed Serlaid and Domhnull would marry. Practically everyone in the village had. She was more taken aback by Domhnull's proposal than anyone. She had been smitten by him as a young girl, but she always believed he was Serlaid's man, not hers. When Domhnull surprised everyone by asking Flora's father for her hand, she didn't know what to do at first. She truly didn't want to hurt her sister in that way. But Domhnull had come to her and spoken such words of love she couldn't refuse.

FLORA'S THOUGHTS drifted back to that day. It was Imbolc, Brigid's festival, and Flora was surrounded by the other girls of the village, all dressed in white with their hair unbound and hanging loose. The elders had chosen Flora by lot to play the role of the goddess. The girls sang the *Ballad of Brigid* as they paraded from house to house throughout the village. Flora sung the words in solo, and the rest of the girls echoed the lines in response.

Down by the loch where the willow tree grows
In the glen on an early spring day...

It was Flora's favorite song. Her father often played his harp and sang it to her as a lullaby when she fell asleep at nights. Now she was acting out the role of the goddess, bringing blessings to the village homes. A light snow drifted down from the heavens, as if Brigid, herself, wept tears of crystalline joy at the sound of the melody.

Flora had a circlet of bronze on her head with a brilliant crystal set in the center that shone like a hearth fire—the *reul-iuil Bríde*, the guiding star of Brigid. She carried a shield made of rushes with a three-pronged cross woven into its heart as a tribute to the goddess. As they visited each house, the families gave gifts of food to her attendant maidens and tied strips of cloth to Flora's dress—tokens of tribute in hopes of receiving the blessing of the goddess. After the festival was over, Flora would return the strips of cloth back to each home, where they would provide powerful protection against fire, lightning, illness and evil spirits until the next Imbolc festival the following year.

They finished the parade of blessings and came to the home of the village chief. The girls slowed their pace and circled the roundhouse sunwise three times. From inside the house, the chief's powerful voice cried out, "Brigid, Brigid, come to my home tonight. Open the door for Brigid and let the goddess come in."

The family swung the door open wide and the girls all filed inside with Flora at the head. They sat down at a feasting table lit by the gentle glow of a hearth fire and partook of a sacred meal from the food offerings given by the villagers. They had roasted duck and oatcakes and steaming loaves of emmer bread made from the most finely ground flour she had ever seen.

The chief's wife had made a nettle soup with lentils brought from beyond the Great Wall, seasoned with marjoram and thyme. The warriors of the tribe had hunted down a boar and roasted it in a pit.

Though the whole village would share of this delicacy, the choicest part, the tender loin, was served to Brigid and her maidens.

The cheese was Flora's favorite. This was not the hard, moldy cheese she carried to the fields when she gathered herbs for Nandag. This cheese was soft and creamy, with a flavor like the faintest hint of hazelnuts and butter. It virtually melted in her mouth. And they washed it all down with a spiced tea made from blackthorn and mint.

The feast culminated with a sacred tribute to the goddess—oat cakes made from the last remaining grain of the previous year's harvest, combined with the first fruits of this year's bounty. It symbolized Brigid's continued care for the clan all throughout the year. It was also a prayer for the idealistic hope of eternal spring.

It was the most lavish meal Flora had ever eaten. And she was seated at the head of the table, in the position of honor, for the whole thing. Being the center of attention made her a little uneasy, but she found comfort in the role she was playing. Had this extravagant celebration been set out for her, she would have wilted with embarrassment. But somehow, it was made bearable, knowing the reverence and splendor were really for Brigid, while she was merely a stand-in for the goddess. So, it was Brigid they honored with their gifts of homage, not her.

With a mixture of apprehension, gratitude, and pride, she received the final honor of the feast. Her attendants all raised a tribute to her from the first milk of spring. Her own cup had been filled with the pure milk of the white cow—a holy honor only Brigid's personal representative could partake of once each year at the Imbolc feast.

As soon as the sacred feast was over, the door was thrown open once again, and a throng of boys rushed in the room to peals of laughter and jubilant songs. The girls, stuffed with delicacies from head to toe, could barely stand. But the boisterous young boys lifted them from their seats and began dancing them around the room. Catriona was among the youngest of Flora's attendants, but Serlaid was not there. Ever since Serlaid had completed the ordeals, she was considered to be a woman, and only girls could play the part of Brigid and her maidens. Indeed, this would be Flora's last year among the village girls during the festival, before she would pass through that mystical transformation from youth to womanhood.

Flora, as goddess for the night, had to dance with each and every boy. It was a sacred rite that brought a blessing to the families represented. But Flora was startled when she was finally passed over to the last of the divine suitors. A strong hand held her gently at the waist, and a tender touch caressed her outstretched hand. She looked up into hazel eyes, flecked with embers of gold, and trembled deep inside.

For a moment, she melted into his embrace, their bodies floating and drifting as one to the rhythm of the lyre and the fife. She was lost in in the mists of fantasy, as if she had slipped through the veil into the Otherworld, and felt the colors and hues of eternity in the very depths of her soul. But then, just as suddenly as it had come upon her, an abrupt realization shook her free from the magic of the moment, and she stopped in place, standing still as a statue. Domhnull was gazing deeply into her eyes, as if he too were lost in the Otherworld of her heart. And the way he was holding her... it was not like a boy holding a girl playing goddess, but like a man holding his woman with passion.

Thoughts rushed through her mind. Why was Domhnull here? He wasn't a village boy. He was a warrior and a man. She had not even seen him for two turns of the moon. He had been off in the wilds of the highlands and the islands with the Great Chief's *còmhlan* of elite fighters and scouts. But most of all, she wondered why he was dancing with her this way? Why was he gazing into her eyes in the kind of way he should be looking at Serlaid? What was happening? Though these thoughts raced wildly through her mind, they couldn't keep up with the beating of her heart.

Domhnull pulled her close and gently guided her back into a dancing step. He placed his cheek against the crown in her hair and whispered softly in her ear. "Tonight, on Imbolc, you are Brigid. This autumn, at Lughnasadh, would you be *my* bride?"

The surreal nature of the night, the headiness of her role as the goddess, the richness of the feast, the warmth of his embrace, and the shock of his words—it was all more than she could take, and she collapsed in his arms.

FLORA AWOKE and struggled to figure out where she was? The night of feasting and revelry was all a blur. She sat up and the sheepskin cover fell off her shoulders. She fumbled around aimlessly with her hands, trying to remember how she had gotten home, when she suddenly realized her fingers were twiddling with the blessing cloths tied to her dress. Then she remembered the Imbolc parade, the feast, the dancing, and...Domhnull.

She glanced about and her eyes lit on her mother's concerned face. "How did I get here? What time is it? Is the feast over?"

Her mother frowned a way that told more of a tale than a bard's ballad. "Domhnull carried you home from the Imbolc feast. Apparently, being a goddess was more than you could handle. You slept all through the night."

"It's morning?" Flora panicked. "It's morning already? I missed the great fire last night?" She leapt to her feet and scrambled for the door.

"Flora, where—"

"The blessings! I have to distribute the blessings! I can't let everyone down. Oh, what have I done?"

After running a dozen paces out the door, Flora hastily scuttled back to the house, fumbled with one of the little strips of cloth, and hurriedly handed it to her mother. "Here's our blessing, *Mamaidh.* Sorry I have to run. I'll be home soon."

And then she darted down the path to the next home, wishing she had taken time to slip on her deerskin *brogen* to protect her feet from the thin blanket of snow that covered the ground. She didn't begrudge the snow one bit. When the serpent came out of its den on the sacred day and encountered snow, it meant the *Cailleach* would not gather more firewood for her hearth. So winter would end soon, and spring would come in all of Brigid's glory.

As she hurried down the village path, Flora couldn't remember which blessing cloth belonged to which family. Normally, the matron of each family would come to her at the great fire on the night of Imbolc and retrieve her family's blessing. But Flora, in her role as the Queen of Heaven, had been absent from the sacred event and the blessing cloths were all still tied to her dress. So now, as she came to each door, the woman of the home retrieved her household's cloth from among the colorful array tagged to her dress. The blessing cloths were all dyed and woven with distinct patterns of checkered blocks and lines, so each one was unique to its associated family.

When Flora completed her final task as the reigning goddess of Imbolc, she turned toward home, hoping she had not goofed up the ritual and denied Brigid's fortune to the people of the village. As she rounded a corner in the path, she heard a whispered voice call her name.

"Flora. Flora, it's me."

Domhnull motioned her to silence and beckoned her to follow him, and her heart skipped a beat. Was it all true then? Had it really happened? Or was it just a dream?

Domhnull reached for her hand and pulled her behind a tree. They faced each other, and their breath came out as thin wisps of smoke that danced and swirled in the air before being swept away by the morning breeze. Domhnull grinned broadly and his hazel eyes glinted with joy.

"Last night... Well, that wasn't exactly the reaction I was hoping for. I'm not quite sure if it was an 'aye' or a 'nay.'"

So it *had* been real! Flora's head spun. She must have grimaced, because the sparkle faded from his eyes and he cocked his head to one side.

"You do know what I was askin', don't you lass? To be plain clear, I was askin' for your hand." He dipped his head and pulled her hands up close between them.

Inside, Flora was melting, like a single crystal snowflake under the warm rays of the morning sun. But outside, her expression must have still been frosty cold, for Domhnull's brow furrowed in sudden concern.

"Flora, you must know how I feel about you, how I've always felt about you. I thought…" He cocked his head to the side again and his gaze drifted inward as he considered whether he had gotten it all wrong.

When Flora finally found her voice, all she could manage to whisper was, "What about Serlaid?"

Domhnull looked at her with a quizzical expression. "Serlaid?"

"Yes. Serlaid. Isn't she the one you want? Isn't she supposed to be your wife?"

The laughter returned to his eyes, and his smile warmed her heart. "I admit, Serlaid is an amazing woman. The way she handles those dogs of hers, and her accuracy with that bow, well, there's no one I would rather have at my side on a hunt or in a fight. Serlaid is my sister in arms. But you… Flora, you are my morning sunshine and a cool summer breeze. You're like moonlight dancing on Loch Rannoch and a whisper on the wind calling my name. You are tender hands that heal a wounded hart and the gentle kindness of a doe with her fawn. You're the sweetness of ripe raspberries I discover along the path and the mystery of the Otherworld reflected in a mountain spring. I remember once, when I was just twelve summers old, watching you across a field gathering herbs in the glen, with the breeze fluttering your dress and rustling your hair. That moment is when I was surprised by love for the very first time. And I've never stopped loving you since. You are my heart song."

His words caused her heart to race and her head to spin. She felt dizzy at his touch. She dared not look into his eyes. With her head down, she mumbled, "Everyone thought you and Serlaid–"

"Hmm. Are you tellin' me you don't feel the same? I thought I felt it in the warmth of your smile. I thought I saw my love reflected in your eyes." He paused and looked up at the sky, into the distance that never ends. "Serlaid is strong. She doesn't need me. She can take care of herself. I need a delicate flower I can provide for and protect."

Now it was Flora's chance to play. Her voice brightened with new life. "Oh, so I'm weak, huh? I need you because I can't take care of myself, hmmm?"

Though she mocked him with her words, inside her feelings echoed with a longing for the safety and stability he proposed. She had always felt secure in her father's home. She found shelter in his strength and confidence in his faithfulness. But someday she would have to leave the protection of her father's roof, and what Domhnull was offering calmed her fears and made her feel safe.

"No, I don't think you're weak. I think you are a priceless treasure, and precious things need to be protected. Your gentleness inspires me. I want to be a strong warrior and maybe even a leader in our clan. But I want to have a good reason to be strong—not so I can boast among the hunters and fighters, or so I can be proud among the chiefs, but so I can protect what is precious and guard what is gentle and true. I want to be strong for *you*."

Flora finally found the courage to look into his eyes—the way she had always longed to do, but never dared. And she was suddenly lost in a deep pool of warmth and love. "Then hold me with that strength. Hold me like you did last night. Hold me close and never let me go."

Flora slipped from her father's arms and melted into Domhnull's embrace.

"FLORA! Hello, Flora. Are you in there some place?" Serlaid's grating voice tore her from the memory.

"He chose me," she whispered to herself. "He chose me."

"Something is definitely still not right with you, little sister. You keep disappearing inside that confused little head of yours and almost can't find your way out."

Serlaid backed up a few steps and sat down on a small bench made from a split log and draped with a sheepskin cover, set back against the wall of the little hut. She hooked the oil lamp on a crooked knot that poked out of the support beam just above her head, and the dim glow wobbled about the room as the flame flickered and danced in the night.

"Now that you are back for a moment or two, why don't you tell me the rest of your fantasy story."

Flora had expected Serlaid to be angry at her comment about Domhnull's choice, but she seemed to have brushed it aside.

"If you're so sure it's all just a delusional dream, why are you so anxious to hear it, anyway? What's the point, if it's not *real*?"

"Because even delusions can be wrapped around kernels of truth. Behind your imaginary veil, maybe I can pick out what really happened. So, what did you do after you climbed to the top of Badger Hill and supposedly saw the village burning? I know you were there, but where did you go next?"

Serlaid didn't talk with her hands like other people often do. She just sat there, motionless, staring at Flora with a piercing gaze that penetrated even the dim glow of the lamplit room. Perhaps that was part of her training as a warrior—to remain still and to avoid wasteful, useless movements that could give away her position or intentions. Or maybe it was just her way.

"How do you know I was really on Badger Hill? How do you know that wasn't just part of some imaginary fiction concocted by my unstable mind?"

"I know you were near there because my dogs found your sack of herbs."

Flora thought about that for a moment. So, Serlaid had sent her dogs out to look for her. Had she actually been worried about her little sister? Had she been trying to find her out of genuine concern?

Probably not. Flora decided that Serlaid had probably just sent the dogs out because the villagers would expect her to.

"That's the strange thing. I honestly can't remember what happened next. Some of my memories are as clear as the Fairy Pools on a sunny, windless day. I can picture the images in my head in vivid detail. And other parts are just missing."

"So, you're sure you didn't run, but you don't know what actually happened? That's very convenient."

Flora was normally a very gentle person. She really didn't have a violent bone in her body. But there were times she just wanted to slap that smug smile off Serlaid's face. Of course, she would never have a chance. Serlaid was astonishingly quick, and was much stronger than Flora. A slap would never get close. But right now, she had to fight hard to keep the impulse from taking over.

"If you're so smart, why don't you tell me what happened next? Surely your dogs picked up my scent. Why didn't you just have them track me down?"

Serlaid frowned. "That's the odd thing. They found your sack of herbs, and followed your trail for a few dozen paces, but then the path went cold. It's like you just disappeared without a trace."

That thought struck Flora as strangely coincidental. Her scent disappeared right about the same place her memory lapsed. Could it have something to do with the gods? Or maybe the "others" weren't just the paranoid hallucinations of a mind on the edge.

A fleeting image flashed through her thoughts and she shuddered. It wasn't distinct, but just a vague impression. She remembered a ring of fire surrounding a tattooed man with the wings of an eagle, and severed heads mounted on gnarled posts. The image was there, faintly, like the moon behind a veil of clouds, and then it was gone.

Flora shivered again. She wouldn't share this kind of impression with Serlaid, nor would she tell her about the "others," or mysterious voices, or visions of a goddess in a spring. She would limit her story to the concrete facts she clearly remembered. She wasn't completely certain she would even share those more nebulous things with Manas or the other druids. Perhaps she should forget those details altogether.

"The next thing I remember is waking up in the middle of the night in a forest on a large hill. I had no idea where I was or how I had gotten there. All I knew was I had never been there before. Everything felt strange and unfamiliar. It was nowhere near Loch Rannoch or our village. There was a slow, steady, drizzling rain. I was cold and afraid, so I found a hole under the roots of a fallen tree and crawled inside to hide."

Serlaid still had a smug look smeared across her face. It was annoying, and Flora forced herself to hold her tongue, as any snide remarks would undoubtedly be turned against her. Serlaid's haughtiness—no, her contempt—had gorged its way under Flora's skin, and lay there, festering. Her disparaging comments just inflamed the lesion, even more.

Serlaid interjected, "Well, it just goes to show what a little training will do for you. Any hunter or warrior worth their salt would have staked out a position and began scouting the terrain, instead of cowering under a rock from wraiths in the night. The rain and darkness would have been a bonus. They would help mask your movements and cause you to blend into the shadows."

"Yeah. Well, I'm not a hunter or a warrior. I'm a healer. And healers are more cautious. Maybe that's because we spend enough time trying to patch you warrior types back together when you get mauled by a bear or cut up in a mindless brawl. I happen to think there is wisdom in playing it safe."

"Whatever. Then what happened?"

"Well, I couldn't get any sleep. All night long I kept hearing sounds like people walking around searching for me. I thought it must be the Roman soldiers who had burned our village. So I stayed hidden and prayed to the gods for help. When it finally got light enough to see, the noises had faded."

Serlaid cut in. "Isn't it funny how daylight always scares away the things that go bump in the night?"

"Yeah. Well, I wasn't taking any chances. When I was sure no one was nearby, I crawled out of my hiding place and crept away. Once I got far enough, I started running. It was still raining and I couldn't tell where I was or where I should go. I ended up slogging through an endless maze of bogs with mud up to my knees."

"Hmmm," Serlaid chimed in with another of her incessant jibes. "I would have thought even healers would know how to find the dry ground along ridge lines and mountain sides. You do go into the forests searching for herbs and roots and such things, right?"

"Do you want me to tell you this story or not? At this point, I don't really care what you think I should have done differently. I am just telling you what happened."

"Okay, fine. Get on with it."

For the next little while, Serlaid held back the snide comments and let Flora tell her story. Flora described how she had wandered through the forest for at least a couple of days, hiding at night time, but never getting any sleep. She hadn't found anything to eat since before she had seen the village burn. She had felt lost in a strange land and had been utterly exhausted from the lack of sleep and nourishment.

"The whole time I was wandering through the woods, I felt like someone was just over my shoulder, searching for me—like when you've snuck out of the village to go pick foxgloves in the glen, and you're certain mother has found out and is coming after you."

"Nope. Pretty sure that's never happened to me."

"Okay, fine. But it was creepy. Anyway, I finally made my way off the mountain and to the edge of the forest. The rain had broken and the clouds cleared completely from the sky. It was the most amazing crystal blue color. Even the wind had stopped. I was at the edge of a millpond, looking out across the perfectly still surface, watching the almost flawless reflection of the mountains and the trees. I felt a sense of peace, like all the land had paused for just a moment to take a breath."

"A sunny day this spring?" Serlaid asked quizzically. "We haven't seen the sun in almost two moons. It has been raining constantly, with just a few breaks in the clouds for the sun to peek through. At least, that's how it's been at Loch Rannoch. I wish I had been in your dream world. It sounds much nicer there."

Flora scowled, concerned to discover that even the weather in the real world didn't correlate with her memories.

"Well, it didn't last for me, either. The calm was shattered by the roar of an approaching locust swarm. But I suppose that didn't happen in your world either, right?"

Flora chose not to mention the spooky feeling she got when the water from the mill wheel failed to make a splash, or the strange voice that prompted her to flee. She didn't think Serlaid needed to know those details.

"And you ran, didn't you? Without stopping to see if there was any food in the mill house? Am I right?"

"Look, if you want to hear what happened, then enough with the critical comments. I don't have to continue this, you know. You can wait to find out after I've talked with the druids. I can stop now and go back to sleep. Is that what you want?"

Serlaid dropped the pretense that this was all for Domhnull's benefit. "Alright, alright. I'll hold my opinions 'til the end. But I expect to have some questions when you're through."

Serlaid leaned back against the wall of the hut, and Flora dropped her gaze to the small piece of twine she found her fingers twiddling with. She continued the story without looking up at her sister. Her thoughts drifted back into the dark recesses of her mind, and she spoke to no one in particular.

She told of how she had scrambled up the mountain to get away from the locust swarm, and how she had found the small cave in the rocky crag where she hid from the ravaging little beasts. She described the wildfire that had raged for day after day, scorching the land and destroying everything the locusts hadn't devoured. She recounted her scramble down the mountain in the pouring rain that had quenched the fire, but which had also turned the hillside into a treacherous quagmire of muddy ash. She related the sudden terror of the wolf attack and how she had evaded the mighty beast by jumping into the raging torrent, which then swept her back into the very millpond she had fled from just a few long, terrifying, miserable days before.

"Well, did you at least go check the mill house for food this time?" Serlaid apparently couldn't hold back the comments any longer.

"Yes," Flora whispered, feeling exasperated and drained by the terror of the memories. "Yes, I checked the mill for food."

"And?"

"And there were sacks of oats, barley, and spelt all ground and waiting for me. As far as I could tell, no one else had survived the holocaust for a day's journey in any direction. I was delirious from lack of food, and so I ate it."

"You were delirious, alright. But I'm not so sure it was from lack of food."

"Yeah. Well, that's not even the worst of it. But I'll get to that in a minute.When the rain stopped, I ventured out of the mill. The whole land was scorched and black with ash. Everything was devastated. I was certain that a Roman army had set the fires and slaughtered anyone who tried to flee. I figured I was the only person left from our entire tribe—maybe the only person left anywhere."

Flora could imagine Serlaid piping up with something like, "Being just a wee bit melodramatic, don't you think?" But she actually held her tongue and let Flora finish the tale.

"Finally, in the sunlight, I looked across the barren glen and saw a splotch of green in the middle of the black-gray ash. And suddenly I knew where I was. I knew that green spot had to be the sacred yew tree. I thought if the gods had protected the holy tree from the swarming locusts and the fiery inferno, maybe they had rescued the druid community as well. So, I left the mill and set out across the devastated glenn. When I got close to the stone circles... You remember? The ones where they held the special ritual during the tribe gathering six summers ago?"

"Yeah, I remember."

"When I got there, I stumbled past what I thought was a small hill. Well, I noticed a horrid stench in the air, and then realized the hill was really a mound of bodies." Flora stopped, closed her eyes, and turned her head aside. It was all that she could do to keep herself from retching all over again at the memory of the pile of decomposing corpses. Her next words were hollow and shaky. "The hill was a pile of bodies—druid bodies. It looked as if the entire community had been massacred and piled up to rot." Flora shuddered again and remained silent for a long time.

"And?" Serlaid prompted.

"And I crawled toward the yew tree. I figured if the druids were gone, then surely the land was dead... everyone was dead... everything was gone. The gods were the only hope I had left. And the only thing the gods had spared was the tree."

Flora stopped and took a deep breath. She sighed and her shoulders slumped. She had hoped recounting the tale for Serlaid would bring some clarity and meaning to her memories. But there was nothing. She felt despondent of hope and drained of energy. What had happened to her? It had seemed so real. And yet apparently it had all been a delusional horror, conjured up by her own unbalanced mind.

After a moment of silence, Serlaid prompted again, "And?"

"And nothing. The next thing I knew, I woke up here. That's it. That's all there is." And she whispered, almost to herself, "Thats enough, isn't it? That's all I could take."

SERLAID, unbidden, commenced with her analysis. "So, like I said, it is all a delusion, because none of that actually happened in the real world. No sacked village. No locust swarm. Oh, and locusts don't eat people or animals, by the way, only plants. I assumed a healer would know that."

"Well, this healer didn't know it. And I was afraid, alright? I'm sure that never happens to a mighty hunter. I was hungry, and alone, and tired. So, forgive me if I didn't have my bug lore down exactly straight."

Serlaid rolled her eyes, and continued. "As I was saying, our village wasn't sacked. There was no locust swarm, no wildfire, and no massacre in the druid community. But here's the odd thing—you *have* been missing for almost a complete turn of the moon. Yet the story you told only covered seven, eight, or maybe ten days at most. So, what was going on in your fantasy world for the rest of the time? And how did you get all the way to the sacred yew tree? That is where they eventually found you. How did you get all the way there from Loch Rannoch? And how did you survive that long? You must have found food somewhere. You couldn't have gone a whole moon without eating anything. It's all very strange."

"Don't look at me. That's everything I can remember. I told you to begin with that I couldn't make sense of it all. It's just a jumbled mess of confused memories."

"Oh, one last thing. Why did you run away from the millpond when you saw the locusts? I know they weren't actually real. But if you *thought* they were real, why climb a mountain? You know locusts can't swim. Why didn't you just jump into the millpond and wait until they moved on? You would have been safe from the fire there too—though that didn't happen either, of course. But in your fantasy world, you would have been safe from a fire in the millpond too. And you would have had a source of food and water. Everyone knows it's better to be near water than to get trapped in a cave on the top of a mountain, so why did you climb up that hill?"

"I don't know, okay? I was scared. Apparently I wasn't thinking straight. Don't you suppose I've asked myself those same questions? I just did. That's all I can say."

Flora knew it sounded like a lame excuse, but she certainly wasn't going to tell Serlaid about the "others," or the mysterious voice, or the omens from the gods. Serlaid already thought she was insane. All those things would just make it worse.

"Hey, I'm really tired now. I'm going back to sleep. Are you staying here?"

"Have to. I'm on watch, remember?"

"I'm not exactly sure why somebody has to be on watch, but whatever you say. Hey. You're going to tell Domhnull, right? I don't want him to think it's all his fault for not protecting me."

"What? Oh, yeah. Sure. I'll tell him."

They both knew Domhnull wasn't the reason Serlaid had asked to hear the story. Then again, Domhnull really wasn't the reason Flora had told her, either. But the pretense had to be honored.

Flora rolled back onto her side, facing the wall with her back to Serlaid. She closed her eyes and tried to sleep, but sleep would not come. The images from her memories churned through her mind, mixing together in a confused jumble with all the unanswered questions.

But something else nagged at Flora. It came indirectly from Serlaid's last question. She, of course, knew why she had run from the millpond, and why she had climbed the hill. She had listened to the voice that commanded her. But that raised a new, more sinister question. Why had the voice driven her from the safety of the millpond and the provisions in the mill? She had assumed the voice meant to help her, but now she questioned if that was the case at all. If the voice had really known about the locusts and the coming fire, wouldn't it have urged her toward the mill and the pond, where true safety could be found? Had the voice been trying to protect her after all? Or had it been luring her into a trap where she would have likely perished?

"Trust me," the voice had pled. Now, Flora wondered if she should have ever done that at all.

In the swirling tempest of blurred reflections and muddled feelings, the darkness finally won out, and Flora slept.

CHAPTER EIGHT

W *hy I am I so cold?* Flora thought to herself. She shifted under the sheepskin blanket as the morning sun filtered in through a small gap between the thatched roof and the stacked stone walls of her little hut to cut across her eyelids.

Flora's sleep had been restless and filled with a confusing mix of images from distant memories and recent delusions. She sensed a rustle near her head and shot up in a bolt. Her heart pounded, and she drew a sharp breath as she spun in her bed and prepared to face whatever sinister menace prowled in the shadows.

Her mother yelped in reaction to Flora's sudden movements and dropped the pot full of urine and excrement she had just retrieved from the small back room. She had been on her way to empty it outside the village proper. Now its contents spilled out and mixed with the wool and flax straw covering the floor.

"Flora! What's wrong, girl? What's gotten into you? Look what you've made me do."

Flora's mind focused once again, and her breathing slowed. Her nerves were so taut she overreacted to the slightest disturbance. Things that would have merely startled her before, now threatened to push her over the abyss and into a panicked frenzy. What indeed had gotten into her? It felt as if some wicked force had reached deep into her mind and wrapped its gnarled talons around the last vestiges of her sanity.

Flora took a deep breath and settled her racing heart. "I'm so sorry, *Mamaidh*. I was having a bad dream. I didn't realize you were here. I'm so sorry I startled you." Flora gestured down to the spilled refuse bowl. "I can take care of the mess. *Dadaidh* said you have been cleaning up after me ever since I was found. Thank you for doing that."

Flora's mother bent over and began scooping the fouled flooring of bracken and wool back into the pot. She busied herself with the task and didn't look up at Flora while she was speaking. "I'll get it. You just calm down and get ahold of yourself. Of course I cared for you when you were ill. That's what a mother does for her children. We were all so very worried about you. We didn't know where you had disappeared to or what kind of danger you might have been in."

"I know, *Mamaidh*. I've been so confused about what happened and so relieved to be home, I never really stopped to think about how it must have made you feel. I'm sure I would have come back sooner if I had known where I was or what was happening. It's all still very hazy and confusing to me. I..." Flora was about to tell her mother about how she had tried to piece the story together for Searlaid the previous night, but then remembered she wasn't supposed to discuss it with anyone except the druids. "I'm hoping Manas and the druids will help me figure it all out."

"Perhaps," her mother whispered, almost inaudibly.

There was an awkward moment of silence as her mother continued to clean up the mess. Finally, Flora spoke again. "Where are you and Father staying? And Serlaid and Catriona? Have you put up a temporary shelter?"

"No, child. I have relatives here in *Incheskadyne*—in the village of the Great Chief, *Toiseach* Guaidre. They are hosting us in their home."

"Are you staying with Grandmother? I thought she lived near the druid community."

"No, not with your grandmother. There are others here."

Her mother's response seemed unnecessarily vague, but then, she had rarely been long on details when they spoke together. Flora was curious about the reply. She never knew her mother had kin in another village, much less in another clan. But then she thought back on her extended family in their own village and realized almost all of her aunts, uncles, and cousins were from her father's side of the family. Why had that fact never occurred to her before?

It was strange her mother had never mentioned other relatives than her grandmother and grandfather. Or that they had never even met her family when they came to the great tribal gathering several years ago. She wondered about this secret side of her mother's past.

Flora realized she was absent-mindedly watching a dung beetle crawling through the carpet of bracken toward the spillage from the waste pot—attracted by the smell, no doubt. She shook her head and focused her attention.

"You never mentioned any family in another village, Mother. Who is it? Why have we never met them?"

"Well, they're rather far away from Bunrannoch, now aren't they?"

"Who, Mother?"

"I've a couple of brothers here. They have families of their own. You must be hungry. Let me empty this pot, and I can bring you some porridge."

Flora let the family issue drop for now, since her mother was being so evasive. Her gaze fell on the two sheep skulls glaring into the room, and she suddenly felt an overwhelming need to leave this place.

"I can empty that pot. I would really like to get out into the sun for a bit."

"No, dear. I'll take care of it. And I'll get you some food."

Flora reached out and grasped the edge of the clay bowl. "Mother, I'll do it. I really want to get out of this hut for a while."

Her mother stared her down and tugged at the bowl. "No, Flora. I have it."

"Mother! Please!" Flora tugged harder at the bowl and it shattered, spilling the foul mess onto the floor again and causing both of them to stagger backwards.

Flora's mother scowled at the waste strewn once again across the floor. Then she glared at Flora. "You can't go out! It is forbidden."

"Forbidden? Forbidden by whom? And why?"

Before her mother could reply, a cowled figure ducked through the low doorway. "I forbade it." The man pushed the hood back off his head, and Flora recognized Manas, the healer who had tended to her when she first woke up. "I instructed your parents to limit your guests and to keep you inside until we have examined you."

"Examine me for what? I'm just fine. I'm a little weak, but I'm well enough to go home and forget all this ever happened."

"I'm afraid that's not possible, at least not yet. I am fully aware of your physical condition. That's not the main issue at the moment. I'm glad to hear you feel well enough to travel. I have instructions from Bhatair Rhu to bring you to *Feart Choille* right away. We will examine you there."

"Examine me for what?" Flora repeated with an exasperated tone.

"When?" Flora's mother interjected. She was still holding the broken pot in her hand. "When will you go?"

"Right now. We will leave straight away. There is an escort waiting outside. Flora gather your things"

"But she hasn't eaten yet. And her father and sisters will want to see her off. Let me go get them and bring Flora some food." She began edging toward the door, still gripping the remnants of the clay vessel.

Flora thought she had a wary look on her face. "And Domhnull," Flora blurted out. "Please bring Domhnull as well."

Manas held out his arm and blocked Flora's mother on her way to the door. "That won't be necessary. We have plenty of provisions, and it is less than a half-day's walk from here. Flora can eat while we travel. And if everything works out as I expect, we'll have her back here by evening on the morrow. Then you'll all be free to go home. We're short on time and must head out straight away. Flora..." He gestured toward the door, indicating she should precede him outside.

Flora's mother bleated out, "Please. Please let me gather her family to see her off. We didn't expect you back until tomorrow. You said you would return in three days, remember? Flora's father and little sister have barely had a chance to see her since she woke from her ordeal. They'll be heartbroken if they don't have a chance to bless her on her way."

"And Domhnull," Flora reiterated, insistently.

Manas' tone became more forceful, and he repeated his gesture toward the door. "I'm afraid we have no time. There is some urgency in the matter. We shall leave immediately and return on the morrow. Now if you please, good woman, we must go. Flora."

His suddenly brusque manner and the authority tone in his voice left little room for argument. Flora slipped her *brogen* onto her feet and took her small flint knife from where it hung by its leather thong on one of the support posts. She had no other possessions.

Briefly she thought with regret about her little pouch of treasures, lying lost in a forgotten cave on some faraway hill, she knew not where—if there even was such a cave, or such a hill to begin with. In any event, the pouch was gone. That was certain. She sighed and her shoulders slumped. She whispered a silent prayer to Brigid that she might someday find those little missing pieces of her soul. Then, yielding to Manas' insistent urging, she ducked her head and stepped past the two sheep skulls into the sunlight.

Outside the door, Flora stopped, straightened up, closed her eyes, and took a moment to bask in the warmth of the daylight. The incessant clouds and constant drizzle had broken, and the sun shone down in the full glory of Lugh's splendor. Flora felt so good to be outside the dank, dark hut, she almost forgot about Manas and the imminent journey to *Feart Choille*. Then the healer prodded her in the back, urging her to take a few steps so he could follow her out the doorway, and the momentary spell was broken.

Immediately in front of her, Flora saw a small company of four armed warriors and four hooded druids standing in a formal formation. Beyond them, a few villagers had gathered to see what was happening. The druids stood in a square and all faced in the same direction. They were wearing normal, brown, everyday robes, with the hoods pulled up over their heads, obscuring their faces. Each carried a pole with a ram's skull mounted on its top. The skulls faced into the center of the square. Two of the warriors were positioned in front of the druids, and two were behind. They wore green belted tunics, but were also painted with the loops, swirls, and beasts of their spirit armor. This seemed very odd to Flora, and it caused her to wonder why they were adorned in this way.

Ever since her people had started fighting the Romans many generations ago, the warriors had gone into battle wearing only small belts of cloth around their waists to hold their private parts in place. Roman soldiers donned heavy armor with bronze or iron helmets and large shields—or so she was told by the bards and warriors of her clan. But the highlanders did not have access to the necessary materials, nor did they have the skills to fashion armor in great quantities for all their fighters.

The combat style of the highlanders was also very different from the rigid formations used by the Romans. Her people could not equal the Roman armies in terms of raw weight and power. Instead of trying to match the Romans with sheer force, the highlanders employed speed, stealth, and cunning. And so their warriors went into battle unencumbered by bulky armor or shields. This tactic was a disadvantage when fighting on the flat, wide open plains of the lowlands where the massive Roman battle arrays were almost unstoppable. But the advantage shifted in the hills and forests of the highlands. This is where speed and agility gave her people the upper hand.

The highlanders also understood the spiritual side of every military engagement. As men fought face to face with swords and spears, the gods battled in another realm. Sometimes the gods strove against each other in immortal combat. And sometimes they interceded on behalf of the people who had worshipped and honored them with gifts and sacrifices. So highland warriors painted their bodies with the sacred symbols and emblems of their gods, woven across their chests and arms, buttocks and thighs, in blue dyes coaxed from the roots of the woad plant. It was their spirit armor, and a highland warrior never went into combat without it.

Flora was confused by the appearance of the four soldiers who waited to escort her to *Feart Choille*, the Forest Stronghold. They wore the everyday tunics of peacetime or hunting, but also the spirit armor of war. What kind of battle had they prepared for today?

Flora's little hut was located some distance away from the village proper. She remembered her father saying it was a healing hut, whatever that meant. Presumably, it was a special building set back away from the village where people who were gravely ill could be treated and rest in relative peace. Her own village didn't have such a place. In her village, people were usually tended by family members in their own homes. But *Incheskadyne* was the village of the Great Chief, and it was much larger than her village of Bunrannoch.

A short distance away, she saw villagers going about their daily tasks, mostly unaware of the small procession assembled in front of the healing hut. Beyond the thatched roofs of the round houses, she spotted a vast body of water nestled in between mountains rising to either side. Flora knew this must be Loch Tatha. Though most in the village were oblivious to her situation, a small group had noticed the arrival of the druids and come to see what was happening. Word would undoubtedly spread quickly.

It seemed odd to Flora that the druids would enter the village to take her away without consulting with Chief Guaidre. Village chiefs almost always kept close control of who came and went from their settlements. She assumed a tribal chief would want to maintain even greater control. But the Great Chief was nowhere in sight.

Flora hoped word would spread fast enough so her family would come in time to see her off. Out of the corner of her eye, she glimpsed her mother edging around the hut and hurrying off toward the village center. She felt Manas place a hand on her back and guide her toward the middle of the formation. She had expected to walk casually together with Manas and a couple of escorts, but it seemed as if he intended for her to march in the center of this odd formation, with sheep skulls watching her from all four corners. She felt more like a dangerous prisoner than a patient going for treatment. The gathering crowd gazed upon them in wary curiosity.

Manas stepped up beside her, and the formation started forward without anyone saying a word. No commands. No directions or instructions. They just began a slow, steady pace away from the village. When they had gone a few hundred paces, Flora heard her father's voice calling out behind them. She stopped and turned to meet him, but Manas gripped her arm tightly and bent his head close to her ear. "Keep walking. Don't look back."

Flora ignored him. She did look back, and she could see her father running to catch up with them. She also saw one of the hooded figures slowly shake his head. The two warriors in the rear stopped and turned to bar her father's path. What was happening here? Was she being taken to someone who could help her sort out her strange nightmare? Or was she being taken captive as a prisoner? Every fiber of her being screamed at her to break free and run to her father. He would protect her! He would keep her safe! But she also sensed the power and the authority of this small group of druids and warriors. If they truly had been sent by Bhatair Rhu, no one who would give her refuge. Not even the Great Chief would cross the will of the Arch Druid.

Manas gripped her arm once again and turned her back around. "Keep walking. Don't look back." He repeated the words as if she hadn't heard him the first time. Then he turned and slipped through the back of the formation.

Flora did glance back again, despite his admonition, and saw him stop to speak briefly with her father. Her father gestured wildly toward her, but she could not hear their words. Eventually, his head dropped, and he nodded sullenly. He turned once more and caught her eye. He waved to her, then lifted his thumb to his lips. It was a special sign only they shared. She could hear his voice whispering in her mind, "I love you, my wee *fauth*," and a tear trickled down her cheek. Despite Manas' earlier reassurances, she had the distinct impression she would not, in fact, be coming back—back to this village, back to her family, or back to her home.

Flora glanced up at the dark, eyeless sockets of the rams' skulls glaring down at her and shuddered. Images flashed through her mind from an elusive nightmare she could not recall, and her knees went weak. She stumbled, but Manas' strong hands caught and steadied her. Where had he come from? How had he gotten back beside her so quickly after speaking with her father? Had she been lost in her thoughts for so long?

Manas held her arm, placed another hand on her shoulder, and guided her on. His grip on her was firm, but surprisingly gentle. It felt, somehow, like a hand of compassion holding her up. She clung to that sensation as the darkness once again threatened to engulf her mind. She focused on Manas' guiding hand and yielded to her fate. The small group tightened up their ranks and walked forward—away from the village, away from her family, away from Domhnull and her father, toward the Forest Stronghold and the sacred yew.

ONCE THEY WERE out of sight of the village, Manas opened a bag he had slung over his shoulder and offered her some food—two oatcakes, a chunk of hard cheese, and some dried pork. She accepted the meager meal and gnawed at it hungrily. Over the past couple of days since she woke up, she had eaten mostly gruel and porridge. It tasted good to chew on some solid food, even if it was mere trail rations.

After she had eaten the oatcakes and cheese, Manas offered her a skin of water.

"I'm sorry for the abrupt departure from the village and for not letting you see your family. When the weather broke this morning before the sun rose, we could see the moon was full. Our calculations indicated that another day would pass before the full moon, but they were apparently wrong. Bhatair Rhu insisted we get you back before the end of the day so the rites can be performed tonight. We simply didn't have time to wait for explanations or long goodbyes. Don't worry, you'll be back with your family again soon enough."

Flora took a drink to wash down the dry crumbs in her mouth before speaking. "Rites? What ritess are to be performed? What will happen when we get to *Feart Choille?*"

"It will all become clear in time. Be patient."

"Will these 'rites' help me to remember what happened over the past month? Will they clear the foggy images in my head? Is that what they are for?"

"I'm really not the person to answer those kinds of questions. I'm just a healer. I was sent to make sure you had recovered enough to travel and then to convey you back to the ones who can take care of all the rest."

"And these men?" Flora gestured to her party of escorts.

"They are here to ensure your protection."

"I'm no druid, but even I know that the skulls of a spirit fence face toward danger, not away from it. The skulls in the hut faced inside, not out. And these skulls are all staring at me. This doesn't seem like a spirit fence to protect me from dangers out there. It seems more like a cage."

She took a bite of the dried pork jerky and began chewing the tough meat. It had a surprisingly tangy taste. It must have been cured with salt, rather than by smoking. Flora momentarily wondered where it had come from. Salt was uncommon this far inland. She had rarely tasted it and took a moment to savor the delicacy. Perhaps this druid's trail rations weren't so meager after all.

Manas frowned at Flora's comment. "Sometimes the greatest dangers come from within."

Flora wondered at what this could mean. *Are they afraid of me?* "Do you think I pose some kind of threat to people? Is that why the warriors have their spirit armor on?"

"I expect this will all become clear to you in time. Like I said, I am not the right person to answer those kinds of questions."

Flora glanced at the warriors. They all looked oddly similar with the same tall, muscular build, dark red hair pulled back and tied in leather thongs, and close-cropped beards. Each one appeared to be about thirty summers old. Their faces were stern with intent expressions, and their eyes shifted constantly, scanning the forest and valley for any signs of danger. She noticed they never really looked at her—only outward.

"Who are the warriors anyway? Are they from *Toiseach* Guaidre's clan?"

"One of them is," Manas replied. "The one with the bull tattoo on his right shoulder. There is one from each of the tribe's four clans. They are part of *Ard-Draoidh* Bhatair Rhu's personal detail."

Flora looked more closely at the right arms of the two warriors she could see from her position in the middle of the procession. She could make out the bull Manas mentioned, swathed in a shroud of blue spirals and swirls, on the shoulder of the guard in the left front of the formation. A glance back revealed a boar similarly portrayed on the guard to her left rear.

She expected the other two warriors would display a hawk and a wolf if she could see them. These were the emblems of the four clans of the tribe. She wondered which of the two had a hawk on his shoulder. That man would be from her clan. She strained to see if she could recognize either of the two as someone she knew from her village, but neither looked familiar. They all looked more like each other than anyone she knew from home.

A question occurred to her and she asked Manas, "They are his guard, then? The Arch Druid needs a personal bodyguard?"

It seemed like an odd notion that a powerful druid—indeed, the *most powerful* druid—would need guards.

"They're not guards, exactly. They're warriors who do special tasks for Bhatair Rhu."

"And the druids? Who are they?" Flora couldn't tell what they looked like because hoods shrouded their faces and concealed their features.

"They are part of the community near *Feart Choille*."

Flora knew that much without asking. What she wanted to know was why they were here and why they were carrying a portable spirit fence. But she sensed that Manas would resist providing more detail, so she turned her questions on him instead. "You are part of the druid community as well, right?"

"I am," he affirmed.

"Then why haven't you shaved your forehead? Why don't you wear a druid's tonsure?"

Manas smiled. "You certainly are full of questions. I've heard that about you." He looked down at her intently and continued. "I am part of the druid community and was trained as a healer. But I have taken a special vow not to cut my hair or to trim my beard. Now, I need to walk ahead, so the rest of your questions will have to wait. All things will become clear in time. Be sure to stay in the center of the square. We will be at *Feart Choille* soon after midday."

Then Manas strode through the center of the formation and took up a position about twenty paces ahead of the front two guards, leaving Flora to wrestle in silence with her worries and her fears.

THEY WERE WALKING on a well-worn path that threaded its way between the River Tatha on their right and a steep, forested hill to their left. The sun still shone in all of its glory as small, puffy clouds drifted lazily across the sky. Pink and purple stalks of foxglove decorated the fields to either side of the trail. The beautiful flowers hid a more sinister core deep within the plant—a poison that, if eaten, could kill a grown man in moments. This had earned the flower its more common nickname, Dead Man's Bells. It was indeed a dangerous beauty.

But Flora also knew that the same lethal saps within the stalks, when properly prepared, produced a powerful balm that could soothe burns and ease labored breathing. She wondered that both fatal danger and powerful healing could be wrapped together behind such an alluring disguise. Only the wisdom of the gods could enable someone to discern and exploit the two truths veiled behind those soft lavender petals.

Suddenly, a shiver coursed through her body. A terrifying realization made her stop still in her tracks. Her name... Flora. Was she just such a flower as these Dead Man's Bells? Were both poison and healing hidden inside *her* heart? Did goodness and evil inhabit her soul? Was something deadly and malevolent mingled inside her mind along with the healing arts Nandag had taught her? If so, how could these two selves be controlled? How could she keep the toxin contained while letting the elixir of life flourish and grow?

Her mind spun with the recognition of her capacity for good and evil, and she grew dizzy with nausea. The two druids at her back took a firm hold on each of her arms and prodded her into motion. They supported her while she regained her footing and then released her to her own volition. And the skulls stared down at her in mute condemnation.

Flora forced her thoughts outward and turned her attention to exploring the countryside. As they rounded the point of the steep slope to their left, a massive hillfort came into view. One of the hill's rocky cliffs grew up into a sheer earthen berm topped with imposing stone ramparts. From this vantage, the fort looked virtually unassailable. It towered over the valley below, like a sentinel standing guard over the mighty River Tatha at the confluence of waters where a major tributary yielded its lifeblood to swell the flow of its greater sibling. Flora didn't know the name of this second river, or the god who claimed its banks, but it seemed to come from the great glen where she knew that *Feart Choille* and the sacred yew must surely be hidden.

Then images flashed through her mind, unbidden and unwelcome. A wolf. Pouring rain. A raging torrent. Involuntarily, Flora gasped for air as the memory made her feel as if she were drowning all over again. Could this docile stream be the same surging flood that snatched her from the wolf's jaws of death? Surely it must be the same coursing flow from her nightmare of horror that hurled her down the mountainside, over jagged rocks, and through churning pools to deposit her in the millpond at the mouth of the glen. How very different it appeared now, meandering its way across the valley floor under golden rays of the summer sun. Like the pink flowers along its shores, the river seemed to have a dual personality of life-giving nymph and lethal serpent.

Flora scanned the fort again, and she felt an odd sense she had been there before, atop the lofty walls, gazing across the lush green valley below. She could even smell the scent of spring flowers wafting up on a cool breeze from the memory hiding in the recesses of her mind. But Flora knew for certain she had never been here, at least not in this waking life. Perhaps in her dreams.

The breeze shifted slightly, and a chill crawled across the flesh of her back and crept down her arms. The vague recollection took on a darker, more sinister mood. She felt the towering stone walls boxing her in ever more tightly. Lifting her arms, she groped at the air, while her inner thoughts clawed at the stones, trying to climb over or through them to escape the flaming horror within its courtyard. And then, as suddenly and eerily as it had come, the feeling vanished, and she was walking again, arms flailing in the air, at the center of the formation. As they rounded the corner and started across the glen, Flora took one more furtive glance back at the hillfort and shuddered.

THE LITTLE FORMATION walked in silence between the base of the hill to their left and the river to the right. It was really odd. No one said a word. The druids held the spirit fence and the warriors flanked them to the front and rear, while Manas lead the way. Flora wasn't sure why he had left her to walk in front of the procession. It wasn't as if the others didn't know the route. She would have preferred to ask him some more questions about what would happen when they reached *Feart Choille*. Instead, she walked in silence like the rest and listened to the wrens chirp, the bullfinches sing, and the redstarts chatter. She noticed the birdsongs were much more animated than usual here beside the stream and in the bright morning sun.

At a break in the trees, Manas turned toward the river, though the path continued straight along the base of the hill. The current was slow and lazy, but it was a good stone's throw to the other bank, and Flora could see there was no bridge. Yet Manas kept walking straight toward the water with no apparent intention of slowing down. He strode into the river, followed closely by the two warriors and the two druids in front of her.

The water came up to their knees, but no farther. The river was surely deeper than she was tall, but the members of the entourage ahead of her didn't appear to sink. Apprehensively, she approached the shore. Were they stepping on stones hidden below the surface of the river? If so, how was she to follow?

Tentatively, Flora placed her foot into the water, testing for a firm surface on which to put her weight. She did *not* want to slip on a mossy rock, plunge into the water, and get swept downstream. She felt a hand on her back prodding her forward, and so she took a cautious step. She found what felt like a pebbled surface just below the waterline. It gave a little with each step but was certainly firm enough to bear her weight.

Flora waded in until the river was at the height of her knees but then descended no deeper. As she looked to her left and right, she could see telltale ripples up and downstream. This was apparently some sort of underwater bridge. Stones lined each side, breaking the force of the water's flow, and small pebbles formed a raised pathway between them. Flora wondered who had made such a construction and why they had taken such pains to conceal its existence instead of just building a normal bridge above the water, fashioned from the trunks of trees.

As she stepped up out of the water on the far shore, Flora saw a wide valley of cleared pasture land where cattle and sheep grazed freely. In the distance, mighty mountains rose on the far side of the glen. Though it was still concealed from view, she knew that *Feart Choille* sat atop one of the lower ridgelines, standing guard over the sacred yew tree on a small hill below.

The yew didn't stand out as starkly against the lush green of the pasture and the wooded hill as when she had seen it in her nightmare. In that context, it had been the only live thing against a black and gray backdrop of death.

Flora shivered at the image in her mind and then trudged on, penned in by the invisible confines of her moving spirit fence. She hoped they would not have to slog through the mud and muck of pasture and bog. But they remained on firm, dry ground as the small retinue wove a circuitous route across the valley floor. This pathway must have been well known to Manas and her other traveling companions, though it was not even slightly evident to her. So she followed, trusting in the navigation skills of her escorts, until they reached the dry ground that surrounded the sacred yew a little past midday.

Flora recognized this place, not so much from the recent horror of her ordeal, but from the great gathering several summers before, when the fields around the holy tree were filled with the tents and fire circles of the tribe's many clans. But the people and the camps were all gone now. Only cattle and sheep grazed in the open fields.

They advanced toward the standing stones of the gateway, and Flora wondered if they would perform a ritual and pass through the portal to approach the yew tree. Great pyres of wood had been erected in patterns around the stones, as if a special offering were to be made to the gods. Apparently, the druid community had prepared a full-moon ceremony to honor Cerridwen. She wondered if they would allow her to attend. It must have been arranged in advance for this evening. She wanted to ask Manas about it, but he walked wordlessly past the fire circles, past the stones, and past the tree, without so much as a glance back in her direction.

Flora felt frustrated at the lack of information. She desperately wanted to discover what had happened to her over the month that she had been missing, and she hoped that kind of revelation would be waiting at the end of their journey.

CHAPTER NINE

F lora's entourage turned to follow a winding path up the steep
hillside. The track narrowed so the members of their troupe
collapsed down to a single file. She was still in the middle, but the
spirit fence no longer surrounded her on all four sides. Somehow, it
made her feel less confined, though the steep slope did more to
prevent her from dodging to either side than the quadrangle of sheep
skulls ever did.

The path was steep and narrow, and Flora felt fatigued. Her
injured knee ached from the long walk, and though she had feigned
bravado about the progress of her recovery, in truth she was still quite
drained from the ordeal. When they finally broke onto a saddle on
first ridgeline, she whispered a prayer of thanks to Brigid for giving
her the strength to make the climb.

They turned right along the ridgeline and followed it east. The
view across the glen was spectacular, and Flora caught a glimpse of
Loch Tatha to the northwest. The great hill which they spent the
morning walking around must lay directly between their present
location and *Incheskadyne*, the village of the Great Chief. In

retrospect, she was quite happy they had walked around the imposing hill, rather than taking the straight path over the top.

While trying to keep her attention on the rutted pathway, Flora stole quick glances along the river at the far side of the glen. She traced it upstream with her eye, along the base of the great hill to the far end of the valley where it took a sharp turn to the south, and there she spied what she was looking for. The millpond! It was real after all!

Perhaps the whole experience had not been some delirious hallucination. She couldn't have conjured up the images and pieced them together in a demented twist of imagination, because she had never seen that mill before in her life. She had known about the sacred yew tree and had seen the standing stones of the gateway, but she had never even heard about the mill. Regardless of whether mad delusions had blurred the lines between reality and fantasy over her last month of terror, parts of what she had experienced were real. The mill proved it.

And if the mill was real, then maybe the rocky crag and the cave were real as well. Perhaps her pouch of treasures wasn't lost after all! At that moment, she was nudged in the back by the druid at her heels and had no chance to scan the distant hillside in search of her secret place. Filled with a mix of hope and regret she turned her back to the glen and trudged apprehensively forward toward her enigmatic fate.

As they rounded the next turn in the trail Flora was surprised by two distinct and startling sights. First, an immense red mare reared up immediately in front of Manas. Mud and twigs showered down onto their party from the horse's flailing hooves. Apparently, the rider had been just as startled to see them. Two more horsemen lurched to an abrupt halt directly behind the first. As the whinnies of the horses echoed into stillness, and the riders regained control of their mounts, the second unexpected sight burst into Flora's awareness. A sparrow's flight beyond the horsemen, atop a steep and jagged crag, rose the walls of an immense fortress unlike any Flora had ever seen before.

One side of the hillfort was perched on the edge of a sheer cliff that plummeted breathlessly to the valley floor below. The fort was surrounded on all other sides by a thicket of holly bushes so dense that a hare surely couldn't navigate its way between the entanglement of trunks and limbs. A stone wall about twice the height of a man formed a barrier in front of the fort to hold the tide of holly at bay. But the most startling aspect of the fort's construction was its ramparts. The fort itself was formed out of the interleaved trunks of massive live ash trees, with the canopy above supporting various platforms and catwalks.

Flora ignored the horsemen for the moment, overwhelmed by the sight of the colossal, imposing fortress. This had to be *Feart Choille*, the Forest Stronghold. Flora mused that it was aptly named, not because it was hidden in a forest, but because it was literally built out of one.

Any force powerful enough to hack its way through the sea of holly would find itself facing a towering wall of trees—living walls that would be many times sturdier than ones made of cut timber, and much more resistant to fire. Surely, such an edifice could only have been constructed by the most talented of druid woodsmen, guided by the wisdom of Cernunnos, the god of the forests, over many generations. It was a marvel to behold.

Flora snapped out of her wonder and amazement when she suddenly realized the man on the lead horse was speaking to Manas about her. Manas bowed his head to the horseman in apparent deference.

The man, himself, was a sight to behold. Perched atop his magnificent sorrel steed, Flora could tell that he was tall and lean, with broad shoulders and fluid movements. Though his forehead was shaved in the traditional druid's tonsure, the rest of his head was crowned with a mane of flowing golden hair, while his face was beardless, smooth, and clean. He appeared to be comparatively young, considering the deference Manas displayed and the apparent respect he garnered from the rest of her escort. He wore a deep forest green cloak with a purple thistle sewn onto the right breast. And though he spoke with the easy authority of one used to giving commands, his expression was light and his smile broad. Flora sensed life emanating from this enigmatic man, and she wondered who he could be.

His two companions were no less bewildering. One was a druid, wearing the traditional white robe reserved for sacred ceremonies. His face was a bit paunchy and round, but otherwise unremarkable. And yet there was something about his eyes—something odd and unsettling that Flora could notice, even at this distance. They were deep and black, like wells that disappeared into a cavernous emptiness from which even sound would not return. He carried a gnarled tree branch, fashioned into a staff. A large knot near the top was inlaid with silver along the natural pattern of fissures in the wood. It looked like a spider's web, glistening with morning dew.

The other man was apparently a warrior. He looked just like the four guards in her entourage, with the same close-cropped beard and the same reddish hair pulled back in a leather thong. But this man exuded authority. His face was taut and chiseled, and he wore a grim expression that contrasted starkly with the broad grin of the lead man. He was clad in a formal tunic with a red and green checkered pattern and knee-length leather boots. His body was covered with the interlaced spirals, geometric designs, and mythical creatures of his spirit armor. Like her own guards, he was equipped for spiritual warfare. She could not see his right shoulder to identify which clan his badge represented.

Apart from his stern demeanor, his most striking feature was a deep, jagged scar that sliced down from above his left eye, across the bridge of his nose, and through his right cheek. Flora shuddered to think what might have caused the disfigurement, or what kind of unseen scars might be concealed deep within the hard man's soul. She was also startled to see a silver torc at his neck—a thick, twisted cord of silver wire with wolves' heads at the ends. Usually, these badges of authority were reserved for the chiefs of clans or tribes, and he didn't seem to be one. Perhaps he was an extraordinary warlord who had won a place of distinction through his skill at leading men in combat. She could only guess at his identity.

The lead man finished his conversation with Manas. "The preparations for the rites are nearly complete. I am off to confer with the leaders of the delegations. There is no need to stop in at *Feart Choille*. Please escort our guest directly to Fedelma at *An Dun Gael*. She is prepared to receive her for the assessment. It must all happen tonight. It is time."

Manas bowed his head again. "As you say, *Mhaighstir*. It shall be done."

Flora stared in wonder as her party stood aside while the horsemen rode past them and down the trail. Who would Manas refer to as "Master?" Could that man have possibly been the Arch Druid, *Ard-Draoidh* Bhatair Rhu? Surely not. He looked as though he were only about forty summers old—an age of respect, for certain, but not one of such ancient wisdom that he should hold the position of the highest druid in all the land. Surely, this must have been some other man of regard among the woodsmen or the seers or the judges. Flora was curious to know, but that revelation would apparently have to wait.

Manas followed after the horses, while the other members of her entourage simply turned in place without a word, and the whole group proceeded back down the path from where they had come. Flora was bemused and disappointed. She had desperately wanted to see inside the magnificent fortress. But even more, she wondered what role she would play in the events of the evening. She puzzled over who this "Fedelma" was, to whom she was being taken, and what kind of "assessment" would be done. Was this woman a healer who could help her understand her recent nightmarish experiences? Would she be able to make the panic and the night terrors go away?

Such questions swirled through her mind along with a torrent of other bewildering thoughts. Who were these "delegation representatives" that the rider would meet? What and where was *An Dun Gael*, the White Fortress? And most of all, why was she here?

It seemed as if momentous events were taking place all around her—powerful people meeting together in sacred places to perform special ceremonies in honor of the gods. How did she become embroiled in it all? Of what significance could a young novice healer possibly be among such prominent and influential men? She groped about for answers, but her escorts were mute, the forest was silent, and the skulls stared down at her in wordless contempt. So she walked in confusion toward her unknown destiny.

THE ODD LITTLE formation of escorts and guards followed the path back along the ridgeline to where it met the trail twisting like a serpent down the mountainside. Flora wondered if they would return to the gateway stones and the sacred yew tree, but they didn't go down that way. Instead, they crossed that path and picked up another trail that continued along the ridgeline away from the setting sun.

Flora's perplexity suddenly swelled at the realization. How could the sun be going down already? Days were very long in the highlands during the summer. Indeed, tonight, there would be almost no darkness at all. Instead, a faint pallor of crimson and orange, low across the horizon, would persist from dusk till dawn. So how had the sun now gone down so low? Had she been lost in her thoughts for the whole of the afternoon? It didn't seem possible. Nor could she believe that they had walked more than a stag's dash from *Feart Choille*. And yet dusk was creeping up behind them like a wolf stalking its prey.

The trail they followed seemed to be slowly vanishing amidst a tangled mass of bushes and shrubs. Manas threaded a circuitous route through the underbrush, while the warriors and the druids fanned out in different directions, spreading to a distance of about a doe's leap between each man. Flora wasn't exactly certain where she should walk, but a tight, twisting path seemed to open up before her and then close back as she passed.

She was so intent on picking her way through the thicket that she unexpectedly burst into a clearing and then gasped at the sight. The nearest druid glanced over his shoulder at her sudden exclamation of awe, and a faint smile crossed his lips before he looked away and the hood once again concealed his features. Flora was astonished at what she beheld. It could be nothing other than *An Dun Gael*, and it, like *Feart Choille*, was aptly named.

In the center of the broad clearing stood an immense stone tower. The foundation was an enormous circular ring from which its walls rose like a giant storage jar to the height of twenty or thirty men. The face of the edifice was stark and unadorned, with only a single low doorway at the base and no openings or windows of any kind in the sides as they rose to the sky. The stones from which the tower was built were like nothing Flora had ever seen. They were solid, bright, gleaming, white blocks that shone radiantly in the light of the setting sun. Each was as wide as twice the span of her arms. They weren't covered with a white wash of lard or with dyed goat skins. The stones, themselves, were white, through and through. And they had been meticulously carved to form a perfectly smooth curve, with seams that were barely discernible.

Flora just stood and gaped at the magnificent structure, overwhelmed by its unique beauty, its simple elegance, and its potent aura of raw power. She marveled at the fact that she had never even heard of such a place before. And, with a sudden chill, she wondered why she would be brought here. Indeed, what mysteries and what horrors lay concealed behind those dazzling, foreboding walls. She was absolutely certain she didn't want to find out.

The members of her guard detail emerged from the thicket into the glade and coalesced back into the structured formation with Flora at the center. Manas moved forward toward the opening at the base of the great tower, but the rest of the entourage remained still.

As Flora peered closer at the details of the glowing white bastion, she realized that it tapered in a slight curve toward the top, so it looked like an enormous jar standing in the center of the field. It was perched on the edge of a cliff, just like *Feart Choille*, and Flora wondered why she had never seen this awesome structure from the valley below. She understood why *Feart Choille* blended into the forest background, since it was formed from living trees. But surely, this glaring white stone edifice should be visible from anywhere within the entire glen below. And yet, not only had she never even glimpsed it, she had never even heard of it. Was it concealed from sight by some kind of spell? Or did some trick of the terrain cause it to blend in to the striations of the cliff face when viewed from the ground? Flora could not comprehend how such a spectacular tower could be kept secret.

As she continued to gape in wonder at the imposing structure, Manas disappeared inside the darkened doorway. Flora watched her escorts to see if they would reveal any clue as to her purpose at this place. She even tried prompting them to speak. She didn't know any of their names, so she just tossed a comment into the air, hoping a reply might echo back from one of the warriors or druids.

"This is an amazing place. Is this *An Dun Gael*? Why have I never heard of it before? Have any of you been inside? And what will happen to me here?"

But the guards just stared forward and didn't utter a sound. It was as if they were oblivious to her presence among them, except for the fact their entire purpose was to ensure she remained within the confines of the spirit fence. Flora was a curious person and not always terribly patient, so the lack of information had become rather irritating. The wait seemed to drag on interminably.

The rider on the horse had told Manas that some woman was prepared to receive her, so she wondered what the delay was all about. She fidgeted with a small fray in the seam of her *leine*. Finally, she became exasperated and tired, so she decided to sit down on the ground. She wondered if that would provoke some kind of reaction from her chaperones, but they just continued to stare at the tower and ignore her.

Eventually, Flora realized the air around the fortress was absolutely still. She could hear a breeze rushing through the trees in the distance and see them swaying under its influence, but the air in the clearing was utterly motionless. Then, just as she was musing over this fact, a forceful rush of wind broke the stillness. It emanated from the tower doorway and blew violently, straight toward them. The warriors leaned into the gale, bracing themselves against its force, and the druids' hoods were blown back, revealing their faces for the first time. Flora was curious to examine their appearance but was too distracted by the wind. Since she was sitting on the ground, it had less of an impact on her. And yet, its sudden arrival seemed to presage ominous portents, so distinct was it from the absolute stillness that had so recently captured her attention.

Amid the howling gale, Manas strode purposefully out of the doorway, across the clearing, and straight toward her. Her escorts parted slightly to make way for him, and he stepped right up in front of her, his long hair and shaggy beard fluttering haphazardly in the wind. Flora stood to meet him.

"It is time," he said. "The preparations are complete. Go to the doorway. Fedelma will meet you there."

"What? Aren't you coming with me?"

Flora yelled to be heard over the wind, but her question came out more like a desperate cry. Although Manas wasn't exactly someone she would call a friend, he was at least somewhat familiar by now. She was disturbed at the thought of going alone into the unknown darkness of the daunting edifice.

Manas shook his head slightly. "My task was to escort you here safely. That, I have done. Now, I turn you over to Fedelma's care. She will conduct the assessment. We are needed for the ceremony at the sacred yew. You will be fine here. I am confident this will all be over soon, and you can return to your family." He stepped to one side and motioned her toward the fortress.

Flora's eyes pleaded with Manas to stay, but he simply canted his head and gestured once again toward the doorway. "Go."

And so she steeled her nerve, squared her shoulders, and took a step into the wind. At that very instant, the gale ceased to blow, and the eerie calm settled back over the clearing. The renewed stillness was even more unnerving than the tempest had been.

As FLORA MADE her way across the clearing toward the tower's gaping entrance, she stole one more glance back at Manas and her escort team, but they had already vanished back into the thicket. A tremor of fear caused her legs to go weak, and she nearly fell to the ground. She stopped and took a moment to refocus her mind. "Get a grip!" she told herself. What was she afraid of, anyway? If they had wanted to harm her in any way, they could have easily done so already.

Then another thought occurred to her. Why couldn't she just run? What would stop her? Manas and the guards were gone. No one was watching her, or if they were, they would be in the tower. Surely she could disappear into the forest before anyone could catch up with her. Her mind leapt at the thought of freedom from the nightmares, from the intrigue, from enigmatic assessments, and from ceremonies to the gods.

She half-turned to act on the impulse, took one step, and then stopped short. She couldn't do it. First of all, where would she go? If she went back to her family, the druids would just come and hunt her down. And the next time they dragged her here, they might not be so civil. But even more than that, she desperately wanted to discover what had happened to her and to understand why she was being drawn into this disconcerting drama. Apparently, the only way to find out was to walk through that ominous portal into whatever awaited on the other side. So, she turned back and continued on toward the fortress.

As she neared the doorway, she saw that it, too, was protected by a spirit fence. But this barrier was more powerful than the one used to confine her on the journey here. Instead of ram's heads, it was formed with human skulls mounted to the corners of the doorframe. This was much more potent magic—an enchantment conjured from the life force of human sacrifices.

Flora instinctively checked her stride and came to a halt. Only a druid could emplace a spirit fence, and only a more powerful druid could break its spell. Anyone who crossed the fence unbidden would suffer a terrible curse. The specific nature of the curse depended on the druid who set up the fence and the gods he called upon to protect the place. Often, it involved a slow, painful wasting disease that would turn the victim's bowels to a foul mix of blood and pus which would seep out of their anus for days on end until their entrails had completely turned to mush, and they died an agonizing death.

Flora shuddered at the image such a curse conjured in her mind. Whole war bands, even whole armies, would turn from their paths if they encountered a spirit fence and didn't have a powerful druid along to abate the magic and break the curse. Whatever was hidden inside this enormous vault of white stone, it was protected by the most potent magic her people possessed.

Though the door stood open, Flora could not see inside because of the darkness within and the brightness without. But she dared not proceed across the spirit fence to enter the edifice, despite Manas' instructions to do so. If the matron of *An Dun Gael* wanted to speak with her, she would just have to come out.

CHAPTER TEN

F lora stood motionless before the entryway to the fortress. She heard a soft voice address her and saw a slim hand reach out into the light to beckon her in. "Come in child. There is nothing to fear."

"I cannot. I will not cross the spirit fence and suffer its curse." Flora wondered if this was some kind of test. Manas had walked through the doorway with no ill effects. But he was a druid, albeit a somewhat unconventional one. She was just a healer's apprentice. "Did you place the fence? Is it yours to command?"

"I did not erect this spirit fence. It is very old and has been protecting this portal since ancient times. But I am the custodian of the mysteries here, and I determine who comes and who goes. You may enter. No harm will come to you."

Flora felt very uneasy about the situation. She didn't like the idea of some present-day druidess trying to control enchantments that had been emplaced ages ago by unknown peoples for unknown purposes. She questioned her decision not to flee, but it was too late to change her mind. By now, she was committed to this fate, whatever it might bring. She drew in a deep breath and stepped across the threshold, out of the light and into the blackness.

A moment later, Flora exhaled slowly. Everything felt okay, at least for now, although she wasn't exactly sure what a curse felt like. Perhaps it took days or months for symptoms to manifest. But for now, she didn't feel out of sorts. She took another deep breath to calm her racing heart and settle her nerves.

Very slowly, her eyes adjusted to the dim light inside the fortress, and she took in her surroundings. She was in a single, very large room. To her right she saw a small storage nook with what appeared to be the underside of stairs forming its ceiling before winding their way up the inside wall of the tower. The structure apparently had a double set of walls with stairs in between them, which spiraled their way to upper levels. At least that's how it appeared.

Though the exterior walls were constructed of the strange, solid, white stone blocks, the inside walls were completely black. Flora could not tell whether they were coated with some kind of black pitch, or whether, like the white stones outside, they were solid black to the core. Whatever the case, they seemed to virtually drink the light out of the few lamps scattered throughout the room and to leave behind a darkness that permeated her very soul. She could almost feel the room sucking the life out of her.

"I know," the voice beside her said softly. "The effect can be somewhat disconcerting. But it facilitates the implementation of my craft."

"And what craft is that?" Flora asked, the forcefulness of her tone surprising her as anxiety and frustration broke through her natural timidity.

"I am Fedelma. I will be conducting the assessment."

Flora turned to see a slight, middle-aged woman with dark hair and what appeared to be rather striking features, at least in the dim light. For some reason, Flora had expected to see a wizened old hag. But this woman was much younger and much more fair than she had imagined. Her face was narrow, her cheekbones slightly angular, and her brow arched high, giving her an air of quiet dignity.

"What assessment?" Flora blurted out, followed by a flurry of questions born of exasperation. "What does that mean? Everyone keeps talking about an assessment. I just want to figure out what happened to me since the last full moon—and to get the night terrors to go away. Are you a healer? Can you help me do that?"

"I'm a seer, child, not a healer. I understand Manas helped care for the illness of your body. I am going to look into your soul."

A chill ran up Flora's spine. What did that mean? Look into her soul? Whatever that implied, it didn't sound good. "A seer? I thought seers were blind."

"Not all seers are blind. And not all the blind are seers. Normal vision can, indeed, be a distraction to those who desire to develop the second sight, but that just forces them to concentrate harder on their task and to focus their inner eyes more deliberately. The atmosphere in this place helps. But, as you can you see, it was even more difficult for me."

Fedelma smiled and gazed intently at her. Flora's eyes had finally adjusted to the dim light of the lamps and she returned the stare. She looked deep into Fedelma's eyes and gasped in astonishment. This mysterious woman had triple sight! Flora had heard tales of triple vision among the gods, but she knew of no mortal who had ever received such a gift. Yet it was clearly discernible in Fedelma's gaze. Each of her eyes had three colored rings, and each of those was inset with its own dark circle. They overlapped each other at the edges, like the leaves of a clover. Flora saw three images of herself, reflected from the lamplight, within each of the three deep pools. It was eerie and disconcerting.

In a moment of total impertinence, Flora failed to contain her curiosity. "What do you see? What does the world look like to you?"

Fedelma's face took on a reflective guise, and she cocked her head slightly to one side. "I see depth, child, which others fail to perceive."

"And what do you see when you look at me?" The question

surprised Flora, and she didn't know what had prompted her to utter it aloud.

"Before, now, or after?"

The question was odd, and Flora didn't know how to respond. Then she suddenly realized what the woman implied. "You mean my past, my present, or my future? Is that what your eyes allow you to see?"

"I see depth, child, which others fail to perceive."

"And so I ask again, what do you see when you look at me?"

"One doesn't need my eyes to see inside your spirit, child. It is written on your face and echoed in your voice. I see fear when I look at you. Insecurity and fear. You don't know who you are."

The comment struck a nerve deep within Flora's core, and it filled her with anger. Her image of the woman abruptly changed. The awe and respect she initially felt quickly faded, to be replaced with contempt and scorn.

"Why do you keep calling me 'child?' I've had my flow. I'm a grown woman."

"I see you as you see yourself, child."

"Well, I'm a woman. I'm a fully apprenticed healer, and I'm betrothed to a mighty warrior. I am no child. I'm a woman."

"As you say. Perhaps that is true. Then again, perhaps you are less. Or perhaps you are much more. We shall soon know the truth of it."

Flora was annoyed, frustrated, and confused. And she was tired of people giving her vague answers to her questions. Her exasperation came out in full measure. "Could you please give me a straight answer for once? *Why am I here?* Why did they bring me to a seer? Are you going to look into my past and help me understand the ordeal I just experienced? I've been trying to piece it together in my mind, but it's still a jumbled mess. Do you want me to tell you what I remember so you can help me make sense of it all? I just want to figure out what happened and then go home to my family."

The woman looked at Flora with what might have been

perceived as empathy or compassion in the dim light of the keep, but her voice was flat and detached. "I already know what you witnessed and what you experienced. You saw villages destroyed and people slaughtered. You watched locusts ravage the land and saw an inferno consume what remained. You were harried by wild beasts and savaged by the elements. You were stalked by famine and menaced by plague. You became bereft of hope and felt utterly lost and alone. There is no need for you to resurrect those pallid memories. I have seen them all."

Her words shocked Flora. How did this woman know what she had experienced? She had said nothing of this to anyone except Searlaid. But even more, how did the seer know what Flora had *felt*—her remorse and despair? She had told absolutely no one of those thoughts and feelings. Yes, Fedelma's summary was somewhat general and abstract, but it was also far too specific to have been a mere guess. Flora was taken aback and was more bewildered than ever.

"What happened to me? It wasn't real. It couldn't have been real. Everyone is fine. The villages weren't destroyed. The land wasn't really devastated. But it *felt* real. Am I going mad? Is it all a delusion—some sort of demented nightmare? You saw it all? What happened to me?" Her last words were a whispered prayer of desperation.

"You've been touched by the gods." Fedelma made the declaration with a note of awe in her voice. "You've been touched by the gods."

Flora shrank back from the seer and sank to the floor. She curled up against the wall and hugged her knees to her chest. She was stunned by Fedelma's words, but somehow, deep down, she knew they were true. She had no idea what it meant for her now. She *feared* the gods, and she dreaded the thought of becoming a game piece in one of their dramas.

After a moment, she whispered, "And why am I here?"

"We know you've been touched by the gods. But we need to

know *which* gods and for what purposes. That is what we will discover this night."

"How? How can you possibly discover that?"

"This is a powerful night. The moon is full. Ceredwin is awake and walking through the heavens. But Lugh will not depart. He will tread around the edges of the horizon and while the night away, dancing with his bride. When the gods are thus engaged in love and joy and peace, they are ofttimes well-disposed to heed the petitions of men. The druid community is assembled in the glen below, arrayed about the sacred yew, to offer supplication and to lift our prayers up before the swooning deities, that they might hear our pleas and grant you the answers we seek."

"Grant *me* the answers? How? Why *me*?"

"You were the one who was touched. You were led to the sacred tree. You were allowed to approach the consecrated ground without conducting the rituals and yet without being consumed by fire. Either you were chosen by Lugh and blessed by him, or you were lured by another for a more nefarious purpose. If Lugh and Ceredwin accept our acts of veneration and harken to our appeals, then they will reveal the truth of it to you."

Flora pressed herself farther into the floor, farther back into the wall, until she was curled up into a ball. She trembled all over.

"I don't want this. I don't want any of this. I didn't want to see those horrible things or to have those terrible nightmares. I don't want to be touched by the gods. And I don't want to be a part of these special ceremonies. I did want to touch the sacred tree, because I'm a healer. But not like this, not this way. All I want to do is go back home to my family and my friends."

Fedelma's tone was flat, and Flora couldn't tell if it was filled with compassion or scorn. "Well, child, I'm afraid that decision is not up to you. You didn't choose this path. The gods chose you. And now we must follow its course to the end. For your sake, I pray that Lugh hears our appeal and shows you a sign."

Flora didn't know what to do. She wanted to leap up from the floor and flee out the door, away from this place and away from this horror. But she knew she couldn't escape. Sure, she might outrun Fedelma, but she could never hide from the gods. They would find her. And when they did, she somehow knew all the terrors of her recent nightmare would spring to life again, and this time without a reprieve.

Was Fedelma right? Was she just a child? A poor, pitiful, pathetic, whimpering child? A long, involuntary shudder coursed through Flora's body, and then she fell still, absolutely still. She went numb all over—not just her body, but also her mind. Her dread gave way to apathy as she resigned herself to this awful fate. She cursed the Morrigan for weaving her life thread into this convoluted tapestry. Then she stretched herself out, rose from the floor, stiffened her back, and frowned at Fedelma. "So what do I have to do?"

Fedelma stared at her for what seemed like eons. Flora felt as if the seer was peering into her soul and weighing her in the balances. Would she be found wanting?

Finally, Fedelma spoke. "There isn't much time. Dusk breathes across the land and Ceredwin awakes to her lover's beckoning call. You must be cleansed. There are many more preparations that should be done, but we have no time. The fires will soon be lit. The rituals will soon commence. This will have to suffice. You must be cleansed."

"What does that mean? Cleansed?"

Fedelma pointed to the far side of the dimly lit room. For the first time, Flora noticed a large pool of water that occupied about a third of the floor space—at least she hoped it was water. She also just realized that the floor of the fortress was not dirt, covered with wool and bracken, as was typical of most other structures. Instead, it was made of the same cut and polished black stone as the interior walls. She didn't know how she could have overlooked the cold, hard texture beneath her feet until now, nor how she had failed to notice the pool.

SINCE HER EYES were now much better adjusted to the faint light within the keep, Flora could also make out the room's other features—the most striking of which was a large, carved, stone altar in the center of the immense circular space. It was engraved with many of the same symbols that adorned the memorial stones erected on important battlefields all over the land. Those memorial stones were usually left in their natural shape, except where a face was sometimes flattened and smoothed to create a surface upon which the symbols would be called out of the stone's heart. This altar, in contrast, was carved into a perfect rectangle with horns shaped at each of the four corners.

Flora could only see the front face from where she stood. On it, she recognized the double disk of Lugh set opposite Ceredwin's double shaft and crescent moon. Below them lay the triple shaft of the Great Goddess with a serpent entwined around it. In this configuration, Flora immediately recognized the preeminence of Brigid's aspect of the Great Goddess, for the serpent was Brigid's symbol of rebirth and regeneration. The Dagda's harp was inscribed to the left of Brigid's sign, while his great club was engraved to the right, and his cauldron beneath. All three together signified the Good God's order, justice, and provision.

A host of tribal animal figures were arrayed around the symbols of the gods—the bull, boar, wolf, stag, goose, hawk, salmon, horse, and a variety of others. The appearance of so many clan icons puzzled Flora. Memorial stones, erected upon battlefields after a great triumph, usually only portrayed one or two of the tribal beasts, along with the signs of the gods to whom the chiefs attributed that particular victory. But Flora guessed that every clan's emblem was represented on this majestic altar, as if to signify that here, at this place, was where all men assembled to encounter the gods.

A single, silver chalice stood on top of the great altar. The cup was more ornately carved than any vessel Flora had ever seen. It was covered from base to rim with symbols of gods and men interwoven with the swirls, spirals, and geometric shapes of a warrior's spirit armor. The relief was so complex and the detail so intricate, the figures appeared to leap from the goblet's surface to swim amid seas of sunshine and rivers of gold. Surely no human artisan could have crafted such a vessel. It must have been forged by Gobannos, himself, the smith of the gods, under Brigid's watchful eye. Flora was mesmerized by its radiant beauty.

Fedelma beckoned to Flora, and she snapped out of her trance.

"Come here, child. Normally, we would garb you in a sacred robe adorned with the emblems of Lugh and Ceredwin—the double disk, the half crescent, the spear, the lightning bolt, and the cauldron. But in this moment, I believe it would be best for you to approach the gods cloaked in humility instead."

Flora wondered "cloaked in humility" meant.

Fedelma took her by the arm and led her to the pool of water. "You must be cleansed. These waters are holy—holier than those drawn from any spring. They have been collected from the dew of heaven, which descends from the gods. They are the captured tears of Brigid when she keens a mourning dirge. You must enter these waters to cleanse both your body and your spirit before you approach the gods. Remove your clothes. You shall be garbed in the cloak of humility."

Flora hesitated, and Fedelma hissed at her in a low, ominous tone, "Do it, child! Do it now!"

Flora obeyed the powerful authority that echoed in Fedelma's voice. She lifted the *leine* over her head and laid it close to the wall. Then she removed the flint knife on its leather thong and slipped the *brogen* from her feet, setting them all together beside her dress. She stood naked at the edge of the pool and resisted the urge to cover herself with her arms. Flora shook out her hair and held herself erect. She would retain some dignity, even in humility.

Fedelma led her into the pool and down a series of tiered steps, until they were both waist deep in the captured liquid jewels of Brigid's tears. Fedelma remained in her dappled robe, which billowed up beneath the surface of the water.

Flora had flashbacks to the time when Nandag led her into a similar spring for her initiation as a healer. Just like Nandag, Fedelma placed her hand on Flora's head and pushed her down under the water. But this time, the experience was very different. Flora didn't feel the burning, tingling sensation in her limbs or sense all of time imploding onto her consciousness. Instead, all she perceived was stillness—nothingness—as if she were floating in a sea of forgetfulness. She dared not open her eyes, but she could literally feel the blackness engulfing her. And then it burst upon her so suddenly she almost opened her mouth to take a shocked breath—a breath that would have drowned her soul in lethal liquid.

A light, brighter than the sun, burst upon her mind. It blinded her eyes, so that she could see nothing but herself. Then it engulfed her in its brilliance, and its searing heat burned every pore of her skin. She longed to scream, but she dared not. She thought about opening her mouth to let the waters douse the flames that seared her heart. Her lungs burned and struggled to take in a breath, but she clamped her mouth shut and clenched her teeth. She felt as if the skin and flesh were seared from her bones and blown away in a desert wind. Whatever was left melted into a small puddle of gleaming liquid that settled to the bottom of the pool and shimmered in the light's radiance. The dross was burned off and only pure silver remained. Then suddenly it was gone, as abruptly as it had arrived, and there was only blackness and silence and stillness once again.

Flora felt Fedelma grasp a wad of hair and pull her head up out of the water. A shriek exploded from Flora's throat and she gulped in an ocean of fresh air. Her body trembled and her lungs heaved in spasm after spasm until the spinning stopped and her mind finally cleared. She opened her eyes to find herself standing alone in the center of the pool, water dripping from her hair and trickling down her cheeks to fall in droplets from her chin. She glanced down, expecting to see charred flesh and singed hair, but her skin was healthy and clean, with a ruddy flush. And oddly, she felt pure. She felt uncontaminated by the filth of the world around her—untainted by the corruption of her own inner demons. She stepped from the waters with a sense of strength and purpose she had never experienced before.

She walked straight toward Fedelma, who stood next to the altar. "I'm now cleansed. And I come before the gods, cloaked in humility."

Fedelma grinned a wan smile and turned her gaze upon Flora. Flora saw herself again, reflected in triplicate from within the depths of those unsettling eyes. What she saw staring back at her wasn't the sudden burst of courage she felt when she emerged from the pool. It wasn't the pure, spotless, shimmering silver spirit that had momentarily stepped through the veil into the Otherworld and returned as a queen. Instead, she saw a small, wet, shivering, naked little girl. And she wept.

In one smooth, deliberate movement, Fedelma snatched the silver chalice off the altar and thrust it into Flora's outstretched hands. "Drink!" she commanded.

Flora reluctantly grasped the goblet and peered into the dark, pungent liquid that shimmered in its gaping mouth. Oddly, though the solution cast off a luminescent sheen and flickered with the radiance of hidden lamps, she could see no reflection in the cup. It appeared more like a window she was looking through than a mirror that would cast her own image back to her.

"What is it?" she asked in a timid voice.

"It is a portal to the gods and a doorway to your soul. Drink! It is time."

Flora thought back to the foxglove flowers along the river, and she suddenly dreaded what the elixir would reveal. If this seer indeed peered into her soul, what would she discover? Would the poison be revealed—the darkness that threatened to overwhelm her and push her over the abyss? Or would she fail to see the wicked parts hiding in the shadows and only discern the healing arts revealed by the light?

With trembling hands Flora lifted the chalice to her lips and took a sip of the bitter draught. It was thick and had a noxious smell that made Flora's stomach want to retch. She struggled to hold back a gag reflex that threatened to spew the liquid from her mouth. She clenched her lips shut and forced herself to swallow.

As quick as the flutter of a sparrow's wings, the flavor morphed into the sweetest honey she had ever tasted. It was rich and smooth, and it beckoned her to drink her fill. Overcome by the heady fragrance of lavender and rue, and drawn in by the succulent essence of cinnamon and ginger, Flora drank deep of the delicious potion and instantly yielded to its spell.

She sank to her knees beside the altar, the precious chalice slipping from her grasp and clanging on the floor. Vaguely, she sensed hands grasping her head from behind, and then she slipped, almost imperceptibly, into the vision.

SHE SWOOPED through the gap in the trunk of the yew and time stood still.

Darkness. Stillness. A small patch of light. Just a point. Growing larger. Moving toward the light. Faster and faster. The light is bright and growing. A rushing noise, like the wind in a gale. Suddenly emerging into the light, like breaking through the surface of a lake into the brightness of day.

She was flying again. She stretched her wings to their full extent and caught the currents of air rising from the flames that did not consume the tree—the flames of light and life and hope and renewal. She arced higher and higher, gliding on currents of power emanating from the life force of the sacred tree, and joy filled her heart to see the rebirth of the land—its restoration from the ashes of doom and despair.

And then the scene was complete, for the land was not only covered again by the trees of the forests and the grasses of the glens, not only teeming with fish in its rivers and sheep on its hillsides, but was once again filled with people in the villages and farms. They were her people, her tribe, her clan, her family. The regeneration was complete. The countryside was whole again—no, better than whole. It had somehow been reborn with a new vitality even greater than before. It now radiated peace.

She soared higher and higher until she could see the oceans on either side of the highlands. Everywhere she cast her gaze she could sense goodness and purity, life and strength. The land shimmered with a surreal luminescence, as if the veil had been lifted and the colors of the Otherworld were shining through. She glided serenely over the lakes and streams, the mountains and hills, the valleys and glens, and her soul exulted in worship of the gods who have given her back hope and love.

She slowly turned back toward the fount of renewal—the great glen of the sacred yew—and watched in rapture as Lugh and Ceredwin danced across the far horizons. As she descended, she saw an ocean of people, heaving and surging in waves that lapped upon shores where three huge pyres lit up the night sky. The bonfires were dotted between three great stone circles, which gazed into the sky like Fedelma's triple eyes, where men in feathered garb spun and twirled, and leapt and swayed.

These were the gateway stones, the guardians of the ancient tree. Rows and rows of white-robed figures, like stalks of waving grain undulating in the summer breeze, encircled the stones in every direction as far as she could see. They were all on their knees, bowing and rising, bowing and rising, with arms extended to the heavens, all except one who stood apart from the rest, holding a curved staff, a shepherd's rod, high in the air.

Suddenly, one of the feathered men uttered a horrific shriek and leapt into the sky. With powerful strokes of his wings, he took flight, spiraling higher and higher in a great arc around the tree. Mighty storm clouds gathered on the horizon and swirled in a massive vortex that darkened the sky and shrouded the waltzing deities, Ceredwin and Lugh, in a cloak of gloom. Behind the enormous eagle, a swath of destruction and devastation trailed in its wake—a great scar of desolation opening up like a gaping wound on an injured land. The skeletal remains of blackened trees reached up from a sea of ash, like charred finger bones grasping for freedom from a muddy grave. Devastation spread out in every direction, consuming the land and devouring the life force emanating from the tree.

Lightning flashed from within the mighty cauldron that filled the sky, roiling and churning like a tempest in the depth of the seas. But these bolts that split the heavens from east to west were different and strange. They were not like those which come from Lugh's spear to herald the coming rains. No, this lightning, and the thunder that crashed in its wake, were more like those that announce the anger of Taranis when he lusts for blood.

Amid the flashes that knifed across the dead blackness of the night and the roaring booms that reverberated throughout the heavens, a torrent of rain erupted from the clouds, drowning the maelstrom in a deluge that threatened to quench the flames of the druids' pyres. The white-robed figures on the ground erupted into a chaotic frenzy of activity, trying in desperation to keep the ceremonial fires burning amid the flood of rain and wind and fear. From the air, they looked like a colony of albino ants whose mound had just been kicked over.

She gazed down upon the mayhem in horror and dismay and suddenly realized the eagle was racing directly toward her with malice in its eyes and destruction in its wake. She banked and dived as a bolt of terror ripped through her heart. An owl couldn't fight off an eagle. She envisioned its talons ripping into her flesh as its razor-sharp beak slashed her all-seeing eyes. Owls rely on wisdom, not on power. So she had to think and think fast.

She dove toward the only source of refuge she could find. Folding her wings, she plummetted toward the sacred tree. Surely its life force and holiness would shelter her from the wicked predator, if only she could reach it in time. The eagle detected her tactic and stealthily maneuvered to intercept. Its wings were so mighty, its strokes so powerful, there was no way for her to win the race. She was certainly lost.

Then suddenly, a hole ripped through the clouds and a single moonbeam from Ceredwin's brilliant face pierced through the maelstrom to illuminate the sacred yew in a dazzling display of color and hue. The tree's fine needles scintillated with silvery flecks of light that leapt from the glowing flames which burn without consuming. She swept into the shaft of light and felt an immediate surge of vigor and strength. From the corner of her eye, she saw the menacing eagle veer sharply to avoid the brilliance. She has been rescued. She has been saved.

But as she rode the moonbeam toward the sacred tree, the clouds moved across the sky and the circle of light left the yew to dance across the glen. Terror rushed over her anew, and she flapped her wings in a wild panic to keep from colliding with the ground. The tree would not be her refuge from the beast. Its boughs would not be her shelter from the storm. What would she do? She could not survive in the field. She could not elude the terrible eagle in the grasses of the glen. Would the protective light itself disappear? Would it leave her alone and defenseless amid the horrors of the sky?

She gazed up and saw Ceredwin's face shining through the rent fabric of the clouds. She was mesmerized by the sight and drawn toward the brilliant light. She focused all her attention and all her energy on flying directly toward the shining beacon of truth and hope. Higher and higher, not in the swirls and arcs she would normally use to catch currents which would lift her to the heavens. No, she bolted in a straight line, with the powerful strokes innate to a creature of the Otherworld. If only she could escape through the hole in the sky through which she saw Ceredwin and Lugh spinning and twirling in each other's arms. And yet, her stalker was not to be deterred. He looped in great circles around the shaft of light, matching her pace toward the heavens.

Suddenly, the clouds closed again, and the silvery light flicked and faded. And all at once her hope evaporated amid the waning glow of the vanishing moon. She would never make it through the misty veil. She would never escape through the dim shadows into the eternal light. Blackness engulfed her. She felt the darkness of death sweeping up behind her. She stilled her wings and glided to a halt, hanging motionless in the night sky for what seemed like an eternity, resigned to her fate.

And then she saw it in the last fading moments of the dwindling rays. If an owl could gasp, her breath would be gone. While she had been surging ever higher, entranced by the dazzling light, the moonbeam had glided slowly across the glen to hover over a shimmering pool of water—a pond fed by a small river with a mill at its end. It was her millpond, the source of her terror and dread, and her refuge from the mighty storm. Then, just as the light of the moon had previously beckoned her ever higher, the millpond called her home.

Hanging motionless in the air, she spread her wings wide and bared her breast to the savage attack of her executioner. The eagle darted toward its prey with a savage squall and an evil glint in its eye. He sank his razor talons into the soft flesh of her belly and hacked mercilessly at her face with his beak. And while he ripped and tore at her very soul, she wrapped her wings around him, holding him tight with all the strength she could muster, and they began to plummet straight down.

The moonbeam was gone—the protection once offered by the light was engulfed in a cloak of malevolence and doom. But she held on tight and wouldn't let go, despite the blades knifing into her heart and the spear stabbing at her eyes. She clutched her feathery arms around the vile menace and wouldn't surrender. And they plummeted, like a shaft released from a bow, straight down, faster and faster, while the lifeblood spilled from her veins and consciousness slipped silently into the night. She clenched her grip tighter and tighter until her strength failed, her energy died, and her hold on her enemy collapsed. They plunged through the surface of the millpond, through a portal in space, through a window in time. The air exploded with the brilliant, dazzling light of the Otherworld, and she knew that she was finally home.

FLORA'S EYES FLICKERED OPEN, then shut and opened again. Her vision was blurred. She lay curled into a ball on the hard, stone floor, with her back resting against the altar. An arm's length away she could make out the cloaked figure of Fedelma, sprawled in a heap on the ground.

Just then, a dazzling figure, crowned with flowing, golden hair, emerged from the light and strode over to Fedelma's motionless form. He knelt down and nudged her gently until she stirred. Fedelma's weak, raspy voice drifted faintly on the currents of air that followed the man into the tower. "She is the one." A cough and a pause. Then, again, "She is the one."

The man moved his lips close to Fedelma's ear, but Flora could still make out his whispered tones in the stillness of the chamber. "I know. I know. It was written on the sky for all to see. You've done well."

The words echoed in Flora's mind as she slipped once again into the peaceful abyss of exhaustion. "She is the one."

CHAPTER ELEVEN

When Flora awoke, she found herself lying in a bed lined with beaver pelts to keep her warm. The images and sensations from the dream rushed back into her mind and she hurled the furs to the floor, feeling in them the deadly embrace of the eagle's wings. The impressions blurred with those from her ordeal, and she saw the furs morph into a great grey wolf that spun from its lunge and turned to resume its attack. She drew herself back and shrunk into the bed, trying to make herself disappear in the protective arms of the remaining furs, as if they were a rocky crevice in a cliff where she could retreat to safety. And then, just as the huge beast sprang toward her, its jaws open wide, its fangs poised to shred her flesh into a bloody pulp, the vision dissolved, and the creature disappeared into a black pit of horror and dread.

Flora was shivering with cold and drenched with sweat. Slowly, her mind cleared, her body stopped quivering, and her awareness returned to the current time and place. But was this reality, indeed, any more true than the visions of the night? She just wanted them to go away and to leave her alone—to let her return to her home, and to marry her man, and to work the healing arts among the people of her village. She just wanted to go home.

Flora let the awful memories fade into the back of her mind and took stock of her surroundings. She was in a room with a flat wooden floor—not a dirt floor covered with flax straw and wool, but a floor where large timbers had been scraped smooth and laid out next to each other. The outside wall was curved and made of stacked stone, while upright timbers, woven with hazel rods, divided the large circular space into smaller sections. A stout stone hearth was set in the center of the space beneath a round hole in the ceiling that appeared to go to another floor above. Gazing through that hole, Flora guessed there might be even more levels above that one, with a thatched roof at the very edge of her vision.

A fire burned in the hearth, casting a flickering glow around the room that mixed with light from several oil lamps to illuminate the space. A wolf-headed fire dog supported a large copper cauldron above the central hearth where iron utensils and wooden bowls were scattered haphazardly about. Dried herbs hung in clumps from the rafters, but Flora could see they were not the kind of plants used to flavor foods. She recognized some as the ingredients for poultices and potions, while others were completely unknown to her.

Across the room, on a bench formed from the base of a tree that appeared to be growing up out of the floor, Fedelma sat in her dappled robe, apparently fully recovered from the nightmare they had experienced together in the dream chamber the evening before. Fedelma fingered a strand of wool, her hands deftly stretching and thinning the fibers while she kept the spindle whirling—a skill learned from a lifetime of practice. But Flora noticed there was no loom in the room and wondered just exactly what kind of yarn Fedelma was preparing. Was she actually the Morrigan, weaving the life-strands of Flora's fate? Would she, even now, sever the thread and cut Flora off from the land of the living, from her family and her friends? She shivered at the thought and hesitated before moving, afraid that she might distract the seer from her task and bring evil upon her future.

Flora stirred, and Fedelma turned toward her. She hastily stopped the motion of the stone-weighted shaft and lay the yarn aside in a basket woven from river reed. "Mistress, you're awake. Are you well?"

Flora instantly noticed the seer's change in demeanor. Where she had seemed haughty and almost condescending the day before, her posture and her voice now carried a note of respect or even deference.

Flora sat completely up in the bed and her head swooned. "Where am I? What is this place?"

"You are in *An Dun Gael*, mistress. These are my personal quarters. The great hall is below." Then she repeated, "Are you well?"

"I'm fine. Just a little weak. And maybe a touch dizzy. I'm actually quite hungry. Would it be possible to get some food, and maybe a little water to drink?"

"Certainly." Fedelma disappeared behind a partition and returned promptly with a bowl of warm pork and a mug of hot, spiced thistle tea. "I hope this will do. The tea should help renew your energy and restore your strength. You've had quite an ordeal."

Flora thankfully accepted the offering and wondered at the strange transformation in Fedelma's manner. She took a bite of the meat and was momentarily swept away by its succulent flavor. It was seasoned with garlic, marjoram, and thyme, and yes, even salt, which all mixed together into a savory essence like she had never tasted before, even at the Imbolc feast. The thistle tea was likewise laced with nutmeg, honey, and cinnamon to produce an elixir that would bring vigor and strength to even the most exhausted warriors returning from battle.

Flora gaped in disbelief. What was happening? Why was she being lavished with such extravagant delicacies? She decided to push the questions aside for just a few moments and to relish the delectable treats. Fedelma sat in silent patience as Flora finished her meal.

But the questions would not remain at bay for long, and they eventually forced themselves to the surface as soon as the little feast was complete. "Fedelma, you said something last night...Was it truly only last night?"

"Yes, *bean-uasal*, it was last night."

This caught Flora even more off-guard than Fedelma's odd tone or the sumptuous food. *Bean-uasal?* Lady? Last night, Fedelma had repeatedly addressed her as "child." But now she had abandoned that term for an honorific due to the wife of a chief. Something very strange was going on, and Flora feared it as much as she feared the night vision.

"You said the gods would show me the truth of what I had experienced. Well, I remember the vision, but I have no idea what it might mean."

"Indeed, *bean-uasal*, the gods provided the answers we sought."

As Fedelma spoke, Flora noticed she never turned the gaze of the triple sight directly upon her as she had done before, and that, too, was as unsettling as her own triple reflection had previously been.

"You said the gods would speak to me, but I didn't hear their voice. And I don't understand the vision at all. What happened? What does it mean?"

"The gods spoke to me through you, *bean-uasal*. They showed us the path behind and the way ahead."

"Tell me, then. What did they reveal?"

Fedelma lifted her gaze then and looked into Flora's eyes. "It is a wonderful thing, *bean-uasal*, but it is not mine to tell. *Ard-Draoidh* Bhatair Rhu is below. He will recount the tale and share the mysteries with you. I will summon him now." Fedelma rose and turned toward a doorway in the wall.

"Fedelma," Flora stopped her from leaving. "Yesterday you called me 'child,' but now you address me as '*bean-uasal*.' Why the change?"

Fedelma turned her head and once again locked Flora's eyes with the triple sight. "I no longer see you as you see yourself. I see you as you are to be." She held Flora's gaze for a long moment, and then turned back toward the doorway.

Before she disappeared, Flora called to her. "I heard you say, 'she is the one.' What one? What did you mean?"

But there was no response as Fedelma vanished down the stairs hidden between the stone walls.

SEVERAL MOMENTS PASSED IN SILENCE, followed by a longer time that seemed to stretch into ages. Flora found a comb made from the antler of a red stag and began teasing the knots out of her hair. She hoped Fedelma wouldn't mind her using the well-crafted tool. Combs were often considered to be very personal items which weren't shared even among family members. The thought made her instantly feel guilty, and she hurriedly wiped it off and set it carefully where she had picked it up. Just then, she heard voices echoing up the stairway, and she quickly returned to her bed, fearing she might get caught in her transgression.

The voices spoke in hushed tones, just above a whisper. But they carried clearly enough up the stone passageway. "Remember to proceed carefully. The bride must be a willing sacrifice."

"Yes, I'm well aware. We have gone to great lengths to ensure everything was properly prepared. It is time." This voice was not as quiet or as muted.

The steps grew closer, and Flora turned away, trying to feign unawareness of their approach. She sensed two men entering the room but waited for one of them to address her before turning.

"Mistress," the first voice called out to her. She turned and saw the paunchy druid that had been on horseback the previous day. He was still in a white ceremonial robe and carried the peculiar staff with the silver web entangled about its head. His eyes looked even more eerie and haunting in the dim light of the room. He gestured toward the second man. "I would like to introduce you to *Ard-Draoidh* Bhatair Rhu. He has some matters to discuss with you."

Flora tensed and then gaped as the man stepped more clearly into the light. It was indeed the young, handsome horseman they had encountered near *Feart Choille* the previous day. He was dressed, as before, in a deep, forest green cloak, while his golden hair framed his face like a waterfall cascading down a fern-carpeted hillside. His eyes shone bright blue, as if they were lit from within. He tilted his head slightly to the right, and the hint of a smile turned up the corners of his mouth.

Her wonder must have been apparent, for the man immediately commented on her obvious amazement. "You appear to be somewhat dumbfounded. You needn't worry. I intend you no harm."

Flora didn't know if she was supposed to stand, or to bow, or to kneel, so she ended up just sitting where she was on the edge of the bed. "It's not that," Flora stammered. "It's just... well, I expected someone older, to be the Arch Druid of the whole land, that is."

"Yes. Well, things are not always as they appear, now are they? Nor as we expect them to be. I would have thought your recent experience might have illustrated this truth to you in a very poignant way."

"Fedelma said you had the answers I am looking for. Please, sir, can you tell me what this is all about. Why was I touched by the gods? Why me? What was the purpose of all those horrible experiences? And what is the meaning of the visions? Did Fedelma tell you about the visions? Can you tell me? I just want it all to go away, so I can return home to my family." Everything came out in a flustered rush. She was so tired of the waiting and the uncertainty. She just wanted it all to make sense.

The Arch Druid glanced briefly at his companion, who nodded slightly and backed out of the room. He addressed Flora. "Why don't we slow down and take this all one piece at a time, okay?" His smile broadened and a warmth filled his expression that set her mind at ease.

"Okay. One piece at a time." She supposed maybe she was learning patience the hard way. But patience had never been one of her strong points.

"May I tell you a story?"

Flora fidgeted anxiously and was certain that her impatience was written all over her face, but she took a deep breath and tried to hold her anxiety inside. She just wanted straight answers to her questions, that's all. But if she had to endure a story from this rather charming man, well then, she would bite her tongue and listen patiently. "Certainly. Of course."

The Arch Druid nodded graciously and began. "Many generations ago, a great chieftain ruled over the people of a rich land, not far from here. His name was Caradog, and he was a mighty warrior who fought bravely against the Roman invaders. The gods held him in high regard because of his piety and his many sacrifices. One goddess in particular, Rigantona, the King-Maker, took an oath to protect Caradog and to make him powerful."

Flora clutched her arms across her breast, trying to contain her impatience. Normally, she could be captivated by the ancient tales of her people. But right now, she just didn't see how this had anything to do with her. And so she stewed with irritation, trying to keep her mind from wandering away from Bhatair Rhu's words and getting tangled up in all of her more pressing questions.

"Rigantona grew to admire the warrior-chief more and more. She frequently appeared to him in dreams to give him wisdom and insights before great battles. But she found herself wanting even closer contact with the man to whom she was oath-sworn. So one year at Samhain, she took on the form of a spirited sorrel mare and crossed over into the land of men."

Bhatair Rhu leaned back and crossed his legs, settling into the tale. "Though Caradog should have been present at the Samhain festival, he felt compelled to go hunting in the forest. And there he encountered a magnificent horse stepping out of a stream. His admiration for the elegant steed compelled him to approach it. But as he drew near, the horse turned and walked slowly away. He spurred his own mount in pursuit. Though the mare never even broke into a trot, and though he, himself, rode at a brisk canter, Caradog was not able to close the distance.

"Finally, in resignation, he gave up the chase and pulled his mount to. He looked longingly at the red mare and called out, 'You are a grand and glorious creature! I only wish to stroke your neck and admire your beautiful coat.'

"At his words, Rigantona sauntered over and nuzzled his arm with her nose. Surprised by this sudden show of affection, Caradog slowly dismounted his own steed and began rubbing his hands over the glistening pelt and powerful muscles of the enchanting mare. She tossed her head in a clear indication for him to mount, and he eagerly complied."

Despite her anxiety over her own situation, Flora found herself being pulled in by the story. Horses had always fascinated her. She nodded her head, and Bhatair Rhu proceeded with the tale.

"Caradog rode the beautiful horse long into the night—through wide open glens, lush forests, and hillsides carpeted with heather. He had never known a mount with such an easy gait, or one that responded so readily to the slightest tap of his heel or the gentlest nudge of his knee. It was as if he and the mare were extensions of each other's will. They both knew what their companion desired and trusted each other's instincts.

"When the morning sun broke over the horizon, the mare reacted strangely. Caradog suspected the horse was from the Otherworld and had somehow crossed through the veil on Samhain night. But he wasn't ready to give up on this glorious steed. So he pulled his sword belt from around his waist. It was studded from end to end with silver plates. He removed the scabbard and looped the belt over the horse's head. The talisman bound the mare to him and identified her as his steed to everyone in the land."

Flora interjected, "Do you mean he trapped her in this world, against her will? A goddess?"

The Arch Druid considered her question carefully before replying. "Let's say he *enabled* her to stay beyond the bounds of Samhain night. You see, the goddess had fallen in love with the gallant man. She knew him to be strong in spirit, brave in battle, and wise in judgment. But throughout that night, she also discovered him to be tender of heart. She welcomed the opportunity to spend a year with him in this way."

Flora thought about it for a moment. "I suppose one year would go by quickly in Otherworld reckoning. What's a year to someone who measures time as a thread with no end?"

"So they spent that year together and were virtually inseparable. She carried him into combat against the Romans, in the funeral procession of his son, and on long winter rides in the moonlight. But when Samhain came again, the Otherworld called for Rigantona to return. Her place was not in this world. They went for a long, glorious ride that night, much like the one that had bound them together a year before. Caradog was lost in joy, and he gave her a loose rein when she headed toward a pond to get a drink. But she didn't stop at the edge of the water. She walked all the way in. Only then did Caradog realize that they were standing in the holy spring of *Treffynon*—a fabled gateway to the Otherworld."

Bhatair Rhu uncrossed his legs and leaned inward. The intensity in his voice grew stronger.

"In the shimmer of the veil, Rigantona assumed her true form. Caradog fell into the spring with noisy splash. He opened his eyes beneath the water and saw a wondrous light emanating from the bottom of the pool. It shone with an iridescent glow in colors more vivid than any he had ever seen. The sight held him rapt in awe and wonder until his lungs burned to take a breath. As his head emerged from beneath the surface of the pool, he beheld Rigantona in all her glory, standing nude before him in the center of the holy spring, with green eyes shining brightly and long red hair flowing in the gentle breeze. The silver belt was draped around her neck."

Flora was spellbound by the tale. She had heard countless stories about the vagaries of the gods. But the ones where the gods interacted directly with people always captivated her. "What did he do?" she asked almost breathlessly.

"When he realized what he had truly done, in binding the goddess to this world with a chain of silver, he immediately went to her and lifted the belt from around her neck. How could he hold her here against her will? But she reached out to him, stroked his cheek with her hand and pulled him into a passionate embrace. They made love there, on the shore of *Treffynon*, below Samhain's silvery moon."

SENSING that the story was coming to an end, Flora's attention once again returned to her own plight. Though she had been drawn in by the magic of the tale and had been charmed by Bhatair Rhu's lilting voice, her thoughts now returned to the myriad questions still swarming around her mind, like a cloud of midges buzzing around her head on a hot summer day.

"That's an interesting legend. But I still don't see what it has to do with me."

"Be patient. Everything will be revealed in time."

Flora humphed in exasperation. "Everyone here keeps telling me that, but things just keep getting more confusing. If you're trying to help my patience grow, it isn't working."

"Patience is a foundational virtue to the druid order. It is a core part of who we are."

"Yes, but I'm not a druidess."

"No, you are not. But you will be much more."

Flora was taken aback and confused even more by this comment. "What do you mean?"

"There is still more to the tale. Be patient a little while longer. I promise this will all make sense when I'm through."

"Okay. Fine," Flora said with a somewhat disgruntled huff. She really just wanted straightforward answers to a few questions, but it appeared she had little choice.

"Where was I? Oh yes, the night at the sacred spring. When the morning sun broke the horizon, Rigantona slipped back through the veil and disappeared into the Otherworld. She promised Caradog they would see each other again, and that she would visit him in his dreams.

"Unbeknownst to Caradog, their night of passion had produced a son. Though Rigantona gave birth in the Otherworld, she knew she could not bear to keep the boy from his father. But neither could she give up her own child. And so she committed herself to another path."

"A baby?" Flora exclaimed in surprise. "Can a goddess get pregnant by a mortal man?"

"Indeed," the Arch Druid replied. "It has happened many times before. Anyway, the next year at Samhain, Rigantona stepped out of the sacred spring carrying the wee bairn in her arms. She found Caradog sitting on the shore, waiting for her, as she had hoped. She lifted the child to him with a smile. As he cradled the unexpected bundle of joy in his big arms, Rigantona unstrapped the silver sword belt from around his waist and draped it about her neck. Astonished, and realizing what she intended to do, Caradog tried to convince her to take the boy and return to the Otherworld. But she wooed him to sleep with a charm. When Caradog woke the next day, he found the baby nestled beneath the boughs of a nearby oak tree, being watched over by a magnificent red mare."

"She stayed?" Flora asked in amazement.

"She did," Bhatair Rhu replied, "for love. Caradog raised his son to be a warrior. He was tutored by the finest riders and most skilled swordsmen. Whenever the young man went into battle with his father's warband, he was mounted on the sorrel mare.

"Caradog, himself, always disappeared with the horse on the evening of Samhain. While the rest of the tribe was immersed in the reverie of the night's celebrations, he and Rigantona returned to the sacred spring where they could spend one night each year in the arms of love."

Flora's mind drifted to her own man, Domhnull, hoping they would also share that same kind of affection and devotion. The story made her long to be held in his embrace once again.

"It soon became apparent the boy was not merely a capable soldier. He was also endowed with the gifts of a druid. He had the special abilities of a bard, a seer, and a judge. And so Caradog directed his training to be refocused on developing those skills.

The Arch Druid's smile waned and his face took on a sterner, more serious expression.

"Caradog's life mission was to drive the Romans out of Britannia. It was a goal he never achieved. He successfully united the tribes of the south and confronted the armies of Rome amid the hills of his homeland, but his forces were overcome. His mortal wife and daughter were captured, and he was betrayed by a fellow chieftain—a woman—into the hands of his enemy. Legend says he was taken to their capital city and paraded through the streets in chains as a trophy of war, but his spirit never broke, and he never bowed his knee to the emperor of Rome."

"So Rigantona was free to return to the Otherworld?" Flora asked.

"No, unfortunately not. You see, her son had bound himself to this world with an oath to the gods that he would not return to the Otherworld until he had avenged his father's disgrace and driven the Romans from the land. Rigantona, likewise, vowed she would remain with her son until the deed was done."

A sudden chill swept over Flora's arms and crept up her spine. She stared long and hard at Bhatair Rhu. "It's you, isn't it? You are Caradog's son, aren't you? And the red mare I saw you riding…"

The Arch Druid didn't even have to answer. She could see the truth of it in his eyes. His gaze was distant and clouded for just a moment, and Flora guessed he was lost in thoughts of times gone by.

"My father passed over to the Otherworld many ages ago. Now

he visits us every year on the night of Samhain. For a few sacred moments, we get to be a family and to dream how life would be together in the Otherworld. But I can't go until the task is done and my oath is fulfilled. And my mother has vowed never to leave my side until it is accomplished."

He paused for a long moment, and then said somewhat mournfully, "Actually, I'm not even sure that it *can* be done at this point. The Romans have entrenched themselves so deeply in this land that our people beyond the wall have become just like them. Even if the Romans were driven out, their spirit would linger on."

Flora stared at Bhatair Rhu in silent awe. "So you... you're a god?"

The Arch Druid's attention drifted back to the present, and he smiled briefly before replying. "No. No, I'm not a god. My mother is a goddess. But my father was a normal man. I'm something in-between—trapped between two worlds, and belonging to neither."

Flora eyed him quizzically. "How long ago did all this happen?"

"Many generations ago. I told you, things are not always as they seem. I'm a bit older than I look."

Flora was still shocked at the revelation, but her former confusion returned in an even more powerful wave. "Okay, *Mhaighstir*." Flora struggled with how to address this god-man. "So, now I know a little more about who you are, but I still don't understand what this all has to do with me. Why am I here? Why are you telling me this?"

Bhatair Rhu took a long moment before replying. "I cannot go back to the Otherworld, at least not until I fulfill my oath." He paused again, as if weighing his words carefully. "The gods are offering you something that I long for, but cannot have."

"Me? What would the gods be offering me?"

"They are inviting you to become a goddess. They have chosen you to become Brigid, the Bride."

Flora gaped at Bhatair Rhu in total confusion. She wasn't sure she had heard him correctly. "Me? A goddess? Brigid? What are you talking about? What does that even mean?"

"I know this is a lot to take in. The reason I told you my story was so you would understand that I'm serious, and that I know what I am talking about."

Flora was shocked, and her mind raced with even more questions now than before. "I still don't even know *what* you are talking about. How can a person become a goddess? How can that even be possible? And *why* would it happen? Brigid already *is!* We honor her at Imbolc every year. She lights our hearth fires and causes springtime to bloom. She guides the healers and pours out her blessings upon our flocks. How could someone *become* her when she already *is?*"

"I know this is hard to understand." Bhatair Rhu's voice was gentle, and Flora saw empathy reflected in his bright blue eyes. "Let me try to explain. Do you remember the great gathering of the tribe six summers ago? Here at *Cridhalbane?*"

Flora remembered the gathering but did not recognize the name the Arch Druid had just used. Her confusion must have been apparent, so he responded to her puzzled expression. "It is an ancient name for this place. It means the 'Heart of Alba,' for the soul of our land—the whole land, not just Caledonia—emanates from this place. It is a sacred name you should know, but which you must not use casually. Do you understand?"

"Yes. I understand." Flora was amazed the Arch Druid would share sacred place names with her—names which could evoke the power of the gods when they were used as part of special rituals. "And yes, *Mhaighstir,* I remember the gathering."

Bhatair Rhu grinned before speaking. "You need not call me 'Master.' I shall very soon address you with an even higher honorific. Do you remember why the gathering was convened?"

Flora nodded. "Because of the great sign in the heavens."

"Yes. The gods sent that sign to get our attention. It was an unmistakable warning from them—a harbinger of grave consequence.

But we did not know its exact meaning, so we summoned the whole tribe and performed special rites to gain an understanding of the oracle and learn the will of the gods."

"I remember the gathering. I came with my family—my whole village, actually. But what does the gathering have to do with me? I was there, but no one took any special notice of me. I was just one young girl amid a great throng of people, a nobody. You, for example, didn't even know I was there, did you?"

"Before the ceremonies, no, I did not. But after the rites were performed, after we had received a clear answer from Cerridwen and Lugh, we knew. We knew you were there. We just didn't know exactly who you were. And we have been looking for you ever since."

"Looking for me? Why?"

"I've gotten ahead of myself," he said. "Let me back up and explain what the gods revealed to us that night. You know the three aspects of the Great Goddess, don't you?"

"Yes. Of course. Brigid, the Morrigan, and the Cailleach—the Maiden, the Mother, and the Crone."

"Correct. And do you know they exist in a perpetual cycle?"

"Do you mean winter, spring, and fall?"

"Not exactly. Though, of course, the Great Goddess in all her aspects does govern the changing seasons as you suggest."

"That's what my mother and Nandag have taught me. The Cailleach is the mistress of winter. She yields to Brigid when we honor the sacred rituals on Imbolc, and so spring comes along with early summer. Then the Morrigan oversees the transformation from late summer to fall before the crone once again demands that winter rule the land."

"Indeed, that is the cycle of summers and winters. But there is also a larger cycle of generations. I doubt Nandag would have spoken of this. It is a deeper and more ancient lore."

"No. I've never heard of the cycle of generations. What does that mean?"

"Once every age—that is once every five generations, or every hundred summers—on the sixth day before Imbolc, the Cailleach leaves *Schiehallion*, her great mountain fortress, to immerse herself in the waters of Loch Ba on the Isle of Mull. Then, on the day of the festival, she emerges from the loch with her youth and beauty restored. She is reborn as the Maiden, Brigid. In that same year, Brigid transforms into the Mother, and the Morrigan transitions into the Crone. This is the larger cycle of regeneration and restoration, without which the land, itself, would age and die."

"I never knew about such a thing," Flora said, beginning to see how the two puzzles fit together. "Is that why Brigid is sometimes represented by the snake? When the snake sheds its skin, it is reborn in a way?"

"Precisely. That's a very astute observation. I can see why the gods have chosen you."

"Well, I don't see why." Flora exclaimed, spreading her hands in exasperation. "I still don't understand any of this."

"Patience, remember. I'm getting to that." Bhatair Rhu's expression turned grave. "The great cycle ended seven summers ago. The Cailleach immersed herself in the waters of Loch Ba as normal. There is a seer on Mull who watched her walk into the loch. It is a rare and special occurrence, and he had been preparing for the moment since the early days of his druidic training. He was certain of the signs. But then the Great Goddess never emerged from the waters as Brigid on the day of Imbolc."

Flora sat in stunned silence as she considered the implications of his statement. If the Cailleach did not emerge, then the cycle of generations was halted. She wasn't sure what the consequences would be, but it couldn't be good. She gave her full, focused attention to what Bhatair Rhu said next.

"Lugh searched for an answer throughout the skies by day, and Cerridwen sought for the goddess among the stars at night, but neither could find an answer. They continued their daily dance across the heavens, but they knew a subtle shift had occurred in the balance of time. They could maintain the natural order for a while, but eventually the imbalance would grow worse until it tore the world apart."

Flora gasped as the implications of his statement settled into her mind. "What happened to her? To Brigid?"

"The Dagda, the Good God, scoured the Otherworld for any sign of his daughter. Eventually, he discovered the truth. Taranis craved total control over the winds of spring and the storms of summer, so he'd trapped the Cailleach in Loch Ba until her hundred years expired. Unable to shed her skin and return to this world with her youth renewed, the Cailleach passed away."

"She died?" Flora gaped at the Arch Druid in disbelief. "How can a goddess die? How can the *Great Goddess* die?"

"She didn't die, exactly. She just wasn't reborn. And so, she just ceased to be. At least, the Brigid aspect of the Great Goddess ceased to be. The other two aspects continue on. It's rather complicated when you get into the details, I'm afraid. Under normal circumstances, such things are not possible. But the schemes of the gods can unleash unstable forces and cause extraordinary consequences. And Taranis is a powerful god.

"Anyway, in the meantime, the other two aspects moved on through the cycle. The former Brigid had grown through the summer of years into the motherhood of the Morrigan, and old age had likewise ushered the Morrigan into the winter time of her life as the Cailleach."

Bhatair Rhu got up from the stool where he was sitting and walked over to the stone hearth in the center of the room. He retrieved a small log and tossed it on the fire. Sparks leapt up from amidst the flames and danced in the air above the wolfs' heads on the firedogs, as if taunting them to snap at wraiths in the night.

"By Lughnasadh, the gods discovered what Taranis had done, and determined to find a replacement for Brigid among the daughters of men. They sent us the great sign in the stars, so we would know to search for her. The sign, itself, was a vision of the future—a vision of Brigid restored to her rightful place in the heavens. During the day, the star took on the appearance of a withered crone, but at night it shone with the beauty of Brigid in all her glory."

"The gods chose a replacement for Brigid," Flora mumbled absentmindedly.

"Yes. They had selected someone from among our clans. Her identity would be revealed to us after seven summers had passed."

"And, you think I might be the one the gods chose... to–"

"–to become Brigid," Bhatair Rhu finished Flora's sentence. "No. We don't think you *might* be the one. We are absolutely certain you are. The timing. Your appearance at *Cridhmathairnaomh*, the sacred yew. But most importantly, the vision last night. It left no doubt."

Flora shrunk back, shaking her head slowly. "No. No, there must be some mistake. I can't become Brigid. I can't be the maiden. I'm not... I'm nobody. I'm nothing."

Flora almost didn't hear Bhatair Rhu's response. Her mind raced in a hundred different directions. *They don't know!* She thought. *Surely the gods would know. This has to be a mistake.*

"Well, apparently you are someone to the gods—someone very special."

"But I can't... I don't... I just want to go home and be a healer in my village—to care for my family and my people."

Bhatair Rhu reached out and grasped her shoulder, giving it a gentle squeeze. He looked her straight in the eye, despite her efforts to fade away. "Look, if you want to be a healer for your people, what better way than to become the patron goddess of all healers? You could bless them in ways you can now only imagine."

"But I can't. What if... What if I don't want to do it? What if I refuse? I mean, they can't actually make me become Brigid, can they?"

Bhatair Rhu was still holding her steady, still looking into her eyes. "Look, Flora, I know this must be a bit overwhelming. But the gods chose *you*. We weren't certain at first. We didn't know if this might be another ploy by Taranis to secure his victory and assert his control over summer. But the rites we performed last night were very powerful, and the response was as clear as the waters in *An Tobar* Spring on a bright sunny day. The gods chose *you*. And it is an incredible honor."

Flora looked deep into Bhatair Rhu's eyes. She saw strength there, and compassion. But it wasn't enough to quell her doubts, her uncertainties, and her fears. "But, what if—"

"Flora, you asked me about the ordeal you experienced while you were missing from your village. I know what it was all about."

"You do?" Flora breathed the words in a whisper. This is what she had longed to find out ever since she had woken in the healing hut. "Please, tell me."

"It was a vision from the gods. No, more than a vision. An encounter. The gods let you experience what would happen to our land if Brigid isn't replaced and if the natural cycle isn't restored. War. Famine. Plague. Fire. Death. The people will all die—your people will all die, your family and your friends—and the land will tear itself apart."

Flora twisted free of his grasp and tore her eyes from his gaze. The horror of her nightmare sprang to life in her mind. He was right. It had been more than a vision. She hadn't just *seen* it, she had *lived* it. She had heard the dull roar of the swarm, felt the wildcat rake its claws across her arm, coughed from the choking smoke that filled her lungs, and tasted the bile in her mouth as she retched in front of the mound of putrefied bodies. But more than anything else, she had felt the oppressive loneliness and the knot in her gut at seeing her village destroyed.

"Can't someone else do it?" she whispered. "Can't someone else take her place?"

Bhatair Rhu's voice took on a bit of an edge and his tone became matter-of-fact. "No." And then he repeated the declaration again, more forcefully. "No. The gods have chosen *you*—for whatever reason. We may never know why, but they have made their will clear. You understand the decision before you, and you understand the consequences at stake better than anyone else possibly could. I'll leave you to think it through. Once you have settled it in your mind, as I know you will, we will begin the preparations. We will present you to the druid community tomorrow. Fedelma will look after your needs until then."

Flora avoided his gaze as he stood and left the room. Her village had not been destroyed. Her family had not been killed. The land had not been ravaged by locusts and by fire. Instead, she had been invited to become a goddess. And yet right now, in this moment, she felt more lost and alone than ever before. She curled into a ball on the bed of furs and wept.

CHAPTER TWELVE

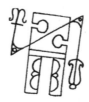

I t had been eight summers ago, when she was only nine. Flora had stolen away into the woods near her home. She always had an excuse ready that she was gathering herbs for Nandag. But sometimes she really just wanted to sit in the sunshine beside the pool at the base of the little waterfall where the burn ran over the rocks on the other side of *Sionnaich* hill. It was a peaceful place where she could be alone for just a little while.

That day she found a whole meadow filled with bluebells. It looked like a huge flutter of azure butterflies on a blanket of green bracken, their wings flickering in the sunlight as they danced in the gentle breeze. She decided to pick a bunch for her mother to set in a jar on the sill and dig some bulbs which Nandag could use to make the poultice that caused blood to clot in open wounds. But first, she would just lie down in the bed of flowers and enjoy the rare spot of summer sunshine.

Her heart almost jumped out of her chest when she saw her Uncle Cruim emerge from the wood line just a few paces away. He had caught her dawdling among the bluebells while everyone else in the village was busy working. But she could always try her excuse.

"What're ya doing all alone out here, lass?"

"I... I was out looking for herbs for Nandag," she stammered.

"Looks like ya found a bed o' flowers to lie in, to me." He walked close and towered over her, blocking the sun.

Flora was still sitting on the ground, and she cowered beneath his wilting gaze. "No... no, really. Nandag uses the bulbs to... she crushes them up to make a poultice."

Flora noticed that her uncle wasn't really listening to her. Instead, he was scanning the field and the forest, as if looking for someone else. Then he lifted his tunic and untied the rope belt that held up his *braies.*

"You just lay right there and keep quiet, hear me? If you cry out, everyone'll know what you've done. What will yer momma and daddy think about that?"

Flora could see the madness burning in his eyes as he knelt down over her. She felt the terrified scream rip through her throat and erupt from her lips just as her uncle's large, powerful hand clamped down over her mouth and stifled the sound.

Her eyes filled with tears and her mind went blank. She tumbled over a precipice and felt herself falling and falling and falling. Clouds poured across the sky and thunder roared through the heavens. She kept falling, terrified that she would be dashed upon the rocks below —until the foul business was done, and she opened tear-filled eyes to find herself curled into a ball, lying amid bluebells in the warm summer sun. Tremors shook her tiny body, and she wept. She begged the rains to come—to wash away the pain, and the blood, and the filth, and the black stain on her soul.

It was the first time, but it had not been the last.

CHAPTER THIRTEEN

Flora rode in the center of an entourage much different from the one that had escorted her to *Feart Choille* just a day before. *Had it only been one day?* So much had happened in one short turn of the sun that it seemed like a whole different lifetime. Indeed, she was a completely different person, in more ways than one. Even her name...

Her current retinue included a detachment of warriors in spirit armor, just like the previous one. But this time her guard detail was much larger, with over a score of men—and even a few women—flanking her from front to rear. The contingent of druids was even more dramatic, numbering more than a hundred, all garbed in the white robes reserved for holy ceremonies. They walked with heads bowed and hands folded together within their sleeves, humming a low, vibrant refrain that melded, almost imperceptibly, with the nature song of the thrushes and starlings, the buzzing bees, the gurgling river, and the whispering wind.

A spirit fence surrounded her this time as well. Yet it too was radically different than the one which formed her previous cage. This time twelve druids, dressed in green cloaks with purple thistles embroidered on the breasts, held silver-tipped ash shafts mounted with human skulls. Bhatair Rhu himself cast the spell which imbued the spectral barricade with its supernatural force. But the eye sockets faced away from her this time, keeping evil out and protecting her like the most valuable treasure in all the land.

The sun drove the incessant rain north and shone down on the procession with a warmth and intensity the highlands rarely enjoyed. While her entourage snaked its way through a lush green glen, nestled between steep hills to either side, gashawks performed their sky dance across the heavens. Eliavres assured her that Lugh's dominance over the clouds, accompanied by the *ceilidh* of the birds, was indeed a good omen.

Eliavres was the stubby, thick-bodied druid who attended Bhatair Rhu. He had come to her earlier that morning to prepare her for the day's ceremonies. She had been sitting in a pile of furs in Fedelma's lair, deep inside the white keep of *An Dun Gael*, brooding over the heavy burden that was being laid upon her shoulders. Her thoughts returned to that moment.

IS THERE ANY WAY OUT? She searched the depths of her mind for any escape from this insidious web into which the *Morrigan* had woven her life thread. She felt trapped in that net of gossamer strands, like a cricket struggling in vain to free itself before tasting the spider's deadly venom. She could *not* become the virgin goddess. She could *not be* the Maiden, pure. Surely the gods knew about the dark stain on her life. There must be some mistake.

Shuffling footsteps plodded up the spiral stone steps that encircled her lair. Expecting Fedelma or Bhatair Rhu, Flora was was surprised and a little unnerved to see a silver-laced staff poke through the doorway, followed by the lumpy form of Bhatair Rhu's companion.

"I'm afraid we have not been properly introduced. I am Eliavres. I will oversee your preparations for the *Annunciation*."

Flora felt herself being sucked in to those dark, black eyes, and shrunk deeper into the pile of furs. "What is that?" Flora's voice emerged as almost a cracked whisper. "What is the *Annunciation?*"

Eliavres shuffled across the room, dragged over a short three-legged stool, and took a seat in front of her. "We shall present you to the druid community as the one betrothed to the god Bres and soon-to-be daughter of the Dagda. The bards have been prepared and songs have been written. Your presentation to the assembly is just the torch that lights the beacons. This news will spread like wildfire to every clan. It is the *Annunciation*. Brigid shall return to heal our land."

Flora gritted her teeth and felt her face flush. No one had bothered to ask her about this decision. Apparently, they all just assumed that she would accept the role which was being foisted upon her. She opened her mouth to speak, but Eliavres pressed on.

"After the assembly, you will be escorted in a procession to your betrothal quarters at the Oak Bank of Fearnan on Loch Tatha. There you will undergo the rites of preparation."

"When can I see my family? When can I go home to Bunrannoch?" Flora overcame her reticence and blurted out the questions in rapid succession.

Eliavres cocked his head slightly to one side and his gaze intensified, his dark, black eyes boring deeply into her soul. "My dear, I'm afraid you misunderstand. In taking this step forward you have entered a new life. You have left your old life behind. You belong to the gods now. They are your family. Your true home is in the Otherworld. You are no longer Flora, daughter of Kellina from Bunrannoch. That life is in the past. You are now Fiona *Taghte*, the Chosen One, the betrothed of Bres, and she who is to become Brigid, the Bride."

"But what if I refuse? What if I don't want to become the goddess? What if the gods made a mistake?" She didn't give voice to her other concern. *What happens when they discover the truth that I'm not pure?*

"I'm afraid it is too late for that. The gods have made their decision. Their will is clear. You *shall* become Brigid. The fate of our people depends on it. The preparation rites begin today."

Eliavres' stare bore down on her, and Flora wilted beneath his gaze. She lost all will to fight back and hung her head in resignation. Loss and loneliness engulfed her as she was stripped of her family, her home, and her very identity. She felt as if she had been cast adrift into a vast, churning sea with storm clouds on the horizon and no land in sight. It was an emptiness as bleak as the horrors of her ordeal.

Flora heard nothing else that Eliavres said. The next moments passed in a blur. Fedelma arrived with two other women, clad in the white robes of druid apprentices. Neither of the newcomers spoke to her, but kept their hoods over their heads and eyes cast to the ground. Busily, the three wove heather into her hair, and dressed her in a long-sleeved linen tunic dyed a deep red with Brigid's sigil exquisitely embroidered in rows along the edges, surrounded by interwoven ivy leaves. They placed interlaced silver bands on her arms and a modest silver torc around her neck, crafted of two intertwined serpents facing each other at the gap.

Fedelma painted thin black lines along the contours of Flora's eyes and then smeared an ochre-colored powder across her eyelids. She used the crushed red berries of the Rowan tree to brighten the hue of Flora's lips. Realizing what the red paste had been concocted from, Flora initially flinched and turned her head aside.

"Don't be concerned," Fedelma reassured her. "The berries were cooked to make the paste. The toxins have been rendered harmless." She peered deeply into Flora's eyes with the triple sight of the visionary seer. "Though I doubt such a trivial, earthly poison could harm one destined to reign in the Otherworld." She held her gaze for a long moment and then looked away. "Your outward adornments are changed easily enough, mistress. The inner transformations will take more time. Nevertheless, we will ensure you are prepared for your wedding day on Lughnasadh."

Lughnasadh? Flora was momentarily confused, and then immediately brightened. "Do you mean it, Fedelma? Am I still to be wed to Domhnull come harvest time?"

"Domhnull?" Fedelma looked at her quizzically, then dropped her eyes and shook her head. "Nay, mistress. Bres. You are Fiona *Taghte*, Fiona the Chosen One, the betrothed of Bres. You are to become the goddess, Brigid."

The fleeting glimmer of hope that had sparked in Flora's heart evaporated in the wind, like the mist of a waterfall blown away by a summer breeze, while the sullen dread of storm clouds filled her mind and darkened her mood. She was trapped in a drama she could not escape, and her old life was being completely stripped away. Who was she, anyway, deep down inside? Flora? Fiona? Brigid? ...A healer? A nobody? A bride? No, *the Bride*? What did it all mean? And who was this "Fiona" anyway? Someone lost between two realities? A no one with no family or clan? A will-o'-the-wisp that would glow brightly in the night and then vanish in the light of dawn? Amid the pall of confusion, she felt certain of one thing—she was no goddess. Of the other possibilities, well, she no longer knew for sure.

Their work done, the seer and her companions escorted Flora down the outer stairs of the keep. She got the briefest glimpse into the inky blackness of the dream chamber on the ground floor and reflected momentarily on her own night vision in that chamber—the vision that had sealed her fate—and shuddered. What was in the cup Fedelma had made her drink? Flora shook her head and turned away from the darkness of the shrine, with its burning pool and mystical altar, and walked through the doorway toward the brightness of the day outside.

She felt carried away by events completely out of her control. Fedelma guided her to the top of a small cliff overlooking the sacred tree and the glen beyond. What had the Arch Druid called this

place? *Cridhalbane*—the Heart of Alban. Bhatair Rhu was there, atop
the rocky crag, wearing the full regalia of his office. He was flanked
by Eliavres and the old warrior. A myriad white-robed druids were
arrayed throughout the valley, undulating in wave upon wave to the
hills on the far side of the glen. Six great pyres stood between the trio
of stone circles that formed the gates to the holy precipice, unlit by
flames and waiting to take the torch. The scene was almost identical
to the one she had witnessed in her vision while riding the unseen
currents of wind as an owl.

Flora teetered with dizziness. The whole scene was surreal. Her
experiences in the ordeals seemed more tangible to her now. An
image leapt to her mind of those white-robed figures as corpses, piled
in heaps, covered in pustules, and rotting with decay. Would that
gruesome specter indeed come to pass if she refused the role the gods
had chosen for her? It seemed impossible. Yet the visions she had
seen and the horrors she had experienced retained more substance in
her mind than this waking fantasy which had overtaken her soul.
Flora wavered on the verge of collapse, and Fedelma grasped her arm
to steady her.

The moments sped by in a dizzying blur. Bhatair Rhu delivered a
fervid panegyric, which sent ripples through the sea of assembled
druids. All Flora heard were bits and scraps of words: Fiona *Taghte*,
the Chosen One, Brigid, the goddess, heal our land. Cheers erupted
from the multitude. Chanting voices filled the air. "Fiona. *Taghte*.
Fiona."

Bhatair Rhu lifted a brand high in the air and a hush fell over
the assembly. Then Eliavres muttered an incantation under his
breath. He touched his silver-laced staff to the torch, and it erupted
in flame. The entire valley was silent from one end to the other.
Only the endless rush of the distant river and a gentle whisper in
the breeze gave voice to the ominous moment. Bhatair Rhu coiled
back his arm and launched the burning brand into the air. It
toppled, end over end, and landed in a spray of sparks in center of
the stone circle. There was a sudden rush of wind, and flames leapt

from amidst the stones to each of the unlit pyres, instantly setting them ablaze.

The crowd gasped in one great collective exhalation, and then the chanting resumed with increased fervor. "Fiona. *Taghte.* Fiona."

Bhatair Rhu turned to look farther up the cliff toward *Feart Choille,* and Flora followed his gaze. She saw a great signal fire blaze up from the far side of the Forest Stronghold. Moments later, another pyre flamed to life down the glen at the distant end of Drumainn Hill, and another and another on even more remote hills in places Flora had never even been.

Fedelma whispered in her ear, "It is the *Annunciation.* Word of your betrothal spreads throughout the land, even now. The bards have been waiting with songs on their lips and harps and lyres in their hands. The Ballad of Fiona will bring new hope to our people. And *you* shall become a goddess!"

THE TORRID SCENES from the morning spectacle faded from her thoughts and Flora returned her attention to the movement of her entourage through the glen and the rhythmic chanting of the druid retinue that accompanied her. Up ahead in the distance, she could see Bhatair Rhu on his great sorrel steed leading the procession, with Eliavres and the great warrior on each flank.

As they worked their way across the glen toward the river, Flora could vaguely make out a small lake with a structure at the far end. Within moments, the realization hit her. It was the millpond, and the structure was the mill house. It looked so different now—smaller and less imposing. Amidst the sunshine, the gentle breeze, and the lush green vegetation of the glen, it reminded her of the scene when she first encountered the old mill. She felt a warm flush of hope wash over her at the sight, followed almost instantly by a foreboding sense of dread as she recalled the "Others" who had stalked her through a barren wasteland of ash and mud. The mill house had come to symbolize a place of refuge for her and also a prison which she could never escape. She shuddered and a cold chill stabbed at her heart.

Flora looked up to scan the hilltops beyond the millpond. Desperately, her eyes searched the ridges and draws, seeking for some sign of her other secret refuge. When she spotted the rocky crag, her heart leapt. The voice that had led her to the cave had all but faded into the foggy mist. But she remembered her little leather pouch and the treasures it held, now spilled across the cavern floor, and wondered if they were still there. Were they safe from prying eyes and scavenging hands? Her heart reached out to recover the little tokens of her past life—memories from a time which seemed like ages ago and relationships which were being severed by the Morrigan's merciless shears.

Lost in her thoughts, Flora was almost unaware that Manas had stolen up beside her. She flinched and momentarily stumbled when she noticed him at her side.

"Forgive me, *Thaghadh*. I didn't mean to startle you."

"No, Manas. I'm fine. I just expected to walk this lonely path alone, hemmed-in within my little protective box. I did notice, however, that the skulls are facing outward this time. I assume I'm no longer considered to be a threat to the tribe."

She immediately regretted the sarcasm reflected in her tone. Manas had never been unkind to her. He was, perhaps, overly formal and somewhat aloof, but never unkind. "So what brings you back into this drama. I thought your responsibility was to assess my health and deliver me to *Feart Choille*."

"You've changed in these last couple of days. It's curious what can happen in just one or two turns of the sun."

"What do you mean?"

"But then again, I suppose you are a new person, after all. Isn't that right? Fiona, *Thaghadh*."

"*Thaghadh?*" Flora echoed the word. "'One who chooses?' I thought I was supposed to be Fiona, *Taghte,* the Chosen One."

"It seems to me you are the one with a choice to make."

"No one else appears to think that way. Eliavres, Fedelma, and even Bhatair Rhu believe the decision has already been made—that I was chosen by the gods and my fate is set."

"Hmm. Perhaps. But in the end, we hall have choices to make—choices about who we are and who we will become." Manas lifted his gaze and looked Flora in the eye. "Who are you, mistress? And who will *you* become?"

With her attention focused on Manas' gaze and the provocative question he posed, Flora lost focus on the path beneath her feet, and she stumbled. Manas instantly reached out a hand to grasp her arm and steady her.

"The path of life is treacherous, *Thaghadh,* fraught with unexpected dangers. Some, we can control. Others we cannot. Eventually, we all confront that critical instance which ushers us from this world into the next. At that moment, the most important thing is for us to be certain about who we are. All we take with us into the realm beyond is our identity."

Flora was silent as they progressed several paces down the road. Eventually, Manas released her arm.

"You didn't answer my question." The challenge caused Flora's voice to take on a slight, unintended edge.

"Didn't I?"

"Why are you here? Your task is done, isn't it?"

"Who is Brigid?"

"Why do you always answer questions with questions? And, for that matter, why do you ask questions with obvious answers?"

"If the answer is so obvious, then it should be no problem to provide."

"Okay. Fine. I'll play your game. Brigid is a goddess. An aspect of the Great Goddess, to be more specific."

"Can you now see how you have begun to change?" Manas, didn't wait for a reply, but continued on without interruption. "Yes, Brigid is a goddess. But she is the goddess of what?"

"Of course I've changed. Who would not have changed given the circumstances I've experienced and the things I'm being called to do? But I still don't get your point."

Manas walked on in silence, his deerskin *brogen* squishing in the muddy mix of grass and muck churned up by the marching feet and horse hooves ahead of them. It would take more than one day of sunshine to dry out the boggy ground of a highland glen. Flora refused to give in to his stubborn air and chose to wait him out in a silence of her own.

Finally Manas spoke. "Deep within *Gleann-Linne,* the Valley of Lakes and Pools, there is a sacred oak grove—a place almost as holy as the ancient yew tree itself. It's not a mixed grove, like so many others. It contains only oaks. That's one reason it is considered to be so sacred. It's almost completely pure."

"Almost?" Flora felt herself being sidetracked from the main conversation by what appeared to be the beginnings of a mystical story.

"Almost. There is one, single willow tree perched in among the mighty oaks. Just one. And not in the center of the grove, which would make it a focal point of immeasurable power. No, this willow is offset about a stone's throw to the southeast. Frawart Stezer, the master of the grove, is convinced the presence of the willow is a distortion which saps the immense potency of this holy place. He wants to cut it down or move it to a field of its own. But, of course, a willow is sacred in its own right. So he is afraid of offending some god by imposing his own will on that one, single tree which doesn't seem to belong where it is."

Flora continued to listen, expecting more, but Manas fell silent. After several more steps down the path, when he still did not elaborate further, Flora shook her head and let the odd story fade into the murmuring chant of her druid entourage. She didn't see its relevance to her situation and decided to steer the conversation back on track.

"Brigid is the goddess of many things. Lakes, springs, and holy wells. Hearth fires and smiths. Springtime and ewe lambs. Serpents and wisdom. Fertility, poetry, and healing. She is my patron. I'm a healer—or at least an apprentice."

"As am I," Manas responded. "And so, I requested to attend you during your preparation."

"But you're a man. My attendants are to be women. No man can be alone with a betrothed woman, especially one promised to a god."

"Hmm. Just so, *Thaghadh*. Just so." Manas paused, as if to give more weight to his next words. "You said my task was complete, but perhaps that's not the case. Perhaps there is still more healing to be done."

Manas stopped, bowed his head slightly, and allowed the trailing ranks of the entourage to engulf him, while Flora continued, step by step, along the narrow path carved out for her by fate.

BHATAIR RHU LED the processional through a glen with steep hills on both sides. Before long, Flora glimpsed a large body of water she assumed was Loch Tatha. It stretched out as far as she could see to the east and west—a deep azure blue surface nestled in among majestic mountains on the north and south shores.

Flora realized that these large lakes were the only truly flat places anywhere in nature's treasure trove of landscapes. Even the broadest glens were not actually flat, but rather undulated with small hills, dips, and depressions. Yet these huge lakes, like Loch Tatha here and Loch Rannoch near her home, and even small pools, like the spring she drank from near her rocky crag, were actually flat. Yes, the surfaces rippled with waves most of the time, while on rare occasions they shone smooth as silver mirrors, reflecting images from the sky and the shoreline. But those variations only decorated what were, to all appearances, truly flat surfaces.

However, the hidden reality was far different. Though a loch's surface gave the illusion of a sheer, even expanse, it hid a whole world of flora, fauna, and rolling hills beneath. Not even the wisest druids completely understood the mysteries concealed within those depths. But Brigid knew. Brigid was the goddess of lochs and pools and springs. Because of Brigid, these places were holy.

Flora wondered if she would, herself, gain the sacred knowledge concealed in the fathomless reaches of the abyss if her transformation into the goddess actually occurred as the druids believed it would. If that wisdom one day became hers, she might understand how these hallowed bodies of water could act as portals to the Otherworld. And if she knew that, then she could return to visit her family one day. Even more, when the time came, she could be the one to hold her father's hand as he made the fateful journey from this world to the next.

Lost in her musings about lochs and goddesses and the secret knowledge of the Otherworld, Flora was only vaguely aware that her entourage had come to a stop. Shaken out of her reverie, she watched as the ranks of warriors and druids filed into ever widening arcs around the end of a bridge which extended out to a crannog—a thatched-roofed, wooden roundhouse built on stilts out in the water.

Flora had seen crannogs before. There were several on Loch Rannoch, which village chieftains used for various purposes. Many served as trading posts where excess village goods could be stored before being loaded onto canoes for transport to other villages or even downriver to the seas. Some sheltered young sheep and goats from predators that stalked the night. Others acted as gathering places where the villagers could pay homage to the gods or hold ceremonial feasts. And a few hosted the families of chieftains, though Flora thought a lake house on stilts would make for inconvenient quarters, given the winds and rains which continually assaulted the waters of the loch. Besides, families living in such a home would have to go by bridge or by boat to get anything they needed. Still, some chiefs viewed crannogs as symbols of power and so dealt with the minor annoyances in order to gain prestige in the eyes of kinfolk and enemies alike.

Bhatair Rhu dismounted from his sorrel steed and approached

Flora. She stared past him, marveling anew at the fact the horse was not truly a horse at all, but the concealed form of his mother, herself a goddess trapped in a self-imposed exile from the Otherworld. If Flora indeed became a goddess, would they one day be friends? It seemed so hard to even imagine, as if she were living in a fantasy world of elves, and fairies, and enchanted gardens.

"Fiona *Taghte,* I present you with a palace worthy of the Bride." Bhatair Rhu motioned her toward the bridge.

Eliavres and the old warrior flanked the approach, both still perched atop their own mounts. Flora watched as two druids drove staves into the ground on either side of the pier, with human skulls secured to the top of each—setting the Arch Druid's spirit fence in place to guard the bridge from all but the most foolish or powerful of assailants.

"Am *I* to live in *there?*" Flora asked with a visible shiver.

"You are soon to be queen of the lochs and pools. Could there be a more fitting residence in this world for the future daughter of the Daghda and the Bride of Bres?" The Arch Druid beamed with a radiant smile, as if he were bestowing a treasured possession upon a favored daughter as a priceless gift. Clearly, he expected Flora to be both pleased and impressed.

"Of course it cannot compare with the vast estate you will inhabit in the Otherworld. But the villagers of *Incheskadyne* and the druid community of *Gleann-Linne* would be honored for you to enjoy the hospitality of their ceremony house during the time of your preparation. I assure you that your every need will be gladly supplied by those who attend you." He gestured again toward the bridge.

Something inside Flora urged her to turn and flee, as if taking a step onto the row of severed saplings which formed the span from the water's edge to the stilted roundhouse would finally and completely seal her fate. As tiny waves lapped upon the shore, Flora felt as if similar swells were lifting her up and propelling her forward, against her will, into an unknown abyss which was deep and dark and full of portent.

No one had asked if she would accept the offer of the gods. No one had even considered the idea she might deign to refuse the honor being bestowed upon her. No one believed she would reject the opportunity to save her people and their land from the terrifying fate she had witnessed in her ordeals. Everyone was nudging her, measure by measure, to take the crucial step and so secure her destiny. Yet, even as she lifted her foot to place it on the first wooden rung, deep in the hidden recesses of her mind she heard the faint echo of a voice calling out to her, "Run, Flora. Run."

But she took the step. And the next. And the next. Bhatair Rhu guided her down the timber path, like a father escorting a bride down the lane of flowers toward her awaiting groom. And the voice faded from her thoughts as she lifted her foot over the threshold into her palace on the loch.

Even before her eyes could adjust to the dim interior of the crannog, Flora heard a voice from her past that made her heart leap.

"Oh, Fiona, my girl. I'm so happy to see you safe."

"Nandag! *Bean-teagaisg*! Is it really you?"

Flora practically leapt across the room and into the arms of her old teacher. They held each other in a tight, almost desperate embrace.

With a choked voice that belied her failing attempt to hold back tears, Nandag whispered in Flora's ear, "I was so worried for you, my child. When you disappeared from the village so many nights ago on an errand to find herbs for me..." her voice cracked with emotion. "I'm so relieved to see you, alive and well. I had feared the worst."

"Oh Nandag. I can't believe you're here. I thought it was all gone. I was afraid I had lost everything. But you're here!"

Flora heard the Arch Druid clearing his throat behind her. Then Nandag broke their embrace and stepped back a pace.

"Forgive me, Fiona *Taghte*. I forget my place."

Flora felt a chill fill the air and dampen the warmth of the reunion with her mentor. She furrowed her brow and searched the eyes of her old teacher. "Nandag? What is it? It's me. I'm here. I'm okay. I'm still your Flora. You're still my *bean-teagaisg*."

Nandag frowned, and pursed her lips in a thin, taut line. When she spoke, her voice was terse and formal. "No, mistress. I am no longer your teacher. You are Fiona *Taghte*, the Chosen One. I am no longer your *bean-teagaisg*. You are soon to be the goddess of all healers—to be my goddess. I am here to serve you during your preparation."

Tears pricked at the corner of Flora's eyes. She shook her head. "No, Nandag. No. I'm still your Flora. I'm still the young apprentice who peppers you with an endless string of questions. I'm still the girl you immersed in the pool."

Nandag looked her in the eye one last time, and Flora could see she struggled to hold back tears. Then Nandag simply bent her head and cast her gaze to the ground at Flora's feet.

An icy pain struck at Flora's heart. Her old life truly was slipping away. The relationships she held most dear had been cruelly stripped from her. Even if the people in her life still lived—even if she could see them and interact with them—they were gone from her in every way that mattered. Nandag was standing right before her, but it was as if she were a stranger Flora was meeting for the very first time. Flora's heart ached and she reached out to Nandag to renew their embrace, but Nandag merely backed away. Flora's spirit was crushed within her. A tear welled up in her eye and trickled down her cheek.

Bhatair Rhu broke through the silence that bound the two women together. "Fiona *Taghte*, I trust you are pleased with your quarters. It was most recently configured as a ceremony house for the community of druids and the village of the Great Chief. But we've had it rearranged and equipped to meet your needs."

Flora's eyes had adjusted to the dim light inside the crannog and she gaped at what she saw. The lake house could indeed be regarded as a palace. The space was large enough to shelter an extended family of at least twenty people, or to accommodate a feast for fifty. It was decorated with the finest linen fabrics of deep reds and dandelion yellows. These were intricately embroidered with the symbols of Brigid's authority and power—serpents, ewe lambs, Imbolc crosses, the eternal flame, and the triple shaft of the Great Goddess which appeared on silver cups and symbol stones.

The thatched roof of the crannog extended up to a height of eight or ten men. The timbers holding it aloft were so large Flora could barely have reached her arms all the way around them. How the old people first sank these enormous beams into the depths of the loch's bottom would remain a mystery to her, at least until she gained the knowledge of the goddess.

The floor had been spread with a thick layer of wool and bracken, as was common even with roundhouses on land. But then ornately woven carpets, with the intricate spirals of a warrior's spirit armor, were laid over the floor's padding in the main areas. Flora had heard about carpets before. She even had a vague idea of how they were woven, like something of a mix between cloth and a basket. But she had never actually seen one. She poked at the nearest rug with her foot.

"Exquisite, aren't they?" Bhatair Rhu slowly nodded his head in appreciation of the elaborate craftsmanship. "The druid community tasked the finest weavers in the land to prepare them for this very purpose."

"So you've had this planned for quite some time now, have you? You knew I would be called by the gods for this role?"

"You?" The Arch Druid shook his head. "We didn't know that you had been selected until very recently. But we've known for over six summers that the gods had chosen someone for this purpose. I don't think you understand just how portentous and perilous this situation is. You experienced the horrors of what our people will face if Brigid is not replaced and the cycle is not restored. Winter will devastate the land—not the winter of freezing temperatures and snow and a scarcity of food. No, not that kind of winter. This will be the deep, dark winter of the soul. And you, Fiona *Taghte*, have been chosen to fill the void and to reestablish the eternal cycle within its normal balance."

He gazed down at Flora, and she saw a flicker of something dark and sober veiled behind the usual kindness that normally brimmed over from those beautiful blue eyes.

"Our salvation is not yet assured. Do you understand that? You have been chosen, but you have not yet ascended to the position. You must be confirmed. You must be found worthy by the gods for this honor."

"Worthy?" The word escaped from Flora's lips in a thin, fearful whisper, for she knew she wasn't worthy at all.

"What the gods are asking of you is not a casual task. It is not the work of a long summer. It is an eternal calling to live among the gods forever—to watch over the people of our land and to exercise Brigid's sovereignty over the domains she controls. This is no small thing. It is of great and eternal import. The gods must be assured you have the character for what you must become."

Flora hung her head. "And if I fail?"

"Then what you witnessed shall surely come to pass. There is no more time. If one more cycle passes without the balance being restored, the eternal system will be thrown out of equilibrium forever, and chaos will reign."

Bhatair Rhu reached out and grasped her chin. He tilted her head up so he could look her straight in the eye, and he punctuated each of his next words with the force of a smith's hammer, beating out Avallenian steel in the forge of the gods. "You. Must. Not. Fail."

He held her gaze for a long moment, and then the usual warm smile returned to his face. "You saw the Eternal Flame of Brigid in the fire circle, I'm sure. The mantle is crafted from a rare type of stone called marble, acquired during the raid of a Roman villa beyond the wall. It is part of the original ceremonial hall and we considered it apropos to the domicile of a goddess. But look just past the altar. Do you see it?"

Flora shifted to the left a few paces and peered around the fire circle and the altar. In the dim light, she saw a shimmer dance across the floor. "What is it?"

"It's a cleansing pool, similar to the one in the white fortress of *An Dun Gael*. It's a true miracle such a thing could be constructed in a crannog. A cleansing pool suspended in the air above the waters of a loch. Surely even the gods marvel at such a feat."

Flora recalled her recent experience in *An Dun Gael's* dream chamber, and a chill ran across her back. "It is truly remarkable. But, what is it for?" Flora wasn't sure she wanted to know the answer.

"Brigid is the goddess of sacred pools, so you will bathe yourself twice a day to begin your transformation. The waters are Brigid's tears. They have been collected from alba lilies growing in the lochs of the western isles. They were gathered and carried here by hundreds of adept healers for this very purpose. Alba lilies are an ancient symbol of purity, and you shall purify yourself in a bath of dew captured by their blossoms and leaves."

"I... I don't know what to say."

"Our people throughout the highlands and islands of Caledonia, as well as those from the Isle of Eire, and even the Gaels across the great sea, have all placed their hopes in you. Collecting the dew of heaven from lily plants is a symbol of their devotion to the goddess. It is just one of many such acts performed on your behalf."

Flora tried to speak, but the words stuck in her throat. She was taken aback by all of this—the lavish palace, the elaborate ceremonial features woven into the fabric of the crannog, and the extraordinary efforts made to create such a place. But most of all, she was totally overwhelmed by the weight of the expectations being heaped on her shoulders. She was *not* capable of what she was being asked to do. She *could not be* what her people needed her to be. She was nothing. She was nobody. Yet all these people expected her to become a goddess—no, more than just a goddess. They expected her to be their savior.

Flora had gathered lilies before. Nandag had taught her how to use the petals to calm nervous fears and help to people sleep. But to make that potion work, she had to dry the blossoms and use a pestle to crush them in a stone bowl. The petals were only useful when they had been ground to a fine powder and mixed with other herbs and oils. Was she, Flora, just such a flower? For her to calm the people's fears, must she be crushed and ground to a powder. The great burden foisted on her back was, even now, beginning to do that very work.

Bhatair Rhu drew her attention back from the murky depths where they had again become mired. "Nandag will coordinate the efforts of your attendants. And Manas will supervise your preparation, under the guidance of Eliavres, of course."

"And you?" Flora liked Manas well enough, but the thought of Eliavres being in control of her future gave her a queasy feeling in her gut.

"I have additional matters to attend to. I will be present for the ceremonies that mark the rites of passage, but your ascension will be the catalyst for a series of events which must be carefully planned and managed. These are portentous times. They involve great risk, but have the promise of great opportunity for our people and our land."

Flora felt like a tiny piece in a *fidchell* game being maneuvered around the board by powerful forces in a high stakes gambit for control of her people and their homeland. She apparently had no voice in how she was moved from square to square or what her own fate would be.

Bhatair Rhu continued. "There will be two adept druidesses stationed outside the door of the palace at all times. Nandag and the other attendants will provide everything you might need. But these women outside are there to watch over the spiritual realm. Two of my own personal guards will be posted at the end of the bridge. These are backed by a contingent of druids and warriors staying in the huts on the shore. You will be perfectly safe."

"Safe? What kind of danger could I be in? Who would threaten someone destined to be a goddess?"

Bhatair Rhu looked at her with pity in his eyes, as if she were a naïve little child. "Have you ever been to the great sea?"

Flora shook her head and muttered, "No."

"But you have seen a thunderstorm beat the waves of Loch Rannoch into a fury, yes?"

"Yes, of course."

"Just such a thunderstorm is, at this very moment, erupting in the Otherworld. There is a great deal of jealousy and animosity between many of the gods. And when there is a struggle for power in the Otherworld, it can drive a violent change of tide in our own. Chaos has many agents who are more than willing to do her bidding. But we have taken strong measures to protect you during your preparation. You will be safe."

As Flora struggled to unravel the implications of the Arch Druid's words, a small, thin man ducked through the doorway, sidled up beside Bhatair Rhu, and bowed slightly in her direction. The man had a somewhat whimsical expression on his face, and the light from the fire pit danced in his eyes.

Bhatair Rhu inclined his head, acknowledging the new arrival. Flora was curious how the man had sauntered right through the spirit fences at the head of the bridge and over the entrance to the crannog without any apparent hindrance at all.

"Now let me introduce you to another member of your preparation team. Finnan '*Breabadair Uirsgeulan.*'"

"Finnan, the 'Legend Weaver?' Flora asked. "What does that mean?"

"Finnan is the greatest master bard of our time. He hails from Eire and has come to compose the ballads that will preserve your ascension in the lore of our people. This is one of the most significant moments in our history. The sagas Finnan creates about you will be sung for generations to come. This is a task for the best minstrel in the land. Finnan will be present with you throughout the entire process, so that he can capture every nuance in story and song."

Finnan bowed his head toward her once again. "Mistress, it is my true delight to serve you."

The instant Finnan spoke, shock tore through Flora's mind, and she was suddenly jerked back into the horror of her ordeals to confront the one enigma she had never resolved. She heard it ringing out, again and again, in the midst of every critical situation—the voice. It echoed, now, in the dark recesses of her thoughts, threatening to drown out every other memory.

Flora fought to restrain the panic raging inside her. It took all her willpower to maintain her composure as she peered deeply into Finnan's eyes, striving to see beyond their fanciful twinkle and to discern the true nature of what lay behind. For the voice which had pierced through the fog of her nightmare—the voice which had either guided her, or lured her, through every step of the gods' horrific labyrinth—was Finnan's voice. Though it had never uttered more than just a few short words, she now knew its identity. She was certain of it, with an absolute assurance that filled her with two conflicting emotions—eternal hope and abject fear. And she didn't know which one to trust.

CHAPTER FOURTEEN

T iny droplets of water fell onto Flora's eyelids, wrenching her
out of a deep sleep and halting the dreams which had plagued
the night. She lay in a huge pile of luxurious furs and listened to
undulating waves of rain beat a pulsating rhythm on the crannog's
steep thatched roof. She listened to the sound of the raindrops
splashing into the water of the loch. That was a unique melody all its
own, which differed greatly from the harsh splatter of rain hitting
rocks, or the soft thump it made on marshy ground. She remembered
first hearing that special music as a child when storms crossed Loch
Rannoch, near her home. It was as if a thousand tiny voices of
individual drops blended together into perfect harmony as they
melted back into a great choir of their own kind—single, weary
travelers returning to the mother waters of the loch.

Nandag stepped through the front door, followed by two novice
druidesses. Their cloaks were soaked with rain and dripped rivulets
of water onto the finely embroidered rugs. Flora wondered how long
the carpets would retain their delicate beauty once they were
exposed to a regular procession of muddy feet.

"Good morning, *Taghte.* I hope you slept well. We'll start with your morning cleansing. Perhaps by the time we are done, the storm will have passed."

"Oh, Nandag. Please don't call me that. It sounds so... I don't know, so formal and sterile coming from you."

"Well, 'Fiona', then, if you prefer."

"Or what about 'Flora'? Nandag, it's me, your Flora. I'm the same person. I haven't changed. Surely here in private we can still be the people we've always been."

Nandag cast a quick, furtive glance at the novices behind her and cut Flora off with a quick shake of her head. "You are Fiona, *Taghte*, she who will become Brigid, the Bride, and patroness of healers, from your throne in the Otherworld. I am your servant. Using your personal name, Fiona, seems too intimate a thing. But if you command it, I will obey."

Flora stared at Nandag in shock and dismay. This woman, whom she had once venerated as her mentor, her *bean-teagaisg*, now bowed in subservience to her. It all felt so terribly wrong. She was still the same person she had been when the moon was last full. Other than the intense fear which continued to ripple outward from her ordeal, she still felt the same way and thought the same way as the young woman she had always been. But now, because of some random twist of her fate in the cruel hands of the Morrigan, her life thread was being pulled in a completely new direction. She had a new name, "Fiona." And a title, *"Taghte."* And a destiny, to become a goddess. To everyone else, she was a completely different person. But she had not truly changed, deep down inside?

"Taghte– uh, Fiona. We need to complete the cleansing. Manas will be here soon to escort you to the *Inauguration."*

"The *Inauguration?* What's that?"

"Manas will explain everything. For now, we need to get you up and into the Pool of Brigid's Tears."

The two novices bowed deeply without saying a word and helped Flora up from the bed of furs. She passively allowed them to undress her and lead her toward the pool.

Flora shuddered involuntarily as she approached the edge of the bath. Images leapt to her mind from two previous experiences with similar "cleansing waters." On one occasion Nandag had pushed her head beneath the surface of a pond. On another, Fedelma had performed a similar rite. In each case, the experience had been both exhilarating and terrifying.

What would happen this time as she was once again plunged into the mystical realm between this world and the next? Would she again experience all eternity being pressed into a single moment of time? Would she feel the intense burning that would refine her soul in the fire, separating the pure silver from the dross within? Would she strain to breathe, but fight against the impulse to open her lungs to a lethal flood of liquid?

Nandag gave her a gentle nudge from behind, and Flora stepped into the pool, muscles taut with anticipation and fear. But she felt... nothing. As she waded deeper and deeper into this cleansing pool, suspended above the waters of a loch, it just felt like she was walking into any normal pond. She sensed no change. She felt no sudden transformation. She just got wet.

It was disappointing, in a way. She thought about all the efforts of all those people who had gathered the drops of dew from thousands of lilies, and her spirit sagged. Apparently, even this vast accumulation of mystical waters and sacred power was not enough to change her into a goddess. Given all she had hoped and feared, nothing significant seemed to have happened. She exited the pool physically clean, but emotionally discouraged.

They dressed her in the same outfit she had worn at the *Annunciation*. At least it looked the same. But it felt new, as if it had never been worn before.

"Nandag."

"Yes, *Tagh*– yes, Fiona?"

"Do you remember the day you caught me exploring the stone circles near the sacred yew tree during the great gathering six summers ago?"

"I do."

"Do you remember what you told me?"

"Not exactly. I have taught you many things, before that time and since. I'm afraid they all tend to run together in my mind."

"I remember that moment distinctly, as if it were but a day or two ago." Flora twisted a stray lock of her hair between two fingers. "I mentioned that I had been exploring near the stone circles. You became very angry with me and warned me about meddling around them in a very stern voice. You said, 'Be very careful in this place. There are forces here which must be handled in a particular manner —forces which must be feared and respected—traditions which have endured for endless turnings of the moon. If you meddle with these forces in the wrong way, you could cause dreadful consequences not only for yourself, but also for our people.'"

"You remember exactly what I said?"

"I do. Word for word. It wasn't just what you said, but how you said it. It was one of the few times I was actually afraid of you." Flora turned away from Nandag so she wouldn't see the tears that threatened to spill over her eye-lids.

"You know I have always loved you. If I was severe with you, it was to protect you from harm. You know that."

Flora just nodded her head. "Is that what caused all this? Is that why I'm trapped in this horrible situation? Did I get too close to the stones and offend the gods? Did I somehow unleash those dreadful forces which threaten to destroy our people and our land? Is this all happening because of my careless curiosity?"

Nandag apparently forgot herself for a flicker in time. She reached out to Flora and pulled her into a close embrace. "Oh no, child. No. It's not your fault. Great powers have been stirring in this land long before you ever tiptoed near those stones. They're like massive waves, churned up by a mighty storm. You just happened to be standing near the shore when they broke upon the rocks. You've been caught in the spray." She squeezed Flora tighter, a loving embrace like Flora had never known from her own mother. "No, my darling. You did not cause this terrible gale. You've merely been trapped in its wake."

Nandag held her close for several more heartbeats. Flora buried her face in Nandag's shoulder and sobbed. "I just want to go back. I want to go back to the way it was before. I just want to be a healer in our village. I don't want to be a goddess. I don't want to be Brigid. I only want to be your Flora."

Nandag patted Flora's back once again, then stepped back, held her at arm's length, and looked deeply into her eyes. Flora saw a sincere empathy in her old teacher's gaze. "A few very fortunate people get to choose their own path in this life. But only a few. For most, that path is chosen for them. I suspect your fate was laid out in ages long past. It has merely waited for time to wash over it—to make it come to life. You are Fiona, *Taghte*. You are the Chosen One. And I... I am your servant."

Footsteps on the bridge caused Nandag to drop her hands from Flora's shoulders and to step back a pace. But her gentle gaze never dropped Flora's eyes until Manas ducked through the doorway with Finnan following closely behind.

"Is she prepared for the *Inauguration?*" Manas inquired.

Nandag's eyes never left Flora's. "Yes. She is ready."

Finnan sounded as upbeat and cheerful as ever, despite the water dripping from his hat so profusely that it formed a puddle on the floor. "Well, if she goes along in that get up, she'll be soaked to the bone in the whisk of a cockerel's tail. Have ya got a cloak for the dear girl? We can't have our new goddess melt away in the storm, now can we?"

Manas cleared his throat and scoffed at the bard. "Though I might have stated the issue in slightly different terms, I will agree with our Master Minstrel. This rain will not abate anytime soon. Fiona *Thaghadh*, will need a cloak with a hood for the ceremony."

"Yes. Yes of course." Nandag gestured to one of the apprentices, and she turned to fetch a thick, black, woolen cloak from a hook against the outer wall of the crannog.

Flora felt a bit disgruntled. Everyone had been treating her with such deference, and she had been given such lavish quarters in which to live, somehow she expected this ritual service, this *Inauguration*, to be delayed until the rain at least let up a bit. What was so important it needed to happen during a downpour?

With the cloak wrapped tightly about her shoulders, and the hood pulled low over her head, Flora started to move toward the entrance of the crannog. But Manas raised his hand and stopped her short.

"Forgive me, *Thaghadh*, but we will be going out the back." He motioned her past a curtain which hung near the rear of the crannog. Flora looked at him quizzically, and then realized there was a doorway behind the curtain. It led to a small platform, with a ladder down to the water. She hadn't noticed it before.

As FLORA DUCKED her head and stepped out into the pouring rain, she glanced up to see two human skulls above the doorway, facing out. Apparently, this entrance to her little palace was also protected by a powerful spirit fence. No one but a druid, and one approved by Bhatair Rhu, himself, could enter her sanctuary through either doorway. She wasn't sure if she felt safe or just trapped.

Flora stepped out from underneath the shelter of the thatched roof, and the rain wrapped her in a cocoon, drowning out all other sights and sounds. Slowly, she inched her way down the ladder leading from the rear platform of the crannog to the water below. The rungs were slick with water, and each step brought with it the peril of a rapid plunge into the loch.

At the base of the ladder, two warriors waited in a dugout canoe. The boat was long enough to accommodate about ten or twelve people, but only Manas and Finnan followed her down. Apparently, Nandag and the apprentices would not accompany them. Given the circumstances and the heavy rain, Flora wished she could stay behind with them.

They settled into their spots, and the two warriors, bodies naked and painted in spirit armor, rowed toward the east end of the loch. Manas sat in front of Flora, and Finnan reclined against the side of the hull at her back.

"What is this *Inauguration* ceremony all about? And what is so important that we need to do it in the pouring rain?" she asked.

"Rain?" Manas called out over his shoulder. He almost had to shout to be heard. "Showers of blessing from the gods. It's one of their greatest gifts to us. Without the rain we would have no water to drink or food to eat. Our crops would not grow, and our flocks would die off. I think this powerful storm is, perhaps, an ardent sign of approval from the gods of your ascension. I'm no oracle, but that's how I see it."

Flora rolled her eyes, and though Manas could not see her gesture, Finnan chuckled softly behind her, as if he were watching her face and saw her every expression.

"You didn't answer my question. What is this *Inauguration?*"

"The druids are intermediaries between the gods and our people. We speak to the gods and communicate their will to the village chiefs and elders. We bring the petitions of the people to the gods through the sacred rights and ceremonies. You understand all of that, yes?"

"Yes. Of course." But, she didn't know what it had to do with the question she had just asked. Still, she waited for Manas to continue his thought.

"When the great sign appeared in the heavens six summers ago, the druid community gathered the whole tribe together to seek understanding from the gods about the bright star and its portent."

"Yes. I understand that. I was there."

"My point is this. The druid community could not divine the will of the gods alone. All the clans of the tribe had to come together in worship for the answer to be revealed."

"Okay, I *don't* understand that. The gods had a problem. The Cailleach entered the sacred pool, but Brigid never emerged. The cycle of seasons progressed, but Brigid was gone. And the gods needed a replacement. So, why did they need to call the whole tribe together to reveal their intentions? You would think they would want to communicate their will in the fastest and simplest way. Why the ominous sign in the heavens and all the grand ceremonies?"

"Ah, Manas, my friend. Fiona, here, doesn't know the dirty little secret, now does she?" Finnan interjected.

Manas glanced back over his shoulder and shot a scornful look past Flora to the bard behind her. "Our people are well aware of the influence the gods hold over our lives. We thrive under their blessings and suffer under their curses. And so we make sacrifices to them and conduct sacred ceremonies to honor them, in order to appease their wrath and to earn their good will. Most of the gods are receptive to these humble gestures of veneration and reverence."

"It's why we hold the special services at Imbolc, and Lughnasadh, Beltane, and Samhain, right? But that still doesn't answer my question. And what's this 'dirty little secret?'"

"Please disregard Master Finnan's impertinent comments for the moment. Our people understand that we must appease the gods. But there is something else the common people do not know. Long ago, the chief druids discovered the gods actually draw their power from our homage. If we ceased to worship them, their strength would fade away."

"You mean, they would die? The gods are immortal. They can't die."

The two warriors kept stroking their oars in the water, propelling the canoe forward at a rapid pace. The swift motion of the boat, along with the driving wind, made the rain sting Flora's face.

"No. They wouldn't die, exactly. They would simply fade away. They would still have power in the Otherworld, but their influence in our world would wane. If we stopped worshipping the gods, they would disappear from our land, and our lives would be entirely in the hands of the fates. As you know, the fates can be fickle companions. The wisest oracles in the training center of *Gleann-Linne* are convinced that without the gods, our civilization would devolve into chaos, and misery would reign."

"So, the gods sent a sign to prompt us to hold a special ceremony?"

"Yes. You see, the gods could not simply resurrect Brigid or even choose a person to fill her role. Even acting all together, which they can rarely manage to do in the best of times, they do not have the power for such a feat. They needed to draw that power from the people. They need our worship, our holy rites and services, in order to restore the balance brought about by Brigid's disappearance."

A moment of realization washed over Flora, like when a torch is lit in a dark cavern. She took a deep breath. "The *Inauguration* is one of those special ceremonies?"

"It is. It's a holy ritual of the ordinary people. The *Annunciation* was also a special rite observed by the druid community. But the druids can't act alone. We are intermediaries, as I said. Real power is only *channeled* by the druid community. It originates from the people and from the land."

"So what will happen? And what am I supposed to do as part of this ceremony?"

"You? Oh, my lady, you just have to stand there and look divine," Finnan quipped.

Manas ignored the comment. "Your role is simple, *Thaghadh*. The ceremony will be held on the commons of *Incheskadyne*, the village of the Great Chief. You've been there, remember? In the healing hut, where you recovered from your ordeals."

"Unfortunately, I didn't get out to see much of the village. It seems there was a spirit fence keeping me inside. I think I was considered to be a danger to the community, right?" Flora didn't bother to hide the sarcasm in her tone, though it was probably drowned out by the rain, anyway.

"Bhatair Rhu and Eliavres will preside. The villagers already know the story by now."

"How could they possibly know? This all just happened yesterday."

"Ah, Fiona. We bards can be quite resourceful when the occasion calls for it," Finnan interjected.

"Master Finnan is correct. The songs and sagas were all prepared in advance. When the signal pyres of the *Annunciation* were lit, bards across the whole land began sharing their tales in every village and every clan. Not just the clans of your tribe, either. The news was spread from the highlands to the islands, and even across the great sea."

They were approaching the end of Loch Tatha, and Flora could see the huts of *Incheskadyne*, the village of the Great Chief. A group of white-robed druids was waiting at the pier to receive them, along with a contingent of warriors in spirit armor.

Manas continued, "You will be presented to the Great Chief's people and to representatives of other clans, who have all been assembled for the occasion. The druids will offer sacrifices to Cerridwen and to Lugh, to the Daghda and to Bres. Three great pyres have been prepared in the center of the commons—one for each aspect of the Great Goddess. Two of the pyres will be lit for the Mother and the Crone. But the third one will remain dormant for now. It is the hearth fire of Brigid, the Maiden. Bhatair Rhu will light a torch from the Crone's fire, and bring it to you."

"What am I meant to do with it? Will I use it to light Brigid's pyre?"

"No. You are Fiona, *Taghte*, the Chosen One. You are not yet a goddess. Brigid's pyre will remain dormant. But the torch is a symbol of the promise of what you will soon become. You simply need to hold it up while the people worship the gods."

"Like I said," Finnan chuckled. "You just need to stand there and look divine."

THE CEREMONY PROCEEDED JUST as Manas had described it to her. Flora had not expected many people to be present for the rituals because of the heavy downpour, but crowds thronged the commons and spilled down almost every path in the village. Flora scanned the crowd, desperately trying to catch a glimpse of someone in her family, but if any of them were there, they were concealed in the vast throng.

When Manas said sacrifices would be offered to several of the gods, it had been a huge understatement. More bulls, goats, rams, and pigs were slaughtered that day than at all of the sacred festivals she had attended in her whole life combined. Blood saturated the ground. Rain water washed it in muddy streams down to Loch Tatha, and Flora wondered if the entire lake would turn red.

Just as he had at the *Annunciation*, Eliavres used his silver staff to ignite a torch in the Arch Druid's hand. It flared instantly to life, despite the deluge pouring from the sky. Then Bhatair Rhu threw the firebrand directly into Brigid's pyre. The assembled crowd gasped, thinking he had made a terrible mistake. But the flames leapt through the air, first to the Mother's bonfire, and then to the Crone's, without igniting the piles of timber stacked together for the Bride.

Then a master craftsman approached the Arch Druid, accompanied by the Great Chief. He unwrapped an exquisitely carved wooden staff and handed it to Bhatair Rhu. It was formed from two intertwined serpents. The vipers' bodies were etched with the symbols of Brigid's power. They held a large, intricately woven iron basket in their mouths at the top of the staff, in which several yellowish-brown stones were encased.

Bhatair Rhu turned to Flora and extended the staff to her. Instantly, she felt the eyes of everyone in the assembled crowd bearing down on her. What was she supposed to do? Manas said she had no active part in the ceremony. She was only to hold the torch of promise up in the air after Bhatair Rhu lit it from the Crone's pyre. But this staff had not been lit. What did the Arch Druid expect her to do now?

Bhatair Rhu smiled warmly at her and extended the staff to her again. Then he nodded toward the Crone's bonfire, which blazed with flames licking the very sky. Flora took a deep breath and grasped the staff from his hands. Struggling to maintain the kind of poise and dignity expected of a goddess, she strode slowly over to the raging mass of burning timbers. In her mind, she saw images of her village engulfed in a blaze that swept out in every direction, turning the whole land into an inferno which could not be quenched. The devastation of her nightmare sent shivers through her body, and she almost dropped the staff.

Flora squeezed her eyes shut, forcing the images out of her mind, and tipped the end of the staff into the flickering tongues of fire. Immediately, the rocks in the basket at the top of the staff erupted into a bright blue ball of light that sprayed a shower of sparks high into the air. A pungent, noxious odor wafted out of the beacon in her hands, but only Flora was close enough to smell it. The stench made her dizzy and almost caused her to retch, until she grasped the serpents' tails and thrust the staff high into the air.

A collective gasp rippled through the crowd, and then they roared together with great shouts of acclamation. "Fiona! *Taghte!* The Chosen One is here! Fiona! *Taghte!*" They chanted her name and her title over and over in a fevered pitch that rose to shake the heavens.

At that moment, the rain halted, the clouds broke, and a single ray of sunshine pierced through the gloom, resting directly on Flora and bathing her in the light of heaven. The crowd broke into a frenzy of awed exclamation and pressed in around her, trying to touch her.

Immediately, a line of warriors appeared and formed a barrier between her and the ecstatic mob. Eliavres snatched the staff from her hands, while Manas and a team of druid adepts formed a thick circle around her. They maneuvered her toward the dock, where a canoe was prepared to evacuate her back to the crannog. Quickly, they deposited her aboard, and the craft pushed out into the loch, leaving the slaughtered animals, the raging pyres, and the frenzied mob all behind.

From over her shoulder Flora heard a familiar, whimsical voice.

"Well, so much for just standing there and looking divine. That little drama will make for a fine stanza of verse."

Flora just collapsed into a heap in the bottom of the canoe and tried desperately to calm her racing heart.

THE CANOE GLIDED across the water like a swan, smoothly and gracefully. This time they had the wind at their back, and the sun shone overhead. Flora sat in stunned silence as she contemplated what had just happened. She was beginning to believe the gods truly had chosen her for this unimaginable role, but the reaction of the crowd both thrilled and terrified her. The display of approval from the gods had exhilarated them, but that arousal had turned to intoxication in the blink of an eye. Flora's path ahead was an opportunity to serve her people in a whole new way, but it was a dangerous opportunity, balanced on a knife's edge between order and chaos.

Flora glanced to her right and watched the shore of a small island slide by. Something about the island looked slightly odd, as if the tiny mass of earth and trees jutting up out of the water didn't quite belong there. Manas glanced over his shoulder and caught her quizzical expression.

"It's not actually an island. It's a crannog from long, long ago. The ancient people built it as a tribute to Brigid—a place of sacrifices and offerings on the lake itself. Now it is used by the druid community for similar purposes. A small—"

His words were cut off as an arrow shot out of the tree line and struck the warrior in the front of the canoe. He slumped over and dangled in the water, half in and half out of the boat. A scream erupted from Flora's throat, but was instantly stifled when a heavy weight slammed her forward and forced her face-down in the bottom of the canoe.

The craft teetered in the water and threatened to flip over, as another arrow buried itself in the side of the hull, a handbreadth in front of Flora's face. She tried to look up, but Finnan's voice rang out in a terse command, "Keep down." She instinctively obeyed his order, just like she had responded to the voice during her ordeal. She shuddered again at the uncanny similarity between Finnan's voice and the one from her dreams.

Then Finnan grunted in a sudden exclamation of pain, followed by a colorful string of epithets. Flora heard a splash and the boat wobbled from side to side for a moment before resuming its swift forward movement. She was only vaguely aware that Manas had pushed the wounded warrior overboard and taken his place with the oar. She heard more arrows thud into the outside of the wooden hull, but they did not pierce through the canoe's thick wall.

After what seemed like an eternity, Finnan crawled off her, cursing in pain. When Flora scrambled back upright, she saw Manas and the other warrior rowing with strong, rapid strokes, propelling the craft away from the island. Finnan, on the other hand, gritted his teeth and bit back an anguished howl as he pushed an arrow through his jerkin and out the other side. There was a small rush of blood, but he pressed hard on his side, and it appeared to stem the flow.

"Finnan, you're hurt! Here, let me help."

"I'm fine," he growled, but didn't resist when Flora reached over and pulled his jerkin aside to reveal the wound. It looked ugly, but she could see that the shaft had only pierced through the fatty tissue on his side.

Flora tore a swatch of cloth from the hem of her dress and folded it into a thick wad. She reached outside the canoe and dipped the fabric into the water. Then she slipped the rope belt from around her waist and used it to tie the clump of wool over the wound. It was a terrible bandage, but it would have to do for the moment.

"Push down on that cloth and hold it in place. The pressure will help stop the flow of blood."

Finnan gritted his teeth and did as she instructed.

Flora shouted up to Manas, "What's happening?"

The warrior from the back of the boat called out, "We're away. No one follows."

Manas paused from paddling to hazard a glance over his shoulder and nodded his head slightly. "Keep rowing. We need to get Fiona *Taghte* back to the crannog as quickly as possible." Then he asked Flora, "Are you okay?"

"Yes. I'm fine. But Master Finnan has taken an arrow to the side. I believe the wound is superficial, just through the outer layer of skin. A handbreadth closer to his gut, and it could have been much worse. What happened to the other warrior?"

Manas just shook his head and resumed rowing. Flora wondered at his silence. She had seen a number of men wounded by arrows from the raids which frequently occurred between her clan and warriors of other tribes. A single shaft seldom proved deadly, at least not right away. Then she realized the man had probably not been killed by that single shot. Manas had pushed him over the side to hasten their escape.

Manas was a healer. He had a sacred responsibility to preserve life in every way possible. Yet he had sacrificed the warrior to the cold waters of the loch to save their own lives. As Flora's mind grappled with the implications of that thought, the reality of the situation struck her like a blow from the Daghda's mighty club. Manas had not sacrificed the man to save *their* lives. He had sacrificed the man to save *her* life. Someone had just died in order to keep her safe. Manas had violated his sacred oath as a healer to get her out of danger.

Flora's gut gnarled itself into a tight knot. She had been devastated by the experiences in her ordeal of people dying and the land being ravaged. But in the end, those had just turned out to be fanciful visions from the gods. But this was all too real. Someone had just tried to kill her, and a man had died to preserve her life. Flora realized this would likely not be the last time such a thing would happen. Bhatair Rhu had warned her that powerful forces had been unleashed in the Otherworld which would contend mightily against each other. And somehow, she was trapped in between this order and chaos.

The craft soon slid to a stop at the base of the ladder leading up to the crannog. Flora was thankful to leave the boat and its nasty business behind, and retreat to the sanctuary of her abode. Half-way of the ladder, she turned to see the canoe paddling away. She called over her shoulder, "Manas?"

"I must dress Finnan's wound and report to the commander of the watch. Your security detail will need to be increased. This is most urgent. Nandag will attend to your needs. I shall see you again on the morrow."

Flora watched the boat glide away toward the shore and then finished her climb to the platform above. She glanced up at the skulls of the spirit fence guarding the doorway and wondered if even their potent magic could keep her safe from the wrath of angry gods and their agents in this world. She hesitated briefly before crossing over the line demarcated by the gaze of their eyeless sockets, but then pressed on. If she could not enter her own refuge, she would not be safe anywhere.

When Flora stepped through the doorway and pushed the curtain aside, she was startled to see her mother sweeping mud off the carpets inside the front doorway. Without thinking, she cried out, "*Mamaidh!*" and rushed across the large room to wrap her mother in a huge hug. Tears sprang to her eyes as the trauma of the day broke through the dam she had erected in her mind and washed over her in a flood.

"*Mamaidh!* Oh *Mamaidh!* I was afraid I would never see you or Father again. They said I had no family anymore. No family. No home. But you're here. Oh *Mamaidh*, you're here!"

As Flora sobbed into her mother's shoulder, she slowly became aware that the older woman didn't return her embrace. She was just standing still, like a cold, hard symbol stone in the middle of an ancient battleground. Gradually, Flora pulled back, holding her mother's arms in her hands, not wanting to let go.

"*Mamaidh?* What's wrong? What's gone wrong? Is everyone alright?" The attack on the boat flashed through her mind. "Have they hurt Father? Or Catriona?" Flora gulped in air to try and quell her rising fears.

But her mother just shook her head. "No, mistress. Cinead and Catriona are well. They've suffered no harm."

Cinead? Flora's mind reeled. Her mother had never used her father's given name when talking to her. She had always spoken of him as her father. And what had her mother called her? Mistress?

"Mother, what are you saying? Why do you talk to me like this? You're speaking like a stranger."

"Forgive me, Fiona *Taghte*. I am here to serve you. *Ard-Draoidh* Bhatair Rhu thought it well to have someone attend you who was familiar with your needs. I'll do my best to stay out of the way while I'm about my work."

Flora pulled urgently on her mother's arms to draw her in to another embrace, but she stiffened in resistance. "*Mamaidh*, it's me. I'm your daughter, Flora. I haven't changed."

Flora looked into the eyes of the woman standing in front of her, and realized the horrible truth. This woman no longer considered herself to be Flora's mother. She now only thought of her as a goddess in the making. *Taghte*. The Chosen One. Bhatair Rhu didn't really need someone to clean up after her. He needed someone from her past who would embrace her new identity. And he knew her mother would be compliant to his demands. She dropped her hands from her mother's shoulders and backed away, shaking her head.

"I am who I am. I am who I have always been. Regardless of what the gods have done, they can't take that away. I am Flora. I'm your daughter. You can't change that just by using a different name."

Her mother dropped her eyes to the floor in a posture of subservience. "As you say, *Taghte*." Then she turned away and resumed sweeping the mud from the carpets.

Flora felt the icy blade of despondency stab at her heart. In less that one turn of the sun, she had been hailed as a goddess, shot at with arrows, and now disavowed by her own mother. Surely her father had not disowned her as well. The very idea brought tears to her eyes. It was all more than she could bear. She pressed her fists to her temples as the mounting frustration bubbled over. Suddenly overcome with rage, she shouted in a voice that echoed up to the crannog's high pitched roof. "Get out! All of you, get out right now!"

The women all stopped in the midst of their tasks and stared at her.

"GET OUT!" Flora bellowed, emphasizing each word.

The two apprentices jumped at her command and scampered toward the door. Her mother slowly laid the broom aside and edged her way out.

Nandag took a step toward her. "Fio–"

"Now! Go!"

Nandag bowed her head and backed toward the exit. A moment later she ducked through the opening, and Flora was left alone to brood in private over memories of a childhood that were, even now, fading into the mists of time. A deep sense of loss wafted over her for the life that was slipping away.

CHAPTER FIFTEEN

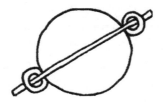

F lora tossed and turned on her bed of furs, drifting in and out of
sleep. The images that plagued her dreams were a confused
mix of childhood memories and scenes of horror. She heard her
father calling out to her repeatedly, "Flora, my girl, my wee *fauth*,"
while her mother's voice fought to drown him out. "Fiona, *Taghte*.
Fiona, *Taghte*. Fiona, *Taghte*."

Finally, Flora drifted into a deeper sleep, and the memory of an
earlier, distant dream sprang back to new life. It was as if she were
reliving an experience she had never really had in the first place. But
this time, she was watching herself from outside, while hearing the
thoughts of her other self echo in her mind—a dream within a dream.

*Tiny raindrops fell on Flora's face and roused her from sleep. As
she propped herself up on one arm and stretched, it took her a moment
to remember where she was. She had that groggy, but somehow
refreshing feeling you get when you wake up in a grassy meadow on a
cool spring day with a slight breeze ruffling your leine and causing
wisps of hair to dance across your face.*

*She looked down, seeing the bag of herbs she had been collecting
for Nandag, her bean-teagaisg—her mentor—who was teaching her the*

art of healing back in her village. Nandag had sent her to gather wild garlic, ivy, cowslip, harts tongue, and marjoram from the spring growth in the forests and glens. She had been successful in her quest and her sack was full of the leaves, flowers, roots, and berries they would use to prepare all manner of tonics, poultices, and other soothing balms.

Flora glanced up at the sky to see thunderclouds darkening the horizon. Rain was a perpetual part of the highlands' landscape. It was the lifeblood of the land. It caused her healing herbs to grow. It filled the sacred pools and springs with water from the heavens that mingled with waters from the earth to form a holy union. Flora liked to think of raindrops as the tears of the goddess Brigid when she sang a keening song to a tune her father, the Dagda, strummed on Uaithne, his enchanted oaken harp. But, for now, she would be drowned in those tears if she didn't get back to her village soon.

Flora never dreamed she would be out this long or wander so far in her search to fill the flaxen sack with herbs. She had been lured steadily onward by the abundant produce of nature and spring—a patch of harts tongue blossoming in the glen, sprigs of garlic hiding among the grass, and fresh ivy leaves creeping up the trunks of trees. Time had flittered by like a meadow pipit dancing in the wind.

And then there was that little nap in the meadow. How long had she slept there, anyway, basking in the rare afternoon sunshine? For that matter, how exactly had she fallen asleep to begin with? That bit was somewhat of a blur. But then again, she was still halfway immersed in the hazy fog that lingered at the edge of wakefulness.

She glanced up and noticed for the very first time that she was floating in a sea of bright red flowers, each one with a cluster of black seeds at its center. The field stretched as far as she could see in every direction.

It was the dream she'd had in the cavern about finding her village destroyed—a dream about a reality that had never actually occurred. It wasn't real, but here it was again, in all its vivid detail. Every little nuance of scent and sound and touch, exactly as it had been before.

All except that last bit about the little red flowers with the black centers.

She drifted back into the dream and the vision folded her into its arms. She began to run through the tide of scarlet blossoms, laughing and dancing. She felt light as air, as if she could fly away. She reached down and picked one of the flowers and breathed deeply, expecting to savor a fragrant aroma. But the bright crimson petals gave off no odor at all. Disappointed, she dropped the blossom to the ground and then the whole world began to spin out of control. She teetered with dizziness and fell to the ground, and the flowers engulfed her, growing in a rapid frenzy to bury her body beneath a flood of blood-red waves.

Flora awoke from the dream suddenly, gasping for air. Her body was drenched with sweat and her heart raced. Then a scraping sound wrenched her gaze over to the far side of the crannog. She groped with her eyes through the dim light and twisting shadows, trying desperately to separate fantasy from reality. Just then, a dark figure rose up out of the floor, and Flora shrank back in terror. She tried to scream, but the nightmare had robbed her of breath, and the shriek was choked off deep in her throat. Instinctively, she rolled off of the bed and began scrambling toward the back door. The specter crouched, turned in her direction, and began stealthily inching toward her.

Just as she reached the curtain that concealed the rear exit of the crannog, she heard a voice calling out to her in hushed tones.

"Shhh. Shhh. Flora, it's me. It's Domhnull."

The voice was sweet music to her ears. In an instant, her panic ebbed, and she collapsed to the ground, gasping for breath.

"Domhnull. Oh, Domhnull. You scared me to death. I thought you were—"

"Shhh. Shhh. Keep your voice down. The guards outside will hear you."

She could just barely make out his face in the dim light cast off by the coals in the fire circle. He slowly made his way over to her and lifted her into his arms.

He was dripping wet, but Flora grasped onto him and held him more tightly than ever before. She clung to him as if he were the only tiny scrap of her past life that still existed. Indeed, that may have been true, in a way. And then she suddenly realized how he had addressed her. He had called her "Flora." Not Fiona. Not *Taghte*. But Flora. She buried her face into his chest and wept.

"Shhh. Shhh. There now, my darlin'. It's okay. I'm here. Everything's gonna be okay."

He continued to hold her in his strong, tender arms until her sobs subsided and her tremors ceased. Then he bent his head down, found her lips with his, and kissed her deeply. A flush washed over her body and she melted into his embrace, returning his kiss with the hungry desperation of a woman drowning in a well of sorrows. He threaded his fingers through her hair and cradled her head in his palm, while his tongue probed deep into her mouth and danced with her own.

Flora floated through the air, buoyed by Domhnull's passion and the heat rising in her breast. She felt safe in his arms—safe from the lurking assassins who sought to take her life, and safe from the hidden forces stalking through the shadows that threatened to steal her sanity. Then slowly, gently, he drew back from her and guided her down to sit on the floor.

Domhnull spoke in hushed tones. "Sorry to frighten you. I just had to see you, and there didn't seem to be any other way."

"How did you get in here? Past the guards?" Flora looked up at her betrothed with a sudden look of shock. "And past the spirit fence. Oh, Domhnull. You didn't cross the fence! It's very powerful magic. You–" Her voice had risen in both intensity and volume, and Domhnull covered her mouth to stifle the noise.

"Shhh. They'll hear you." Slowly, he removed his hand, but held her eyes with his own. "No. I didn't cross the fence."

"But how–?"

"There's a door in the floor over there. When they used to shelter young lambs and goats in here to protect them from wolves, the pens were over agains that far wall. They used the small door to sweep the dung and fowled flooring into the loch." He smiled and motioned his head back toward the trap door. "I climbed up from the water below, so I did not, in fact, cross the spirit fence." He grinned again with a self-satisfied look, apparently pleased with his cleverness.

"How did you know about it?" she whispered.

"I have a friend on the Great Chief's special detail, named Alisdaire, who grew up in *Incheskadyne*. His father is a carpenter and helps to maintain all the crannogs near here. They have to sink new support beams into the bottom of the loch every so often, because the old ones shift in the tide. Anyway, he helped his father's crew put the new supports in a few years ago and discovered the old trap door. He knew I wanted to see you, so he told me about the secret entrance."

"I'm so happy you're here. You can't possibly know what it's been like." Flora reached out and wrapped her arms around his broad shoulders, drawing herself close against him. "But, this is a huge risk. I don't know what they'll do to you, or to us both, if they find you in here. No men are permitted to be alone with me. And only druids approved by Bhatair Rhu, himself, are allowed past the spirit fence."

"Exactly. No one would ever suspect I could get inside. So they would never even think to look. I'm pretty sure we're safe. Besides, I had to see you. I miss you so much. I had to hold you."

Flora's mind raced. She was dizzy with joy to be held in Domhnull's strong arms once again. But thoughts of their situation gnawed at her conscience.

"Domhnull, I'm supposed to become Brigid, a goddess. I'm betrothed to Bres. How can I do that and still marry you?"

"I don't know. I don't know what to think. I'm a warrior, not a druid. How does that even work? How exactly does someone become a goddess? Does Eliavres say some kind of incantation and touch you with his silver staff or something?"

Flora twisted her brow and pressed her cheek against his chest. "I don't know, actually. I never thought to ask the Arch Druid about how it happens. I've just been shocked at the idea it could happen at all." She turned her face up to his. "But what about us?"

Domhnull pushed back a little and ran his hands across the top of his head in frustration. "I don't know what to think. But I know I don't want to lose you. You're my heart. You're my strength. You're the reason I train harder and fight harder than all the other men. I want to be the best warrior in the whole tribe, all for you. I want to be worthy of your love."

"Oh, Domhnull, don't ever think that. You don't have to earn my love, you already have it. You don't have to win me in battle, I'm already yours."

"Except, now you're not. You'll be a bride, but not *my* bride. You'll be a goddess and live in the Otherworld with Bres. You'll lie in his bed and have his children."

"No. No, it's not like that."

"Then what is it like? Tell me that's not what's happening here."

"I don't know. I just don't know. But I'm absolutely certain of one thing. They can change my name and they might even be able to make me into a goddess, somehow. But they can't change who I am inside. And they can't give my heart to someone else. My heart is mine to give, and I've already given it to you."

Domhnull had been twiddling with a clump of bracken straw in his fingers. Then he stopped and flicked it across the room, where it dropped and lay still on one of the ornate rugs.

"So what do we do?"

"I don't know." Flora hung her head and breathed out a sigh of resignation. "What can we do?"

Domhnull shook his head several times. "I'm not gonna to let this happen. I'll figure something out. Lughnasadh is still almost a full moon away. I'll think of something by then."

He turned toward Flora and took her back into his arms. She could see a fierce determination in his eyes, and she loved him all the more for it. It didn't seem likely that he would be able to fulfill his promise. But she pulled together a tiny bit of hope and tucked it deep down inside where it could keep her going. Maybe he *would* find a way to make everything right again—to change everything back to the way it was before.

A thought struck Flora, and a spark of possibility kindled an idea. "How did you get to the trap door?"

"I swam from the shore and climbed up the support beams. Why?"

"Can you get me out that way?"

"No, Flora. No, it's way too dangerous."

"Why not? I can climb. And I can swim."

"But if you get caught outside, *with me*—"

"What exactly will they do?"

Domhnull shrugged. "I don't know. But it couldn't be good."

"Well, they won't catch me with you, anyway. I don't need you to come with me. I just need you to sneak me out to the shore and then back in again. The rest of the time, we won't be together."

"I don't know. I don't like it. There's too much risk."

"You took a risk to come here."

"But that risk is just to *me*, not to you."

"Well I'm prepared to take the chance of getting caught, if it means we could be together again. I want my old life back. I want you back. I don't want to be a goddess. They can find someone else."

"I'm not sure exactly how this all works, but I don't think that's possible. What are you planning to do if I get you to shore?"

"I can't tell you that. You'll just have to trust me. But I think it might be our only chance."

"I'll think about it."

"No. Don't think about it. Just come tomorrow night and get me to the shore. And if you have any doubts, think about *this* instead." She tilted her head up and kissed him with a long, wet, passionate kiss.

When they finally broke their embrace, his smile was broad and his eyes were on fire. "Okay. Okay. You win. That's a powerful motivation. I'll figure out a way and come to you."

He moved back toward the trap door and she followed, her hand resting lightly on his waist.

"I have to go. If they discover I'm gone, they'll start asking questions I can't answer."

"But you'll be back tomorrow night to get me out, right?"

Domhnull nodded, hesitantly. "Tomorrow night."

He drew her in to one long, final embrace, then pulled back and disappeared through the door and down a support beam. Flora listened closely but couldn't hear as he slipped into the water and stroked silently away toward the shore. Then her mind started racing with plans. She lay back down in the bed of furs but couldn't even begin to fall asleep.

THE NEXT MORNING, after another ritual cleansing in the Pool of Brigid's Tears, which again appeared to have no effect on her, Flora received a visit from Bhatair Rhu. He arrived during a lull between rain showers, accompanied by Eliavres. They dismissed Flora's mother and the apprentices, but indicated that Nandag should stay. Apparently, not even Bhatair Rhu, himself, could speak to her without a woman present.

Flora wondered what had prompted the Arch Druid's visit, and what had caused him to dismiss her attendants. Her heart quickened and she struggled to maintain a calm demeanor as her mind wrestled with the possibilities. Had they discovered Domhnull's midnight foray? If so, what would the consequences be? Or had Finnan's wound been more serious than she thought? Would Manas be replaced as the overseer of her preparations because he allowed her to be put in danger? Could it have been her performance at the *Inauguration* ceremony and the frenzy that resulted? None of these boded well for her situation. Then again, perhaps they would deem her to be an unfit candidate and let her go home.

Bhatair Rhu smiled with his usual amiable grin, but it didn't set her mind at ease. Her hands unconsciously fretted with the cuffs on the loose sleeves of her *leine*. Eliavres wore his typical expression of stern reproach, as if he were constantly analyzing everything around him and disapproved of what he saw.

"Fiona, *Taghte*, I trust you slept well," said the Arch Druid.

Flora grimaced. They knew about Domhnull. She was less concerned for herself than for the consequences to her one-time fiancé. It would also put a swift end to any plans he might devise to free her and restore their relationship.

"No, actually. I did not sleep well. Apparently, there are people trying to kill me. So my mind was not exactly at ease."

"Yes. I can see how that might be a bit disconcerting. We seem to have misjudged the level of security required. You can rest assured. We have doubled the size of your guard detail and positioned warriors in boats off the back side of the crannog. Though, I doubt anyone was trying to kill you. It's more likely they would want to abduct you and take advantage of your special status."

Flora breathed a sigh of relief. Maybe they had not found out about Domhnull after all.

Bhatair Rhu apparently mistook her reaction for one of reassurance about her safety and continued on.

"This all just affirms the powerful response of the gods and the villagers at the *Inauguration*. We could not have hoped for a better outcome."

"A better outcome? What could you possibly mean? That crowd went crazy. As soon as the staff caught fire it ignited them into a mob. I thought they would tear me apart."

"It wasn't the staff, though that did have a nice effect. No, it was the ray of sunshine that split the clouds and rested directly on you. You probably couldn't tell from your vantage point, but the image it presented was stunning. You were positively bathed in radiance from the heavens. It was a clear and distinct sign of approval from Lugh, himself."

"But the people went crazy. That can't be good."

Bhatair Rhu's smile broadened and he shook his head slightly, as if he were laughing at a naive little child. "On the contrary, that is extraordinary. We need that kind of passion. We need the people to react in awe and wonder at the signs from the gods."

Flora thought back to Finnan's "dirty little secret" in their conversation in the boat. "You mean, you need the people to honor and worship the gods so they don't lose influence and power in this world." It was a statement of fact, not a question.

The ArchDruid was taken aback slightly, and Eliavres' frown deepened. "Ahh. You seem to be more perceptive than I've given you credit for. Indeed, the gods need the worship of our people in order to have the power necessary to effect your transformation and restore balance to the system."

"Worship? Or fear?" Flora blurted out the words without thinking.

Bhatair Rhu's smile faded ever so slightly. Then he snorted cheerfully. "Hmm. Even so." He paused for a moment, then continued. "In any event, we will allow the fervor to temper a bit before opening access to petitioners."

Flora looked at him quizzically. "Opening access to petitioners? What does that mean?"

"Well, my dear, you will soon be their goddess. The people will want to seek your blessing and pay homage to you, so you will remember them favorably when you take up your mantle in the Otherworld."

Flora groaned. She hated being the center of attention. She really didn't like crowds. She preferred to deal with people one-on-one or in small groups. She certainly didn't want to be put up on some kind of throne and receive a waiting line of hopeful people seeking the blessings of Brigid.

This was all some huge mistake. Surely the gods knew. Surely they knew she *could not be* the pure mistress, the immaculate bride. She was dirty. She was tainted. She was defiled. Surely the gods must know. She could not let this charade continue.

"I... I can't—"

"Of course you can't grant blessings yet." Bhatair Rhu misunderstood her hesitance. "You have not yet become the goddess. But you can accept the petitions of the people for such a time when your transformation is complete. It will give the people hope."

"I'm..." The words stuck in her throat. Then she thought about what Domhnull had asked her the night before. "How exactly does that transformation happen, anyway. You said the gods chose me to become Brigid, but you never indicated how that will occur. The cleansing baths don't seem to be having any effect as far as I can tell."

Bhatair Rhu studied her for several breaths, as if he were deciding how to address her question. But Eliavres broke in and pushed the conversation forward.

"The transformation is the work of an instant. It doesn't proceed slowly over time. Brigid is the goddess of the springs. On the appointed day, you will walk into the holy waters of a spring as a mortal woman and emerge in the Otherworld as a goddess."

It took a few moments of reflection before Eliavres' words sunk in. "You mean, I will drown myself in a spring?"

Bhatair Rhu took the conversation back into his own hands. "A goddess cannot drown. But yes, you must shed this mortal shell to take on immortality. The gods will cause the metamorphosis to occur, like a butterfly emerging from its cocoon. I assure you, the moment will be the most exhilarating experience of your life."

"How do you know all of this? Please forgive me if I'm skeptical of your assurance. You're asking me to drown myself."

Bhatair Rhu breathed a deep sigh and shook his head. "Don't trust me. Trust the gods."

"You didn't answer my question. How do you know? How do you know this is what the gods want? How can you be sure?"

Bhatair Rhu smiled a wan, thin lipped smile, then said, "My mother. My mother has been through the experience—not exactly the same, but very similar. She has crossed between the two worlds. She has taken on flesh and left it behind. I trust her, and so can you."

Flora paced back and forth in front of the two druids. "Assume I do trust you. Assume I walk into a sacred spring and drown myself."

Eliavres cleared his throat in a gesture of admonition.

"Alright. Alright. Suppose I do walk through a watery portal into the Otherworld, shedding my mortal body and transforming into a goddess. If all that happens in an instant, then why all the rituals on this side? Why all the cleansing baths, and the *Annunciation* rites, and the *Inauguration* ceremonies? What is the point of all this pomp? Do the gods have to be certain they didn't make a mistake—that they didn't make the wrong choice?"

"No. They did not make a mistake. You are Fiona *Taghte*. You are the Chosen One. The preparation time is for you. It's all for you."

"For me?"

"For the people, in part. But mostly for you. You must decide that you want to become a goddess. The Bride must be willing."

A vague memory tugged at the back of Flora's mind. It was something she had heard, but couldn't quite place where.

Eliavres echoed Bhatair Rhu's declaration, "The Bride *must* be willing."

When she heard Eliavres speaking, the memory crystalized in Flora's thoughts. She knew where the recollection came from, and it made her blood run cold. Back in *An Dun Gael* she had heard Eliavres' voice echoing up the stone staircase making a similar proclamation—similar, but different in a very important way.

Flora spit out a bitter retort. "You mean sacrifice, right? The bride must be a willing *sacrifice*."

Bhatair Rhu shot a quick, irritated glance at Eliavres, but rapidly regained his composure. "Of course it is a sacrifice. To become a goddess—to transform into Brigid—you must be willing to give up this life completely. You have to take everything that's most important to you and leave it behind. Your family. Your village. Your loves and desires. You must sacrifice them all for the sake of what you will become."

"Why? Why do I have to give it all up? Why would I even want to?"

"You remember your ordeals—the visions of horror and desolation from the gods? That's why. Those weren't just fanciful delusions. If Brigid is not replaced, and if the cycle is not restored, then winter will come and chaos will reign. You are the *only one* who can re-establish the natural order. *You* are Fiona *Taghte. You* are the Chosen One. But the Bride must be willing. You must choose. Will you be Flora, an insignificant healer in a minor clan in the village of Bunrannoch. Or will you be the goddess, Brigid, savior of her people and healer of her land? Only you can decide."

With that, Bhatair Rhu and Eliavres turned on their heels and strode out the doorway into the drizzling rain, leaving Flora to contemplate the import of what they had revealed.

NANDAG EMERGED from the shadows where she had been waiting while Flora spoke to Eliavres and Bhatair Rhu.

"It must not seem fair, mistress."

"No. No, it does not seem fair. Oh, Nandag, what did I do to bring this impossible situation on myself. What god did I anger? Which of the fates did I offend?"

"Some people might consider it an honor—to become a goddess." Nandag was twisting something in her hands that Flora could not see.

"But how do I know it is even real? How do I know that I won't walk into that pond and just drown? What if the spring is not a portal to the Otherworld, but only the entrance to my own watery tomb?"

"The signs from the gods have been very potent. You saw Brigid's star in the sky with your own eyes. You participated in the sacred rites that were used to divine the will of the gods those many years ago. And you alone experienced the terror that will result if the gap is not filled and the balance is not restored. Those all seem to be powerful omens which should provide some sense of certainty. Are you sure that's all? Is something else bothering you?"

"What if the gods made a mistake? What if I'm not the right one? What if I can't be what they are asking me to be? Surely there's someone else better suited to the task."

She turned slightly away from Nandag, afraid her old mentor might see through the expression on her face and read the dark thoughts that afflicted her mind.

"What would make you such a bad choice? The young woman I know is a gifted healer, with a deep love of her family and a compassion for her people. What better qualities would suit someone to be a goddess?"

"But it's not just any goddess. It's Brigid."

"Ahh. And you were already promised to that young warrior. Is that it?"

Seeing an opportunity to steer away from the real issue, Flora took up the thread of Nandag's conjecture and used it to weave a way out of the conversation. It was true, even if it wasn't her most pressing concern. "I do love Domhnull very much. Life with him would have been so simple. He is a strong fighter. He would be a good protector for our children. He might even become the village chief in time. I could raise sons and daughters for him, and teach them the healing arts. I know that might sound rather plain and ordinary. But for me, its all I really ever wanted—a home, a family, a good man to love, and a chance to serve my people."

Nandag finished fiddling with the object in her hands and held it out to Flora. She had woven a twist of river rushes into a three pointed cross—one of Brigid's symbols that young maidens carried at the Imbolc feast and that people displayed on their doors to keep evil out of their homes.

"Do you remember bearing one of these through the village during the spring festival? For some girls acting as Brigid's representative is a fearsome chore. For others, it is an excuse to show off and a display of foolish pride. But for you, it was something different, something natural, as if you were born to the role. I don't think the gods chose you for anything special you've done. I think they chose you for who you are, deep down inside. And the very fact you hesitate to embrace the calling is, perhaps, a testimony to the wisdom of their selection. You're not the kind of person who would use the power of the goddess to make onerous demands of our people. No, you will use that power to serve."

Flora wished Nandag's words were true. But she looked into her own dark heart, blotted with a black and evil stain, and turned away to hide the dreadful truth from her mentor.

Flora intentionally changed the subject. "Nandag, what kind of flowers have bright red petals with black centers and clusters of seeds in the middle?"

"Why, there are many such flowers here in the highlands. Cowberry, bearberry, lousewort, marsh cinquefoil, sheep's sorrel, and even red clover. I'm sure there are others as well. What makes you ask?"

Flora thought she sensed a slight tentativeness in her teacher's voice, but it could have just been an imagined phantom dredged up by her own expectations. "No, I know all of those. You taught me many of them. Others I already recognized from when I was a child. This one is quite distinctive, and I suspect it has medical uses."

A voice behind Flora startled her. She spun to see Finnan several paces inside the door.

"I believe it's the poppy you're describin'. Or so it seems to me. As for medical uses, well–"

Nandag interjected. "It could be that, yes. In certain circumstances, these plants can have some medicinal uses."

Flora turned to look at Nandag when she spoke and briefly saw a scowl disappear from the older woman's face.

"What the good healer is meaning' to say is that the pretty red flowers can be used to control pain, but it takes huge fields of them to get enough of the juice to be effective, and that precious liquid, the milk of the poppy, generally has a more sought after purpose."

"And what would that be?" Flora asked.

"Why, it is the key ingredient in the elixir of the gods—a powerful tonic that enables our oracles and seers to communicate with the immortal rulers of the Otherworld."

"But it can also be very dangerous," Nandag cautioned. "It must be mixed very carefully, in precise ratios with other moderating herbs."

"Or what?" Flora prompted her to continue. "What can happen if the mixture is not properly prepared."

"If it is not made correctly, the elixir can cause death," Nandag replied.

"Oh, not just death. A nasty, horrible death. It will cause a man to go mad—to see horrific visions which cause such terror his heart will explode if he doesn't first dash his own brains out with a rock. It's a rather disturbing sight, I'm afraid."

"And *that* is the special, valuable use of the poppy plants, this elixir of the gods?" Flora asked.

"Yes," Nandag affirmed.

"That, and its power to open the mind, which can also be quite helpful in certain situations," Finnan again interjected.

Flora noted how free Finnan was to share information, while Nandag seemed much more reserved.

"What does that mean? To open the mind?" She inquired of the bard.

"Well, many suspect that it is all one and the same thing as conversing with the gods—that it is, indeed, the gods themselves who speak through lower doses of the elixir to reveal truth."

Flora looked at him quizzically, and he continued.

"You see, when the milk of the poppy is administered in controlled amounts, it can open the mind to... How would you say it? ...to suggestions. In such cases it can prompt people to disclose truths which they might not otherwise wish to reveal. You can, I assume, see the usefulness of such a quality for interrogating prisoners."

Flora reflected on what Finnan said for a moment. "Could it open the mind of someone to see things that weren't real?"

"Well, now. There're your treading on a fine line. Certainly people see visions when they imbibe the elixir. But are those simply wiles of the imagination, or are they truly revelations from the gods? The wisest among us contend it is the latter."

Nandag interjected herself back into the conversation. "You didn't answer my question. Why do you ask about this particular flower?"

Flora ignored her mentor and pressed forward with questions of her own. "Do these flowers grow in great fields? Fields that stretch as far as the eye can see?"

"Aye. They can. Though they have usually been planted in that case. I don't think they would occur in large groups naturally."

"Where do they grow that way? Where are they planted in great fields?"

"Why, in *Gleann Dubh nan Garbh Clac* of course—the Black Glen of the Crooked Stones. The druid community relies on the elixir of the gods for oracles and divination. It is critical to their task of communicating with the Otherworld."

"You mean *Gleann-Linne*? I know it as the Valley of Lakes and Pools."

"The very same. Though there can be much in a name. Choose whichever you wish."

"Poppies grow there? In great fields?"

"They are cultivated by druids, along with the help of the *Searbhantan*—those who serve. Mind you, the flowers don't really like our wet, marshy weather. They come from hot, dry lands. So it takes some work to get them to grow here."

Flora turned her attention back to Nandag. "I saw them in a dream. Great fields of these poppy flowers. They pulled me down and covered me, like I was drowning in a huge red sea. So explain that to me. How do I have visions of flowers that I have never seen before—flowers with the special power to open minds and to channel revelations from the gods?"

Flora abruptly turned her back to both of her companions. She flushed with a sudden rage that she did not quite understand—rage mixed with confusion.

She heard Nandag's flat, impassive reply. "I'm sure I don't know, mistress. I'm a healer, not a sage."

"I," offered Finnan, "am a bard and not a sage. But my question to you is why you would *not* dream of such a thing. If you are to become a goddess, why should your mind not be open to visions from the gods?"

∾

FLORA AGAIN MARVELED at the similarity between Finnan's voice and the one from her ordeals. They had to be the same. She was certain of it. But she knew nothing about this man. She had never met him before in her life.

She turned and walked closer to Finnan. "How's your wound? Are you okay?"

"Ahh, yes. They told me I would be writing great songs and sagas about you, mistress. But I didn't know I'd be called upon to take arrows for you as well. However, Manas assures me I will mend quite handily."

"Thank you for that. For taking an arrow for me. I may owe you my life."

"Not at all. The rascals might actually have been targeting me all along. Who's to say? Manas was quite complimentary about the temporary bandage you applied to the laceration in my side. Perhaps it was you who saved my life." Finnan twisted his mouth up into a lopsided grin and canted his head in her direction in an odd sort of bow.

"Well then, we both seem to have done our best to serve the other. Tell me about yourself, Master Bard. Why were you chosen above all the minstrels in the land to write my story into song? Forgive me for saying it, but you look a bit too young to be the most accomplished musician from all the tribes. Do you share the Arch Druid's affliction?"

Nandag had faded into the background again, though Flora knew her old *bean-teagaisg* would be keeping a watchful eye on them both from the shadows.

"So Bhatair Rhu told you his own tale, did he? I should guess he might have done."

"And yours?" Flora prompted.

"No. I am not the supposed offspring of a king and a goddess. I just happen to be fanciful with words. And I've a good memory, they say."

Flora noticed his use of the term "supposed" when alluding to Bhatair Rhu's parentage, but decided not to pull on that thread. Instead, she prompted Finnan for more detail about himself. "And?"

"And I've traveled quite extensively, though not all it being of mine own accord."

"Perhaps you could fill me in on the whole account of Finnan, the Legend Weaver. I expect we have the time. The Arch Druid assured me I would not engage in another outing today."

"Well, if you must know the whole sordid tale...though I'm not so sure it's worth the tellin'. Of course you'll be aware, I hail from Eire."

"So the Arch Druid has said."

"Well I started out there. I had shown some affinity for lyrics and tunes when I was a wee lad, so the druids stole me away for training at an early age. I did so love to learn the sagas and the tales. And I was quite handy with a lyre and a flute, if I do say so myself. The tunes seemed to make it all so much easier to remember. Within a few summers' time, the masters told me I had well-nigh committed all the lore of our homeland to my mind, so they conspired to send me across the narrow sea to study the history of the Caledonian tribes."

"That sounds like quite a feat. How old were you, then?"

"Oh, just a tike on the way to becoming a man. On your own

island, fair, I quickly came to discover that we share a similar heritage. The stories are much the same, all the names just being changed. Same miraculous acts of the gods, but on different hills and in different dales, and with different heroes performing the deeds. Eventually, I was able to sort out how all the bits fit together to form the bigger picture. There's no doubt in my mind that our tribes and yours share a common legacy which has been woven afresh in every village and every home to make it fit into the local garb. I wondered if it might be the same south of the wall."

Flora stared at Finnan with a scowl on her face, aghast at what he implied.

"You mean you went to the Roman territory? Surely they don't share our heritage? They stole our lands. They renounced our gods and brutalized our people. The Romans can't be our brothers from ancient times. Is that what you thought?"

"Nay, mistress. Not the Romans. You're getting ahead of the story. I meant the people in the hinterlands of the west—the ones in those wild, borderless regions which the Romans claim as their own, but don't actually rule. If it weren't for the tin mines, the Romans would've left there long ago. It is a land called Cymru, and the people there speak a tongue quite similar to ours."

"You mean the people of the south who surrendered to the Romans?"

"Actually, they're people much like our own, who have not quite given up the struggle. Anyway, their own legends tell much the same tales as yours and mine, but with different names and different tunes. Those stories fascinated me, and I learned to spin them all."

Flora could tell this would take a while, so she sat down on her bed of furs and bid the bard to take a seat on a bench not far away.

"How were you able to travel south of the wall, anyway? I didn't think the Romans allowed it."

"Well, by boat, of course. There's still a bit of trade takin' place, north to south and back. And bards have a sort of special status, if you will."

"But the Romans hate the druids. Why do they allow druid bards to travel freely across the border?"

"Aye, they hate the druids. But they think they destroyed them ten generations ago. And they don't know that bards are part of the druidic orders. They think we're traveling entertainers. But mostly, they like to hear the stories we tell about the tribes to the north of the wall. They think if they can understand our stories, they'll know how to conquer us, when the time comes."

Something Finnan said piqued Flora's curiosity. "You said they destroyed the druids ten generations ago. What do you mean?"

"I said they *thought* to have destroyed the druids, and indeed, they nearly did. Our Arch Druid didn't tell you that part of his tale, then?"

"Apparently not."

"Well, I shall digress for a moment, by your leave." Flora nodded enthusiastically, and he continued. "Before the Romans came to the isles of Britannia, the bardic school for the whole world was on an island off the coast of Cymru, which the local people call Ynys Mon. Young apprentices came from all over the known world—yea, even from across the great sea—to study from the wisest masters of their time."

Flora unconsciously leaned in closer, fascinated by these sorts of ancient stories.

"From encounters in the lands of Gaul and Germania—"

"Wait, from where?"

"From lands across the great sea called Gaul and Germania. These are places far from here, and near to the Roman homeland. The people in these places worship the old gods, just as our ancestors have for generations. And, like us, they have druids who interpret omens, divine the future, decipher oracles, judge the laws, and preserve the heritage and lore of the tribes. The Roman generals soon discovered that druids were the link between the people and the gods and were, thus, the true power within the tribes. They reckoned if they could destroy the druids, they could conquer our lands."

"And they tried to destroy the druid school on–" Flora fumbled to remember the name of the island Finnan had just mentioned.

"Ynys Mon. Aye, they did indeed. And by all accounts they succeeded. Mind you, their soldiers feared the wrath of the gods for attacking such a holy place. But their commanders forced them on, driven by their mad general, Suetonius Paulinus, to show no mercy. The druid masters, dressed in black robes, formed giant circles in the clearings and around the sacred groves, calling on the power of the gods to avenge them. And a contingent of warriors, men and women alike, lined the shores. But they were no match for the power of the Roman legion crossing the channel in thousands of boats. Once it began, the slaughter was horrific. There are somber dirges put to morose tunes which describe the scenes in great detail, but few can bear to sing them, except in the gravest of times."

"Do you..." Flora began, but then hesitated. "Do you know these songs?"

"Aye, for certain. But I care not to share them unless I must."

Flora shook her head, not wanting to reawaken the torrid memories of her own ordeals. Instead, she turned the conversation back to the present situation. "You said this had something to do with Bhatair Rhu. How does he fit in to it all?"

"Well, you see, Bhatair Rhu was an accomplished adept in the school at Ynys Mon at the time, so the story goes. When defeat looked certain, the Arch Druid and master of the center, *Ard-Draoidh Naomh Teine*, charged Bhatair Rhu to lead a small remnant—the most capable young adepts from every druidic discipline—to escape the island and flee north to a sanctuary in the wilderness. There he would restart the druidic school and prepare for the time when the Romans could be driven from the islands for good, and when the old gods would again rule Britannia. Or, so the story goes."

"*Feart Choille*, the Forest Stronghold," Flora whispered. "They came to Gleann-Linne, didn't they?"

Finnan nodded, gravely. "Aye. To *Gleann Dubh nan Garbh Clac*, the Black Glen of the Crooked Stones. To *Cridhalbane*, the Heart of

Alban. It is the safest, most desolate place in all the highlands and the islands—a sanctuary with mountain walls and ramparts of stone, where a sacred yew, *Cridhmathairnaomh*—" Flora heard a gasp from the shadows at the use of the sacred yew tree's secret power name, but Finnan ignored the exclamation and continued, "—the most ancient living thing in all the world, pumps its lifeblood throughout the land. Bhatair Rhu led them *here*. Or so the story goes."

Flora noted Finnan's repeated use of that phrase and gave him a quizzical look. "It's true, though, isn't it? The story?"

Finnan grunted. "Truth? Ahh, young Mistress, what is truth? What indeed?" The Master Bard looked introspective for several long moments.

Flora realized she was holding her breath, waiting for him to continue, but he didn't elaborate further on the curious comment.

"Well, back to mine own tale," he began again in a cheerier tone. "Unfortunately, as things may happen to occur, I chanced to be at an alehouse in the countryside of Cymru, among the company of some bright, fine lassies—studying the local lore, of course—when a Roman patrol came knockin' at the door. It seems they were rather taken with the young ladies of my acquaintance, and decided we should all accompany them to their camp, just a few days' walk away. The leader of the troop kept asking questions about a band of cattle thieves roaming the land, which we, naturally, had no knowledge of. But he thought maybe his own centurion might want to confirm that fact for himself, so off we went to a place in the Roman dialect called Segontium."

Flora mouthed the word, awkwardly. "Segontium." It tasted strange to her tongue.

"Aye, that's the place. Anyway, I sang a couple of tunes for the pleasure of the commander, and he decided I might be a useful source of information, so he kept me on with his unit, even after they rotated out of that camp to other stations of duty."

"You were a slave, then? A slave to the Romans?" Flora spat the words out as if they left a foul taste in her mouth.

"I suppose it depends on how you look at it. They wanted me for the knowledge in my head. So they fed me well and didn't force me to labor. But I wasn't exactly free to come and go as I chose. So, yes, in that respect I was a bit of a captive."

"And you gave them the information they asked for? You told them the secrets of the tribes? You divulged the sacred ancient lore?" Flora could not hide the hint of accusation in her tone, but Finnan apparently took no offense.

"Oh, dear. I'm afraid you misunderstand the calling of a bard. Our role is to preserve the heritage of the tribes in sagas and songs and to spread those tales far and wide. Such accounts of the power of the gods and the valor of our heroes enhance the reputation of our people and strike fear into the hearts of our enemies. Most of our lore is intended to be shared abroad with vigor and zeal. And so I sang those tunes for the Romans with great delight, for they magnified the renown of our highland warriors in the eyes of our foes."

Flora still balked at the idea that Finnan gave up the tribe's information so readily, especially to the Romans. "But the ancient lore, the sacred power names, the–"

"Oh, no, mistress. Those things are not for sharing outside of the tribes. The sagas provide a tantalizing sample. But the secret of the sauce remains buried deep in the minds of the druid community, not to be disclosed."

Flora felt a bit relieved, but her revulsion of the Romans with all they had done to her people and their land always made her tense, uneasy, and bitter. She flicked a bit of ash from her sleeve which had drifted over from the fire circle in the middle of the crannog.

"How did you escape?"

"Well, I suppose that might have to be a story for another day. It appears our host has arrived." Finnan nodded to Manas, who strode purposefully through the door, and came to a halt about three paces in front of Flora.

"*Thaghadh.*" Manas bowed his head in Flora's direction. Flora glanced at Finnan to see if he reacted to the slightly different title

Manas used to address her—"One Who Chooses" rather than "the Chosen One." If Finnan noted the distinction, he didn't show it in any way.

"Master Bard." Manas nodded toward Finnan, then returned his gaze to Flora before continuing. "We have increased the security arrangements in accordance with the Arch Druid's instructions. You will be quite safe from now on. Please forgive the inadequate preparations which had been made prior to yesterday's incident."

"Who was it, Manas? Who attacked our boat? What were they trying to do?" The words spewed out of Flora's mouth in a flood of anxiety and curiosity.

"I'm afraid we don't know for certain, but the circumstances are somewhat disturbing. The arrows came from Druid Island, the ancient, overgrown crannog I told you about on our journey back from the ceremony."

"Druid Island?" Flora asked, incredulously. "Why would druids try to kill us?"

"I doubt that druids actually loosed the shafts. It is not our way. But whoever it was could not have been there in force without the help and knowledge of the custodians of the island shrine. It's quite disturbing. However, I doubt they were trying to kill you, mistress. I expect they wanted to take you captive. Fortunately, we didn't row as close to the island as they had anticipated. We were too far out of range for their weapons to be effective."

"Captive? Why would someone want to take me captive."

Manas eyed her intensely before responding. "You truly don't understand, do you?"

"No!" Flora blurted out in frustration. "I don't understand. Make me understand!"

"As *Ard-Draoidh* Bhatair Rhu explained to you earlier, our people believe mighty forces are at work among the gods, and you are the key to the power struggle. They surmise that only you can fill the gap in the cycle and restore the balance. *Only you.* So whichever faction has possession of you, has the most leverage in the conflict."

Flora threw her hands up in exasperation. "Why me? Why does it have to be me? Why not some other girl from among the tribes? Surely there is someone else who could fill the role. What is so special about *me*?"

Manas looked past her as if he were gazing through the very thatch of the crannog's roof and into the depths of the heavens, so that he might discern the will of the gods. Then he shook his head. "Each conclusion follows the next in the Council's chain of reasoning. You are Fiona *Taghte*. You are the Chosen One. The cycle is ending. There is no time to select another. The gods have chosen you."

"I thought I was '*Thaghadh*' to you. I thought the choice was mine to make."

Finnan's eyebrows lifted in response to her remark. She could tell he was listening intently to Manas' reply.

"You are both. According to the oracles and seers, the gods have chosen you. That is done. But you must also choose."

"Yes, I know. The Bride must be willing. Eliavres has made that abundantly clear. And Bhatair Rhu has likewise made it perfectly clear that if I refuse this calling, then winter will come, chaos will reign, and the curses from my ordeals will be released upon our land. So it doesn't seem like I really have a lot of options. Some choice!"

Flora turned her back to the men so they would not see the tears pricking at the corners of her eyes. But Flora noticed that Nandag, concealed in the shadows, caught her downcast look. Nandag undoubtedly saw what Flora tried to hide from the men. Did Nandag also see what Flora hid deep inside her soul?

"Nonetheless, you must still choose. And I sense you have not yet crossed that threshold in your own mind. It will come, in time."

Flora still faced away, tossing the question over her shoulder at the Master Healer. "Well if I'm so important, why would the opposing side try to capture me? Wouldn't it be better if I were dead?"

"No. I'm afraid it's more complicated than that. Neither side actually wants chaos to rule. The diviners tell us the Cailleach would like for winter to come and never end, so her domain would hold eternal sway over the seasons of men. Accordingly, she and her compatriots—Tyrannus, Arawn, Babd Catha, and Bel—don't want the cycle to be broken either. They just want to control it. And if they control Brigid, they can manipulate the cycle as they see fit."

Flora turned toward him now, the tears replaced with a bitter petulance which she didn't bother to hide. "So this whole great wheel of gods and men and worship and seasons all turns or fails on the choice of one apprentice healer from the village of Bunrannoch? It seems to be a rather fragile apparatus indeed."

"Just so." Manas nodded.

"Then why shouldn't I just allow it all to fall apart? Why not just permit the whole order to devolve into chaos?"

"Because you are an apprentice healer from the village of Bunrannoch." Manas echoed her own words back to her. "Because it is against your nature to consign your family, your village, your clan, and your tribe to such a fate. This is what they are counting on."

"But that's Flora, the village girl from Bunrannoch. Maybe Fiona is a different woman altogether."

"Is she? Is she indeed? Perhaps *that* is precisely the choice you have to make after all."

They stared at each other for several heartbeats, neither blinking. Indignation raged in Flora's heart—bitterness at being forced into this impossible situation. But she saw something entirely different reflected in the Master Healer's eyes. What was it? Contempt? Annoyance? Derision? No. None of those. Then Flora noticed the flicker of a sentiment which she recognized from times when her own father gazed into her eyes, and she knew it for what it truly was. Compassion. Somehow, Manas saw through to the emotions that tore at her heart, through the fear and loneliness and despair. Yet he didn't look down on her or judge her. Rather, he empathized with her. And perhaps, in his own way, he was walking with her through this trial, gently guiding her with wisdom and concern. Flora softened her expression. Whoever else Manas might be, he was not her enemy. He did not deserve her scorn.

"I'm sorry, Manas. This is not your fault. You don't deserve to be the target of my frustration. Please accept my apology."

Manas bowed his head in deference to her. "*Thaghadh*. There is nothing to forgive. I am here to serve you as I may." Then, turning to Finnan he gestured toward the doorway. "Master Bard, I believe it's time for us to go."

Flora reached for a woolen cloak and draped it about her shoulders. "Manas, let me come with you for a bit. The rain has let up, and I would like to go for a walk and get some air."

Manas turned and lifted his arm to block her way. "I'm sorry, *Thaghadh*, but it is not safe for you to go out just now. The Arch Druid insisted you stay inside until we can ensure the danger is passed. I'm afraid you will have to remain within the crannog for the moment. I'm sure your preparations will take you out and away soon enough."

"But—"

Manas just shook his head. "*Thaghadh*, please be patient. All things will happen at the appropriate time."

Frustrated, Flora took the cloak off and tossed it to the floor. Despite all the fine rugs, the elaborate furnishings, and the lavish meals, it turned out her palace was just a prison by another name. Maybe it was true the gods were battling over her life. Or maybe it wasn't. But one thing was certain, Bhatair Rhu was pulling her strings. She came and went at his behest. Well, she would see about that. When Domhnull came tonight, she would get out of this cage.

But Domhnull did not come, either that night or the next. And Flora felt trapped, abandoned, and betrayed.

CHAPTER SIXTEEN

A fter three days of being pent up inside her palace prison, Flora was about to go mad with frustration. She allowed the apprentices to lead her once again through the morning ritual of bathing in the Pool of Brigid's Tears. She never felt any different after the ceremonial cleansing and wondered about the point of it all.

She tried speaking to the apprentices on occasion, with very little success. They only ever responded with single words or short phrases, and never elaborated on their families or clans. Their typical reply was a bow of the head and a brief, "yes, *Taghte*" or "no, *Taghte*." They revered Flora and their awe made her uncomfortable. Just one turn of the moon ago, they would not have given her a second glance. Yet now, they showed her a deference reserved only for the gods.

There were four apprentices, but only two came each day. They were pretty young women, and all looked very similar, so it was sometimes difficult to tell them apart. They wore simple *liene* tunics bleached white in the sun, indicating a ceremonial purpose. Apparently, attending to Flora was considered to be a holy and ritualistic act. They also wore small white shoulder cloaks with hoods that mostly concealed their faces, though Flora caught the occasional glimpse of flaming red locks or a flash of bright green eyes. She noticed each one had the smooth, alabaster skin of a dove, unmarked by scars from the pox that afflicted most girls by the time they reached womanhood.

Flora had tried to ask their names on the very first day, but the two in waiting at the time gave each other a quick glance before responding in unison, "We are your attendants, *Taghte*. You may call us '*Brighanta*.'" This wasn't terribly helpful, as the term just meant, "Servant of Brigid." Flora soon learned that all four of them would respond to the name, so it was very difficult to specify a particular one.

Oddly, Nandag was not similarly clad. Instead of a white tunic, she wore her usual black robe, trimmed with Brigid's emblems embroidered in bright red thread. It was the same clothing she had worn in the village as Flora's mentor—the typical garb of an adept healer.

After the morning's cleansing ritual was complete, Flora again tried to engage one of her attendants in conversation, though she expected no success. "How were you chosen to serve me?" Flora asked the girl who held her hand as she rose to exit the pool. "Was it a duty you requested?"

Neither of the two responded, and Nandag quickly interjected. "These women have been preparing for this task for almost six summers, *Taghte*–, uhh, Fiona. Forgive me. They were selected from each of the four clans by the gods themselves."

Flora stepped out of the bath, her body glistening with Brigid's tears, which trickled in tiny rivulets down her cheeks, falling back into the pool and making little circular ripples across the water's shimmering surface.

"And just how did the gods indicate their choices? Did these girls experience ordeals similar to mine?"

"Nay, mistress. Each one was marked from birth."

The two adepts began scraping the water from Flora's skin with dull blades carved from deer antlers as she stood just inside the edge of the bath. None of the precious tears were to be wasted, but were carefully collected and redeposited back into the sacred spring.

"Marked?" Flora asked. "How were they marked?"

"Each has the red crescent moon of Cerridwen embossed on her inner thigh. When the druids discovered the girls among the clans, they knew they had been set apart for a holy purpose. But they didn't know the nature of that purpose until after the tribe gathering six summers ago, when Brigid's star appeared in the sky, and when the druid council learned of the broken cycle."

Flora sat on the edge of the pool and allowed the apprentices to remove the last few drops from her feet before pulling them in and hugging her knees to her chest. She pondered Nandag's words, and something struck her as odd.

"You said they were marked by Cerridwen from birth. That had to be long before the star appeared. How did the gods know they would need special apprentices even before the cycle had been broken?"

Nandag cocked her head to the side, considering the question, and finally shrugged. "I don't know, mistress. I had not thought about it before. Perhaps you should ask Eliavres or Bhatair Rhu. I am sure they would know."

Flora wasn't so sure about that, but let the question lie for now.

She rose from the edge of the bath and turned around to allow the apprentices to clothe her. But Nandag took her arm and led her toward the far side of the crannog. "Today, we have special preparations to make. Please, Fiona, lie down on this table."

Flora looked quizzically at Nandag. "What for? What is this all about?"

"There is a special ceremony today. Eliavres will give you more details when he arrives. But you will need to don the spirit armor of Brigid for this occasion."

Flora took a couple steps back and gently pulled her arm free from Nandag's grasp. "Spirit armor? I'm no warrior, and I'm certainly not going into battle. Why would I need spirit armor?"

"It is the spirit armor *of Brigid.*" Nandag stepped forward and reached for Flora's hand. "Please trust me, Fiona. All is well. The Arch Druid has instructed us to prepare you. The seers have interpreted oracles about this day. I, myself, don't know the nature of it, but they assured me it will be a great day in the course of your preparation. Please, lie down here."

Flora's instincts told her to resist. Her mind yelled at her to flee from this place, but she had nowhere to go. And though her old mentor insisted on treating her like a new person, like one who would become a goddess, she knew Nandag would not betray her. So she sat down on the edge of the table, lay back, and swung her legs up until she was prone on top of the platform.

The two apprentices stepped back into the shadows at the far side of the roundhouse and three adepts ducked through the entryway. They also wore white tunics, but with deep red hooded cloaks, which identified them not only as masters of their druidic order, but also as priestesses of Brigid. They carried silver bowls full of liquid and thin reed styluses with splayed ends. Flora guessed the bowls contained bright blue dyes made from the leaves of the woad plant.

Flora had prepared the pigment, herself, on many occasions. Healers, of course, did not use the dye to emboss spirit armor on a warrior's skin, as that was a task for a druid. But the plant's extract, when applied to open wounds, would prevent them from becoming rotten and inflamed. And, naturally, it was also quite useful for coloring wool. Her mother had shown her how to make the dye when she was a young girl, and Nandag had taught her about its healing properties.

Flora thought through the process as she lay on the table, preparing to be covered with the intricate blue interwoven designs of spirit armor. The woad leaves had to be collected during the height of summer on a warm day and only from new plants in their first year of growth. Her mother would tear the leaves into small pieces and steep them in copper bowls of simmering water while she sang the first two verses in the Saga of the Great Mother. Then she chilled the liquid rapidly by setting the bowls in the cool waters at the shore of Loch Rannoch.

After straining out the leaves, Flora's mother added fine ash from a fire pit and whisked the mixture to a froth until it turned a deep green color. She did this while singing the next two verses from the Saga of the Great Mother. Then she allowed the solution to sit, undisturbed, until the sun crossed one fourth of the sky, and the dark blue pigment settled to the bottom of the pot. Finally, she poured off the cloudy liquid on the top, leaving behind just the pure dye.

The finished extract could be used right away, or set to dry for several days. If dried, the mixture formed small flakes that could be ground with a stone and stirred into clear water to reconstitute it as a paste. The process was complicated and time-consuming, which made the dye very valuable.

"Why are there three of you?" Flora asked one of the adepts. "Isn't spirit armor usually the work of one artist?"

"Shhh, *Taghte*," Nandag cautioned her. "The ceremony is sacred, and the *Bandrui* must listen in complete silence to the voice of the gods directing their designs. Now, lie back and pray."

Flora did lie back, and she tried to pray, but her attention was constantly drawn away to the sensation of the stiff brushes tracing lines across her skin. Sometimes it tickled, and she had to concentrate hard to keep herself from pulling away. She tried to figure out what shapes they were making, but she couldn't tell from the feel alone. She would have to wait until she could see the final result.

Flora was surprised that the three adepts were working in sequence. She assumed they would each concentrate on a different portion of her body, but it seemed like each one was following the other, tracing complementary figures around what the previous one had just created.

The process went on for the greater part of the morning. Finally, they stopped scrawling lines on her skin and began chanting the *Bandia mor Chruthac*, a melody about the beginning of all things when the Great Goddess created the land. Flora kept her eyes closed, not wanting to interrupt the sacred ritual.

When the song came to an end, Flora assumed they had finished their work. Her arms and legs were cramped from lying still for so long and her naked body shivered from the cold, so she was anxious to move.

Nandag touched her lightly on the shoulder. "Please turn over, Fiona, so they can proceed with the other side."

She groaned and sat up. "Can we take a break? I'm hungry and thirsty."

"I'm afraid not, mistress. This ceremony is holy. Your body is being consecrated to the Great Goddess. Once the process has begun, it must be completed without interruption. Fasting is part of the sacred rite. Now, please turn over and lie still."

A lifetime of reverence for the gods kept Flora from complaining further. Fearing their wrath, she quietly obeyed the instruction, but inside, her mind was reeling. This was very different from what she expected. She wondered at the length and intricacy of the process. She had never been dressed in spirit armor before, but Serlaid had told her about the procedure, and it was nothing like this. A single *Bandrui* could complete Serlaid's warrior armor in less time than it took to bake a loaf of bread. Indeed, an entire war band could be prepared for battle in a single morning. But now, three adept priestesses were working from sunrise to sunset to enshroud her, alone, with the spirit armor of Brigid.

Flora dozed off while she lay on the table with the brushes scratching lightly across her back. In the half-state between wakefulness and sleep, visions danced through her mind. She got the vague impression she had experienced this process before. In her dreams she felt herself lying on a cold stone slab. She wasn't restrained with cords, but could not seem to move. She felt the tingling sensation of reed pens being traced across her skin. All around her, shadowy figures gyrated and flowed in a rhythmic dance to chanting and beats hammered out on drums. Flames blazed up in every direction. Then a beast with a woman's naked body and the head of a stag rose up beside her, brandishing a bone dagger. Firelight glinted off its silver hilt as the creature raised the blade high in the air and then drove it toward Flora's breast.

Flora screamed as she woke from the nightmare and threw herself off the table. The three adepts jumped backward and Nandag rushed to Flora's side.

"What is it, Flora? Are you alright, child?"

Flora only dimly registered the fact that Nandag had called her by her real name, reverting back to her old mentor role in the moment of crisis. Flora lay trembling on the ornamental rug which covered the crannog's floor as the horrific images slowly faded from her thoughts. Were they, indeed, some sort of hallucination concocted by an unstable mind? Or were they elusive memories floating at the edge of her awareness from experiences she couldn't quite recall. They seemed surreal, and yet they felt far too tangible to have been totally imagined. Could these be additional visions sent by the gods? But for what purpose? To warn her of impending dangers? Or to keep her focused on the consequences of fleeing from the task they had assigned her?

"No more," she whispered to Nandag. "I can't do more of this spirit armor, right now. Not now." She curled herself into a ball and shivered.

Nandag glanced back at the *Bandrui*. Through her sobs, Flora heard one of them say, "It's okay. Our task is done. We completed the inscriptions almost the very instant the panic seized her. This may, in fact, have been a spiritual attack. Our labors will no doubt have angered the forces arrayed against us. If so, the spirit armor of Brigid has done its work. It has deflected the blow and protected her from harm."

Flora remained quivering on the floor, wondering at the adept's ominous words, while the three priestesses gathered their implements and retreated to the door. Before exiting, one of them called back, "Be careful not to smear the patterns on her back. The ink must have time to dry. Marring the designs at this point would create a weakness in the armor and leave Fiona *Taghte* vulnerable to further assaults."

Nandag eased Flora up onto her bed and, heeding the *Bandrui's* caution, helped her lie down on her stomach. "Try to lay still until the dyes set. The spirit armor will protect you. Manas told me to expect Eliavres shortly before sunset. Your preparation ceremony will occur under the full moon of Ceredwin's watchful eye. Unfortunately, your fast must continue until the rites are completed."

Nandag retreated into the shadows at the perimeter of the crannog, but Flora could tell she had not left. She felt comforted knowing Nandag would be nearby. But even her old mentor could not keep her safe from the terrors that plagued her mind. Flora's stomach grumbled, and she fought to ignore its incessant complaints. She tried to rest, but feared the demonic *Coroniaid* who haunted her dreams, so true sleep would not come.

FLORA COULD NOT TELL if Eliavres disliked her or merely disapproved of her as a candidate to replace Brigid. His attitude toward her was always terse, brusque, and almost disdainful. Perhaps he just had a disgruntled nature and was sour to everyone.

This evening was no different. Virtually everyone who attended Flora showed her a deference that bordered on worship. But Eliavres strode purposefully through the doorway of the crannog without announcing himself in any way.

"The *Bandrui* tell me the spirit armor is complete, though the rites were cut short due to a bout of anxiety which apparently overcame our bride-to-be." He looked at Nandag and motioned her in Flora's direction. "Stand her up so I can inspect the designs."

"And good day to you as well, Eliavres." Flora's annoyance at his attitude overcame her and she spoke before thinking. It was a problem she struggled with, though her impetuous nature usually stemmed from unbridled curiosity and normally took the form of questions rather than irritated outbursts.

Nandag ignored Flora's remark, nodded her head to Eliavres, and grasped Flora's elbow to help her off the bed. Save for a thin loincloth and the interlaced spirals of the spirit armor, Flora was completely nude. She felt uncomfortable being placed on display, like a slave being presented to a new owner. She resisted the temptation to cover herself with her arms or to reach for a fur, deciding instead to capture Eliavres' gaze with her own eyes and pull his attention away from her body. But then she caught a glimpse of the *Bandrui's* exquisite creation and gasped. It was the first time she had taken notice of their art work on her skin, and she was astonished at the elaborate design.

The priestesses had used three colors instead of just one. The azure blue of the woad dye was complemented with accents of deep scarlet and forest green. The three colors, grouped together, symbolized the triple union of the Great Goddess, of Brigid, the Morrigan, and the Cailleach—the Maiden, the Mother, and the Crone. They blended together to form an intricate collage of interlaced symbols which sprang to life with an essence of their own, reshaping the very contours of her limbs and torso.

She could identify the many power symbols of the Great Goddess which represented the separate domains each aspect controlled. Brigid's crosses accented her breasts and her navel, while serpents writhed around her arms and legs. The eternal flame burned above her heart and a ewe lamb grazed upon the fertile ground of her womb. Flora scanned for sacred pools or springs, but could not find them anywhere. Surely, the *Bandrui* would not have neglected such a potent sign of Brigid's most reverenced domain.

Nandag watched Flora's reaction and must have guessed what Flora was thinking. Her finger slowly traced an inverted triangle on Flora's back. "The Morrigan's raven escapes from the three-sided circle of life between your shoulders. It grasps a spear in one talon and a shield in the other. I'll find a mirror so you can see."

Flora continued to survey the interconnected spirals and

geometric figures which covered her body, providing a rich backdrop for the power symbols. The Cailleach's wand seemed to grow up along the soft skin of her forearm, emerging from cat's paws which had once been her hands. The storm clouds of winter brewed across her stomach, unleashing bolts of lightning so vivid Flora could almost hear the accompanying thunder.

After seeing the astonishing beauty and intricacy of the designs, Flora almost regretted they would not be permanent. Unlike the clan tattoos which warriors commonly had seared onto their shoulders, spirit armor was painted on with dyes that eventually faded over time. Though they would not wash off immediately, day by day, they would slowly wane until they had finally vanished altogether. A warrior usually had fresh spirit armor applied before every new battle or dangerous patrol.

"It's incredible," she murmured.

"Indeed," Eliavres replied, apparently so taken with the montage he forgot to be his usual cynical self. "It's astonishing. Turn around so I can see the other side."

Though his command rankled her, she complied with the directive and turned to face Nandag.

"I see most of the Great Goddess's symbols, Nandag. But the sacred springs are missing. Are they hidden on my back?"

Nandag slowly shook her head, and her face softened with a smile. Flora almost thought she saw a tear trickle down her old teacher's cheek. "No, child. The sacred pools were already there. They've always been there. The *Bandrui* need not inscribe them on your body, for they shine forth through your eyes. Those deep blue pools are the wellspring of your soul." Nandag smiled again and her face beamed with affection and pride for her one-time apprentice.

Eliavres' perturbed exclamation broke the tenderness of the moment. "What happened here?" He jabbed a finger at a spot on Flora's lower right side, and the sudden contact made her jump. "Given their exquisite attention to detail, I seriously doubt the

Bandrui would have made such a mistake. Did you smear the ink before it could dry?" He scowled at Flora and Nandag.

Before either could respond, Eliavres continued. "It creates a vulnerability I don't like. No, I don't like it at all. But we will have to take the risk. There is no time to correct the fault." He shook his head in annoyance. "The rites must be performed tonight at the height of the full moon. I should have inspected the work sooner."

His statement roused Nandag and concern filled her voice. "Will Fiona be in danger?"

"I don't know. If Lugh and Cerridwen approve of her, they will intervene where they can. And the Daghda. He is certainly capable of protecting his future daughter, if he so chooses. We have done our part. The rest is up to the gods."

Flora wondered where the apprentices were. Surely, if there was to be a holy ceremony, they would need to dress and prepare her. She reached for a tunic hanging on a nearby peg, but Eliavres cut her short. "No. For tonight's consecration you will wear only the spirit armor of the Great Goddess."

Flora gaped at him. This was going too far. "I'm not a warrior going into battle. And I'm not about to be paraded around completely naked in front of a huge crowd of druids or villagers." Flora looked to Nandag for support, but her mentor remained silent.

Eliavres shook his head. "No, you're not. It's not that kind of ritual. This is a solemn affair between you and the gods alone."

"What do you mean? What kind of ritual is it, anyway?"

"Be patient. Everything will be made clear at the appropriate time."

Flora didn't like this at all. She scowled at Eliavres. "Where is Bhatair Rhu? Will he take part in the ceremony?"

"Not this one. The Arch Druid is attending to other matters this evening. I have been directed to oversee this sacrament."

Flora threw her arms up in exasperation. "Other matters? You have all gone to great lengths to convince me the fate of our people and the future balance of the natural cycle relies on *me* becoming

Brigid. What other matters could possibly be more important than the sacred rituals which cause that transition to occur?"

"This is a garment with an intricate pattern, woven from many different threads. The *Comhairle*, the Druid Council, has planned the process in great detail, after consulting with many seers, judges, and elders. The gods, themselves, have guided the preparations. The different strands must be handled by the right person at the right time." Eliavres' expression took on a haughty, self-confident air. "I have been appointed to weave this particular fiber into the grand design. The Arch Druid is managing other, equally delicate affairs."

Flora looked at her mentor. "Nandag?"

Nandag just frowned. "It's important for us to follow the guidance of the *Comhairle* with great care."

"Can you at least tell me what all these complicated plans involve? I seem to be an important part of the whole process. Don't you think I deserve to know what's going on?"

Nandag sighed and looked down. "This is a complex situation. I, myself, don't know how all the moving pieces fit together. Do you remember the process we use to make the tincture of foxglove? If it's done properly, the healing properties are very powerful. But if the slightest error is made, the mixture becomes a deadly poison."

"I remember."

"These circumstances are very much the same. The Council has taken great care to discern the will of the gods. We must each trust and play our part."

Eliavres took back control of the conversation. "There are certain things which you must not know in advance. For the gods to assess your character and your suitability to the role for which they have chosen you, they must see how you respond to different circumstances. It is like the ordeals our young warriors go through to earn their spears."

"I'm not a warrior," Flora insisted.

"So you keep reminding me. And these are not the ordeals of a fledgling soldier. These are the preparations of a *goddess*." He placed great emphasis on the last word, stressing its significance.

Eliavres stared her down for a long moment. Finally, he motioned her toward the rear of the crannog. "Now, if you please. It is time."

"We're going by boat?" Flora blurted out, her uneasiness growing even more intense. "That didn't work out so well last time. Besides, I'll freeze with no clothes on." She glanced at Nandag and noticed her brow was furrowed in concern.

"I assure you," Eliavres's tone grew more insistent. "We have taken every precaution against further assaults. This is a spiritual issue. There will be no assassins where we're going. And the spirit armor will protect you both from attacks and from the chill of the night air."

Flora didn't trust this man. She didn't trust the situation. And she didn't like the lack of information. But she didn't seem to have any options. She knew if she didn't comply with his instructions, then Eliavres would direct warriors to come and force her into the canoe. Or perhaps he would deem that the Bride was not "willing." Flora wondered what would happen in that case, but she wasn't sure she wanted to find out. Before following his direction, she reached for her flint knife hanging from it's leather thong on one of the upright timbers. She glared at Eliavres, daring him to challenge her, but he did not react. So she slipped the cord over her neck, allowing the blade to dangle on her chest. Then she stepped out the back door onto the platform and climbed down the ladder to the boat waiting below.

There were just two warriors in the boat. It was long and narrow, having been shaped from the trunk of a single oak tree. The two oarsmen sat at opposite ends of the boat, and the one in the back held tight to one of the crannog's huge ash wood stilts to steady the craft while she climbed aboard. Eliavres followed and motioned for her to sit.

Flora was surprised to find no one else in the canoe. It furthered her unease. She had hoped Manas would accompany them to the ceremony, but perhaps he was already waiting there. She found herself to be oddly disappointed that Finnan was also not present. The bard, with his quirky personality, was starting to grow on her. And there was still that odd connection with the voice from her dreams.

"Where is everyone else? Are they already at the ceremony site?" Flora had to look over her shoulder to speak with Eliavres, while the two warriors silently pushed the boat away from the crannog and began paddling slowly away from the shore.

"As I said, this is a solemn affair between you and the gods alone. No one else will be present. You need not have concerns about modesty. No one shall see you."

Flora's feelings of anxiety grew even more intense. She was alone in a boat with a man she didn't trust and two warriors she didn't know. Someone had already tried to kill her once. Could Eliavres have been behind that previous plot? Her mind screamed for her to jump out of the canoe and swim for shore while it wasn't too far away. She was kneeling in the bottom of the craft and it would take no effort at all to dive over the side. She could be out and away before anyone could stop her.

Flora placed her hands on the sides and began to push herself up, when she felt a hand on her shoulder. "Not yet."

That startled her and she sunk back down. Apparently, her thoughts were more conspicuous than she had known. It irked her that Eliavres could divine her intentions so easily. And what was that comment supposed to mean? "Not yet?"

"I urge you to put yourself in the right frame of mind." Eliavres voice crept up from behind her. "Seek communion with the gods. Find wisdom in Cerridwen's face shining down in the fullness of her grace. Listen for the voice of the Great Goddess whispering in the wind. Above all, envision yourself as Brigid, sitting among your peers in the Otherworld, disputing the fates of men."

"Where are we going?" Flora asked, trying to control the quaver of fear in her voice.

There was no response, so she asked again, with more insistence. "Where are we going?"

Again, she was met with only silence. Apparently, Eliavres had offered his guidance and would say nothing more.

The moon was full, shining down with a silver cast that danced across the surface of the lake. Flora gazed at the sparkles of light, shimmering on the rippling waves, and tried to read an omen in the pattern they wove across the tide. They looked like stars twinkling in the depths of the heavens, and for an instant, Flora almost felt as if she could discern the Great Bear treading its way across the heavens. But then the image became warped and distorted by the wake from the lead rower's oar, and it faded into the otherwise random flashes of light reflecting from the water's glassy sheen.

Flora scanned the horizon, looking for the shoreline on the far side of the loch. The boat moved steadily toward the very center of the lake and Flora wondered what mysteries awaited her on the opposite shore. She could see no pyre lit to call the attention of the gods. Perhaps the rites would be performed near a great standing stone or even in a sacred circle. She did not know Loch Tatha and its environs like she knew Loch Rannoch near her home, and had no idea what to expect when they finally beached the canoe on the other side. For the moment, at least, she took some comfort knowing they were far from the arrows of any would-be assassins.

As the craft moved forward, Flora felt herself being lulled to a drowsy state by the slow, steady, rhythmic chant of the paddles and the gentle lapping of waves across the bow. Under different circumstances, this would have been a uniquely peaceful experience. She breathed in the fresh summer air and closed her eyes to feel the cool wind caressing her face.

The serenity of the moment was broken by Eliavres' curt remark, "Here."

Abruptly the two warriors stopped rowing and took a few backward strokes to bring the boat to a halt.

Flora craned her neck to look back at Eliavres. "What's

happening? Why have we stopped?" Panic rose in her chest, and she could hear the pulse pounding in her ears. A chill pricked at the skin on the back of her neck, and her senses jolted to become fully alert.

Eliavres' voice took on an ominous tone. "Brigid is the patron goddess of springs and sacred pools. And the Morrigan has domain over rivers and lochs. The Great Goddess is quite at home in the watery places of our land. This is your induction into your new domain."

Before Flora could even react, Eliavres grasped her under the left arm, and with surprising strength, thrust her up and out of the boat. Flora plunged into the chilled water of the loch and thrashed about trying to regain her equilibrium. Having grown up on Loch Rannoch, she could swim well enough. But being hurled into the water unexpectedly had caught her off guard, and she struggled to reorient herself. In those precious few moments, the oarsmen had resumed rowing, and the boat was gliding slowly away into the moonlight.

Flora cried out, "Wait! Come back!" But no one took any notice of her plea.

Frantically, she began swimming after the retreating canoe. She pulled and kicked with all her strength, but desperation made her strokes sloppy, and she watched the little craft slip farther and farther ahead until it disappeared in the distance.

Flora panicked. She looked around in every direction, trying to determine which shoreline was closest, but it appeared as if they had dropped her in the very center of the loch. Yes, she could swim, but the nearest land was surely more than a thousand bowshots away. She could never make it that far. As fear gripped her mind in its iron talons, she fought to break free of its tightening grasp and to regain control of her senses. She couldn't give in to terror. If she allowed hysteria to overcome her, she would surely drown.

And then she heard it—the voice calling out to her. It was faint, but distinct. "This way."

Flora hesitated, treading water in place to keep her head above the surface. She had not heard the voice since her ordeal, except for its odd similarity to Finnan's own peculiar accent. She had begun to wonder if it had even been real, or if it was just some shadowy wraith conjured up by her own unstable mind. If her experiences had, indeed, been visions from the gods, did they control the voice as well? She had not actually decided whether it was friend or foe—whether it had been leading her to safety or deeper into danger.

"Trust me," it whispered from far away.

Flora wept with frustration. Who *could* she trust? Was there anyone at all? Surely not Eliavres. That was clear. But what about Bhatair Rhu? Or Finnan? Or even Nandag? Her old mentor must have known, or at least suspected, what Eliavres was doing. Had her teacher betrayed her—someone who had been more of a mother to her than her own?

Maybe she couldn't trust this disembodied voice that haunted her memories of horrific times which were yet to come. But what other choice did she have? Once again, she was all alone, facing unimaginable terrors, and the voice was her only companion. Who else did she have? Who else promised hope? With a sigh, she gave in to its urging and began a slow, steady breaststroke toward the distant horizon.

Flora hummed a tune to distract her mind from the precarious nature of her situation. She needed some way to keep her thoughts from wandering down the dark path into despair. And so the Ballad of Brigid kept her company—the song her father had often sung to her as he lay her down to sleep.

> *Down by the loch where the willow tree grows*
> *In the glen on an early spring day*
> *She is born*
> *She is here*
> *The wee bairn in my arms*
> *She has come to set my heart free*

Flora wept for her father now. She longed for his comforting embrace, and for his strong arms to keep her safe. Would she ever see him again? Would she ever again hear his rich, deep voice or feel the tenderness of a father's touch?

A young sprite is she, a fair bonny lass
She bids me raise Uaithne and play
She dances
She sways
She sets right the days
In winter, fall, summer and–

Suddenly, Flora felt a sharp, burning stab of pain in her lower back and a thunderclap rattled the heavens. She winced in agony and immediately stopped swimming. When she reached around to put pressure on the aching wound, she began to sink. A powerful wind whipped up and beat the water's surface into angry waves. Flora thrashed about, trying desperately just to stay afloat, but any movement caused searing agony to rip through her back.

The tempest raged around her, and white froth sprayed from the water's mighty swells. Storm clouds rolled across the sky and burst into a deluge of pouring rain. Flora gasped for air and felt her head slip beneath the surface of the lake. No! She would not give up now. She would not give in to the voracious hunger of the waves. Gritting her teeth against the pain in her side, she forced her arms down in a powerful stroke and thrust her head up above the churning sea. She gulped in air to fill her lungs, craving the life-giving breath, and hoped it would buoy her mouth above the surface. But when she kicked her legs, another stab of pain thrashed her body, and she once again slid down into the watery depths. This time, Flora's hopes descended with her into the liquid grave, and she felt her will give way to despair.

Little bubbles trickled out of Flora's mouth and floated upwards. Time slowed to a heartbeat. She opened her eyes and gazed about at a surreal world. The beating waves hammerred down like a thousand little pin pricks, stabbing the roof above her head as raindrops bombarded the surface of the lake, while a school of tiny fish floated impassively just beyond the reach of the tempest's fierce wrath.

Suddenly, a vision came to her mind—a memory from a similar situation with a raging river and a ravenous wolf. Then she was in the Otherworld, lying on her back in a grassy meadow, basking in the sunshine. She heard the voice whispering in the wind of the trees. It wasn't piqued and urgent this time. It was deep, and strong, and comforting.

"Relax," it said. "Lie back. Trust me."

Flora opened her eyes. The wild winds still beat the surf to a fury and a torrent of rain fell in sheets, but the panic was gone. Slowly and deliberately, she rolled over and shifted her weight. Instead of struggling toward the surface, she simply laid her head back and allowed herself to float upwards. Her face broke through to fresh air and she drew several slow, deep breaths, while the waves buffeted her from side to side, like a piece of driftwood on the swells of Loch Rannoch in a mighty gale. She couldn't stroke her arms or kick her legs without causing sharp stabs of pain from her wound, so she just lay still and allowed the wind and currents to blow her where they may. To keep her mind focused on something other than the storm, she continued the refrain from the Ballad of Brigid.

> *A daughter divine, one sister of three*
> *As her father I see past these times*
> *She searches*
> *She ponders*
> *Toward wisdom she wanders*
> *And soon I must give her away*

Her father was, indeed, giving her away, but surely in a manner he had not anticipated, and to an end he could not have foreseen. She wondered how he had chosen this particular song to grace the special times they spent together. It had turned out to be more prophetic than he could have possibly known. Had the gods inspired him to prepare his daughter for a role beyond what either of them could have imagined?

A maiden in white, a princess to be
With a flame set ablaze in her eyes
She weeps
And she sings
A bride of the springs
To heal the land she will rise

"A bride of the springs..." The water and waves which, moments ago, had threatened to claim her life, were now lifting her up and bearing her home. She would not drown in the depths of despair this night. She would, indeed, rise again. And perhaps she would eventually heal the land. She took hope in the words of the song and the promise they implied.

Flora had no idea how long she lay on her watery bed, being driven by the winds and the waves. She shivered as the wetness drank the warmth from her body. Her mind drifted into a nebulous place, as if she were caught in the veil which separated the Otherworld from the world of men. She was vaguely aware of hands lifting her up, wrapping her in a blanket, and carrying her away. She muttered something under her breath, "Bride of the springs," and allowed the comforting darkness of sleep to engulf her.

A cock crowed in the distance, and Flora's eyes fluttered open. Light seeped around the edges of a curtain flapping in the gentle breeze, causing dim shadows to dance across the room. For a moment, Flora thought she was at her home in Bunrannoch, waking up from a horrific nightmare. Then she saw Bhatair Rhu sitting on a stool a few paces away, and the nightmare came back alive as a grim reality. She wasn't at home. She was being held prisoner in a crannog at *Bruach Daraich*, the druid sanctuary of Oak Bank near *Incheskadyne*, the village of the Great Chief. She groaned in frustration as the previous night's memories came flooding back into her mind.

"Good day, Fiona *Taghte*. I trust you are well," the Arch Druid greeted her with a bright smile.

"Well? Am I well? I was dumped in the middle of Loch Tatha to be drowned by a storm. I was struck by some kind of arrow or spear in my side. And I have absolutely no recollection of how I ended up back here in this miserable cage. No! I am anything *but* well." Flora rolled over on the bed of furs and turned her back on Bhatair Rhu. Oddly, she felt no pain as she moved about—no discomfort at all.

"You completed the *Initiation* ritual rather well, I would say."

It took a moment for Flora to register what he said. Then she bolted up in bed and glared at him. "*Initiation* ritual! Are you serious? Your little game nearly got me killed. It was a miracle I made it back to the shore alive."

"Actually, you were never in any real danger. I was following you in a boat with our Master Bard and a half dozen warriors. We were never more than a few strokes away."

"Then why did you let me almost drown? I thought I was going to die, until..." Flora was going to say "until the voice called out to me," but realized she had never mentioned the voice to anyone before. She didn't know where it came from, and so she decided to keep it a secret for now.

"Until what?"

"Until, uh, I remembered how I escaped a similar incident during my ordeals by lying back and allowing the water to lift me up and carry me away."

Eliavres stepped into view behind Bhatair Rhu. "I disagree with your assessment, *Ard-Draoidh*. A true goddess would have simply stood up and walked across the surface of the loch."

Flora cast daggers at the Master Druid with her stare. "I'm not a goddess. I'm a healer."

Eliavres was apparently nonplussed by her outrage. He smirked. "Indeed. It is as you say. And with that attitude, it may, in fact, remain that way."

Bhatair Rhu interjected to ease the tension, "By whatever method, walking or lying down, Fiona *Taghta* has demonstrated her mastery of the watery domains. She has shown herself capable of becoming the patron goddess of springs and sacred pools."

Eliavres just grunted in response.

"Even more, she has shown a surprising ability to ward off the attacks of Tyrannus, himself," the Arch Druid continued.

Flora assumed he was referring to the fact she had survived the storm, which fell under Tyrannus' domain. Still infuriated at what they had done, she gritted her teeth and bit back her rage. But she had an additional accusation to hurtle at the Arch Druid. "Oh, something else. I thought you had provided protection against assassins. Eliavres and Manas both promised me you had taken every precaution to ensure I wasn't assaulted again. So, who loosed the arrow that hit me in the back as I swam?"

"Oh, *Taghte*. That was no human arrow. When I said you warded off the attacks of Tyrannus, that's precisely what I meant. You were not struck by a shaft from an assassin's bow. It was a lightning bolt, hurled from the heavens by the god of thunder, himself. And you survived the assault. It is, indeed, a miracle."

"A lightning bolt?" Flora cried, reaching to touch the wound on her back. "How...? I should have been killed instantly." Feeling around for the spot where she had experienced the pain, Flora could detect only a small rough patch of skin that caused no soreness or discomfort at all.

Bhatair Rhu grinned at her with his enchanting smile. "The spirit armor of the Great Goddess protected you. It absorbed the power of the shaft and deflected it into the water."

"But something came through. I felt a sharp stab of pain. It was so intense I couldn't swim. I could barely move at all."

Eliavres interjected, the indignation in his voice quite apparent.

"It was the flaw in the design where you smeared the ink. That's what let part of the energy through. You're lucky that little chink didn't allow the armor to be ripped apart and expose you to the full fury of Tyrannus' wrath. I told you it was a terrible risk."

"Yes," Bhatair Rhu retorted. "It was a vulnerability we should have caught in time and corrected."

The "we" apparently referred specifically to Eliavres. The Master Druid, nodded his head in acknowledgement of the rebuke and stepped back a pace.

"In any event," the Arch Druid continued, "you can see the armor is intact, though faded a bit by exposure to the water. It will last long enough to serve you through the rest of your preparation rites."

Flora groaned. "You mean there's more? What's next? Will you drop me in a viper's pit or burn me with the sacred flame to prove my authority in Brigid's other domains?"

Bhatair Rhu stood up from the stool. "There will be no more work today. Just rest and recover from your experience last night. And take pride in how you faced the challenge. You did well." He nodded his head several times in approbation of her accomplishment and then turned to lead Eliavres out the door.

Flora noticed Nandag sitting on a bench at the far side of the crannog. She called over to her. "Nandag, did you know what would happen last night? How could you let them do that to me? I was terrified, and I almost drowned. Why would you let them do that?"

"Oh Fiona, my girl. No, I did not. I knew there would be rites of *Initiation*, but the *Comhairle* did not revealed any details to me. You know I'm not a seer or a judge or an oracle or an elder. I'm just a healer. They assigned me to attend you during this time because they knew I was someone you would trust. But I'm afraid they don't share their specific plans with me. I'm so sorry. If I had known, I would at least have warned you what to expect." She frowned and cocked her head to the side. "Then again, the Council is probably aware of that fact, so I doubt they will be any more forthcoming with information in the future."

Flora shrugged off the fur blankets and got up out of bed. She walked to Nandag with tears in her eyes, and pulled her mentor into an embrace. "I was so afraid. I felt all alone. After all I've already been through, then they paddled me to the middle of a loch and threw me out of a boat. I thought I was going to die. I felt like there was no one I could trust." She buried her face in Nandag's shoulder and sobbed. After a few moments Nandag softened to her despair and returned the hug, gently patting her on the back.

Flora's mother stole through the front door and cleared her throat. "The attendants are here for your bath, *Taghte*."

As Flora and Nandag broke their embrace, Flora's mother edged around the far side of the crannog and went to the alcove to retrieve the large copper pot where Flora relieved herself. Personal homes rarely had such conveniences, but the druids had provided her with every possible luxury. Or perhaps they just wanted to remove any excuse for her to leave the "palace" without permission.

Before stepping into the Pool of Brigid's Tears, Flora once again looked over her spirit armor. As Bhatair Rhu had mentioned, it was slightly faded from the time she spent floating in the water of Loch Tatha. Yet the designs were still exquisite in their detail and astonishing in their multi-dimensional effect. They virtually leapt up from her skin and danced in a shimmering glow around her body.

After she finished her bath, the attendants dressed her in undergarments and a thin linen tunic. She would not be going out in public for the rest of the day, so they clothed her in something comfortable. In fact, she discovered it was already past mid-day. She had been so exhausted from the night's horrific experience that she had slept straight through the morning. In addition to being tired, she was also famished. Part of her preparation for the *Initiation* rite had been an entire day of fasting, and now she was starving.

To her surprise, Finnan entered the front door carrying a platter of food.

"I thought you might be a wee bit hungry after the evening's adventures. Might I offer you a bite to eat?"

"You surprise me. I wouldn't expect a master bard to play the role of a servant. And I'm also impressed to discover you can cook."

"I would it were so. Unfortunately, my culinary skills are somewhat lacking. I believe Kellina prepared this detectible meal, and merely allowed me the honor of bringing it to you."

"Kellina? You mean my mother?"

Nandag interjected. "The woman who was once your mother. Flora's mother, that is. Now she is a servant of Fiona *Taghte*, just as I am."

"Even so," echoed Finnan. "Well, because of this past which never happened, but of which your own memory is quite clear, you will, no doubt, find this particular repast quite to your liking. I understand you might have a special affinity for roasted eel, bannocks with brambles and honey, boiled nettles, and a delightful drink made of sweet cicely, elder flowers, and strawberries. Or at least a young woman of your acquaintance named Flora used to enjoy such delicacies on special occasions. So I'm told." Finnan smiled, bowed, and extended the tray of food toward her.

This must have been Bhatair Rhu's way of trying to make her feel good about getting dumped out of a boat in the middle of the night. Well, it would take more than a nice meal prepared by her mother to make up for being half drowned and struck by lightning. But she accepted the proffered morsels and hungrily began devouring them. She paused for a moment and offered to share with Finnan and Nandag, but they politely declined.

Between bites Flora eyed Finnan, trying to discern his relationship to the voice she heard in the night. "Tell me, Master Bard, were you in the boat with the Arch Druid when I was thrown into the loch and left to drown?"

"Hmm. Well, I'm not certain I would have characterized the event in exactly those terms. But, yes, I was in the boat with Bhatair Rhu. The Council felt it was important for me to witness the occasion so it could be properly documented in the tribe's lore. I'm afraid I had no input into the actions taken. I was only permitted to observe."

"Did you call out to me at any point?"

An uncharacteristic look of surprise crossed Finnan's face. "Nay. I did not. If I'd had the inclination, the contingent in the escort craft would not have permitted it. And it would have served no purpose as they would never have allowed you to board our vessel unless you were in dire need of rescue. But why do you ask?"

Flora ignored his question. "*I* certainly felt like I was in dire need of rescue."

Finnan just shrugged. He didn't seem poised to debate the point.

"And where were you during my ordeals—before they found me at the sacred yew? What do you know of my experience during that time?"

"I'm not sure of the exact timing, but I was visiting my home in Cill Dara when I received the summons from the Council. I arrived shortly after you were found."

"You weren't here before they took me to the healing hut at *Incheskadyne*?"

Finnan looked increasingly puzzled. "Nay, mistress. I arrived the day before the *Annunciation* ceremony. It was then the Council outlined my task. Again, I wonder, why do you ask?"

Something in the timing nagged at Flora, but she wasn't sure exactly what it was. "How long was your journey from home to *Feart Choille*?"

Finnan looked thoughtful. "Why, let me see. Three nights from Cill Dara to the coast. Two nights waiting for a ship. Three nights at sea. It must have been five nights negotiating the mountains and bogs of the highlands. So, all told, nearly a *pythefnos*."

"A fortnight? Half a moon?" Flora asked. Her thoughts shifted from curiosity about the voice to the odd sense that something was amiss with the timing. But she had never been good piecing together numbers to make sense of them. She knew herbs and potions and poultices, but could never quite grasp how someone like Finnan could string together one block of time with the next to come up with the whole duration from beginning to end. But something still seemed wrong. She would have to consider it later.

Nandag emerged from the shadows and retrieved a copper pot hanging between the firedogs over the hearth. "Fiona, this is a tonic made from bog myrtle mixed with lavender and hops. If you take it with your meal, it will help you rest and recover from your exertions in the night."

"Thank you, Nandag, but I'm quite refreshed from my sleep. I'm just annoyed at the things they keep doing to me, and I don't think your elixir will help with that."

Nandag nodded and placed the pot down beside the hearth, in case it was needed again, and Flora finished the eel she had been eating.

"Actually," Finnan intoned, "I'm afraid I have an ulterior motive for bringing your dinner. I was told that you have been clad in a rather unique suit of armor, which must assuredly be memorialized in verse. Indeed, it looks as though it might, in fact, be peeking out from beneath your tunic even now. Once you have finished dining, might you allow me to see the handiwork of the *Bandrui?*"

Flora drew back and felt a little annoyed. She hated being put on display. And she certainly didn't intend to disrobe in front of this man, Master Bard or not.

"Forgive me. I have given you offense. Rest assured, it was not my intention. Surely you can understand what a significant occurrence this is in the history of our people. Three adept *human* artists fashioned a spirit armor design which proved itself against a direct attack from Tyrannis, himself. This is a uniquely singular event. An achievement like this must be preserved as part of our heritage. And it will be a hallmark moment in the saga of your own transformation into a goddess."

"But..." Flora muttered and dropped her gaze to the floor.

"Ahh. Rest assured, it would not be necessary for me to inspect every intricate detail. Certain parts could, of course, remain discretely covered. If I could but glimpse the greater portion of the design as a whole, it would be more than adequate. Any bard worth his salt can fill in missing details in a way that harmonizes with what is readily known."

"I just... Well, bards are used to being the center of attention. I'm not, and it makes me uncomfortable. I didn't volunteer for this whole plan, and I really wish someone else could take my place. I only want to be a healer in my village."

"I do understand."

Flora sensed genuine empathy in Finnan's tone.

"The machinations of the gods often appear arbitrary and capricious. I, myself, have ofttimes felt as if I were merely a pawn in their little game. It makes me wonder, on occasion, if there might be a different way to view the circumstances we encounter in our lives. If there may, perhaps, be another perspective from which to see the world—one that makes sense of it all."

Finnan's voice trailed off and his gaze drifted past Flora into a distant place where she could not follow. She got the distinct impression he had stopped speaking to her and was musing through his own troubled thoughts. She wasn't exactly sure what he was talking about, but sensed that now was not the time to ask.

Then he muttered a soft, "Hmm," and his attention returned to her face. He smiled.

"Yes, well, if you could deign to oblige me, I vow to be discreet in my observations and respect your desire for modesty."

Flora put the last bannock in her mouth and licked the honey from her fingers. The conversation had robbed her of the enjoyment the meal should have provided, but she couldn't blame Finnan. It wasn't his fault. He was just playing his own role in the Morrigan's twisted drama in which she had ensnared them all—a web spun of sticky strands that trapped anyone who wandered into its deceptive embrace.

She rose and stepped behind a thin wall of interwoven hazel rods which acted as a partition. She removed her tunic, folded it into a small square and held it to her chest. A loincloth covered the other parts of her body she preferred not to display. She heard a new voice as someone else entered the crannog, and she hesitated for a moment. When she recognized Manas' formal tone, she decided that he, too, would be respectful of her dignity, and moved around the partition back into the main room in front of the Pool of Brigid's Tears and the Hearth of the Eternal Flame.

Finnan blinked his eyes several times and gasped in amazement. "Astonishing," he muttered. "Absolutely breathtaking." His eyes traced the intricate lines that laced her body in a cloak of ethereal protection. "I have no idea how I could ever capture its essence in verse."

Manas acknowledged Flora's presence with a nod. *"Thaghadh."* He seemed a bit less overawed by the *Bandrui's* creation, as if he had known what to expect. "It is, indeed, well crafted. But I am certain, Master Bard, if your reputation holds true, you can surely do it justice."

Responding to the sarcastic barb with his own repartee, Finnan replied, "Well, since I crafted most of my reputation, myself, I can assure you the tales of my talents are considerably exaggerated. But I shall endeavor to weave a tapestry of words which will enable future generations to recreate this marvelous work of art and power in their own minds' eyes. Mistress, would you do me the courtesy of showing me your back?"

Flora turned and allowed him to inspect the other side of the armor. She hoped he would be able to describe it well, since she could not see it for herself.

"It's not simply beautiful," Finnan remarked. "The symbols are also expertly positioned to project the power of the Great Goddess in each of her aspects and domains?"

"Indeed," Manas acknowledged. "This design is not the work of a moment. It has been shaped over many years with input from the wisest of the seers, oracles, and elders. I, myself, was consulted concerning the symbols of healing power—the serpents, the bag, and the bell. But I grant the implementation has been executed with great skill. It is well done. And it has already proven its worth in protecting our bride-to-be."

"Thank you, mistress. I do appreciate your indulgence of my request to see the armor."

"Is that all? Are you done creating your lyrics? I expected to be standing here for the rest of the day."

"Oh, no. That will take a great deal of time, attention, and prayer. But, as I might have mentioned, I have a rather good memory. If I close my eyes, I can recall every detail. I have what I need to spin the image into the saga."

Flora was relieved and withdrew behind the screen to put her dress back on. When she returned, Manas bowed his head.

"Now, *Taghadh,* if you will pardon us. *Ard-Draoidh* Bhatair Rhu has summoned us to a Council meeting at *Feart Choille.* We shall be back on the morrow."

Flora furrowed her brow. "What is this Council meeting all about? Shouldn't I be present if they are discussing my preparations? I don't appreciate being left in the dark about everything. And I don't want any more surprises like that horrible experience last night."

Manas grimaced. "We would take you if we could, but I'm afraid you have not been summoned. Please be patient. Everything will be made clear at the appropriate time. Now, by your leave, we will be off."

Not waiting for a reply, Manas ushered Finnan toward the door. But the Master Bard stopped before ducking his head through the portal and looked back at Flora to catch her eye. The sympathy and compassion in his expression eased Flora's apprehension, if just a little, and she was thankful to know that someone empathized with her plight.

CHAPTER SEVENTEEN

D omhnull came that night. Flora was sound asleep and didn't realize he was there until water dripped from his hair onto her face. She bolted upright at the sensation, but Domhnull clasped a hand over her mouth until she recognized him. He released his hold on her and gestured for her to be quiet. Her heart raced, and she took several deep breaths, forcing herself to calm down.

Domhnull motioned for her to follow him. He led her to the far side of the crannog where the dung door was hidden beneath the bracken and wool flooring. Domhnull pulled her into a close embrace and held her there for a long while. Flora felt herself melt into his strong arms, and her skin tingled where his fingers lightly stroked her back. She wished she could linger in that moment for the rest of her days, with her head against his chest, listening to his heartbeat.

Finally, Domhnull moved his mouth close to her ear and whispered. "I came last night, but you weren't here. I had to try again. Put your *leine* in this bag to keep it dry while we cross over to the bank."

Flora felt a bit awkward, undressing in front of Domhnull. He had been her betrothed, and she would have shared his bed. But that dream was gone now, cut out of time and replaced by a horrid reality she would escape if she could find a way. She so longed to wake up from this nightmare and to find her cherished past restored.

She felt Domhnull's eyes scanning her body in the dim light of the Eternal Flame. She couldn't tell if the intensity of his stare came from a primal hunger for her or from astonishment at the spirit armor. Finally, he tore his eyes away. He took the leather bag from her, twisted it at the top, and blew air inside. Then he tied it shut with a thong. Flora felt the sticky residue on her fingers from handling the bag. Domhnull must have smeared the leather with animal fat to seal it against the water.

He bent near and spoke in hushed tones. "Can you climb down the pole to the water?"

Flora looked through the door and down to the surface of the loch. It shimmered in the moonlight. But she felt as if she were standing on a high cliff, far above the raging sea. Tentatively, she shook her head.

Domhnull whispered, "Shh. It's okay. I can carry you down. Get on my back and hold onto the bag. Don't let go. It's deep enough, so you wouldn't get hurt if you fell, but the splash would alert the guards. Okay?"

Flora nodded and wrapped her arms around his neck. Domhnull was agile and strong. He began to climb down the huge timber stilt and Flora felt his muscles rippling against her skin. He paused when they were just below the floor of the crannog and looked up at the trap door they had just come through. Flora knew he could not carry her and also reach back to pull the door shut. She wanted to help, but if she let go with even one arm, she would lose her hold on him and fall. After a moment's hesitation, he shook his head and continued the descent. Moments later, they reached the bottom and slipped silently into the water.

Flora kept her voice low. "I can swim to the shore."

Domhnull motioned her to silence and shook his head. He pointed up to the guards outside both the front and back doors. Then, he grasped another leather bag, which was lashed to one of the stilts where he must have left it there earlier. He showed her how it floated and then slowly moved his legs in frog kicks that propelled him silently across the surface of the loch. If someone had been looking closely, they could have spotted his form edging through the gentle swells, but he made no noise that would draw their attention. Domhnull beckoned with his head for Flora to follow him, and she mimicked his movements while holding on to her own float.

They edged far to the east before turning in to the shore, floating in toward the bank until the water was shallow enough for them to crawl up onto the beach. Domhnull crouched and reached for her hand to help her up out of the water. Then he led her silently into the forest. Once they were out of earshot from the little cluster of huts surrounding the crannog, Domhnull stopped and embraced her again.

This time Flora felt heat rising in her breast as Domhnull held her close. With their outer garments in the bag, they each wore nothing but loin cloths, and Flora was keenly aware of the sensation of their bare, wet skin pressed together. Domhnull bent his head to kiss her and she longed to meet his lips with her own. But she pulled back at the last instant, pushing her palms against his chest to create some distance between them. She shivered and turned away.

"Domhnull, we can't. I want you more than you know. But..." Her voice trailed off in the whispering breeze.

"But what?" Domhnull reached for her shoulder and pulled her gently toward him. She resisted and kept her eyes on the ground. She knew if she lifted her gaze to his, and let herself get lost in his deep hazel eyes, shining bright in the moonlight, her resolve would evaporate like a mist in the breeze, and she would give in to their mutual desire.

"Domhnull, I love you. And if I could make things go back to the way they were, I would do it. I would do it in a heartbeat."

"And why can't we? Why can't we go back?"

Flora grasped her head in her hands and pressed her palms

against her temples in frustration. "I don't know. I just don't know. I'm betrothed to a god, whatever that means."

"And?" His voice, too, was fraught with irritation.

"Domhnull, if you had seen the things I've seen, and felt the terror..." she trailed off. "If there's any chance it could actually come true, any chance at all, I just can't risk it. I couldn't allow that to happen to our village, to our families, or to our clan."

"But you were to be *my* wife. You were betrothed to *me*. What right do they have to take you away from me? What right?"

Flora fumbled with the leather thong that tied her bag shut. She tried several times to loosen the knot, but eventually threw the bundle to the ground in frustration. Domhnull reached past her, retrieved the sack, and twisted the knot free with his fingers. He pulled the mouth of the bag wide, and handed it to Flora.

"Would you at least look at me?" he pleaded.

"I can't. If I do, I'll never look away again." She kept her gaze away from his face, but tilted her head up and to the right. "Maybe there's a chance. I need to talk to my grandmother. She might know some way to get me out of this mess."

Flora pulled the linen tunic out of the leather sack and slipped it over her head. She felt a little less vulnerable with some clothes on, so she turned and allowed herself to meet Domhnull's eyes. A tear trickled down her cheek, and Domhnull reached out a hand to brush it away. The sensation of his fingers stroking her face made her body quiver. Flora wanted this strong, passionate man. She wanted him to be her husband. She wanted to hold on to him and never let go—to cling to him and the life he represented. Instead, she turned away and began trudging through the forest toward the far hillside where her grandmother's hut used to be.

Flora heard Domhnull grunt in frustration and begin to follow her. "At least let me lead you through these woods," he said, stepping past her. "Where are we headed?"

"To see my grandmother. She used to live in a hut on the ridge across the valley from the ancient yew tree. Do you know the place?"

"Aye. That's Drumainn Hill. There is a dun on the far end with a signal pyre and huge stone ramparts. It guards the place where the Linnne and Tatha Rivers meet."

"If my memory is correct, Grandmother's hut is toward the middle of the hill, straight across from the yew. We visited her during the tribe gathering six summers ago."

"That seems a little vague. Are you sure you can find it?"

"No, I'm not. I'm not sure she even still lives there. But I have to try. She's the only one I know who might have a way out of this mess."

Flora recalled her grandfather's words in her vision of the Otherworld. "Find your grandmother. She has the answers you seek." Was that dream even real? Or was it just another fanciful illusion her mind had created? There was only one way to find out.

Flora continued, "You can lead me to the foot of the escarpment, but I have to go up alone. We really shouldn't be seen together by anyone. Not now."

Domhnull stopped and turned to face her. His flaxen hair glowed in the moonlight. "Listen, Flora, I don't like this. I didn't know what you had in mind when you asked me to sneak you out. I am meant to be on a patrol that leaves our camp before sunrise. If I'm missing it will cause a lot of trouble. And you have to be back at the crannog before sunup as well. There is no time for this."

"Domhnull, I have to do it. I have to see if there is a way out of this trap. My grandmother may be the only chance I have to get my old life back and for us to be together again. You want that, don't you? Besides what can they do to me anyway, if I'm found out? Refuse to make me into a goddess?" She snorted in mock laughter.

"What am I supposed to do? I can't just leave you out here all alone."

"Actually, you have to. You can't go with me to see my grandmother. And if you miss your patrol, they'll figure out where you've been. Look, I survived for a whole moon out here on my own."

"And came back half-mad!"

Flora felt herself flush with a sudden burst of frustration and anger. "Is that what you think? You think I'm crazy? You think I'm making all this up?" She glared at him for several raging heartbeats. When he didn't reply, she turned away. "I'll be fine. I know my way back to Fearnan. Just get me to the escarpment at Drumainn Hill and I'll be okay. Then you can go back to your camp before anyone knows you've gone."

Domhnull turned toward the hill, muttering under his breath. He led her in a sullen silence that seemed to drag on for an eternity.

Clouds rolled in to cover the face of the moon and a light drizzle began to fall. A chill tremor wafted through Flora's limbs, but she wasn't sure if it was from the rain soaking through her clothes or from somewhere deep inside. Despite her bravado and her confident words to Domhnull, she was dreadfully afraid of everything this night held in store—fear of what her grandmother might say, fear of losing her way in the dark, and fear of discovering that her cage was, indeed, locked and barred against any way back to her old life. This was her last hope.

After wandering through the mist and the trees for what seemed like half the night, Domhnull stopped at the base of a steep cliff. "Is this the place? How do you plan to get up the bluff?"

"There's a pathway cut into the rocks. You really can't see it unless you know where to look. My mother showed us how to find it. I'll be fine."

"You grandmother is pretty old, right? Are you sure she still lives up there? How could she even get up and down that rock face at her age?"

"I don't know if she's still up there or not. But she has people who bring her what she needs. And there is a longer path from the top, down the side of the mountain. We just didn't have time to go that way tonight. Now go, before they discover you're missing."

Domhnull shook his head, agitated. "I don't like this. I don't like this at all. I don't want to lose you."

"If my grandmother can't give me a way out, then you've lost me already."

Domhnull shook his head and started to walk away. Then he turned at the last moment, pulled her in against his body, and kissed her deeply before she had time to resist. As his lips groped hungrily for hers, her taut muscles eventually relaxed and she melted into his embrace. She allowed her longing desire to take control and returned his kiss with unbridled passion. She wanted to just let go—to run away and give herself to her lover for the rest of her life—to lose herself in the heat of the moment and forget everything that had happened.

Suddenly a bolt of lightning split the sky. Thunder echoed through the heavens, and Flora was jolted back to the reality of her nightmare. Her body went cold and she pushed Domhnull away. "Go. Please, just go. And pray to the gods that Grandmother can get me out of this mess."

A look of sheer anguish crossed Domhnull's face. Rain streaked across his brow and dripped from the stubbly beard on his chin. "What kind of warrior am I if I can't even protect my own woman?" He shook his head in bitter irritation and turned to disappear into the woods. He didn't look back.

FLORA GAZED up at the rocky cliff and stifled a sudden urge to flee. What was she doing? What help could her grandmother possibly provide? And how would she ever climb the steep, narrow path to the old woman's lair?

She groped around in the darkness, pushing through underbrush, searching for the start of the path. Everything looked different now than it had during the clan gathering when her mother showed her the way. Perhaps it was the night shadows that shifted the outlines of rocks and trees into an unfamiliar and ghoulish pattern. Perhaps it was the changed perspective of a confident little girl who had grown into a terrified young woman.

Eventually, she pushed aside a juniper branch and found the first two steps of the pathway. She looked up and saw the zig-zag line tracing its way across the face of the bluff. Tentatively, she began slowly scrambling up the rain-slick rocks. It really wasn't far up the slope, a little more than a bowshot from bottom to top. As Flora clambered up the last few ledges, she noticed a light flickering just within the tree line. It came from the direction where she remembered her grandmother's hut to be. Flora expected the old woman to be asleep at this time of night, but the soft glow of a hearth fire spilled out of a window and illuminated the raindrops streaking through the darkness.

She approached slowly, conscious of the muffled sounds every footfall created. This was silly. She was visiting her own grandmother. Why was she so afraid?

The hut was similar to a typical family roundhouse, with stacked stone walls. But instead of rising straight up to support a thatched roof, the walls of her grandmother's small abode curved inward upon themselves to form a shallow point. Some thatch was layered over the top of the stones to repel water, but not in the form of a typical roof. The overall impression was like a giant beehive with a moss-covered top.

The door stood slightly ajar, so Flora hesitantly pushed it open far enough for her to step inside. An ancient woman sat on a cushioned stool just behind the fire circle in the center of the large room. She looked familiar to Flora in many ways, but also strange and distant at the same time. She peered at Flora for a long time without saying a word. Finally, she squinted, as if taking notice of the girl for the first time and spoke in an airy but powerful voice.

"Who am I?"

Flora was taken aback by the question and stumbled through her reply. "Grandmother. You are my grandmother."

The woman repeated the question in an even tone, emphasizing each word. "Who am I?"

Flora groped around for an answer. What was her grandmother expecting her to say? She decided to try her intimate, given name.

"You are Alula, daughter of Kayci the Vigilant, and mother of my mother Kellina."

The old woman's gaze sharpened as she peered over the flickering flames and glowing embers. The inquiry, repeated once more, became more intense, her voice more insistent. "Who - am - I?"

Flora knew how to respond. She knew what the aged crone wanted to hear. It was her most formal title, the one most distant and impersonal. "You are the *Seann Ghliocas*, the Ancient Wisdom of the Tribe."

Flora received the slightest nod in return. The unstated meaning was clear. "I am not speaking to you as a close relative. I am addressing you on behalf of our people."

"Who are *you*?" the *Seann Ghliocas* continued in a flat monotone.

Flora tried, one last time, to turn the encounter into an intimate interaction instead of an impersonal consultation. "I am Flora, your granddaughter."

A log cracked in the fire, spitting a shower of sparks into the air between the young maiden and the wizened crone. But the older woman's stare didn't soften or waiver.

"Who - are - you?"

Frustrated and confused, Flora blurted out. "I'm Flora... or Fiona... Oh, Grandmother, I don't know *who* I am. That's what I'm here to find out. I thought you could help me. I saw Grandfather, and he told me to ask you."

For a fleeting moment, Flora saw a look of surprise waft over her grandmother. For just an instant, her eyes shifted focus, as if she was staring a thousand paces away, lost in a memory of days long gone. But then her attention snapped back onto Flora and the moment passed as quickly as it had come.

"You *saw* your grandfather? When? Where?"

"In the Otherworld. In a vision, or an encounter of some kind. I don't know. Anyway, he said to me, 'Find your grandmother. She has the answers you seek.' Then everything just faded away."

The old woman's eyes narrowed, and she peered deeply into

Flora's soul, as if trying to ferret out a lie. She said nothing for a long moment. The fire popped and spat, and Flora's thoughts were drawn back to the blazing inferno of her nightmares, which had, at that time, wrenched her out of the Otherworld vision and back to the horror of her plight. The anxiety and fear boiled back up inside her, just as they had that day. She felt her grandmother's gaze bearing down on her, like the "others" who stalked her during her ordeals. Finally her grandmother straightened and resumed her former tone.

"You are Fiona *Taghte*. You have been chosen by the gods."

Flora's spirit wilted inside her. Apparently, she would find no rescue here from her plight. Her shoulders drooped and her eyes fell to the floor in front of the fire pit.

"Look at me!" Her grandmother commanded sharply. "You *must* complete the preparations without wavering or disobedience. Do you hear?"

Flora nodded, meekly.

"Be very careful. You have started down a path from which you can never return. Once something, or *someone*, has been consecrated to the gods, it cannot be taken back. You *will* go to the gods, either as a bride or as a sacrifice."

Flora just stared at her grandmother, and her mouth gaped open as she digested the import of the old woman's words. The implications terrified her. Until now, she had assumed that if she was found to be "unworthy" of the calling, the plagues she had witnessed would ravage her people and their land. But suddenly the consequences had become even more personal.

"You mean, they would *kill* me as an offering to the gods?"

"The gods have made their decision. You have been sanctified— set aside for a holy purpose. Your life belongs to the Otherworld, one way or another. Now, the choice is up to you. Choose wisely, Fiona."

At that, the old woman closed her eyes and a blank expression washed across her face. She sat completely still.

Flora cried out, "Grandmother. Grandmother, please." But the *Seann Ghliocas* would not respond in any way.

Eventually, Flora gave up pleading and turned to leave the little hut, more confused and more frightened than before her journey up the mountain.

As FLORA PICKED her way down the steep, rocky, zig-zagging path, she wrestled with the new understanding of her situation. Apparently, she could either work to become approved as the goddess Brigid, or she would be offered up as a sacrifice to the gods. How could her own grandmother, her own flesh and blood, allow such a thing? Did her mother and father know about this? Or were they as trapped by the circumstances as she was? What about Nandag? Surely her old mentor was aware of the situation. She was, of course, first and foremost a druidess and a healer in service to the clan and the tribe. But if she knew, how could she not only condone such a plan, but even support it? Did she feel no sense of loyalty to her student? Was their friendship merely a facade—a thin veil of feigned kinship with no real depth or sincerity?

Of course, Manas would be on the inside of the plot. He was her day-to-day controller. And Finnan? He had to know the whole story, so the ballads he wrote would ring true with the deeper meaning of the saga. Flora despaired, and her heart ached with the depth of betrayal she had experienced from those closest to her. Was there anyone at all she could trust? Or were she and Domhnull alone in their plight?

When she reached the valley floor, the clouds parted and moonlight illuminated the glen with a silvery glow. Flora's eyes were drawn to a rocky crag on the opposite hilltop. It took a long moment for what she was seeing to register in her mind. The stone outcropping on the distant ridge was *her* rocky crag. It was her sanctuary from the locusts and the fire and the storm. It was also where she had left her little sack of treasures.

Suddenly, she was overcome by a powerful wave of remorse, and she broke down in tears. Every last vestige of who she was had been stripped away—her family, her friends, her home, her place within the clan, even her very name. It had all been stolen from her and replaced with an unbelievable fantasy that strained the limits of credulity. Who *was* she now? She barely even knew.

But her treasures—the little trinkets and baubles from the simple life of her past—were real, tangible reminders of who she had once been. In that moment, she determined to retrieve them from the dusty cavern of her ordeals. Regardless of whether the pursuit would make her late returning to the crannog, regardless of whether it would cause her foray into the night to be discovered, and regardless of the potentially lethal consequences for her disobedience, she would retrieve those tiny little reminders of who she was, deep down inside, before she had been snared in this hellish trap.

Flora set off for the hill with a determination she had not felt in a very long time. She strode purposefully through the boggy mire that sucked at her feet with every step. Slowly, steadily, she trudged across the glen until she found herself staring up at the steep slope. Memories flooded her mind of the time, which seemed so long ago now, of when she forced herself to ascend that imposing incline to flee the locust swarm. Back then, it had taken all her determination and will to just keep going.

Now, an even more fierce resolve drove her to face the hill and to climb. Step by step, handhold over handhold, she fought to conquer the slope and her fears. It was as if she fought to preserve her very identity. If she stopped now, she would just slip into the flowing current and be carried away to a destiny over which she had no control. She was being swept along by a tide of someone else's making, and she felt more like she was drowning now than when she had been unceremoniously dumped into the middle of the loch. She would *not* give in. She would not allow others to force her down a path of their own choosing.

Slowly, steadily, Flora made it up the hill, past the jagged scar made by a long-ago landslide, past the little spring where she had quenched her parched throat and first glimpsed the goddess inside her own eyes, to the opening of the cavern that had sheltered her from the locusts, and the fire, and the storm. Tentatively, with a trembling in her limbs she could not quell, she crept into the darkness of the cave. She could not see a thing, but the contours of the rock were familiar to her, as if she had been there only moments ago.

She crawled to the spot where she had once slept, propped against the cold stone wall, and groped across the floor with her fingers, feeling in the darkness for the comforting sensation of the trinkets she had kept close for so long. Her heart raced and her hands floundered as her finger tips felt nothing but dirt and rubble. Were her treasures gone? Had they been whisked away by a wraith in the night? Or carried off by some scavenger hunting for baubles to line its nest? *Or had she, in reality, even sorted through the memories in her leather pouch while an imagined wildfire ravaged the land outside her makeshift tomb?*

The terrifying confusion of those days washed back over her mind, and she began to panic. They had to be here. If they were not, then the locusts had not been real, and the fire had not been real, and the pile of dead bodies at the stone circles had not been real. If her treasures had never existed, then this had all been a horrific nightmare, foisted upon her by arbitrary and capricious gods. But her treasures *were* real to her. They had to be real. For if they were not, if they were just some fanciful illusion of a life that had never been lived, then she was lost—lost beyond saving and past the point of ever knowing who she truly was, ever again.

Then, as her hands floundered about of their own volition, a spiny barb pricked her finger, and she almost collapsed in relief. She lifted up the little tuft of wool snagged about a thorn branch, and the memory of her baby lamb, Caora, sprang back to life. Her treasures were real. Her memories were real. She was Flora, a healer from the village of Bunrannoch, and her old life, which had almost vanished in the mists of time, came flooding back to her. She felt about for the rest of the items, and they returned to her, one by one—her sister's comb,

Catriona's speckled rock, the oak-inscribed antler slice, Domhnull's lock of hair, the amber bead from her mother's wedding bracelet, and Brigid's talisman from the sacred pool. Everything was there. Nothing had been lost. Carefully, she placed each item back into the little leather pouch. Then she sank to the floor and wept.

FLORA PICKED her way carefully down the steep slope and back through the glen toward Oak Bank at Fearnan. A pale glimmer was breaking over the eastern sky, and Flora feared she would be too late returning to the crannog. Hopefully, she would only be discovered by Nandag and the apprentices as they prepared her morning cleansing in the Pool of Brigid's tears. Maybe then she would find out where Nandag's true loyalties lay.

There was still a slight chance she could slip back inside unnoticed. Domhnull had warned her to go back in from the west side of the small village. The loch actually had a slight, but significant flow toward the outlet on the eastern side. If she tried to return from the same direction they had left, she would have to fight the tide. Though she might be a strong enough swimmer to make it to the crannog's stilts, her strokes would likely make too much noise and alert the guards to her presence in the water. If she went into the loch on the upstream side, she could float down under the crannog with the current and more readily avoid detection.

As Flora neared Fearnan's scattering of small huts, she skirted into the forest on the west side. Her nerves were taut, and every step seemed to echo loudly in her ears. She knew extra guards had been deployed around the perimeter of the village to enhance her security. She wished right now she had her sister's skills as a hunter and a warrior.

Suddenly, a loud rustle erupted directly to her left, and she leapt to the opposite side. The shock caused her heart to jump, and she dropped to the ground. Was it a wolf, or a bear? Or worse yet, one of the guards? A dozen heartbeats later, she saw a bird flutter into the sky, and her panic subsided. She took four or five long breaths to calm her nerves. After several more long moments, she stood and patted the little leather pouch to ensure it was still tied to the hemp belt around her waist. She turned to resume her journey through the woods toward the loch and screamed!

The man had crept up behind her, as noiseless as a cat. He grabbed her and held her in an iron grip. The look in his eyes was cold and calculating. For a moment, Flora thought she could see the primal hunger that once filled her uncle's gaze every time he forced himself on her. But then the shock of recognition spread across the soldier's face, and she knew she was found out. That, at least, was preferable to the alternative she had feared if lust had overcome the man.

"Fiona, *Taghte*! It's you, mistress. What are ya doing out here?"

Flora was speechless. She had no idea what to say. She was not terribly quick witted, and she hadn't prepared a story in case she was caught. "I...was...uh... collecting herbs for a healing poultice."

It was the only reason she had ever ventured out in the forest on her own in the past, but it seemed like a lame excuse at the moment. Flora held up the empty leather sack that she had used to float out of the crannog earlier that evening.

"Alone? In the dark?"

"There is a special kind of mushroom you have to collect just before morning. Otherwise the spores dry out in the sun." This was actually true, but she didn't know if it would be very convincing. "Druids sometimes use a tincture made from liberty cap mushrooms to help them cross over to the Otherworld and commune with the gods. They prefer to use an extract from fly-agaric spores, but we can't harvest those until later in the fall."

The warrior eyed her quizzically and just shook his head. "I don't know nothin' about druid magic, but I do know it isn't safe for ya to be out and about in these woods by yourself. We're all pulling double duty to make sure you're protected from any kind o' harm. I best be escortin' ya back to the loch house."

"It's okay. Really. I can find my own way back. I appreciate your assistance. What's your name? I'll remember you one day when I take my place in the Otherworld."

"Oh, mistress. They'd stretch my neck if I left ya alone and somethin' happened to ya. I'll be seeing' ya safely home." He reached out and grasped her elbow in a firm grip to guide her toward the village.

Flora couldn't tell if his concern for her safety was genuine, or if he just didn't believe her story. In any event, she had no justification to reject his assistance. And he didn't seem too inclined to release her arm.

They walked the short distance out of the forest and through the small cluster of roundhouses. No one was out stirring in the pre-dawn morning. The clouds, which had temporarily parted to reveal the glow of the rising sun, rolled back in and shut the sky with a gray, dreary overcast that soon produced a steady drizzle of rain.

Interestingly, the warrior didn't take her to his captain. Instead, he led her straight toward the long, slender pier that stretched out to the crannog. Flora could see the two guards posted on the beach at the head of the bridge. But another cloaked figure was standing near, talking to them with his back to Flora. Her escort tightened his grip on her elbow as he led her up to the man in the cloak.

"Master Druid, I've found Fiona *Taghte* and returned her here, as ordered."

The hooded figure turned, and Flora found herself staring into the scornful face of Eliavres. Her heart sank. From the warrior's words, it sounded like they had been searching for her. In that case, her excuses would be useless. She decided the truth would be her best defense—or at least a partial truth.

"Good morning, *Taghte*. I trust your visit with the *Seann Ghliocas* was beneficial to you."

Okay, so maybe her midnight escapade had not been as secret as she hoped. Apparently, there was no need to defend herself with the truth, since that part of the story was already well known. But was Eliavres aware of her other excursion to retrieve her treasures from the cavern? She decided not to mention that part of her nighttime foray.

"I have not seen my grandmother for over six summers. I value her wisdom, as does the rest of the tribe."

Eliavres bowed slightly. "Indeed. The *Seann Ghliocas* is a great source of counsel to the druid community. I'm certain she provided you with sound advice."

Flora struggled to make her face an implacable mask to hide her internal dismay. Her grandmother's counsel was decidedly *not* what she had hoped to hear, but Flora gave Eliavres the only reasonable reply she could. "Of course."

"Nevertheless," Eliavres continued as he guided her onto the wooden bridge to the crannog, "there are appropriate and inappropriate ways for you to pursue such objectives."

The smugness in his tone galled her, but she bit back her words and accepted the rebuke in silence.

"You need not sneak out in the middle of the night. If you desired to speak with the *Seann Ghliocas*, we could have arranged a meeting. Your security is of paramount importance, *as is your obedience*. The gods do not want a headstrong rebel to join their ranks. The Bride–"

"I know," Flora's irritation got the best of her, and she broke in. "The Bride must be willing."

They passed by the two druid guards posted near the doorway, but Eliavres turned Flora aside. Instead of moving through the door and into the crannog, he led her along the small porch that extended about halfway around the outside of the building's circular wall.

"I see you have a small pouch attached to your belt. Might I ask where you obtained it? It was not included in the wardrobe provided for your use during the preparations."

Flora unconsciously reached for her sack of treasures, to ensure it still hung at her side. Its thong was taut, and the mouth of the bag was closed. Eliavres could not possibly see inside.

"It's mine," she mumbled. "I've had it from before—the pouch and the flint knife."

They had reached the end of the porch, and Eliavres turned her around to face him squarely. "Might I examine the contents?"

Flora wriggled free from his grasp. She didn't like this man. And she certainly didn't like him touching her. "Why? There's nothing of any value, just some keepsakes."

"Precisely the point. Keepsakes are reminders. In your case, they are reminders of a past that has been left behind."

In a surprisingly swift movement, Eliavres snatched the bag with one hand and sliced its leather thong with a small knife.

"Hey! That's mine."

Flora swiped at the pouch, but Eliavres turned his back to her, and the porch was too narrow for her to maneuver around him.

Eliavres opened the sack and spilled its contents into his hand. He poked through the items with a finger until he noticed Brigid's charm among the other un-noteworthy objects.

"This," he held up the amulet with its intertwined serpents, "is a remarkable artifact. I've never seen one quite like it. And I quite heartily disagree with you. It is of exceptional value. Where did you get it?"

"It was a gift from the goddess." Flora glared at him. "She gave it to me at my anointing as a healer." Quickly she added, "If you don't believe me, you can ask Nandag. She was there."

"Oh," Eliavres said, holding the charm up to the scant light of the cloudy morning sky, "I believe you. Only the gods could have fashioned such an item. It is a sign of your favor with the goddess. I wonder if she realized she was giving it to her own successor?"

Flora wrestled with the implications of that thought. Had Brigid somehow known of her future plight? Had she, herself, chosen Flora for the role she was destined to fill? How could that possibly be?

Eliavres finished scrutinizing the amulet and turned, slightly, to hand it to Flora.

"This," he intoned solemnly, "is a symbol of your future life in the Otherworld. I would not presume to take away what the goddess, herself, has given. But these," he shoved the other items back into the pouch, "are mementos from a life that is gone. They can serve no purpose but to dredge up memories best forgotten. You are no longer that young woman. You are Fiona *Taghte*, the Chosen One. You shall be the goddess Brigid, the Bride of Bres. Your place is in the Otherworld. You *must* leave your former life behind."

With that, Eliavres tossed the little leather pouch over the railing and into the loch.

"No!" Flora screamed. "Nooo!" Flora let out an anguished moan as she watched her treasures sink beneath the surface of the water and descend into the depths.

They were the last vestiges of the life which had been stolen from her—the last few reminders of who she had been and who she truly was, deep down inside. She'd had them in her grasp. She had climbed up to the rocky crag in the middle of the night to retrieve them from the chasm of forgetfulness. Now, they were slipping slowly into an abyss from which they could never be recovered. How long would the memories last—memories for which the treasures were her only token reminders? Or would they, too, fade into oblivion and be lost in time like tears in the rain?

"You bastard! How could you?" Flora raised her fist to pound against Eliavres chest, but the Master Druid was shockingly swift. He caught her arms in his own two hands and held them motionless in the air. He stared at her sternly, his eyes boring into hers.

"Actually, I know both my parents, and they were committed to each other until the day they each died. Not everyone can say as much."

Eliavres gazed at her for another long moment and then released her wrists and turned to walk away. He called back over his shoulder,

"It would behoove you to be more compliant in the future. Is that clear?"

Flora gave no reply. Instead, she peered into the depths of the loch, trying to catch one last glimpse of her pouch and the hopes it contained. Tears welled up in her eyes and trickled down her cheeks as it sank beyond the reach of the sun's feeble morning rays and faded forever from her sight.

CHAPTER EIGHTEEN

"Fiona." Nandag tapped her lightly on the shoulder.

Flora felt her mentor shaking her gently, but she just wanted to press her eyelids closed and shut out the waking nightmare of the world outside. Her dreams, terrifying as they often were, presented a preferable reality to the path she was being forced down.

"Fiona. It's time to get up. You have a big day ahead of you."

Flora groaned. It seemed like only a few heartbeats since she had cried herself to sleep on the pile of furs that served as her bed after Eliavres tossed her treasures into the loch. The light drizzle outside had swelled into a pouring rain, but the thick thatch of the roof kept the crannog dry and protected. Finally, Nandag's words registered in her mind and she peeled her eyes open.

Flore sighed deeply. "What's the big day all about?"

"Oh, Manas will be here shortly, and he will tell you everything. But for now, we need to get you up and dressed."

Flora pushed herself up off the bed and allowed the two apprentices to get about their business. She felt exhausted, not only from a lack of sleep but also from her shattered hopes—her grandmother's lack of help and Eliavres' cruel blow. She almost didn't care anymore what happened to her. Let them play out their little scheme. Let the gods push her around like a game piece on the *fidchell* board of life. What did it matter? She would let them have their way with her. In some respects they were no different than her uncle—but this rape robbed her not only of her virtue, but of her very identity. Maybe their goal all along was to strip away her soul and recast her in a new form of their own design.

Drib and Drab, her two attendants, went about their task with smooth efficiency. Okay, so maybe she should be more respectful, but since none of them would tell her their names, she just made something up to call them in her head. They bathed her in the Pool of Brigid's Tears, dried her with soft linen cloths, and rubbed her body with lavender oil infused with thyme and rue. Flora wondered at this particular mixture. It was a potent blend. The thyme attracted spirits from the Otherworld, and the rue warded off magic. They seemed to be preparing her for communion with the gods and protection from evil spells. The slowly fading spirit armor would have a similar effect, but they soon covered it up entirely with a rich red woolen gown, trimmed with black embroidered serpents and crosses interspersed with tiny white flames—all symbols of Brigid's power.

They put the same coloring on her face as they had applied for the *Annunciation* ceremony, so she wondered at the nature of this occasion. Would it be as significant as that event had been? They confirmed her suspicions by placing the silver, serpent-headed torc around her neck. She had only worn this status symbol at the *Annunciation* and the *Inauguration*, so something similar must be planned for today.

She was ready shortly before the sun reached its height at mid-day. Almost on cue, Manas ducked through the doorway, followed promptly by Finnan.

"Good," Manas said without preamble. "I see you are prepared, *Thaghadh*."

"Good day to you as well, Manas," she said with a touch of sarcasm. "I might be dressed and decorated, but I have absolutely no idea what is going on. None of these women would say a word. They told me you would explain everything when you arrived."

"Just so," Manas confirmed. "This is another step in your progression toward becoming the goddess. It is the *Officiation*."

Flora waited for him to provide more detail, but he seemed to think that was an adequate explanation. She, however, disagreed.

"The *Officiation*? What is that supposed to mean?"

"Are you trying to imply," Finnan interjected with a smirk, "that the title, in and of itself, is not sufficient to completely and fully reveal the nature of the event in its entirety? Why, I am astonished at your naïveté and slowness of wit."

Flora stifled a grin. She found Finnan's humor a refreshing diversion in these otherwise somber and portentous times.

"Apparently, I am quite dull. Please, Master Bard, would you care to enlighten me?"

"Well, I'm not privy to the details of what the Council has in mind. They want me to experience these occasions right alongside you, without foreknowledge of their nature, so I can accurately capture the essence and fullness of the emotion in my ballads. Yet, I suspect you might be called upon to 'officiate' in some capacity, perhaps in your forthcoming role as the goddess, Brigid. That's just conjecture, of course." He gave a slight bow.

Flora turned her attention to Manas and gave him a quizzical look. "Would you care to elaborate further, Manas?"

Manas tried to keep his irritation at Finnan's interjections in check, but it spilled out around the edges of his expression and his tone. "As usual, our friend here has correctly identified the general theme, in his own rather unique manner. But he seems to have glossed over the significance of the ceremony."

"And that would be?" Flora prompted.

"The people believe you will one day soon become the goddess, Brigid. As you are aware, our people rely on the goddess for any manner of blessings. So, a few representatives from each of the clans and villages, with certain, special situations, have been selected to present their petitions to you for your judgment and consideration."

Flora's momentary amusement at the banter with Finnan quickly subsided, and her frustration flared up again. "How am I supposed to respond to such requests? I'm not a goddess. I can't cure a child's illness with the wave of my hand or promise an abundant crop at harvest time. I can't make a barren womb fertile or imbue a smith's apprentice with wisdom and skill. You're just setting me up for failure. Even worse, you're setting the people up for disappointment."

Manas looked at her thoughtfully. "Hmm. You offered many of these same services as a healer in your village, did you not?"

"Yes, I did. But, as you yourself well know, healers can't guarantee results. People are satisfied for us to try our best, but they expect a goddess to accept their offerings and to answer their prayers. If they don't receive the blessings they've requested, they feel abandoned or shunned by the gods. I can't guarantee any results, and I won't make promises I can't keep."

"I think you are missing an important point. The people know you are not *yet* a goddess. However, they anticipate that you shall become one in the near future. So these petitions are merely requests for your later consideration. No one presumes you will provide miracles on the spot. They just want to curry your favor for the day when you take your place in the Otherworld. Does that make sense?"

"Aye, lass," Finnan added in a more serious tone. "And you do, indeed, have something else with which to bless them in the meantime. You can give them *hope*, and hope can be a very powerful thing."

"But I won't know how to respond. What will I say? I never had to speak at any of the other ceremonies. I didn't really interact with anyone. I was just presented before the people at a distance. I didn't have to *do* anything. This is very different. What if I make a mess of it?"

"There is a progression in your steps of preparation, *Thaghadh*. Each one is a test, and each one is an opportunity to grow.

Transformation is a process. Look inside yourself. Heed wise counsel. Pray for guidance. Act in faith. You will become what you are meant to be—*if* you follow the path laid out before you. In the end, *you* must choose, *Thaghadh*."

Finnan interjected once again, and the lightness had returned to his voice. "It'll not be such a hard thing, after all. You'll be knowin' exactly what to do and what to say. Imagine every man who comes before you is your dear father, and every child your wee sister. Just answer them the way you would if all the power in the heavens and on earth were yours to command. That won't be so difficult, now will it?"

"It just feels wrong to promise something when I don't have the power to make it come true."

"Perhaps not now," Finnan answered. "But a promise has been made to you, and you are merely passin' that promise on to others, whom you would help if you could. Show them your heart. You'll be just fine."

Manas brought the conversation to a close. "In any case, the ceremony will proceed as planned. Everything is prepared, and you *shall be* presented before the people."

Flora turned her attention away from the men and their words. She thought back to the horrors of her ordeals. She might not be able to guarantee blessings to the people in this moment, but if she failed in her calling, she might cause terrible curses to fall on them all— worse curses than any of them had ever known. It seemed to be an incomparable trade.

She listened closely. The rain had stopped sometime during their conversation. Perhaps it was a sign. Perhaps Lugh would smile down on this ceremony in the same way he had blessed the previous two. She hoped in her heart it would be true.

Manas gestured toward the door, and Flora, feeling like she was stepping out of a cage and into the fire, walked out of the darkness of the crannog and into the light of day.

Flora assumed they would board canoes and paddle to *Incheskadyne*, the village of the Great Chief. To her surprise, she saw a large crowd gathered on a small pap just beyond the farthest of Fearnan's roundhouses. The residents of the little village had constructed the small mound to resemble the much larger, natural hills created by the Cailleach in ages past. Those large paps had been shaped by the goddess to resemble a woman's breast, as a reminder of her blessing of fertility. The clans held special gatherings on these great mountains during Samhain to honor the Crone of winter.

Schiehallion, the largest and most prominent of these great mountains, cast its shadow over Flora's home on Loch Rannoch. Her clan gathered there at least once each year to lift their petitions and offerings to the creator goddess. From that great vantage point, the bale pyres of Samhain could be seen dotting the countryside in every direction.

Most villages had a small mound, like this one, built close by, where the people could gather to make judgments, pass sentences, or conduct other formal proceedings. They would also conduct ceremonies on the small paps to honor the gods. Apparently, her *Officiation* would be held on this spot. Brigid, like the Cailleach, could grant fertility to barren wombs, and so many of the great paps throughout the land were dedicated to Brigid's aspect of the Great Goddess. This small mound would be an appropriate place for her to meet with the people if she were truly a goddess and could bestow the blessings they sought.

A contingent of twenty guards met Flora and her companions at the end of the crannog's bridge and surrounded them as they progressed through the scattering of huts and up the hill. The crowd parted for them, and Flora was escorted to a stone seat constructed on the pap's crest. Oddly, Bhatair Rhu and Eliavres were nowhere to be seen, but a row of twelve druids and druidesses flanked the chair of authority on each side. They stood, passive and expressionless as the entourage came to a halt.

Manas gestured for Flora to sit down and turned to address the crowd. "Fiona, *Taghte*, the chosen daughter of the Daghda and betrothed of Bres, shall receive your offerings and hear your petitions."

Flora noticed that Manas used her formal title, *Taghte*, the Chosen One, in public, rather than his own modified version, *Thaghadh*, the One who Chooses, with which he addressed her in private. That was interesting.

The warriors formed two lines in front of the stone seat, between which the suppliants could approach Flora. She nervously scanned the crowd, feeling entirely unprepared for this. What would she say to these hopeful people?

A heavyset man with a full beard and unkempt auburn hair was first in line. Interestingly, he appeared to be as anxious as she felt. He led a young lamb by a rope through the column of soldiers. As he drew near, Flora could see his hands trembling and he dropped to his knees about five paces in front of her.

People made offerings to the gods all the time, but they never met in person. They would bring their gifts to a sacred pool, a holy grove, or a stone altar. On some occasions, one or more druids might be present to perform sacrificial rituals. But an ordinary person never confronted a goddess face to face. They were truly breaking new ground here, and no one seemed certain how to proceed. Flora didn't know what to do, and she felt her stomach tie itself in knots. She nodded slightly to the man, but decided not to say anything.

The man took her nod as a cue to begin. "Greetings, *Taghte*. I am Balloch of Clan *Donnachaidh* of *Pit Cloich Aire*."

"Greetings to you, Balloch." Flora's welcome seemed to surprise the man, but it appeared to calm his nerves a bit at the same time.

"I am..." he started, and then stumbled for words. "We..." and again, he seemed at a loss in forming his request.

Flora took a deep breath to muster her own courage and smiled warmly. "Who do you represent, Balloch?"

"I'm... here on behalf of the herdsmen of our clan, mistress." He bowed his head and swallowed hard.

"Go on."

"Well, you see, mistress, for the last three summers, we've all been havin' a poor run of luck. Only 'bout half our ewes have gotten pregnant each year. Lambing season, following on from Brigid's own day of Imbolc, has been fraught with all sorts of calamities—freezing rains, wolves, poachers, and thieves. But most of all it's the black leg. Near half the herd has died from the sickness already. If it goes on much longer, it'll wipe out the flock. We're desperate for help, you see."

"Is this one of your infected lambs? Have you brought it here to be healed of the black leg?" Flora gestured to the little sheep, tugging at the end of its rope as it tried to reach a clump of clover to munch on.

"Oh, no. Nay, *Taghte*. This is the best and cleanest of this summer's brood. Not a spot on her. She's a gift, *Taghte*, for you. For your kindness in hearing our plea."

Flora's throat suddenly closed and she found herself unable to speak. These people had experienced such hardship already and yet were willing to send the best of their flock as a votive offering to her? The thought of accepting such a gift caused an ache in her gut, especially when she was being showered with so many luxuries and fine meals.

A concerned look spread across the man's face at her silence. He spoke up in a shaky, almost desperate tone. "Forgive me, *Taghte*, if I have given you offense. Truly, this is the best sacrifice we have to offer. We have nothing more to give."

Flora felt like a fraud. She could not take the finest lamb and give them nothing in return. And she could not promise this man healing for his kinsmen's sheep or better fortune during the mating season. But to refuse the gift would be taken as a sign of rejection by the gods.

Conflicting emotions tore at her heart. As she delayed her response even longer, she watched the man's shoulders droop in despair as his spirit was crushed inside him.

Then Flora remembered Finnan's words of advice. She would treat this man as if he were her own father and as if she had all the power in the world to grant his request. It didn't seem like it could possibly be true. But maybe, just maybe, she could give this man and the people of his village a little hope to carry them through.

"No Balloch. It is a generous gift—a truly fine animal. I am honored to receive it from you." She took a breath and mustered her courage to make a bold pronouncement she desperately wished would come true. "I have heard your request on behalf of your kinsmen and your village. As patroness of flocks and herds, I grant you my blessings in the coming season. Your ewes will be fertile. I will defend your lambs from wolves and thieves. And the black leg will no longer ravage your flock. Now rise and be of good cheer."

A wave of relief visibly wafted over the man, and a broad grin broke out on his face. He bowed several times before rising, and then bowed thrice again. A druidess from the ranks stepped forward, accepted the rope from his hand, and led the lamb off to one side. A strong murmur of approval rippled through the crowd. Flora could sense they were encouraged to see a favorable outcome, and it would bolster their hopes for their own cases. The shepherd backed slowly down the column of warriors, bowing with practically every step, until he reached the end, and the next petitioner stepped forward to take his place.

The line was long, with people from all over the tribe bringing offerings to Fiona *Taghte*, and seeking the promise of blessings in return. A farmer from *Auchnacloich* asked for an extension to summer so they could recover from several seasons of blighted crops. A bard sang a new ballad, prepared especially for the occasion, in exchange for her inspiration for his faltering apprentice. The smiths of Killin presented her with a finely forged cauldron, inscribed with a large cross of Brigid on the inside and a circle of flames around the rim. They were in search of a new iron deposit, as the bog ore they presently relied on was nearly spent. An old woman from *Crianlarich* offered her a finely embroidered woolen tunic, asking that she bless the wombs of the young brides of her village.

Everyone approached Flora as if she were already a goddess, treating her with deference and awe. In the euphoria of the occasion, Flora momentarily forgot she was not actually a goddess and that her promises were, in truth, hollow and empty. She enjoyed bestowing blessings on these poor, unfortunate people, and it warmed her heart to see the hope her words kindled in their hearts.

As the line of petitioners began to taper off, a middle-aged woman approached with a young girl of about four years old hobbling along a few paces behind. The girl had misshapen legs and supported herself on a crudely formed cane with four small wooden feet. The woman bowed and knelt before Flora like the other supplicants had done. She held out a small amulet in the form of Brigid's cross, finely crafted from silver. The woman was clearly of modest means, and the gift was extravagant in the extreme. A muffled gasp erupted from the crowd.

"Greetings Fiona *Taghte*. I come to offer praise and thanks to Brigid on behalf of my son." The woman kept her eyes to the ground.

"Please. Look up, sister, and tell me your name."

The woman glanced up furtively, but clearly struggled to meet Flora's eyes. "I am Tyra, mistress, daughter of Strauna, and widow of Camron. We hail from Aberfeldy, just down the River Tatha from here." The woman lifted the amulet up and extended it toward Flora.

A white-robed druid stepped out of the ranks to accept the offering, but Flora stood and gestured for him to stand back. He gave her a concerned look, but then acquiesced and withdrew to his spot in the line. Flora reached out and accepted the silver cross.

"This is an exquisite piece. Do you know the craftsman?"

"Aye, *Taghte*. 'Twas my late husband who fashioned the cross. He was a silversmith of rare skill. This was his own favorite charm, because Brigid is the goddess of craftsmen and smiths. I know he would want you to have it."

Flora struggled to receive something of such value from a widow. A village chieftain would provide a year's worth of grain in exchange for such an item. A prominent druid might offer much more.

"Your husband's workmanship is very fine. What can I do for you, dear lady, in return for such a priceless treasure?"

"I ask for nothin', mistress. It's a gift of thanks. Last winter, my son was stricken with the croup just before Imbolc. He got worse and worse, despite the healer's tonics and poultices. He could barely breathe, and I knew for sure he was standin' at death's door. I traded my last winter cloak for a newborn lamb and offered it to the Great Goddess. Our Imbolc plaid was returned with a promise of blessing from Brigid, and my son was healed. Now he is well and strong, and I owe great thanks to you."

"Is this your daughter?"

"Aye, *Taghte*. She is."

The little girl shuffled forward awkwardly, fumbling with her crutch on the uneven ground. "I would like to be fixed too, like you helped my brother get better."

"Hush, Mysie," her mother hissed.

"No, please," Flora stilled her. "It's okay." Then to the little girl, "Mysie? Is that your name?"

"Yes, ma'am. It means 'child of light.' My daddy always told me I was the light of his life."

Flora smiled at her. "I'm sure you were. Would you like to sit with me and tell me what happened to your legs."

"Sure," Mysie responded without hesitation and hobbled forward.

Manas bent over Flora's shoulder and whispered in her ear, "*Taghte*, perhaps—"

Flora cut him off with a wave of her hand. These were her people, and she would help in any way she could. She was just heeding Finnan's advice to follow her heart.

Worry lines creased the mother's brow, but she remained silently kneeling.

"Come sit right up here on my lap," Flora said. "Now, tell me about your legs."

"Well, *Mamaidh* says I was born this way. I just wasn't put together quite right."

Flora glanced at her mother, who just nodded.

"But," the girl went on, "*Dadaidh* told me the gods make some people special so they can get good at things normal people can't do."

"And what do you think?"

Mysie frowned thoughtfully and looked a little sad. "I'd really like to run and play with my friends. *Mamaidh* says you made Cailin better from his cough. Can you fix my legs too?"

Suddenly, the euphoria of the day came crashing down, and Flora once again remembered she was not really a goddess. How could she make that kind of promise to this precious little girl—a promise she had no way to keep. As a healer, even just a novice one, she recognized that Mysie's condition was irreversible.

"You know, your daddy was a very wise man. I think maybe he was right, and you were made for a special purpose that a little girl with normal legs wouldn't be able to do."

Flora felt Mysie sag in her lap, as if her spirit were crushed. "Why can the gods make some people better and not others, like me?"

Flora couldn't stand to pile more disappointment on the little girl. Maybe Finnan was right. Maybe she could at least give her a tiny bit of hope. "If you trust the gods with all your heart and say your prayers and offer your sacrifices... You know how to pray, right?"

Mysie nodded enthusiastically, "Uh-huh."

"If you do all of that, then the gods can make everything work out right—maybe not right away, but when the time is best. Do you think you can do that? Can you be patient and trust the gods to make you well?"

Mysie smiled up at her. Then she said, "I trust *you*. I know *you* will make me better."

Flora felt a huge lump in her throat. What had she just done? What terrible thing had she just done? She pulled Mysie into her arms and buried her face in the little girl's hair to hide her own tears. She held her there for a long moment.

When Flora released her, Mysie was beaming from ear to ear. The little girl wriggled off her lap, then reached up and handed her crutch to Flora. "Here. This is for you. I won't need it anymore."

Mysie stumbled down the slope to her mother. "*Mamaidh*, the goddess said my legs would get better. Maybe not now, but I'm sure it will be soon."

She staggered past her mother, and the woman rose hesitantly, bowed quickly to Flora, then turned to grasp Mysie's hand and walk her down the path. Flora felt as if the weight of the world was crushing down on her. Guilt overwhelmed her. She was no goddess. She was certainly no pure and spotless maiden. She knew she could not become Brigid. And so all her promises this day had been hollow pretensions. Maybe she had given people hope, but it was a false hope that would be dashed against the rocks when her fake blessings failed to come true. She watched an innocent and hopeful little girl disappear into the crowd, and she could barely hold back the tears.

As Flora wallowed in her own misery, a hushed murmur rippled through the crowd, followed by a collective gasp. She heard shouts of "Impossible!" and "It can't be!" and "She's walking! She's healed!" "Praise the goddess! Praise Brigid!"

Suddenly, the crowd parted and Mysie came running up the hill. She jumped into Flora's arms and gave her a huge hug. "I knew you'd do it! I knew you'd make me better. I just knew it."

The cry started softly, but grew in fervor and intensity. "*Taghte! Taghte!*" People were cheering and rushing forward to surround her. The warriors quickly drew up in a tight square and formed a shield of protection, holding the crowd at bay.

Manas stepped up behind her and grabbed her firmly by the arm. "I think it would be best if we go now."

The druids, as taken aback as the rest of the crowd, joined in the shouts of adoration and praise. "*Taghte! Taghte!*"

Flora set Mysie down on the ground. "Go find your mama, sweetie." Mysie dashed off into the cheering throng on her newly restored legs, and Flora stared after her in stunned amazement. What had just happened here? Could she have possibly healed her?

The guard detail formed a square around her, two ranks deep, and began pressing their way through the crowd, back toward the crannog. As they left the cheering throng behind with their shouts of "*Taghte! Taghte!*" filling the air, a big man in a hooded cloak strode up to Manas at the head of her retinue.

Flora heard Manas say, "Fiona *Taghte*, can see no more petitioners today. There will be other opportunities for you to present your request."

The man replied, "Oh, I'm sure she'll see me. I'm quite certain of it."

The voice sent an icy chill up Flora's spine. She knew it well, and fear gripped her heart. She wanted to ignore the man's plea and stay tucked away inside the protective wall of her warrior guards. But the consequences of turning him aside might prove disastrous, because this man knew something no one else knew. He knew the secret lie that would bring her down and forever destroy her pretensions of being a goddess.

"Manas, please stop. I would like to hear this man out." She hoped the shouts of the distant crowd would drown out the tremor in her voice.

"As you say, *Taghte*," he replied reluctantly.

The formation came to a halt and the guards parted, allowing the man to approach. He strode forward and pushed back his hood so Flora could see her uncle's face. She tried to hold his gaze, but her eyes flickered to the ground in shame. Her uncle dropped to one knee.

"Fiona, *Taghte*."

Flora wondered if anyone else here detected the snide tone of irony in his voice.

"Yes," she replied curtly. "What is your request?"

"My horse was lamed in a recent raid."

"And you would like for me to heal your horse?"

"Nay, Fiona. Though I'm quite certain a goddess could heal a lame horse, just the same as a little girl's legs, I'm afraid I had to put him down. But I'd be much obliged if you could provide me with a new horse. It's important for the protection of our village, you see."

Manas was quite obviously perturbed by this man and his petition. "What would you offer to *Taghte* in exchange for such a blessing?"

"Oh, I'm a poor man, you see. The horse was my only possession of any value. But Fiona *Taghte* would have my eternal thanks and praise for restoring my livelihood and my position in our village."

The images leapt, unbidden, into Flora's mind of her uncle covering her mouth with his huge hand to muffle her cries as he forced himself on her, time and time again. She shuddered and turned away.

"Manas, please find this man a horse." She glanced briefly up at the man's face. "Is that all?"

Her uncle bowed his head, ever so slightly. "I'm truly grateful to have found favor in your eyes. I trust you will remember me when you take your place in the Otherworld."

"You can be certain of it," Flora replied, trying to mask the utter contempt she felt and keep it from spilling over in her voice.

The man stood and turned toward Manas. "I'll just wait by the shore of the loch for you to bring my gift from the goddess." Then he turned and strode away.

Manas tried to catch Floras eye, but she averted her gaze. "I would like to go home," she said.

Manas bowed his head. "As you wish, *Thaghadh*," he responded, and led the formation of warriors toward the crannog.

Flora supposed this palace on the loch was the only home she had left. But when she asked Manas to take her 'home' she had meant something altogether different—something that was vanishing from her memory as if it had never existed—something that was slipping forever out of her grasp and being consumed by this new reality. She was not a goddess, nor could she ever become one.

CHAPTER NINETEEN

F lora tossed and turned in her bed, the events of the day spinning through her mind. She was plagued with doubts over the false hopes she had spread to so many of the people. She made promises to them she had no way to keep. And yet, what happened to Mysie's legs must have been a miracle from the gods. The girl had been lame from birth, but after her interaction with Flora had almost instantly been able to walk and run. How was that even possible? Surely, Flora had done nothing to effect the cure. She had been hesitant to even give the little girl hope her condition could ever be changed. Mycie had demonstrated more trust in the gods than Flora, herself, could muster.

And then there was the confrontation with her uncle. He was the one person in all the tribe who knew for certain she was a fraud and unfit to become the Maiden Goddess. He knew because he had stolen her virtue and soiled her soul. And clearly, he intended to use this knowledge as leverage to get what he wanted from her. This time it was a horse. But her capitulation to his demands ensured he would be back again—just as he had always come back, again and again, to get what he wanted from her.

Part of her wanted to let him tell his dirty little secret and set her free from this whole charade. She would be free from the manipulation and deception. She would be in control of her life again. But then, she actually wouldn't be. Instead of being groomed as a future goddess, she would be offered as a sacrifice to the gods. As her grandmother had said, she was now consecrated to the gods, and she would be delivered up to them one way or another.

Maybe she could just run away. She knew how to escape from her prison without notice—well, maybe that was true, except Eliavres had somehow found out the first time. Anyway, she could certainly get to the shore undetected. But then what? Where could she go? A young woman like her could never survive long on her own. And Bhatair Rhu would, no doubt, employ every resource at his command to retrieve his prize gift to the gods. No. She was trapped even more by circumstances than by either the crannog or the loch.

Something else nagged at the back of her mind. It was something Eliavres had said during their interchange on the crannog's porch when he threw away her treasures. She remembered feeling disturbed by one of his comments but couldn't pinpoint exactly what it had been. She tried desperately to recall the details of the conversation, but they evaporated in the wind, swamped by the flood of emotions caused by watching her little leather pouch disappear into a watery grave from which they were completely irretrievable.

Somewhere between thoughts of her uncle's threats, the little girl's miraculous healing, and the Master Druid's enigmatic riddle, she slipped into an uneasy and restless sleep.

In the semi-conscious state between wakefulness and slumber, images raced across Flora's mind. Scenes replayed themselves from the day's events, jumbled together with memories from her childhood and nightmares from her ordeals. She saw a broken and deformed little girl suddenly jump up on perfectly healthy legs and begin running, leaping, and laughing. Then she *was* the little girl, dancing and swaying in her father's arms as he swung her in circles, his face alight with joy. She felt her grasp on her father's arms slipping, and suddenly she was hurtling through the air amid a scorched and barren land. She thudded hard on an earthen mound. But when she tried to stand, she found she was lying on a heap of rotten and decayed bodies, just beyond the stone circles which guarded the way to the sacred yew tree. She screamed, and it jolted her awake for just a few moments before utter exhaustion pulled her back into the terror of her night visions.

Flora dreamed she was walking with a vaguely familiar shepherd through a pasture full of sheep. There was just a scattering of newborn lambs, but on closer inspection, she could see their legs were black with putrid flesh. The remorse she felt at their plight caused her to kneel down and comfort one of the pitiful beasts. At her touch, the blighted skin and sinews were restored to healthy, supple limbs. The herdsman looked down at her with delight, and a broad grin spread across his face before mutating into a sinister smile. Then the man was her uncle, clasping his hand over her mouth and forcing her to the ground. She struggled to cry out and to break free, but his hand muffled her screams and his iron grip bound her tight, until a magnificent sorrel mare leapt over his back and kicked him in the head with her hooves.

The scene shifted again, and Flora found herself peering into a shallow spring. The face of the goddess stared back at her with eyes that seemed all too familiar. A tear trickled down her cheek and dropped into the water, making ripples glide across the surface, distorting Brigid's image until it all faded away. Flora felt herself being pulled into the little spring, and suddenly it became a huge loch in a raging storm, dragging her down into its watery depths. As she descended deeper and deeper, her lungs ached to take a breath. She struggled against the impulse to open her mouth and allow a flood of water to fill her lungs. For a moment, she thought about just giving up and allowing the nightmare to end. Instead of becoming a goddess she would be offered as a sacrifice. But the horror would be over, and she would be free at last.

Then she heard it, calling softly to her, as if from far away. It was a strong, powerful voice—one unlike the gentle breeze or the raging storm—a voice filled with the authority to command. "Run, Flora. Run."

Flora was still dreaming, but felt as if she were waking up to the gentle timbre of her father's voice singing a melody from her childhood—the Ballad of Brigid. She opened her eyes to see his smiling face. With tears of joy in his eyes, he scooped her up into a warm embrace, and she felt safe once again. Something subtle changed in the feel of his arms, and when she drew back, she found a strange man with blue eyes, olive skin, and dark brown hair staring back at her. His face was stern, with chiseled features and a beaked nose. In that instant, Flora recognized something shocking and unsettling in the eyes gazing back at her. They were the eyes of Brigid. They were *her* eyes.

Instantly, the jumble of images ceased and the scene became absolutely clear. Flora wasn't certain if she was still dreaming, or if she had been jolted awake. She was reliving a memory, but it was as vivid and real as if she were experiencing it for the very first time.

She stood behind Eliavres as he fumbled through her treasures, pulled out Brigid's amulet, and pushed the other items back into the bag. Then he tossed her little leather pouch over the railing and into the loch.

Flora heard herself screaming, "Nooo!" and she let out an anguished moan as she watched her treasures sink beneath the surface of the water and descend into the depths.

She railed at Eliavres. "You bastard! How could you?" Then she raised her fist to pound against the druid's chest, but he caught her arms in his own two hands and held them motionless in the air. He stared at her sternly, his eyes boring into hers.

Then everything in the scene became absolutely still. The rain stopped, the sound of the waves lapping against the shore ceased, and the rushing wind faded away. Flora's full attention was on Eliavres' face. All she could hear was the crystal clear sound of his voice. The words echoed in the stillness and reverberated in her ears.

"Actually, I know both my parents, and they were committed to each other until the day they each died. Not everyone can say as much."

Suddenly, Flora knew. She knew the terrible truth with a certainty that comes from a lifetime of suppressing a knowledge she couldn't bring herself to admit. It wrenched at her gut and tore at her heart, until she fell to the wet wooden planks of the crannog's porch and curled up into a ball. Both in her dreams and on her bed of furs, Flora wept.

FLORA'S MOTHER skirted around the edge of the crannog, heading toward the chamber pot, when Flora woke from her nightmare. Nandag and the apprentices had not yet arrived to begin her daily ritual. Flora didn't know what new surprises Bhatair Rhu and the Council had planned for her today. She hoped they would allow her to recover from all the tests and trials and ceremonies she'd endured. Her nerves were on edge, and she really needed to get away from all the drama for just a day or two.

But there was something she had to do now, which she could no longer avoid. She had probably always known something was not quite right in her home, but was afraid to face the truth. There had to be a reason why her mother doted over Serlaid and Catriona, but treated Flora with a detached indifference. Now the truth was staring her in the face, and she could no longer push it away into a corner and pretend it didn't exist.

Her mother retrieved the copper basin and headed toward the door to empty its contents. Flora pushed herself up from the pile of furs, her bed shirt drenched with sweat, and moved to intercept her mother.

Her mother looked almost like a cornered mouse. She tried to sidestep Flora and escape to the doorway, but Flora called out and stopped her short.

"We need to talk."

Her mother halted and bowed slightly, albeit more toward the door than in Flora's direction. "Of course, *Taghte*. Is there something wrong with your quarters? I'm doing my best to keep them clean and orderly."

Flora fumed. "I don't need to discuss the condition of my living arrangements with a servant. I *need* to talk to my mother. Is she still in there, somewhere?"

"I'm only trying to follow the guidance of the Council. They–"

Flora grasped her mother's arm and tried to turn her around, but the older woman resisted with more strength than Flora expected. "I don't *care* what the Council wants, or Eliavres, or Bhatair Rhu, or any of the rest of them. I need to talk with *my mother*. And I think it's time you gave me an explanation."

Flora felt her mother tense, but then she sighed in resignation and turned to face her daughter.

The smell of yesterday's waste wafted up from the chamber pot and Flora winced. "Can you please put that down and talk to me?"

Her mother set the bowl on a nearby bench and turned toward Flora, again avoiding eye contact. "An explanation for what?" At least her voice had taken on the old tone of a mother rather than the formal air of an attendant.

"Please. Just sit down so we can talk like mother and daughter for once?"

Her mother nodded resignedly, and they moved over to some benches beside the fire pit. There, in front of the Eternal Flame, Flora began one of the most healing and most painful conversations of her life.

"Why, Mother?"

Her mother sighed heavily. "Why did I never treat you like a real daughter? Why did I never love you like I loved your sisters?"

Tears pricked at the corner of Flora's eyes. Her throat closed and she couldn't give voice to her words, so she just nodded her head in reply.

"I did love you, very, very much. I *do* love you. You have to believe that."

Flora pursed her lips and took a long moment to respond. "But?"

"But every time I glimpsed your face, every time I looked into your eyes, I saw my shame staring back at me."

Flora finally found her voice. She decided to cut straight to the heart of the issue. "Mother, who's my father?"

The crannog walls were well sealed against the elements outside, but Flora, nevertheless, felt an icy chill waft through the room. The Eternal Flame flickered in the fire pit.

A look of incredulity crossed her mother's face, but her gaze was directed toward the dancing flames and glowing embers. She would not meet Flora's eye. "What's that supposed to mean? You know very well who your father is."

"Mother, look at me. *Look at me!*"

Her mother was apparently taken aback by the tone of authority in Flora's voice and complied. For the first time in as long as Flora could remember, her mother looked her in the eye—not merely with a furtive glance, but in a way that established a truly genuine connection.

"Who - is - my - father?" Flora emphasized each word. "My *real* father?"

Flora's mother dropped her gaze to the floor and her shoulders slumped. She was silent for a long while. When she spoke, her voice was distant.

"The men were all down river at the Sentinel Stone, fighting off a Roman raid on *Pit Cloich Aire*. For some reason, the Romans were sending patrols up all the rivers and the glens, probing into the heartlands. And while our men were defending the old outpost at *Tigh Na Cloich*, another small squad had slipped through the lines and made it all the way up to Loch Rannoch."

Flora's mom wrung her hands nervously while she was talking, as if she were kneading a lump of dough.

"I didn't know all of this until sometime later. On that day, I was away from the village, down by the river, gathering rushes. I remember it was hot, deep in the middle of summer, and the rains had let up for a spell. My back was sore from bending' over, and I straightened up to ease it a bit. That's when I saw him, standin' there watching' me."

"Who?" Flora asked. "Who was it?"

"A Roman soldier, all dressed in leather and bronze."

Flora drew in a sharp breath when the significance of what she heard registered on her mind. She had suspected that some other man had gotten her mother pregnant. She thought it might have been similar to what she, herself, had experienced—that a relative from the village or maybe a raider from another clan had raped her. But she had never imagined the horror her mother was describing now.

Her mother continued the story. "I remember his eyes peering out from inside his helmet, as if they were glowing hot with fire and lust. I made to cry out for help, but he lurched forward, wrenched at the collar of my dress, and raised his sword to silence my scream." She paused and shook her head, as if to clear her mind of the painful memory. "Well, there's no need to say what happened next."

Flora's mother raised her head and looked her straight in the eye. There was force and conviction in her voice. "Your father never knew. I never told a soul what happened that day—no one except your grandmother. And even then, she had guessed the truth of it and pressed me for an answer. You must never speak a word of this, hear me? Not a word to anyone, most of all your father."

"My father?" Flora asked, her confusion leaking into her tone.

"Yes," her mother hissed. "Your *father*. It's not blood that makes a father, it's love. And that good man has loved you as his own from the day you were born. He never knew the truth of it, and he never will. Understand me?"

Flora ran her hands through her hair and across the top of her head in frustration. "Why? Why didn't you ever tell him?"

"How can you even ask that? Honor. Pride. If he had found out, he'd have hunted that man to the ends of the earth. It would have gotten him killed. I kept quiet for his sake and for the sake of our family. I needed a husband, and you girls needed a father. There's nothin' could be done to right the wrong, and revenge would have been the end of us all."

Frenzied thoughts tore at Flora's mind. It clearly wasn't her mother's fault, any more than Flora, herself, was to blame for her own rape. Some evil monster had violated her mother in the same way her uncle had stolen her virtue. She longed to reach out in a gesture of compassion for the horror they had both endured. She wanted to forgive her mother for holding her at a distance all her life. Though it still hurt, at least she understood why. But part of her also wrestled with the shock of the revelation. She had Roman blood running through her veins! She was an abomination—the bastard daughter of a savage beast. Her head spun and bile rose in her throat.

Flora teetered and reached out to steady herself against a pole. "Mother, please go. I need to think all this through."

Her mother stood and took a step toward her. "Flora, darlin'–"

"Please," she muttered again and pushed the woman's hand away. "Just go."

Reluctantly, her mother turned, retrieved the copper basin full of Flora's waste, and left. Before she ducked out the door, she turned back to her daughter. "It's not the blood in your veins that makes you who you are. It's what you hold in yer heart."

"And who am I, Mother? I don't think I even know anymore."

THE DAY PASSED IN A BLUR. Flora's masters granted her wish and gave her a short respite from any more preparations. They even let her go for a short walk into the forest outside the village, albeit with a large contingent of warriors shadowing her every move. But Flora could scarce enjoy the fresh air and the brief period of sunshine. The horror of her mother's revelation played itself over and over through her mind.

She was half Roman! She *hated* Rome and all it stood for. She had witnessed the cruel savagery of the Roman armies during the terror of her ordeals—her village burned, the men murdered, the women raped, and the children taken as slaves. No, it had not really happened, at least not what she had seen in that specific vision. But it was a future reality which *could* come true. And it was certainly true of what the Romans were capable of doing. Indeed, it was consistent with what they had already done, both beyond the great wall and even here in the highlands.

S*he* had Roman blood flowing through her veins. The thought literally made her sick to her stomach. She loathed herself for who she truly was, and though it wasn't fair, deep down inside she blamed her mother for allowing it to happen. Even with the threat of a sword at her throat, couldn't her mother have done something? Couldn't she have cried out for help or fought the man off. She hadn't been a helpless child. As a grown woman of the clans, a highland woman with the fire of Brigid in her spirit, she should have waited for the sword to drop and then clawed the man's eyes out or kicked him in the groin. Instead, she allowed a Roman soldier to impregnate her—to create a half-breed aberration who could never truly belong among her people.

But then Flora thought back to her own molestation. Had she reacted any differently? She had not screamed for help. She had not resisted. Instead, she had cowered in fear and, like her mother, buried her shame in a dark pit of silence and despair.

Surely the gods knew all of this. They *had* to know. So how could they have chosen her to become a goddess and to fill Brigid's vacant role? She was a bastard child and a tainted woman. She could never be the pure, virgin Bride. She could never become the chaste and holy Maiden.

Then the terrible truth hit her like a blow from the war hammer of Tyrannis. The gods never intended for her to become a goddess. They planned for her to fail the tests. They meant for her to be exposed for who she really was. And then, instead of becoming one of their own, she would be offered up as a sacrifice—the half-Roman abomination, burned on a Samhain pyre as a pleasing aroma to the gods. Would that oblation somehow break the Roman power over the land? Would her death sever the chains that held her people under the menace of Roman tyranny?

These thoughts circled around and around in Flora's mind, like a pack of wolves hemming her in on every side, until she cried herself to sleep that night in her palace prison on the loch.

Sometime, shortly after she had finally drifted off into the nether realm of hateful visions and terrifying fantasies, a soft touch on her arm and a gentle voice woke her.

"Flora. Flora, wake up. Flora, it's me, Domhnull."

"What–"

"Shh."

Flora opened her eyes to see her true love crouching at her side. Domhnull put a finger to his lips. Then he motioned for her to get up, and spoke in hushed tones, "We need to talk, but not here. Let's go to the forest. I'll have you back long before daybreak. They'll never know you were gone."

Flora shook her head, adamantly. She pushed herself up and brought her mouth close to his ear. "They know. Eliavres knew I got out last time. They'll catch us."

Then it was Domhnull's turn object. He whispered back, "Your grandmother, the *Seann Ghliocas*, sent a messenger to Eliavres that night. She told him about your visit, but he doesn't know how you got out. And he doesn't know about me."

Flora thought this through and then nodded. It made sense, but she still had reservations about trying the ruse a second time.

Domhnull continued. "Come on. I got in without anyone noticing. We'll be alright."

Flora was still unsure, but finally acquiesced. After all, if she was going to be offered as a sacrifice in the end, what did it really matter if they were caught? But she didn't want Domhnull to get dragged into her terrible fate.

She put her clothes into a greased leather bag, and they descended to the water as before. None of the guards raised an alarm as the two escapees glided silently across the surface of the loch and turned toward the shore. A light rain helped to muffle any sounds of their retreat and to obscure their silhouettes as they crawled onto the bank and disappeared into the trees.

When they were finally alone and beyond the range of the patrols, Domhnull pulled Flora into a close embrace and kissed her deeply. For a moment, she felt her body melt into his. She so longed for this man to be her husband. She longed to forget the call of the gods and to return to her village as the bride she was originally intended to become—Domhnull's bride. But thoughts of her impossible situation finally broke through the misty swoon of Domhnull's kiss, and she felt herself go cold. She put her hands on his chest and pushed him away.

A twig snapped somewhere nearby and she jumped. Domhnull's warrior instincts, honed through years of training and experience, must have told him it was just an animal, because he remained steady as a rock. Flora wanted to cling to that rock to keep herself anchored in this storm, but she shook her head and drew back.

"Domhnull, please. Don't make this any harder than it already is. I'm trapped in this surreal game, and there's no way out. I don't want to drag you down with me."

He grasped her arms with his strong, steady hands, and she could almost feel his strength flowing into her.

"I think this game, as you call it, is more complicated than you know."

"What do you mean?"

"The chief's special war band—the one I was recruited for—well, we haven't been going out on scouting missions. Not really. We've been escorting druid emissaries from Bhatair Rhu to all the other tribes in Caledonia. We even went to the islands and to Eire."

His words piqued Flora's curiosity and she prompted him to continue. "Why? What for?"

Domhnull's tone grew grave. "They're planning a raid on the wall. No. Not just a raid, an all-out assault."

"What do you mean? Who's planning an assault?"

"Bhatair Rhu, mostly. Him and Kynwal. They've convinced almost all the tribes to band together and push the Romans out of Britannia, once and for all. Other armies across the great sea have also coordinated invasions of Roman positions in their own territories. There are even rumors that some people south of the wall, who still honor the old gods, intend to help as well. They'll open some of the gates along the wall so our forces can get through."

"Push the Romans out of Britannia?" Flora mouthed in a whisper. The thought was almost too inconceivable to speak aloud. Then she puzzled at the name Domhnull had just mentioned. "Kynwal? Who is that?"

"He's the old warlord who's managing this whole effort for Bhatair Rhu. I'm sure you've seen him. He has a big scar across his face."

Flora remembered the man she had seen on horseback with Eliavres and Bhatair Rhu near *Feart Choille*. "Yes, I think I know who you mean. Who is he? What's his role in all of this?"

"I don't know much of his background. Apparently he has a long history with Bhatair Rhu. But the war bands from all the separate tribes will need a high commander to coordinate the attack. Kynwal will be that man."

"Is he the great chief of a tribe? I saw him wearing a thick silver torc, so I assumed he was an important person."

"No, he's not a chief. He's a warlord. But for this assault, he will be more than just a warlord. He will be an over-lord—head over all the tribal commanders. They're calling him the Pendragon."

Flora mulled over the implications of what Domhnull had said. Was it possible for the Romans to be driven out of Britannia? The Roman war machine had dominated the lands south of the wall for a dozen generations. Even in the highlands above the wall, their shadow cast a pall over everything that happened. Daily life among the tribes was forever shaped by the fear of Roman armies marching north, with death and devastation in their wake. And now, Flora had just discovered that her own life had been marred by Roman influence in a way she was revolted to even think about.

"Domhnull, you said this game was more complicated than I could imagine. The game I was talking about involved the gods and my calling to become Brigid. What does all this war planning have to do with me?"

Domhnull shrugged. "I don't know. I'm a warrior, not a druid or a chief. It just seems like a lot of big, important things are happening all at the same time."

"Yeah. It seems more than just coincidental. When is the assault on the wall planned for?"

"Just after the new moon."

Flora gaped in astonishment. "That's right after Lughnasadh!"

"Yeah. So? I figure they will make sacrifices to Lugh to get his blessing on the raid. What are you getting at?"

"Lughnasadh is when I'm supposed to be transformed into Brigid and make my transition to the Otherworld." She didn't say, "Or maybe its when I'll be offered as their sacrifice to Lugh." Instead, she sat down on the trunk of a fallen tree and buried her face in her hands. Rain dripped from the ends of her braided hair. "I need to think this all through."

Domhnull sat down beside her and put an arm around her shoulder, drawing her close. "Look, that's not what I brought you out here to talk about." He paused for a moment before continuing. "Flora, I have a plan. I want you to run away with me."

Flora's head shot up. "What? What are you talking about?"

"You're always saying that you're trapped in this situation and you want a way out. Well, I think I can get you free."

"How? Where could we possibly go?"

"Look," Domhnull rubbed her shivering shoulder. "While we were out on escort duty for the druids, I met people. And I learned my way around. We could go to Eire. The people there talk a little funny, but they can always use a good hunter and a warrior. We could get by."

Flora was skeptical. "How could we even get there? As soon as they discovered me missing, they would send search parties out in every direction."

"I've thought about that. We could swim out of the crannog, just like we did tonight. There are boats at the far end of the village. No one guards them. There's no reason to. If we take a boat, we could make it to Killin, at the far end of the loch, before sunup. With that much of a head start, they could never catch us."

"But what about me? After the *Annunciation*, everyone in the highlands and the islands knows I've been called to become Brigid."

"Aye," Domhnull smiled. "Everyone knows the news, but not a one of them has ever seen ye. How would they ever know who ye are? They'd know we were a couple on the run. But they'd never know what we were runnin' from until its too late to matter. We'd have to watch over our shoulders 'til after the new moon. After Lughnasadh, they'll all be too busy with the war to worry about us."

Flora considered what Domhnull said. She *had* been looking for a way out of this trap. Running away on her own wasn't an option. She would never be able to evade her pursuers for long. And she wouldn't even know how to survive alone, on the run. But with Domhnull, there just might be a chance.

Flora looked up into Domhnull's face. He was so strong and so confident. She longed to be his wife—to make a home together and have a family, like normal people. But somehow, she suspected their lives would never be normal again.

"I need to think this through, okay?"

"I know," Domhnull replied. "It's a lot to take in all at once. But you'll have to decide soon. If we're gonna do this, I'll need to get things ready."

Flora nodded, pensively. She looked into his bright, hopeful eyes, and a lump formed in her throat. This bold, confident man was willing to give up all he had accomplished and all his future prospects to free her from this devilish snare and live together with her as outcasts in a foreign land. She had never known that kind of love, and it melted her heart. She reached up, drew her face close to his, and brushed his lips with her own. Within moments they were kissing passionately, alone in the forest and oblivious to the drizzling rain.

"Manas, I want to see Bhatair Rhu. I want to see him now."

Manas inclined his head toward her. "Good morning to you, *Thaghadh*. I trust you rested well."

Flora stormed over toward the doorway, catching the firedog near the mantle on a fold in her *leine* and nearly toppling it. "Did you hear me? I want to see Bhatair Rhu."

"Relax, *Thaghadh*, you will see him soon enough. You will hear more petitioners today, and I understand the Arch Druid intends to be present. You can see him then."

Flora shook her head vehemently. "No. No, I need to talk to him privately, not at some public gathering. And *why* do I have to put on another one of those terrible pretenses? I can't stand making promises I have no way to keep."

There was a stirring just outside the doorway, and Bhatair Rhu ducked through the entrance. "As I hear the story, a young crippled girl walked away from your last 'pretense.'"

Flora felt a bit cowed by the Arch Druid and dropped her gaze.

He straightened up after negotiating the low portal and then bowed slightly toward her. "Good morning, Fiona *Taghte*. You seem rather spirited today. I could hear your voice at the other end of the causeway."

Bhatair Rhu broke out into a broad grin, and his eyes shone brightly, as if it had been a delightful start to his day, thus far. This just irked Flora even more, and the fire in her mood was kindled into a blaze.

"I need to talk to you. In private."

"Well now, what has caused all this agitation? I thought you would have been refreshed after a couple days of rest."

Flora turned her attention to the others in the room—Manas, Nandag, and the two attendants. "Please leave us. I need to speak with the Arch Druid alone."

Everyone hesitated, not knowing whether to obey the command. Bhatair Rhu gave a brief nod of the head and everyone began filing out except Nandag.

"Fiona *Taghte* must not be left alone with a man during her preparations. I can remain here, but stay back out of the way to protect her honor," Nandag suggested.

"Thank you, Nandag, but that won't be necessary. I need to speak to him alone," Flora insisted.

Bhatair Rhu sensed the urgency in Flora's mood and acquiesced. "It's okay, Nandag. The gods will take no offense."

Nandag hesitated a moment longer, then bowed slightly. "As you wish." She turned and ducked out the door.

"I hear you had a conversation with your grandmother a few nights back. How did that go?"

Flora ignored the question. "This is all about your father's mission, isn't it? And your vow to drive the Romans out of Britain?"

"Of course it is."

Bhatair Rhu's answer took Flora off guard. She had expected him to deny the accusation. "So this charade about becoming a goddess is just a ruse, is it? I am actually going to be your sacrifice to Lugh—highland blood mixed with Roman blood."

"Ah. It seems you have also spoken with your mother. I had hoped that subject might finally come up between you two."

Flora was taken aback by the Arch Druid's unabashed candor once again. "You knew? How? Mother said she had told no one—"

"Except your grandmother," Bhatair Rhu finished the statement for her. "The *Seann Ghliocas* felt the information might be useful to me."

Flora fumed. "So you figured you would just trick me into

becoming your blood sacrifice to Lugh, to gain his blessing on your little assault on the Wall? Why all the drama? Surely you had the power to take me and bind me to an altar without all the pretense." But then a thought flashed through Flora's mind, and she answered her own question. "Oh, I forgot. The bride has to be a *willing* sacrifice."

The Arch Druid's expression turned grave. "It seems you've had other conversations I didn't anticipate. Who told you about our plans to raid the South?"

Flora faltered, not wanting to get Domhnull in trouble, but she couldn't come up with a plausible lie, so evasion would just have to do. "That's irrelevant. *I* want to know the *truth* about why I'm being deceived and manipulated."

Bhatair Rhu took a deep breath and sat down on a bench near the Eternal Flame. "Why don't you have a seat."

"I think I'd rather stand," Flora said irritably. She actually would have liked to sit down, but at the moment, she just didn't want to do what the Arch Druid asked her to do. Whatever he requested, she would have done the opposite.

"Very well. Suit yourself."

He pulled out an amulet formed from two intertwined serpents. Flora instinctively fumbled in her pocket to see if he had somehow stolen Brigid's charm from her. But it was right there where she left it. The one in Bhatair Rhu's hand was an exact twin of her own.

"Where...?" Flora struggled to articulate her surprise.

"I think there is a rather significant misunderstanding between us." He twisted the amulet in the firelight.

"And what's that?" Flora quipped.

"Your calling by the gods to become Brigid is not some elaborate ruse. It is quite real, I assure you."

"But you do expect for me to fail their tests, so I will be offered as a sacrifice instead?"

The Arch Druid shook his head slowly, as if he were expressing disappointment at an apprentice who failed to learn a crucial lesson. "No. No, we strongly desire for you to succeed."

"Why? Don't you need a blood sacrifice for Lugh to bless your attack on the Romans?"

"Oh, there will, indeed, be many sacrifices, but we desperately need Brigid to fight the spiritual battle in the Otherworld, while we assault the Roman positions here."

Flora was still angry and confused, but Bhatair Rhu's words piqued her curiosity, and she stopped clenching her teeth quite so strongly. She spat out her next words. "What's that supposed to mean?"

The Arch Druid held up the amulet again, as if inspecting it for the very first time. "The workmanship truly is exquisite, is it not? Did you feel its power flowing through you that day when you were immersed in the holy waters?"

Flora gaped at him. Was there anything about her this man didn't know? "How...?" She let the question trail off into the air and evaporate in the morning mist. Of course he knew. If he had an exact duplicate of her amulet, he must have contrived for her to find a similar one in the waters of the spring that day. She shifted her thoughts back to the matter at hand. "What spiritual battle?"

"When men fight against each other in this world, there is always a larger spiritual conflict going on in the background—a confrontation we are usually not even aware of. But make no mistake, what happens in the spiritual engagement will work itself out in the affairs of men. We need Brigid to fight on our side to win this war. We need *you* to fight our spiritual battle in the Otherworld."

"*Me?* Fight against Tyrannis and the Cailleach?" Flora was stunned at the implications of his words. Even if she were to be transformed into Brigid, she could never hope to contend with powerful gods who had ruled their domains in the Otherworld since the beginning of time.

"Oh, heavens no. You won't fight against them. You will fight *with* them."

Now Flora was more confused than ever. "You mean join with Tyrannis and the Cailleach against Lugh, and Cerridwen, and the Daghda? That doesn't make any sense."

Bhatair Rhu actually laughed aloud. "No. No, that would make no sense at all." Then his expression became more sober. "In order to drive the Romans out of our land, we need Brigid to defeat the Roman god."

Flora sat in stunned silence. She was staggered by the Arch Druid's words. Her anger dissipated in an instant, only to be replaced by a flood of terror. The Roman armies were the most powerful armies in the world. According to the stories she heard from her father, the Romans had never been defeated in battle. They had conquered lands she had never even heard of before, subduing ancient civilizations that had ruled for countless generations. If these stories were true, the Roman god had to be more powerful than any other gods. He must have defeated the gods of those other nations, or the Roman armies could not have conquered their lands. What could Brigid possibly do against such a god? What could *she* do in such a war?

Bhatair Rhu apparently saw the understanding dawn in Flora's mind. "*That* is why we needed your Roman blood. We needed Roman blood mixed with the blood of a highlander, not as a sacrifice to Lugh. We need that blood to flow in the veins of Brigid, herself—to give the goddess the power she needs to overcome the nailed god."

The Arch Druid's words did not bring her any comfort. Instead, they just stoked the fires of her horror what she was being asked to do.

"The 'nailed god?' What does that mean?"

"The Romans believe their god came down from the heavens to visit them, disguised in human form. While living on this earth, he was captured and nailed to a cross as a traitor to his people—one who sought to steal the crown of the Roman emperor."

Confusion mixed with Flora's anxiety. "They killed their god? I don't understand."

"Apparently, the nailed god rose from the dead and then demanded their worship."

This was even worse than Flora had feared. Not only had the Roman god subdued the gods of all their enemies, he had even overcome death, itself. The Great Goddess herself could not claim such a feat. Yes, the Cailleach 'died,' in a sense, every hundred years, but she really just shed her old form to be reborn as Brigid. In fact, Flora's own current plight was spawned when the Cailleach truly had died, but then never re-emerged as the Maiden. Brigid was actually 'dead,' and now needed to be replaced.

"I know," Bhatair Rhu said in a consoling tone. "It's a bit overwhelming. But dangerous times lead to great opportunities. This is our chance to gain ascendency over the nailed god and to drive the Romans out of Britain forever. And *you* are the key. Your blood will give you power over the Roman god, maybe not everywhere, but here in our own land. Highlander blood and Roman blood will give Brigid the power she needs."

Flora shook her head in dismay. "I can't do it. I can't fight the Roman god. I could never win such a battle."

The Arch Druid frowned, gravely. "The visions of your ordeals are true as well. If you don't defeat the nailed god, and if we don't drive the Roman armies from Britannia, the horrors you witnessed will become a reality. Our people and our lands will be left in ruin. I can't let that happen, and neither can you."

Bhatair Rhu once again held up the amulet to the light of the Eternal Flame. "If you're wondering where this came from, I received mine in much the same way you received yours. It was a gift from the goddess many years ago. I always wondered why she gave it to me. Then, when Eliavres found yours in your little leather pouch, I knew."

"You knew what?" Flora whispered, almost breathlessly.

"I knew you were the one we had been seeking. There were times I doubted if we had identified the right person. I doubted the oracles and Fedelma's visions. I even doubted your appearance at the sacred yew. But when I heard about your talisman, I knew for certain you were the one."

Flora fished in her pocket and retrieved her amulet. She held it up in the fire light, where it glinted next to its twin. Bhatair Rhu smiled.

CHAPTER TWENTY

This day of petitions had been harder than the first, and Flora collapsed into a pile of furs lying on the floor.

"Was it truly that bad, mistress?" Nandag asked.

"Oh, Nandag. I feel horrible giving all those people false hopes. I have no power to grant their requests. I honestly wish I could. Their needs are real, and many are devastating. I truly, feel their pain, but can't actually do anything to help. All my promises are really just lies."

Nandag knelt beside her and looked at her with the familiar expression of a concerned mentor. "Now there. You may not have the power to help them at this moment, but one day soon you will. After Lughnasadh, you can hand out as many blessings as you choose. You'll be able to make a big difference in these people's lives. That's what they're counting on."

Flora sighed heavily. "I'm glad you're so sure of that. I'm certainly not."

"And what makes you doubt the plan of the gods?"

"I don't doubt them. I doubt me. Oh, Nandag, you know me

better than just about anyone else. Do *you* really think I could become a goddess?"

Nandag reached for Flora's hands and squeezed them gently. "I think you are a very special young woman, with unique talents and abilities. You may just surprise yourself. The love in your heart runs deep, and your sense of compassion is strong. These would seem to be the most important traits for a goddess, don't you think?"

"Hmm," Flora just murmured. She did not add that purity would be a necessary virtue for the Maiden Bride, and she was most certainly not pure.

A shadow momentarily blotted out the sun shining through the doorway, and Finnan's familiar silhouette crossed in front of the altar. "Well done, lass. That was a fine thing you did for the wee bairn at the hearing."

Flora assumed Finnan meant her promise to the young boy who had recently lost both parents to the fever. The hope that he would become a mighty warrior and make his father proud helped lift his spirits. But when she assured him they would all be united in the Otherworld one day, he broke into tears and rushed forward to give her a hug. He asked Flora to take a lock of his hair to his mother, so she wouldn't forget him. How could she deny such a request? She clutched the twisted lock in her hands even now, rolling it between her fingers and wondering how she could ever keep her promise.

"Finnan, I'm glad you're here. I'd like to ask you some questions about the Roman god. Did you learn about their 'nailed god' when you lived among them?"

Finnan looked introspective for a moment, while the firelight of the Eternal Flame danced across his face. "Indeed, I learned much. But what makes you ask such a question?"

Flora looked back into Nandag's face. Her old mentor still held her hands, and Flora squeezed them appreciatively before pulling them free. "Nandag, could you please give us some time to talk?"

"Certainly, *Taghte*. I'll be just across the room. You can't be left alone with a man during your preparations."

"I understand. Thank you."

Flora waited until Nandag had disappeared into the shadows at the far side of the crannog. "Bhatair Rhu tells me I am to fight a spiritual battle against the Roman god."

"Aye," Finnan replied, "to support the attack on the Wall."

Flora pursed her lips in a scowl of irritation. Finally, she said, "So does everyone know about this except me?"

"Well apparently you *do* know, or you couldn't be askin' the question, now could you?" Finnan winked at her.

"Hmph. Well, if I *am* to do battle with this 'nailed god,' then I should learn as much about him as I can. So, what can you tell me?"

"Well, let me see." Finnan stroked his goatee. "First of all, he's not a Roman god."

Flora allowed the perplexity to show in her expression. "What do you mean, he's not a Roman god?"

"Well, I mean he's not a Roman god, of course. That bein', not all Romans claim him as their god. And those who do worship him are not all Romans. Most, in fact, are not."

"You're really confusing me. I don't understand what you're saying. The Romans worship a god who gave them victory over almost every other people in the known world. Isn't that so?"

Finnan grinned. "Well, actually no." He motioned at a nearby stool. "Do you mind if I have a seat? It appears this might take some explainin'."

"Of course." Flora gestured for him to sit down.

"Now then. When the Roman armies were out conquering lands far and wide, they worshipped the old gods, which are pretty much the same gods the highlanders still worship today, just with different names."

"But now the Romans worship this 'nailed god?' Why would they abandon the gods who gave them victory? And why would *our* gods allow the Romans to defeat us?"

Finnan leaned back and pulled a pipe from his pocket. "Do you mind?"

Flora just waved him on, anxious to hear the answers to her questions.

"Well, I'm guessin' I better take those questions on one at a time. Last one first. I can't say I know the mind of the gods, but they might have favored the Romans because the Romans gave them better offerings. Or, our people might have angered them in some way. Sometimes I think perhaps the gods just like to watch we mortals squabble amongst ourselves. But I *will* point out the Romans conquered neither the highlanders of Caledonia, nor my people on Eire. In fact, they built a rather large wall, straight across the island, to keep us out of their business."

"Okay. Okay, but who is this 'nailed god,' and why do the Romans worship him now?"

Finnan took a deep draw on his pipe and then rested it on his knee. "Some do. Some don't. Some still worship the old gods. But about three or four generations ago, the Roman emperor prayed for the Christian god to give him victory in a critical battle. After he won the engagement, he issued a decree honoring this god and then proclaimed his allegiance to the same. Of course, whatever the emperor does, becomes fashionable for the aristocrats as well."

Flora was puzzled by this strange term. "What's an aristocrat?"

"Ah yes. Our people don't have those, now do we? Well, you can think of them like the village chiefs and the leaders of the clans. In any event, not all Romans worship the Christian god. Likewise, many people who do worship him are not Roman. And so, he is not, per se, a Roman god."

"Okay, fine. But our Arch Druid seems to believe I need to battle this god in the spiritual realm so our armies can drive the Romans out of Britannia."

"So he does."

"Wait," Flora mused, "what did you call him? The Chrishman god? What does that mean?"

"It's 'Christian.' It means the followers of the Christ."

Flora rolled her eyes. "That's not terribly helpful. What is a 'Christ?'"

Finnan took another series of puffs on his pipe. The smoke had a sweet, pungent odor. It mingled with the fumes of the Eternal Flame, and they danced together toward the apex of the thatched roof. That was actually why the roof was pitched so high—to allow the smoke from the fire to ascend out of the breathing space. Eventually, it permeated the thatch, keeping it dry and free of bugs.

"The Christ is the 'Anointed One' of the most high god in heaven. Or so the Christians claim. The Romans nailed the Christ to a cross, but then he rose from the grave three days later."

"But Bhatair Rhu said the *Roman god* was nailed to the cross. You're saying it was really this Christ man."

Finnan blew a smoke ring and smiled. "Well, now, that's where it all gets a wee bit complicated. You see, the Christ is the son of the father god, but in human form."

"So this Christ is sort of like Bhatair Rhu, the son of a human parent and a god?"

"Well, not exactly. No. According to the Christians, the father and the son both existed together as one from before time began. The son just took on human form for a little while."

Flora was getting annoyed. She had hoped to learn about the Roman god and possibly identify some weaknesses she could exploit if she had to engage him in battle as Brigid. But she was just becoming more and more confused.

"You mean, there are really two gods? The father god and the son god?"

"Three, actually. Father, son, and holy spirit. But they are also one."

"Okay, so now that's starting to make more sense. This Roman god is like the Great Goddess, with her three different aspects—Brigid, the Morrigan, and the Cailleach—Maiden, Mother, and Crone."

Finnan nodded. "Aye. Similar, but different as well."

"How do you mean?"

"Well, the Christian god—the father, son, and spirit—are three individuals, but are perfectly united in nature, in will, and in purpose. They all work together to uplift and glorify each other. The aspects of the Great Goddess, on the other hand, are very different from one another, and often find themselves at odds. Even now, the Cailleach appears to be conspiring with Tyrannis and others to subvert Brigid, so that winter will remain forever, and summer will never come. The Great Goddess not only squabbles with the other gods, but occasionally even ends up quarreling between her own selves. The Christian god would never do that."

Flora thought about what Finnan said for a while before replying. "Then why did the father god send the son down to earth and allow him to get crucified?"

"Actually, they planned it together, all three of them, from the beginning of creation, or so I'm told."

"Why?" Flora wondered aloud. "What for? That doesn't make sense."

Finnan shook his pipe in the air to emphasize the point, "Ahh. You've struck at the heart of the matter. The Christians believe this plan was intended to redeem them from the curse of this world. Not just them, actually, but everyone who accepts the son's sacrifice on their behalf."

Flora shook her head. "Now you've lost me again."

"I know. It can all be a bit confusing. I'll lay it straight out, as it was explained to me."

"Please," Flora exclaimed, trying to contain her growing frustration.

"Maybe I should start from the beginning. This is how the Christians explain it, you understand."

Flora nodded for him to continue.

"The father, son, and spirit existed from eternity past. No one created them. They have always been. At some point, I'm not sure exactly when, they created beings in the spiritual world which the

Christians call 'angels.' Funny term, that. It really means, 'messengers,' or so I'm told."

Flora mused. "Who did the god need to send messages to?"

"I admit, it is an odd situation. But in any event, one of the highest ranking messengers questioned the legitimacy of the father's government and challenged the son's authority. I don't know what his arguments involved, but they must have been persuasive, because he convinced a large number of the angels to stage a rebellion."

"This is all very interesting," Flora interjected, "but what does it have to do with the Romans?"

"I'll be gettin' to that by and by. About this time, the father, son, and spirit created our world, along with the sun, the moon, and the stars."

"Wait." Flora held up her hand to stop him. "I thought the Cailleach created the world. And what about Lugh and Cerridwen? They rule over the sun and the moon."

"Hold that thought for just a bit, and I'll show you where it all fits together."

"Okay," Flora relented, her patience wearing thin. "But this all sounds very ridiculous to me. I can't believe this is a true story about a god who is so powerful he won over the Romans and subdued the whole world. I think maybe these 'Christians' lied to you to protect the secrets of their god's power."

Finnan's expression lost its whimsical air and he assumed a grave countenance. "I assure you, my lady, this is their true belief. I've spoken to Christian priests from Londinium to Rome, itself. Not only do they tell the same tale, but they would give their lives to defend the honor of their god."

Flora sensed she had offended Finnan and demurred. "I'm sorry, Master Bard. Please go on."

Finnan's manner softened once again. "Of course. Now where was I? Oh yes. After they created the world with all the plants and animals, the father, son, and spirit formed the first two people in their own image. I don't really think this couple looked like their god, at least not in a physical sense. I get the impression they were created in such a way that they reflected the god's nature—more like a shadow than an exact copy."

Flora wondered about this. She always imagined her own people's gods looked like big versions of themselves—like giant humans who strode over the earth and flew through the heavens, just in the Otherworld where they couldn't be seen. Of course, they could change form into animals, if they chose. But she always assumed they looked human in their natural state. Now she wondered if that was really true, or if people simply imagined the gods to be the way they wanted them to be, rather than how they really were. In any event, she motioned for Finnan to continue his explanation.

"After the father, son, and spirit—uh, the Christians call them the 'trinity' for short. Anyway, after the trinity created the first couple in their own image, they drove the rebellious angels down to the earth and trapped them there. And here's the tricky part. The trinity allowed the fallen angels to recruit the humans into their rebellion. The father asked the man and woman to trust him. If so, he would provide for their every need. He also warned them to follow his guidance, so they would be safe from harm. But you know how that goes, right?"

"What do you mean?" Flora asked.

"Well, you and I don't have children of our own. But parents tell me that young ones have willful minds. They can apparently be rather head strong on occasion, and often do exactly the opposite of what they are told. Of course, I never did such a thing." Finnan winked at her. "And I'm certain, neither did you."

Flora knew he made the comment in jest, but nevertheless, she thought of the many times she had defied her father's will and crossed her mother's rules—usually to her own detriment, and certainly to their disappointment.

"So did these fallen angels succeed in winning the people of the world over to their side?" Flora asked, interested now, despite herself.

"Aye, they did. And to a sorrowful end."

"How did it happen?"

"The head angel—the one who had started the whole conspiracy —deceived the woman with trickery and lies. He appeared to her in the form of a serpent, and persuaded her to mistrust the father and to disobey his instructions."

Flora interrupted Finnan. "So these rebellious angels can take on the form of animals, just like our gods can?"

"Apparently so. At least this one did in this case."

"Okay, so what happened?" Flora felt herself being drawn into the story, even though it really didn't help her understand how to defeat the Roman god.

"Well, the serpent wasn't satisfied with disobedience alone, so he didn't stop there. He actually convinced the woman she could become a goddess herself, if she would only trust him instead of the trinity. She believed the lie and joined the insurrection. Her husband, not wanting to lose his beautiful bride, followed her example, and was lost as well. They, and their descendants, have been in rebellion against the trinity ever since."

Flora frowned and her irritation returned. "Wait. You said you would explain what all this has to do with the nailed god of the Romans. I don't see any connection whatsoever."

"Be patient, mistress. I promise to bring it all together."

Flora rolled her eyes. "If one more person tells me to be patient, I think I'll scream. First Nandag, then Manas, and now you. You people can be very frustrating."

"And you," Finnan smirked, "can be very impatient."

"Okay. I'm being patient. Now would you please just get to the point?"

"Certainly. The father, son, and spirit knew the inexperienced humans would be at a disadvantage against the sly cunning of the enemy. They warned the man and the woman against going down the road of mistrust and disobedience. If they started down that path, it would end in death. You see, they had been created to live forever. But rebellious hearts would lead to ruin."

Flora motioned Finnan to pause for a moment. She listened closely, and could faintly hear the guards at the end of the bridge talking to someone. She realized her conversation with Finnan would be interrupted soon. "Hurry up. Someone's coming."

Finnan puffed on his pipe, blew out the smoke, and resumed his story. "Since they knew the man and the woman would fall prey to the deception of the enemy, the trinity devised a plan to reconcile them back to the side of truth and holiness, and to restore the relationship which would be damaged by their mistrust. According to this plan, the son would become a human. He would show them what a life of faith was like. And, more importantly, he would take responsibility for their rebellious actions. He would live a life of perfect harmony with the father and the spirit. Then he would trade his perfect life for the failures and shortcomings of the man, the woman, and all their descendants. All they had to do was trust in him. Then he would suffer the consequences of the curse they deserved, and they would receive what he deserved—reconciliation with the father. He would die, and they would receive eternal life."

Flora saw Manas duck through the doorway and walk up behind Finnan.

"Greetings *Thaghadh.*" Manas bowed his head slightly. "Master Bard." Another nod of the head. "That sounds like the story of the Christian god."

Flora floundered for an explanation. "I asked Finnan to tell me about the Roman god. The Arch Druid told me I will have to fight against the nailed god in the Otherworld. I assume you know about that. Everyone else seems to."

"Indeed. That is precisely what the Council is preparing you for," Manas replied.

"Then why didn't anyone bother to tell *me* about it? I had to put it all together on my own."

"Be patient. Everything is revealed at the appropriate time," Manas replied.

"Uh oh," Finnan intoned with a smile.

Flora exploded. "Quit telling me to be patient! And quit hiding things from me! This is my life we're talking about here. I am apparently the key person to the success of this whole invasion plan. I think I deserve to know *everything* about what's going on."

"Even so," Manas concurred, calmly. "If it were up to me, I would gladly provide all the details. But I'm afraid you must address the issue with the Arch Druid and the Council." Then he tried to change the subject. "Did Master Finnan answer your questions about the Roman god?"

Flora felt like screaming, but realized it wouldn't do any good. Finnan and Manas had been more helpful to her than anyone else except Nandag. It wouldn't be fair to take her frustrations out on them. She would have to insist on speaking with Bhatair Rhu to confront him about anything else they might be hiding from her.

Flora took a moment to calm the fire burning in her gut and then replied in a more reasonable tone. "Okay. I'm sorry for my outburst. It's not your fault. I'll take this up with Bhatair Rhu. And no, Finnan has not answered my question. He has entertained me with a long history of the Christian god, but he has not told me anything useful that will prepare me to confront this nailed god in a spiritual battle."

Finnan gestured at her with his pipe. "I was just getting to that point."

Flora tossed up her hands. "Please. Tie it all together if you can."

Finnan pursed his lips and looked thoughtful. "You asked why the Romans nailed the son to a cross and then later turned around to worship him."

"Yes," Flora replied, barely holding back her agitation. "That's what I wanted to know."

Manas interjected. "The truth is, the Christians conquered the Romans without drawing a sword."

This remark instantly captured Flora's attention. "What do you mean by that? And what do you know about the Roman god?"

"The *Christian* god," Finnan corrected her.

"Unlike our Master Bard, here, I have never traveled to Rome,"

Manas replied. "But I have spent a great deal of time with Greek physicians south of the wall, conferring about the healing arts. Most of them are Christians, and so I learned a great deal about their god from them."

"And what did you mean when you said the Christians conquered the Romans?" Flora reiterated.

"The Christians discovered a power greater than the mightiest army in the world. They conquered Rome from within, not from without."

Flora looked at him with a quizzical look, but Finnan chimed in before she could ask Manas what he meant. "Three powerful forces, actually."

"You mean the trinity you mentioned before?" she asked.

"Nay," Finnan replied.

And Manas again weighed in. "Faith, hope, and love. Faith in their god. The hope of eternal life. Love for their god and for each other."

"Aye," Finnan concurred. "These are the forces the Christians used to drive the old gods out of Rome and to subvert the mightiest army the world has ever known. Or so I'm told."

Flora was disappointed. This didn't give her anything she could use against the god of the Romans to help her people win the war on the ground. "So what is his weakness? The Dagda is vulnerable to light. Lugh is susceptible to water. The Cailleach fears the warmth of fire. What does this Christian god fear?"

"Fear?" Finnan scoffed. "According to the Christians, their god is all knowing and all powerful. He fears nothing at all."

"This is true," Manas concurred. "Since his enemies cannot harm him directly, they do it indirectly. They attack his people."

This notion perplexed Flora. "If he is all powerful, why can he not protect his own people? The Daghda can certainly protect us if he chooses to."

"Aye," Finnan agreed. "But the Christian god honors the free choice of his people. He will protect them if they place their faith in him. But just like the first woman and man, if they decide not to trust him, and to believe his enemies' lies instead, they place themselves outside his refuge."

Manas concluded, "And so the greatest weapon of his enemy is deception. If the Christians can be enticed to abandon their god, or even simply to ignore him, then they become vulnerable to other attacks."

"Finally," Flora exclaimed, "you have given me something I can use. If I become Brigid, I just need to get the Romans to doubt their god, and then their armies will be powerless against our forces on the ground. Is that true?"

"I'm not sure it would be that simple," Finnan reasoned. "The Roman armies are quite formidable, in and of themselves. Many of the soldiers are still loyal to Mithras, one of the old gods. But you are correct that the true spiritual battle lies in the hearts and minds of the Christian people. The only way to harm the Christian god is to lead his followers away from him."

"If," Manas interjected, "that is what you truly want to do."

"What do you mean?" Flora retorted, perturbed at his remark. "Of course it's what I want to do. *If* I become Brigid—and I still consider that a big 'if'—I would have a duty to protect my people."

"Even if it means resorting to lies and deceit to accomplish those ends?" Manas picked up an iron poker and prodded at the logs in the fire circle. Then he looked her straight in the eye with a piercing gaze that surprised Flora with its intensity. "In the end, *Thaghadh*, we all have choices to make—choices about who we are and who we will become."

Flora's thoughts flashed back to her conversation with Manas on the walk from *Feart Choille* to Fearnan. On that day he had looked at her in a similar way and asked, "Who are you, mistress? And who will *you* become?" As the memory crystalized in her mind a chill ran up her spine. Who, in fact, was she, after all? Who, indeed, would she become?

Manas now echoed his words from that auspicious moment,

staring intently into her eyes as if to ensure she would remember the lesson this time. "The path of life is treacherous, *Thaghadh,* fraught with unexpected dangers. Some, we can control. Others we cannot. Eventually, we all confront that critical instance which ushers us from this world into the next. At that moment, the most important thing is to be certain about who we are. The only thing we take with us into the realm beyond is our identity."

Manas bowed. *"Thaghadh."* He turned on his heel and left.

Flora stared at the Master Healer's retreating back and wondered at his words. She remained silent for a long while. Finally, she stood and moved close to Finnan. He looked at her quizzically and took a deep draw on his pipe. Flora bent down and whispered in his ear, low enough that Nandag would not hear.

"Finnan, I need to get out of here tonight. I need to see my father. Can you help me?"

Finnan turned his head to blow out a big puff of smoke, then he looked back at Flora and studied her thoughtfully. Though his expression retained its typical whimsical air, Flora thought she saw something other than mischief in his eyes. Could it be compassion?

Slowly, Finnan nodded. "Aye," he responded with a wink. "That I can do. Be ready after dark—after Nandag and the attendants have gone."

"Thank you," she mouthed wordlessly, and patted his shoulder.

FLORA COULDN'T SLEEP. Anticipation about this meeting with her father had caused her to toss and turn in an endless cycle of frustration and doubt. She reclined on a bench in front of the Eternal Flame and watched the fire spit and pop. It was only "eternal" because Drib and Drab constantly fed its ravenous hunger with an endless supply of logs. Otherwise, it would sputter and die in a pile of gray ash and glowing embers just like any other fire.

The rain came down in a steady drizzle, its soft patter on the thatched roof providing the only solace Flora felt at the moment. She was beginning to wonder if Finnan had either failed in his task or simply abandoned the notion altogether, when she heard muffled voices outside the door. The druidess adepts stationed on guard challenged Finnan. They knew who he was, of course, but they would question his reasons for visiting Flora this late in the evening.

She listened closely to hear Finnan's excuse, hoping it would be adequately convincing.

"Fiona *Taghte* said she has a recurring dream, almost every night. Unfortunately, by morning time the memory of it fades into the darkness. Such a repeated dream could hold great portents, if it is from the gods."

"Okay," one of the guards replied. "But what does that have to do with you? Why hasn't Fedelma or one of the other seers been summoned to interpret the vision? And who is this with you?"

"Indeed, Fedelma has been summoned. Alas, she could not get here this evening, but will come on the morrow. However, in case the dream occurs again this night, perhaps for the very last time, I have been assigned to check on Fiona *Taghte* and document all she can remember of the vision."

"And her?"

Flora heard Finnan reply again, "As you know, the Chosen One cannot be alone with a man during her preparations. My apprentice is here to chaperone me during the visit. We shan't be long. I will wake Fiona, briefly, to determine if the dream has come this evening. If so, I will question her and memorize every detail. If not, we shall leave and come again before dawn. If this is, indeed, a direct communication from the gods, it could be an important part of Fiona's story, to be preserved for generations to come."

"Or," the guard countered, "it could be a warning for the Council." There was a brief pause, and then, "Very well, Master Bard. Be about your business."

Flora watched the door swing inward, and wind blew rain through the opening. Finnan ducked through the entrance of the crannog, followed by a lithe figure in a hooded cowl. They negotiated around the Pool of Brigid's Tears, and came up beside her.

"Nicely done," Flora spoke in a hushed tone. "You got in well enough. But now how do we get out?"

"Not to worry," Finnan whispered. "I have everything under control." Flora could see his bright eyes sparkle in the firelight. "You trade places with Gavenia here. She'll wait while we go to visit with your father. When we return, you can switch back." Finnan grinned with self-satisfaction. "I find a simple plan so much easier to implement, don't you?"

Flora smiled her approval. "You, Master Bard, are quite devious when you choose to be. I'll have to keep my eye on you."

Finnan turned his back as Flora quickly swapped clothes with Gavenia. The rain-soaked cloak made Flora shiver, but the hood would mask her identity and keep her somewhat dry. With the exchange complete, Finnan led her out the door.

"Well?" the guard asked.

"I'm afraid not," Finnan replied. "We'll try again before sunrise. Hopefully, we haven't missed our opportunity to discover the secret."

"If the gods truly want to communicate with us, or with Fiona *Taghte*, they'll make sure the message is clear." The guard turned to Flora. "You're fortunate. Not many people get to meet a goddess in person."

Flora was terrible at disguising her voice, so she decided a wordless response would be best. She bowed her head in a deferential gesture toward the adept, hoping it would suffice.

Finnan stepped away and began striding down the bridge. He called over his shoulder, "We'll be back before dawn."

Flora hastened to follow him, and they made their way across the causeway. The warriors stationed on the other end of the bridge were less of a problem. They were merely charged to keep Flora safe, not to protect her spiritual purity.

Flora followed two steps behind Finnan, as an apprentice should, while he led her through Fearnan's scattered roundhouses. The rain muffled the sounds of their progress and kept most of the warriors inside their quarters.

Finally, Finnan approached a small hut, pushed aside a cowhide flap, and ushered her through the entrance. It was dimly lit inside with oil lamps and a fire in the circle at the center. Flora immediately saw her father across the room. Before she could even say a word, he rushed across the space and swept her up in his arms.

"My wee *fauth*," he cried, "I've missed you so." He almost crushed her in his enthusiastic embrace.

Vaguely, Flora heard Finnan remark, "I'll be leaving you to yourselves, now. I'll watch for you to come out the door when you're ready to return." Then he exited the hut into the rain.

"Oh, Father," Flora whispered into his ear as she buried her face in his hair. And then she could say nothing more. She just wept in his strong arms, feeling truly safe for the first time since this whole ordeal began. They stood there for a long time, holding each other close.

"Hush now. Hush. It's okay. I'm here, my girl." He held her tight. "I'm so sorry, darlin'. I'm so sorry I let them take you away. When Manas came for you that day, I had a sick feeling in my gut I'd never see you again. I tried to follow after you, to talk to you one more time, if only to say goodbye. But the warriors blocked my way and warned me not to interfere. I'm so sorry I let you go."

Eventually Flora pulled back a bit. "It's not your fault, *Dadaidh*. There's nothing you could have done. They've been planning this for a long time. If you tried to intervene, you would have just gotten in trouble with the Arch Druid and the Great Chief." Flora looked around the small room. "Where's Mother?"

Her father beamed down at her, his huge bulk overshadowing her tiny form. "You look so fine. Are they treating you well?"

"Fine? I'm soaking wet. I must look like a drowned rat."

"Nay, you're always my beautiful girl. No bit o' water from the sky can change that."

"Mother?" Flora repeated.

"We're staying at *Incheskadyne* with her kin, while she's here tendin' to you. It's just a way down the loch. Not far. This is Master Finnan's place, while he's here doing his work. He sent for me this noon and said you asked for me. I didn't know he was sneaking you out. But it does my heart glad to see you. Ahh, you're the spittin' image of your mother."

Flora backed out of his embrace and dropped her gaze to the floor. "That's part of why I asked Finnan to bring me here. There's something I need to tell you. Something you need to know."

Flora wasn't sure she could even find the words to say what she planned. Then suddenly, she realized she couldn't speak at all. This was all a big mistake. She should never have asked Finnan to sneak her out or put her father at risk. She certainly didn't need to hurt his heart this way. There was no reason he needed to know. It would only cause him useless pain.

The big man watched her in silence as the struggle raged on inside. But finally he broke the stillness in the room and the tension tearing at her heart.

"So, you know, do you?"

Flora's head jerked up, and she stared into his face. "Know what?"

"You found out about your father. Is that it?"

"You know?" Flora exhaled the words in a breathless whisper of shock and surprise.

Her father sat down on a nearby stool and braced his elbows on his knees. "Aye, lass. I know. How could I not? Your light brown locks. Your olive skin. Those blue eyes full of starlight. Nay. You got none o' those from me."

Flora was still reeling from his revelation. "How long? How long have you known?"

"Oh," he shrugged. "From before you were born."

"But Mother said she never told anyone. She was afraid you'd go after the man and get yourself killed."

"Aye. She was right about that. I wanted to hunt the bastard down and rip his throat out with my own two hands, but I needed to protect your mother's honor, even more. And yours. Didn't want you growing up in shame." He looked down at her, and Flora could see tears welling up in his eyes.

Flora turned away. She couldn't look this man in the face. The shame he had given so much to protect her from was crashing in on her, even now. "But why? Why would you suffer that humiliation in silence for me? I wasn't even your own. I wasn't your daughter."

The big man stepped up behind her and wrapped his strong arms around her shoulders, pulling her close. "Oh, my girl, my precious girl. It's not the blood running through your veins that makes you my daughter. It's a father's love that makes you mine. And you've had that since the day you were born. You are my very heart."

Flora turned in his embrace, buried her face in his chest, and wept like a child. Her body shook with sobs. So many things had been stolen from her—her family, her village, her place in the clan, even her name. She was afraid this revelation would steal her father away from her as well—the one person in this world who had loved her more than anyone else. But his love was the kind that could not be shaken.

Flora whispered under her breath, "I thought I'd lost you too."

Her father squeezed gently and held her close. "You're my girl, my wee *fauth*, and nothin' can ever change that. I love you, lass, not because of where you come from, but because of who you are."

She cried for a very long time. And her father, her true father, held her close and never let her go.

Eventually, her shudders subsided and her sobs grew still. Her father placed his hands on her shoulders and pushed away, slightly, so he could look into her eyes. His face was blurred by her tears, but she could still make out the gentle smile on his lips.

"And now look at you. You're gonna be a goddess. You're going to be *my* goddess—the patron of smiths. Who'd'ave ever thought, all those years when I was singing you the Ballad of Brigid, the words would turn out to be true of you? How could I not see the light of your own life reflected in the rhymes?"

He placed one arm around her waist and grasped her hand in the other. Then he danced with her, while he sang in a deep, rich, resonant voice. Flora closed her eyes, allowing her body to follow his lead, and lost herself in the melody. As she listened to the words, she wondered if they had, indeed, been prophetic. The song wasn't just the story of Brigid's life. It was turning out to be the story of her life as well.

Down by the loch where the willow tree grows
In the glen on an early spring day
She is born
She is here
The wee bairn in my arms
She has come to set my heart free

A young sprite is she, a fair bonny lass
She bids me raise Uaithne and play
She dances
She sways
She sets right the days
In winter, fall, summer and spring

A daughter divine, one sister of three
As her father I see past these times
She searches
She ponders
Toward wisdom she wanders
And soon I must give her away

A maiden in white, a princess to be
With a flame set ablaze in her eyes
She weeps
And she sings
A bride of the springs
To heal the land she will rise

Flora and her father—the man who had raised her from when she was a wee bairn and loved her with a father's true heart—danced and wiled away the night. Flora knew she would cherish this moment for the rest of her days. Her life had been shattered in so many ways. She had been robbed of so many things that were dear to her. But now she would have this one thing to cling to when all else failed. Though her mother might always remain distant and aloof, and though the blood that ran in her veins may be tainted with Roman filth, she had a father, a true father, whose love for her would never fail. It was the love, not of obligation, but of choice. A love not demanded, but freely given. It was the rock upon which she could anchor her soul—a rock that would stand firm against any gale.

Sometime during the night the rain had stopped, and the dim rays of dawn brightened the horizon. Flora left her father with a lightness of heart she had not felt since this whole nightmare had begun. She doubted whether she would ever see him again, at least not to enjoy time alone like this. But the knowledge of his undying love would sustain her through whatever new trials might come her way.

Flora stepped out of the little hut and Finnan appeared almost instantly at her side.

"I owe you a great deal of thanks, Master Bard. If I ever have the opportunity to show appreciation to the people who have helped me through this, you will be at the top of the list."

"It is my pleasure," he replied. "Truly."

"Tell me, Finnan, do you know the Ballad of Brigid? My father sang it to me just now. He used to lull me asleep with that melody when I was a little girl."

"I do, mistress. I know it well. It was one of the first songs I ever composed."

Flora stopped in her tracks and grabbed Finnan by the arm, jerking him to a halt. "*You* created the Ballad of Brigid?" She gaped at him in astonishment.

"Aye. Many moons ago. It's one reason I was recruited for this very task. The druids felt I knew the heart of the goddess better than any other bard, in large part because of that little tune. Who better than the author of that song to document the rise of the maiden who would become the new Brigid?"

As Flora digested this revelation, Finnan changed the subject. "While we're stopped here, I have another wee gift I hope you will enjoy, though you may need to keep it to yourself."

The bard reached within a fold of his cloak and produced a small leather pouch. Flora's eyes instantly shot wide open and her jaw dropped. She gaped at Finnan again as he proffered the little bag, its neck open and its drawstring slack so she could see the contents inside. It wasn't just any leather pouch. It was *her* little stash of treasures.

"But how...?" was all Flora could say in her amazement. "Eliavres threw it away. I watched it sink into the loch."

Finnan winked at her and sported a mischievous grin. "Well, I can't go revealing all my secrets, now can I? It would ruin my mystique."

Overwhelmed with joy, Flora forgot herself, leapt forward, and gave Finnan a huge hug. The bard, somewhat taken aback, nevertheless patted her lightly on the shoulder. "So, am I to understand you are pleased with your present?"

Flora released him and beamed with delight. "I am," she squealed. "More than you could possibly know."

"It makes my heart glad. Truly. Now, it appears dawn is nigh, and we best be gettin' you back to your lair before your attendants arrive.

By the way, you wouldn't happen to have had any recurring dreams of late, now would you? It would certainly help my little ruse to have a story to tell of your visions in the night."

Flora almost skipped along behind him as she sorted through the treasures in her little bag. "Oh," she replied, "I'm sure you can come up with something far more imaginative than I could ever do. If I had to guess, I expect it might have something to do with owls, and serpents, and men dancing in the firelight, dressed like eagles."

"Indeed. Those very images came to mind even as you spoke them aloud. I'm certain the gods are telling us something of great consequence which will add ominous portents to the tale of your transformation."

As she quickly reversed the exchange with her erstwhile double back in the crannog, Flora reflected on the great debt she owed Finnan. In one night he had given her two gifts that helped to restore her sense of identity. Though powerful forces still conspired to transform her into something strange and frightening, she now had two small points on which to anchor her soul—two shining stars that would point her toward home whenever she lost her way—a father's undying love, and a little bag of trinkets to remind her of who she really was. In this terrifying world of gods, and druids, and warlord chiefs, she had found someone she could actually trust. She had found a friend.

CHAPTER TWENTY-ONE

Despite her playful banter with Finnan, Flora did dream. In the dim light of the early dawn, Flora collapsed on a pile of furs, emotionally exhilarated and physically exhausted from her midnight escapade. She hoped to get a little rest before Drib and Drab arrived to begin her daily rituals. But images played through her mind, causing her sleep to be restless and disturbed.

In her dreams, she watched a Roman man in a white tunic trimmed in purple approach her mother. Flora tried to look away, fearing she would witness the rape which had brought her into this world. But the man caressed the woman's face, and she responded lovingly to him. Flora looked on in horror as the couple lay down together. It was no rape after all. Her mother had gone willingly to a Roman bed!

But some hidden urge deep inside forced Flora to peer closer. Perhaps it was something unfamiliar in the woman's manner. But to her surprise, Flora realized the woman was not her mother after all. Rather, it was someone whose look and mannerisms were so like those of her mother to render them as close as twins.

Suddenly, the scene shifted, and Flora found herself in a strange place, surrounded by a mob of people, all shouting words she could not comprehend. The sun was low in a cloudless sky. The air was hot and dry. The path beneath her feet was dusty. Huge stone buildings rose in the background. She saw her mother then, and looked closer to make sure it was the right woman after all. This woman had her mother's features, but she wore Roman garb. She was staring intently up a nearby hill. Flora followed her gaze and was shocked at what she saw.

Flora watched a Roman soldier hammer a huge spike through a man's wrist. She heard the man's agonized cry as the iron nail pierced his flesh and sank into the wood beneath. Moments later, a crew of legionnaires, dressed in helmets and armor, used ropes and levers to raise three pillars on the top of the hill—three crosses with a man impaled on each one. Flora somehow sensed that one of these men, perhaps the one in the center, was the Romans' nailed god. She was seeing the actual event, through her mother's eyes.

The man cried out incomprehensible words, "*Eloi. Eloi. Lama Sabachthani.*" Thunder boomed, and lightning split the sky. The ground shook beneath her feet and time stood still.

Suddenly, the scene changed, and Flora became an eagle, flying in wide arcs over a vibrant land, thick with forests and wide green glens. It was the highlands of her homeland. She winged higher and then dove low, not of her own volition, but carried along where the vision willed to take her. Then she saw it with the piercing vision unique to a bird of prey—an ancient tree, standing out in vibrance and vitality from the rest of the bushes and shrubs. It was the sacred yew, a sentinel watching over the entrance to *Gleann Dubh nan Garbh Clac*, the Black Glen of the Crooked Stones. A pregnant woman walked through the gap in the trunk of the tree and emerged from the other side carrying twins, a boy and a girl, with dark curly hair and olive skin. The eagle shrieked, and its cry echoed over the valley, reverberating into the night.

At that moment, a sharp clang jolted Flora from her sleep. Still disoriented from the vivid dream, she blinked her eyes several times and frantically scanned the room before finally glimpsing her mother in the shadows of a far corner of the crannog. Something tugged at the edge of Flora's awareness—a sense that something important had been revealed in the dream, but that she did not understand. Flora's mother emerged from the shadows, carrying the chamber pot as usual, and Flora had an overriding impression that the secret of her dilemma rested deep within her mother's true identity.

"Mother, wait."

Flora pushed herself up from the pile of furs and hurried to intercept the servant woman. She caught up with her mother just before she exited the door. Flora grasped her arm and pulled her around. She stared intently into the older woman's face and saw the images from her dream gazing back at her.

"Who are you, Mother?"

Her mother dropped her eyes to the ground and demurred. "Whatever do you mean?" Still, she did not look Flora in the eye.

"Who *are* you? Are you a highlander? Or are you a daughter of Rome?"

An ancient, raspy voice crackled from outside the doorway. "Both, actually."

Flora turned to see the stooped, gnarled figure of her grandmother edge through the doorway. The old woman leaned against a rough, twisted staff, and stared at Flora with a piercing gaze. Then the *Seann Ghliocas* repeated her assertion. "She is both highlander and Roman. As am I. As are *you*."

"What do you mean by that?" Flora spat out, without the deference due a grandmother of the tribe.

"I mean," her grandmother replied, hobbling over to a stool set in front of the Pool of Brigid's Tears, "that both highlander blood and Roman blood flow in our veins."

Flora followed her grandmother to the Pool, but her mother stood mutely transfixed where Flora had stopped her in the course of her duties.

"When? How? I know about mother's rape. But you're talking about something deeper, something farther back, aren't you?"

The *Seann Ghliocas* settled herself down on the stool and began stirring the water of the Pool with her staff. Flora wondered if that was a sacrilege of some sort, but let the concern pass. She had larger issues to deal with now.

"The line began," her grandmother intoned distantly, "exactly twenty generations ago."

"What line?"

"Our line. Mine. Your mother's. Yours." It seemed as if the *Seann Ghliocas* was trying to use her staff to wipe away the reflection of the Eternal Flame that rippled on the surface of the Pool of Brigid's Tears. "Exactly twenty generations ago," she continued, "a Roman official arrived in *Cridhalbane*."

Flora was startled at her grandmother's use of the sacred power name for the region. She clearly implied something more significant than the coming of this man to the central region of the highlands. Her words suggested a deeper, more spiritual connotation.

"He came," the old woman continued, "on a diplomatic mission from the Roman senate to seek an alliance with the Caledonians. But the gods were at work behind the scenes."

Flora sat down across from her grandmother, the Pool of Brigid's Tears glistening in the firelight between them.

"The officer and his retinue stayed in the shadow of *An Dun Gael* and *Feart Choille* throughout two summers, while the negotiations dragged on. In that time, he took a young highland girl as his lover. She bore him two children that year. Twins. A boy and a girl. He took the boy with him when he returned to Rome, but he left the woman and the girl behind."

Flora's thoughts flashed back to the couple she had seen in her night vision, and suddenly realized who they were.

"You said the gods were at work behind the scenes. What do you mean?"

"Hmm," the old woman muttered, and then went on,

apparently disregarding Flora's question. "The diplomatic mission failed, of course. The druid Council could see through Rome's benevolent pretensions. But they also knew Rome was a power to be reckoned with. And so they decided to preserve the Roman bloodline within highlander wombs. There is power in blood, and the seers foretold of opportunities to use that power one day. Little did they know at the time how potent that lifeblood would become."

"How could the bloodline be preserved?" Flora asked.

"When the girl was of age, she was given to the Great Chief of the tribe. And since that time, every first girl in the lineage has been given to the tribe's Great Chief, so the strongest highlander blood would sustain and dominate the Roman blood." She paused for a moment to emphasize the next point. "I am in that lineage. Your grandfather was the Great Chief of our tribe."

Flora stared into the Pool as she reflected on what her grandmother had just revealed. Her mother's image, from where she stood in the shadows, peered back at her, and a sudden realization struck Flora like the jolt of a thunderbolt. "But Mother..."

"No. Your mother did not become the wife of a Great Chief. Instead, she violated her sacred duty and fell in love with a blacksmith's apprentice. The Council feared her rash decision had brought over three hundred years of diligent control to an end. There were some who hoped the singular potency of the bloodline could be perpetuated through the offspring of the blacksmith, since such men have been chosen and gifted by the gods. But, alas, Serlaid lacked all the qualities needed to carry on the lineage."

Flora looked up from the reflection of her mother in the Pool and lifted her eyes to the real woman, who shrank back into the shadows —away from the revelation of her character and away from the shame. Flora was shocked to hear about her mother's failure to fulfill her duty to the tribe. But in another way, she was proud of the courage it took for her mother to follow her heart. Flora couldn't imagine growing up with a different father than the one who had cherished her with such unconditional love, and she was glad for her mother's irresponsible decision.

"So, is that why they're planning the raid on the Wall, right now? So they can leverage the power of your blood while you still live?"

"Oh no, child. It's not my blood that will bring victory in this war. It's yours."

Flora stared at her grandmother in astonishment. She saw something deep inside the old woman's eyes that made her shiver with fear. The person who returned her stare wasn't a loving grandmother at all. What she saw instead was the cold, calculating glare of the *Seann Ghliocas*.

"But how?" Flora muttered. "I'm not the daughter of the Great Chief."

Flora knew the answer even before she heard the old crone's reply.

"No, you are not. But you *are* the bastard daughter of a Roman soldier. And so the power of the bloodline has been renewed."

"But I was not given to the Great Chief as a wife. If I was meant to restore the lineage, why was I promised to Domhnull?"

"Oh, my dear child. If you had been wed to Domhnull, he *would* have become the next chief. Of that you can be certain."

The old woman still peered at her with unsympathetic eyes. When she finally looked away she grumbled in disgust, "At one point, I even hoped you would be the Promised One. But I certainly don't see it in you. You don't have the iron in your spine to do what must be done."

"Well," Flora spat out the reply. "Everyone else seems to believe I am Fiona *Taghte*, the Chosen One. *They* apparently assume I have what it takes."

"Yes, they do. And they have proceeded on this course against my advice."

"And," Flora quipped, grasping at some kind of support to bolster her argument, "what about the signs from the gods? The omens all confirm their approval of me."

"Yes, indeed. What about the signs from the gods?"

The *Seann Ghliocas* lifted her staff out of the Pool of Brigid's Tears and watched the drops fall to the floor. Flora was aghast. Each morning and each evening, Drib and Drab went to great lengths to ensure that none of the precious liquid left the sacred bath. They scraped off every drop and returned it to the artificial pond. Her grandmother's blatant disregard for the holy waters bordered on blasphemy against the goddess.

Pushing her abhorrence aside, Flora pressed for as much information as she could glean from the old crone. "Why are you here? What made you come down from your perch in the middle of the night to visit me this morning?"

"Why," her grandmother flashed her a crooked smile, "it was time for you to know the truth of it—time for you to hear of your mother's shame and to learn from it, so you don't repeat her mistakes. *You* must do your duty and fulfill your responsibilities to the tribe. The women of our line must set aside our personal desires and meet the larger obligations to our people."

"And," Flora continued, "what did you mean when you said the seers didn't fully understand the potency of the Roman bloodline?"

The *Seann Ghliocas* turned to look at her with what appeared to be a tiny sliver of genuine respect. "Perhaps you are not as naive as I thought. The original woman, that first daughter of the Roman official—"

"Yes, I remember." Flora didn't mention she had actually seen the woman in her dreams.

"Her twin brother went back to Rome and became a prominent official in his own right. He was later assigned as Governor of the Roman province of Judah."

"Okay," Flora replied. "I don't understand the significance of that."

"His name," the old woman quipped, "was Pontius Pilate. He was the man who nailed the Roman god to a cross."

Flora gasped. Her night vision. She had seen it all happen.

"The blood that flows in our veins," the wizened hag continued, "is the same blood that killed Rome's nailed god. It had that power once before, and it most certainly retains that potency now."

With her revelation disclosed, Flora's grandmother—the old crone, the *Seann Ghliocas,* the Ancient Wisdom of the Tribe—rose from the stool, turned her back, and shuffled out the door. And Flora's mother, head hung in shame, followed her retreating back without saying a word.

FLORA LOOKED out the open door. She saw Nandag and her attendants making their way across the bridge to the crannog. In the village beyond, she spied Bhatair Rhu and Eliavres speaking with Manas.

Flora pulled a cloak from a nearby hook and stepped out the doorway. The startled guards tried to block her way.

"*Taghte,* you must not leave here without an escort," one of the druidesses said, grabbing Flora's arm.

"I'm going to speak with the Arch Druid," Flora replied.

The guard kept a firm hold on Flora's sleeve. "You must have an escort."

Flora stared intently into the guard's eyes. Then she repeated herself, with prominent emphasis on each word. "I'm going to speak with the Arch Druid. Right over there," she added, pointing at Bhatair Rhu.

Apparently satisfied that Flora wouldn't go far, the guard released her grip and motioned for Flora to pass. "Very well."

Flora swept past a confused Nandag without saying a word. She heard her old mentor toss a question into the air, just for it to float away in the wind. "Where—?"

Flora didn't even look back. Instead, she focused on her next obstacle, the two warriors stationed at the far end of the bridge. They had heard the commotion and now crossed their spears to block her way.

Flora tried the same tactic with these two. "I'm going to speak with the Arch Druid," she said, pointing in Bhatair Rhu's direction.

The warriors were unmoved by her declaration. They just stood their ground.

Flora tried repeating herself, with emphasis. "I'm going to speak with the Arch Druid."

The guards remained as still as statues. One of them replied, "We have our orders from the Arch Druid. You may not leave without an appropriate escort."

Flora was about to try the "goddess" angle and suggest that her blessings and curses might be dispensed or withheld once she assumed her role in the Otherworld, when she heard Bhatair Rhu's voice carrying across the compound.

"It's okay. Let her pass."

The warriors immediately uncrossed their spears and gestured for her to proceed. Flora noted where their loyalties lay. Though she would become a goddess one day soon, these men ignored her requests and followed the commands of the Arch Druid without question. They apparently had more respect, or perhaps more fear, of Bhatair Rhu than of a woman who was about to don the mantle of Brigid and wield the power of the Great Goddess.

The ground was wet beneath her feet, and Flora nearly slipped in the mud as she made her way toward the three druids.

"You knew, didn't you?" Flora blurted out as soon as she was within speaking distance. "You knew about the bloodline."

Eliavres scowled at her, but Bhatair Rhu smiled as if he were greeting an old friend he chanced upon along the road. "Good day to you, Fiona *Taghte*. Perhaps we should step into our Master Healer's house to continue this conversation. We seem to be causing quite a stir."

Flora glanced around and saw that people all over the little encampment had stopped their activities to watch the exchange.

Bhatair Rhu was right. This should be kept private, for both their sakes.

"Fine," she said, curtly, "Please lead on." Flora nodded to Manas, who inclined his head in response and then stepped toward a nearby roundhouse.

No one said a word until they had reassembled inside. Flora glanced around the interior of the hut, and saw that it was filled with the accouterments of a master healer. Herbs hung drying from rafters, and small mixing bowls sat in rows near the fire pit in the center of the room. The acrid scent of thistle being seared on an iron grate over hot coals filled her nostrils. But aside from the implements of Manas' trade, the remainder of the roundhouse was sparsely appointed. It was certainly much more austere than her own palace on the loch.

Flora turned to face Bhatair Rhu, and seethed. "You knew about the Roman bloodline, didn't you?"

"Of course," the Arch Druid responded, nonplussed. "The Council has been nurturing that divine gift for centuries now. I, myself, have been the custodian of that secret power for a very long time."

"The gods didn't choose me, did they? You chose me. You chose me because you knew I had Roman blood from both my mother and my father. The gods never needed a replacement for Brigid. You needed a blood sacrifice for your war on Rome. All this is happening so you can fulfill your personal vow."

The smile never wavered from Bhatair Rhu's expression, and it galled Flora. She wanted to slap the smug smirk off his face. But he just sat there and listened patiently until she finished her rant.

After allowing her to vent, the Arch Druid finally spoke. "You keep dividing my purpose from that of the gods, as if they were two different things. They are, in fact, the same. My goal and the will of the gods are like the inside and outside of the same jar. Do you understand?"

"No," Flora fumed. "I don't understand. You have a personal

vendetta against the Romans in Britain. I understand that. I hate them too. But I don't see what that has to do with the gods' need to replace Brigid. One deals with a political problem in this world. The other deals with an imbalance in the celestial cycle of the Otherworld. And somehow, I got trapped in the middle."

"I want to show you something. I think it will clear up all your confusion on this point. Will you ride with me to *An Dun Gael*? There is something in the White Fortress I think you should see."

Flora fidgeted. He had sparked her curiosity, but she wasn't sure she trusted him. "I can't ride," she replied.

"Not to worry. You can accompany me on my mare. She will keep us both safe."

Bhatair Rhu turned to Eliavres and Manas. "Can you both see to the preparations for the *Ordination*? A gathering that large will require a great deal of coordination. And please dispatch messengers to the clans and villages. Fiona *Taghte* and I will return this evening. Fedelma will provide for our needs at *An Dun Gael*."

"Of course," Manas responded with a nod. Eliavres just grunted his assent, appearing a bit irritated at the disruption to their previous plans.

"Shall we go?" Bhatair Rhu asked as he ushered Flora to the door.

Moments later, Flora was mounted behind Bhatair Rhu on the mare.

"Hold on to me," he instructed her.

Flora felt a bit awkward with her arms wrapped around this man, but she had never ridden a horse before, and her apprehension about falling off overcame her timidity. A short distance into their ride, she became accustomed to the horse's gait and relaxed a bit. She felt her face flush when she realized how tightly she had been holding onto Bhatair Rhu. She also wondered at the appropriateness of their close proximity, given that she was not to be left alone with a man during her preparation time. Then she remembered the mare was actually Bhatair Rhu's goddess mother from the Otherworld, and decided the gods would accept her as an appropriate chaperone.

They covered the distance between Fearnan and the sacred yew tree in a fraction of the time it had taken for the retinue to walk the same stretch in the other direction. They headed up the steep trail to *An Dun Gael* before the sun started its decline to the west. The Arch Druid brought the mare to a halt and turned her loose at the edge of the clearing that surrounded the white tower.

Flora stopped short to take in the sight of the astonishing structure. The circumstances were much different than those of her first visit to this place. But its impression on her was no less breathtaking.

They walked side by side to the small door at the base of the tower. Flora had long since ceased to shudder at the human-skull spirit fences which guarded the entrance to the place. They were not so much different than the ones positioned in front of the door to her crannog. Perhaps she was becoming more comfortable in this world of druids and gods and spiritual forces.

Fedelma met them inside the door. "Greetings, *Ard-Draoidh.*" Fedelma used his formal title. "And you as well, Fiona *Taghte*. It must be time for the Chosen One to see the *Iolaire.*"

"It is time," Bhatair Rhu confirmed.

"I have foreseen it," Fedelma said, as she turned the eerie triple sight on Flora. "But will it be enough? Will she believe?"

"*Iolaire?*" Flora asked. "What is it? And what am I supposed to believe?"

"You will see it with your own eyes," Fedelma replied. "But will you see it for what it is? I wonder."

"Before we proceed, I need to give you the history," the Arch Druid said. "We should go into the great hall, and I can tell you the tale."

Fedelma ushered them into the dream chamber where Flora had seen the vision of the owl and the eagle. It was the dream which had confirmed the gods' choice of her to become Brigid. Flora looked across the room and shuddered. She could make out the stone altar and the cleansing pool in the dim light of the torches mounted on the wall. The memories of this place were powerful and intimidating to her. When she had walked out of that pool, she had felt clean, and new, and free from the filth of her past. But as she had looked into the seer's triple eyes, her momentary surge of courage had dissipated as quickly as it had come. She was left just as small and as defiled as before.

"I'm afraid we will have to stand for this little history lesson," Bhatair Rhu said. "No one sits in the sacred hall."

"That's fine," Flora replied. "I just want to get on with it and see this *Iolaire*. That's what you brought me here for, right? That's supposed to enlighten me about the link between the broken cycle of the gods and your war on the Romans."

Fedelma bowed and backed out of the chamber. "I'll leave you to your task. Let me know if I am needed."

The Arch Druid nodded to Fedelma and began his tale. "It is the story of a Roman military unit—a group of around five thousand men called a legion. And though the individual men might come and go, the unit retains its unique identity. It is an entity all its own. It was first blessed by the gods and then cursed."

Flora crossed her arms and leaned back against the wall. She had accompanied Bhatair Rhu on this excursion, and now she would have to patiently endure his lecture.

"This legion was among the first to invade the shores of Britannia. It was the spearhead of Rome's early conquest of the peoples in the south. One of those tribes decided to ally themselves with Rome rather than to be conquered. This tribe was known as the Brigantes."

Flora lifted her head at the name. "They were followers of Brigid? And they betrayed their own people to the Romans?"

"For my own family, it was even worse. When my father, Caradog, and the armies of the south were defeated by this legion, the remnants of his force sought refuge with the Great Chief of the Brigantes—a woman named Cartimandua. She granted them asylum and then promptly turned them over to her Roman confederates."

"She was the woman you told me about before, the one who betrayed your father? And she was a follower of Brigid?" Flora asked in disgust.

"Yes. The same one. And she later supported this legion when it invaded Ynys Mon to destroy the School of the Druids. Do you know about that?"

Flora nodded. "Finnan told me."

"Good. And you know my own role in that story as well?"

"Finnan told me that too."

Bhatair Rhu continued his tale. "Anyway, Cartimandua's husband, sickened by his wife's deference to the Romans, staged a coup. Twice, he rallied the Brigantes against their Roman overlords, but this legion came to Cartimandua's aid, and reinstated her as Chieftain of the tribe. After one more revolt, many years later, the Romans finally invaded the Brigantian lands and subjugated the people."

"Where was Brigid all this time? Why did she not defend the followers who called themselves by her name?"

"I admire your discernment. Your question shows great insight. You are beginning to see the link between the wars of men and the affairs of the gods. The gods, themselves asked this very question. How could Brigid fail to protect her own people?"

The image of the nailed god on the cross flashed into Flora's mind, and she shuddered. "Was it the Roman god? Was he more powerful than the gods of this land? Did he give the Romans victory over Brigid and her people?"

"No, at this time, the Romans still worshipped the old gods, much as we do now. I'm not sure we will ever know exactly why the Romans were allowed to conquer Brigid's people. It is a mystery that remains locked in the meeting hall of the gods. Some of our oracles and judges speculate that Cartimandua's betrayal undermined Brigid's power. The goddess had selected her to rule, and her treachery subverted Brigid's efforts on behalf of the tribe."

"And Brigid's failure in this war somehow led to her demise in the Otherworld?" Flora asked.

"We don't know for certain. The council chamber of the gods often remains closed to us, but we do know what happened over the following years in the world of men."

"And what was that?"

"This legion that invaded Britannia, destroyed the School of the Druids on Ynys Mon, and subjugated the Brigantes, boarded ships and led a campaign against our sister tribes in the north. It destroyed the armies of the north in a great battle at Mons Graupius. I'm sure the men were different men, with different commanders over them, than those in the first invasion of our land. But the unit, the legion, was the same."

Flora recalled the vision of her village being destroyed during her ordeals. Had that just been a fantasy of her mind, a hallucination with no basis in reality? Or was it a glimpse into a possible future, more horrific than she could even imagine? Did it, in fact, reflect what Rome would do to her people if given the chance?

"But, then the fortunes of the legion changed. The influence of the nailed god started to permeate the ranks. It began with the commanders and officers, but then trickled down through the line of common soldiers. And that betrayal by the Romans gave renewed power to the gods of our land. Britannia belongs to the ancient gods, and the worship of our people gives them strength."

"Even to Brigid? Even though the people called by her name were defeated?"

"Especially Brigid. Perhaps that is what made the Cailleach jealous of Brigid's power. Perhaps that is what prompted this coup to make winter rule the land. We may never know."

Flora had become engrossed in the story and wanted to know more. Perhaps she could learn something else that would give her an advantage over the Roman god.

"So what happened? What changed the Roman legion's fortunes?"

Bhatair Rhu gestured around the room. "This changed their fortunes. Emboldened by their victory on the northern coast, they decided to strike at the heart of Caledonia. They tried to invade *Cridhalbane* and conquer the highlands. They tried to capture this holy place."

"And?" Flora whispered, breathlessly.

"And now I can take you up to the sky tower."

Bhatair Rhu gestured toward the circular staircase, encased between *An Dun Gael's* inner and outer walls. "Please."

Flora struggled to restrain herself from rushing up the steps. Her anticipation grew with each footfall. They passed the doorway into Fedelma's quarters and Bhatair Rhu urged her onward. After ascending at least three more floors, Flora came to a massive oak door, guarded by a spirit fence of four human skulls.

"Be very careful here. This is no ordinary spirit fence. The skulls are from the legion's highest ranking officers. I placed the curse on this barrier, myself. No one can enter this sanctuary without my personal intervention."

The Arch Druid removed a sprig of mistletoe from a pouch on his belt and a then a small amulet woven from what appeared to be human hair. He intertwined the two items, held them up before the door, and whispered some unintelligible words. After a long pause, he stepped back.

"I'll enter first. You can follow after I have lit the lamps."

Bhatair Rhu unlatched a black iron hasp and pushed on the heavy door. To Flora's surprise, it swung open without a sound, and the Arch Druid disappeared into the darkness. Flora waited on the landing until a small glow filtered out through the doorway. When Bhatair Rhu motioned her to cross the spirit fence and come inside, she realized she had been holding her breath. She let the air in her lungs out with a gasp as she took in the sight.

The room was empty, save for a single stone column in the very center. Four openings in opposite walls allowed the wind to whip through the space in a howl of rage and roar of triumph. Flora could feel the raw power pulsing through the chamber.

Mounted in the center of the granite pedestal was a short staff, topped with a magnificent eagle, forged from solid gold. Its eyes blazed in the firelight and it glowed with an iridescent sheen that seemed to emanate from within. Flora inhaled sharply. She recognized that majestic and fearsome bird. It was the eagle from her vision that had attacked the owl. It was the one that had sought to rip her life apart with its talons and pierce her heart with its beak.

"But the owl won that battle." Bhatair Rhu's voice echoed against the black stone walls. "*You* won that battle."

"How do you know that?" Flora whispered.

"Fedelma watched the whole thing happen, through your own eyes. It was the confirmation we needed to know that you were the Chosen One—that you were, indeed, Fiona *Taghte.*"

"What is this?"

"It is the standard of the Ninth Roman Legion. It is the eagle of the Ninth. And it is a symbol of the power of the highland gods over the gods of Rome, whoever they may be."

"How did it get here? Was it stolen by a raiding party?"

"The arrogance of the Roman commanders led them to attack up the Tatha River glen, into the center of the highlands. They had beaten the armies of the south lands and the forces of the northern coast. They were certain they could strike at the heart of Caledonia and subjugate our tribes, once and for all. They suspected the School of the Druids had been relocated to this remote and protected place after they destroyed the druid community on Ynys Mon."

"Is that true? Did the school move here?"

"That's why I am here. I led the survivors of the massacre at Ynys Mon here, to the heart of the highlands—to *Cridhalbane* and to *Cridhmathairnaomh*, the sacred yew. This is where our land draws its strength. This is where our world touches the Otherworld, and where men commune with the gods."

"So what happened to the Roman legion?"

"The gods of this land intervened to protect our people. The Ninth Legion pressed up the Tatha Valley. They pushed past *Dun Chailleann*, and *Obar Pheallaidh*. But when they reached Drumainn Hill, the highland warriors rose up, like a swarm of hornets, and the gods rose up with them. Tyrannis gave them strength and the Daghda gave them courage. Lugh gave them dominance over the day, and Cerridwen gave them dominion at night. The Cailleach made them cunning and the Morrigan made them stealthy. But it was Brigid who ultimately saved the day."

"Brigid? What did she do?"

"Brigid gave them the most powerful weapon of all. She made them wise. All the strength, all the courage, all the skill in the world could not have overcome the might of Rome. But wisdom—the wisdom from Brigid—gave the highlanders victory."

"How? I don't understand."

"Wisdom led our forces to retreat up the valley until the Romans had gone too far to escape. Wisdom bogged the heavy Roman soldiers down in marshy ground where their armor made them cumbersome and slow. Wisdom attacked the Roman formations from every side, splitting their forces and dissipating their power. Wisdom put the highlanders in constant motion, striking and withdrawing, striking and withdrawing, so the Romans could not concentrate their might."

"So what happened? Was the legion defeated? Did the highlander armies win?"

"The Ninth Roman Legion was completely and utterly destroyed. Not a single man survived. The highlanders cut down every last one. The victory not only crippled the Roman army in Britain, it struck fear into the heart of their empire. The Ninth Roman Legion had marched into the highlands of Caledonia and completely disappeared, never to be heard from again. Nothing like it had ever happened in the history of Rome. The emperor, himself, ordered the army to build a great wall at the north edge of the Roman lands to keep the wild highlanders at bay."

Flora stared at the golden eagle in the center of the jet black tower. She imagined the battle scenes the Arch Druid described. She envisioned the highland warriors in the blue spirals and sacred symbols of their spirit armor swarming over the helpless Roman army, like the locusts from her dreams.

"Do you see it now?" Bhatair Rhu asked. "Do you see the link between the celestial cycle of the gods and the wars of men?"

Flora nodded, thoughtfully. "I think so."

"And Brigid is the key. Brigid turned the tide of the battle back then. And Brigid will give us victory this time as well. Brigid must be replaced to restore balance to the Otherworld and to unite the gods in support of our armies on the ground. You *must* become Brigid. And your blood, your *Roman* blood, will be the key to destroying their army and driving them from the land—them *and* their nailed god. It will restore the dominance of the old gods in Britannia forever."

Flora heard Fedelma's voice from behind her back. "So she *does* understand after all. Perhaps there is hope yet."

"Yes," Bhatair Rhu agreed. "There is hope, indeed."

The eagle stared at Flora with menace in its eyes, but she no longer feared its wrath. The owl had defeated the eagle in her vision from the gods. And she would make that vision into a reality. She would become Brigid. She would drive the Roman armies out of Britannia, and she would set her people free. She was Fiona *Taghte*, and she would become a goddess.

CHAPTER TWENTY-TWO

Fiona rode behind Bhatair Rhu on his sorrel mare, her arms wrapped around his waist for stability. After their shared experience in the sky tower of *An Dun Gael*—after staring down the eagle of Rome and walking away transformed—she felt closer to this man, somehow. Now, as they rode together, Flora could sense their hearts beating in rhythm as one. It was not a romantic attraction, for she was betrothed to a god. Rather it was a kinship of purpose which united them now.

They rode in silence down the steep patch from the top of the ridge to the valley below, then through the marshy glen, and across a rushing stream. The sun was setting to their backs, and Fiona gazed up at the rocky crag where her life had been transformed during her ordeals—a time that seemed like ages ago. She had hidden in that little cave, sorting through her bag of treasures and cowering in fear. But now fear no longer dominated her life. It had been replaced by a sense of purpose and a new identity that gave her life meaning.

She released Bhatair Rhu with one hand and fumbled inside her cloak for the little leather bag. Eliavres had been right after all. The little trinkets were just memories of a past that held her in bondage.

To move forward and achieve her destiny, she needed to cut the cords and set herself free. As she wrestled with the knot in the leather thong that fastened the pouch to her belt, the horse suddenly reared, and she was nearly thrown to the ground.

Bhatair Rhu pulled the mare around and pointed up to *Feart Choille* on the hill. A bright signal pyre burned above its wooden ramparts. Flora followed his gesture down the glen and saw a similar flame blazing at the far end of Drumainn Hill. Then more sparked to life in dots on hilltops in a zig-zag pattern down the Tatha River valley as far as she could see.

"What is it? What's happening?" she asked.

"An attack by the Romans. But something is amiss. The signal is meant to come up the valley from the sea to warn of a Roman advance. This one originated at *Feart Choille* and is spreading in the opposite direction. I need to get you back to Fearnan immediately and then figure out what's happening. The omens did not foretell a Roman assault. This is unexpected."

As Bhatair Rhu spurred the mare into a thin forest, a huge tree fell across their path. Then men in bronze helmets carrying iron swords emerged from the woods on every side. Flora instantly recognized the large rectangular shields and plated armor of Roman soldiers. But what she saw next stabbed at her heart and caused her blood to run cold.

A familiar figure in a brown robe pointed at her and shouted over the din in a language Fiona could not understand. Then he switched to the Pictish tongue, as if for her benefit. "That's her. And that's the Arch Druid. They're alone." Manas stood at the right hand of the officer who was clearly in charge. "Remember, she's not to be harmed."

The soldiers quickly surrounded them, cutting off every route of escape. The divine steed reared again and again, snorting and neighing and frothing at the mouth, but its desperate cries for help went unanswered. No lightning struck from the heavens and no earthquake shook the ground beneath their feet. Apparently, the gods would not intervene to rescue the Arch Druid and the Chosen One from the clutches of the Roman eagle. Worst of all, they had been betrayed by a friend.

The soldiers worked with cold efficiency. They pulled their captives from the horse and led the mount aside. Clearly not wanting to linger in the road, they quickly bound Fiona's hands and formed a tight square around the two prisoners. Then the whole group disappeared into the cover of the trees.

Oddly, Bhatair Rhu made no effort to resist. Either he understood the complete futility of their situation, or he held out some hope Fiona could not fathom. Perhaps he still anticipated some intervention by the gods. Perhaps he doubted the ability of the patrol to avoid detection in the heart of Caledonian lands. Whatever it was, Fiona did not share the Arch Druid's bravado. The courage she had felt in the sky tower such a short time ago had dissipated like mist in a morning breeze, to be replaced by a terror she could scarce endure.

Images from her nightmares played themselves out before her eyes. Would she be raped by a Roman soldier as her mother had been? Would the Roman war machine roll over the land like the locusts in her visions, decimating everything in its path? Would her village be burned after all? Would her lover be slain, her sisters be ravaged, and her father be led off in chains?

Somehow, the nailed god had seen through their scheme. He had intervened in their plot and cut off her path to become a goddess—*the goddess* with the sacred bloodline necessary to destroy him in battle. In this single coup, at the very moment when her destiny had become clear and her sense of purpose settled, the traitorous act of an ally—a man she had begun to trust as a friend—brought the whole plan crumbling down.

Fiona screamed, not so much as a cry for help, for there was no one around to hear such a plea, but as a howl of frustration and rage. She was answered with a sharp slap across the face from the nearest soldier. Fiona recoiled from the sting and tasted the bitter tang of blood on her lips, while the legionary snarled at her with unintelligible words and shook his fist in her face.

THEY MARCHED ON SILENTLY through the darkness of the forest. Fiona and Bhatair Rhu had been separated so they could not confer together or console one another. Every time Fiona stumbled on a root or staggered from exhaustion, she was prodded forward with the butt end of a spear. They plodded on while the last vestiges of twilight faded from the western sky and darkness engulfed the land.

At one point, Manas edged up beside her. "I don't suppose you'd understand–"

"Get away from me, you traitor," Fiona spat. "I have nothing to say to you."

"Please, just let me explain, *Thaghadh*."

"I have nothing to say to you," she repeated emphatically. "I couldn't care less what your excuse might be. You are a coward and a traitor. You betrayed my friendship and my trust. I don't want to have anything to do with you ever again. Get out of my sight."

Fiona turned her head away from Manas and refused to look in his direction. If her hands had not been bound, she would have slapped him across the face. She actually did want to know what had motivated his treachery, but his words would never have made it past the seething anger in her soul.

They trudged on through the night, stumbling over roots and branches and wading through marshy bogs. The soldiers cursed and swore at the grueling march through the arduous terrain, while trying to maintain their tight defensive formation. Eventually, as dawn broke over the eastern horizon, they came to a stop and prepared to make camp. Apparently, they planned to travel through the night and hide out during the day.

Suddenly, an arrow shot through the morning haze and slammed through the throat of the soldier to Fiona's right. Then, a mighty warrior on a gigantic steed materialized out of the mist, as if by magic, and brought a massive sword down in a mighty blow that cleaved another Roman's helmet in two from top to bottom.

The legionnaires shouted a war cry and tried to fall back into their square formation, but it was too late. The trap had been sprung with lightning speed. Fiona saw more arrows hurling through the air, and then hordes of highland warriors, clad in the blue spirals of their spirit armor, thrust spears in the faces of the foreign invaders. A few of the Romans tried to hurl their javelins or draw their short steel blades, but they were instantly cut down. The rest realized the futility of their situation and lay down their arms at their officer's command. The ambush was over within a lark's cry.

Fiona heard Bhatair Rhu's voice rising above the din. "I want prisoners. Take them alive."

She saw several druids scattered among the highland warriors. They surrounded Manas, bound his hands, and led him out of the fray.

Serlaid emerged from a knot of men and walked over to Fiona. She, too, wore sprint armor, and Fiona barely recognized her sister. "It looks like my dogs saved your neck once again. They sniffed out this Roman dung and led us to our quarry."

Serlaid pulled out a knife, slit the throat of the Roman soldier on the ground at Fiona's feet, and pulled the shaft from his neck. She narrowed her eyes and looked sideways at Fiona. "That's a good arrow. I think I'll keep it to spill more Roman blood one day."

Fiona wondered whether the statement was an oath or a threat.

Bhatair Rhu sought out the old warrior on the horse. It was the warlord Domhnull had told her about. What was his name? Oh yes. Kynwal. That was it. Domhnull said they called him the Pendragon. When he appeared out of the fog and cut his way through the Roman guards, Fiona had thought he might be a god. Interestingly, he was clad in cloak and mail rather than spirit armor like the rest of his men. Fiona wondered about that.

"Well done," the Arch Druid told his warrior friend. "I had a feeling you might appear around dawn. I'm glad you found us right away."

Kynwal nodded his head to acknowledge Bhatair Rhu and then barked some orders to his men. Turning back to the Arch Druid he asked, "Do you want them taken back to Fearnan? Or to *Feart Choille?*"

"No," Bhatair Rhu replied. "Let's go straight to Dun Drumainn. Send for Fedelma and Dornoll to prepare the sanctuary in the Moraig Grove for a sacrifice. They will need warrior guards and some craftsmen to assist them."

The Arch Druid pointed down the valley toward the other signal pyres. "Did the Romans assault the other strongholds?"

Kynwal shook his head. "There were some small scale raids, but they appear to have been diversions to scatter our forces. This patrol seems to have been the primary mission. What do you think? Were they after you or the girl?"

"Fiona *Taghte* was their target. I was just an unexpected bonus."

Kynwal grunted. "It's just like the Romans to grub for gold and leave the iron behind."

"Oh, and send for Finnan. This will all need to be documented. It's the first skirmish in the war that will drive the Romans from Britain. I want this memorialized in poetry and songs."

"As you say," Kynwal replied. He turned his mighty steed and began issuing orders.

The Arch Druid walked back over to Fiona. "We'll be here for a bit to get things organized, and then we'll proceed to Drumainn Hill. Try to get some rest. You walked all night, and we have a busy day ahead."

"Why? What's going to happen now? Aren't we going back to Fearnan?"

"No." The Arch Druid grinned. "Our Roman friends have given us a unique opportunity to win the favor of the gods. And *you*, Fiona *Taghte*, will play a crucial role."

THE SUN WAS high in a rare, cloudless sky as they marched in procession up a steep path through a thick forest. The Romans had been stripped of their armor and bound with leather thongs. A dozen of them had survived the ambush and were now being led as captives up to the fort on Drumainn Hill. Fiona did not know what their fate would be, but expected it to end in a brutal death at the hand of highland warriors.

Finnan had arrived in their makeshift camp before they left, along with Eliavres and a small group of druids. He walked beside Fiona now. She was thankful for his company, but also plagued with a fresh wariness. One loyal ally had just betrayed her. Could she really trust anyone at all, especially this bard whom she barely knew —a druid wordsmith whose voice perfectly matched the one that had haunted her nightmares?

But aside from Bhatair Rhu and Eliavres, Finnan was the only one in their little company she even knew. Serlaid had taken her bow and her dogs and left with a small war band right after the night rescue. Fiona was actually thankful for that. Though Serlaid was a blood relative, she felt less kinship for her than for almost anyone in the clan.

Swarms of black flies accosted the little retinue as they trekked up the rocky path. The flies were each as thick as Fiona's thumb and had a vicious bite that would draw blood whenever they could strike bare skin. Everyone in the party waved their arms frantically, trying to keep the menacing attackers from landing a blow, except the Roman prisoners whose hands were lashed behind their backs. These men uttered a string of what Fiona suspected must be the vilest curses their language could produce, as the black flies continually raised bloody welts on their heads, necks, and arms. The swarms continued their relentless assault as long as the group was in the shade of the trees, but would disappear, for some unknown reason, wherever sunshine broke through the canopy of limbs.

"You know," Finnan muttered, squashing one of the vicious creatures into a gooey pulp on his arm, "they need our blood to fertilize their eggs. So, if you let any of the little bastards get at ya, there'll just be even more of them next season."

Fiona felt she was about to go mad from constantly swatting away the sinister little beasts, when Bhatair Rhu brought the procession to a halt at the edge of a small clearing. He was mounted on his tawny mare, and alone among the retinue appeared to be unmolested by the seething throng of little demons. The Arch Druid motioned to Eliavres, who dismounted and strode ahead into the sunshine where he would be unassailed by the flies. He bent down to the ground momentarily and then rose up again. He lifted his silver-laced staff toward the heavens, muttered an incantation Fiona could not understand, and tossed a handful of dirt into the air.

Immediately, a stiff breeze whipped up and blew the dust away. Then, to Fiona's astonishment, the swarms of black flies disappeared, blown away in the wind along with the dust Eliavres had hurled into the sky. She could tell the Roman soldiers were, likewise, amazed at this display of power. Who was this man that even the winds obeyed his command? Fiona looked on Eliavres with a renewed sense of respect. And she wondered at the fact that he deferred to Bhatair Rhu. Did the Arch Druid also possess such abilities?

"How did he do that?" Fiona muttered to Finnan.

"He did not, actually, do anything at all."

"You just saw him summon that breeze to blow away these horrid flies. What do you mean he did nothing? Could *you* do that?"

Finnan chuckled. "No, I could do no such thing. But neither could he. He merely called on the gods and pled for their intervention. And this time, he got the answer he sought. I expect it was actually the *Sidhe* to whom we owe this momentary reprieve."

"*Sidhe?*"

"Ah," Finnan mused. "Yes. It's the name by which the fairy folk are called among my people on Eire. Of course it could have been

Borrum or even the *Daghda*, himself. It's really quite difficult to tell. The gods can be somewhat capricious."

"Well, anyway," Fiona replied, "it's still an impressive feat. And I am glad to be rid of the little pests."

"Even so," Finnan concurred.

Relieved from the dreaded curse of the vicious, biting insects, the group made faster progress. As they walked along, Fiona took the opportunity to question Finnan about the recent developments.

"Why do you think Manas did it?" she asked the bard. "Why would he betray his people, and why would he betray *me* to the Romans? What would he have to gain?"

"It's an interesting question, I have to admit. What do you think?"

"I don't know. I wondered if they had threatened to harm someone he cares about, but I don't think he has close family, does he?"

"No, I don't believe so. Besides, a druid's loyalty is to the tribe first, and then to kin folk. It has to be that way, for us to act in the best interests of our people as a whole. Even a healer might have to sacrifice a loved one to a plague to prevent an uncontrollable outbreak."

"Surely they couldn't have bribed him, could they? What could they possibly offer that he would want bad enough to commit treason against his own clan?"

"I don't know about you," the bard replied, "but Manas always struck me as a man of convictions. Do you remember what he asked when you were searching for a weakness you could exploit in the Christian god?"

"Yes, I do. He asked if I was willing to use deceit in order to win. He implied that who I am is more important than what I might do, and that sacrificing my values, even to save the tribe, would have consequences for my life, long into the Otherworld."

"So," Finnan asked, "do those sound like the sentiments of a man who would renounce his own convictions?" He didn't wait for a reply.

"I have to believe, for whatever reason, Manas felt he was doing the right thing. I don't know what motivated his actions, but I suspect he thought they were justified."

Flora considered what the Master Bard said, as they continued to march, side by side, along the narrow path. She also puzzled over the fact that she was walking at all. Bhatair Rhu, Eliavres, and Kynwal all rode on their trusty steeds. Didn't a future goddess warrant a mount as well? She wondered what that might imply about how they truly valued her. Was she, indeed, the critical key to the success of their plan? Or was she merely another piece they were maneuvering across their game board?

BEFORE THE SUN had fallen half-way to the far horizon, they broke into a broad clearing at the western crest of the hill, filled with chest-high bracken. Across the sea of leafy green waves, Fiona saw the stone ramparts of a massive hill fort. This must be Dun Drumainn. Though she had never been here before, it felt strangely familiar to her.

Unlike *Feart Choille*, this stronghold was fashioned from earth and rock rather than from the trunks of live trees. It was perched on a rocky crag overlooking the confluence of the River Tatha and River Linne. Though Fiona was no warrior, even she could see how perfectly it was situated to guard both glens from an attack up the Tatha Valley. She could not, however, figure out why they allowed the bracken to grow so thick around the fortress. Surely the thick carpet of vegetation would allow enemies to sneak up to the walls undetected. But she was no military strategist, and she supposed they must have had a good reason.

The group proceeded down a narrow, zig-zag swath which had been cut through the field of ferns and then up to the looming stronghold. They entered the fortress through a wide wooden gate and were immediately surrounded by a crowd of warriors clad in a curious variety of armor and garb. Some wore the dark green tunics with purple thistle badges which identified them as part of the Arch Druid's guard. Others wore the plain brown tunics Fiona was familiar with from the people in her own tribe. But most of the men were garbed in odd clothing, with emblems Fiona didn't recognize and with jewelry and other adornments that seemed strange and foreign to her. Most had thick, silver torcs around their necks and bands of silver on their arms.

Fiona whispered to Finnan, "Who are these men?"

"This," Finnan replied, "is where Kynwal has been meeting with the tribal chiefs and warlords to plan the attack on the wall. These men have come here from all over the highlands and islands of Caledonia, from Eire, and from across the great sea as well. Such a gathering has never taken place in the history of our people. They are all united in a common purpose, which, itself must be a miracle of the gods. If ever the Romans were to be driven from the land, now would seem to be the time."

"Why are they all staring at us? Surely they have seen Romans before. Why would they be so curious about these prisoners?"

"Oh, mistress, they're not gawking at the Romans. It would be you they're fascinated by."

"*Me?* Why would they be interested in me?"

"Why, they all want to see the woman who will become a goddess and guarantee their victory in this war. They're not just here to plan a military campaign. They're here to gain assurance the gods will be on their side."

Fiona suddenly realized Finnan was right. Everyone in the crowd was staring at *her.* She became self-conscious of all these powerful men watching her every move, and she had no idea how to act or what to do.

"Don't worry yourself, mistress. You need not be concerned about how you might appear to these folk. I've discovered, from many years of singing my tunes in the halls of chiefs and emperors, that they are oft just as worried about how they might be perceived in your own eyes. After all, they might be heads of clans and commanders of men, but in their eyes, you will be a deity. They look upon you with fear and tremblin' in their hearts, despite what their faces might show. So take courage and stand tall, for you are a goddess among mere mortals."

Despite Finnan's words of encouragement, Fiona felt terrified and small. Yet like the men surrounding her, she was determined not to reveal her weakness, but to put on an air of bravery and strength.

Bhatair Rhu swung off his horse and conferred with a small group of military commanders. Then he gave some orders to Eliavres and finally turned to Fiona. "*Taghte*, please take a short time to rest from the journey and to refresh yourself. A room has been prepared for you with food and water. Unfortunately, there are no novices here to attend you. There will be an important ceremony just before sunset. And tomorrow morning, we travel to the sacred grove for the *Oblation*."

"What's the *Oblation?*"

The Arch Druid smiled. "It is the next step in your preparation. You will make a special offering to the gods."

For a moment, Fiona wondered if she would *make* an offering to the gods, or if she would *be* an offering to the gods. But she thought back to the golden eagle in the sacred chamber of *An Dun Gael* and felt her confidence return. She would, indeed, become a goddess. She would lead her people to victory. This was her destiny.

As Bhatair Rhu walked away, Finnan edged up beside her. "Manas is here. They're keeping him locked in the base of the corner tower."

"And?" Fiona asked.

"Well, it might be the only opportunity you have to find out what caused him to make the choices he's made. I don't expect he'll be long for this life. The highlanders don't take kindly to traitors." He bowed his head to her and turned away.

One of the Arch Druid's personal guards showed Fiona to her quarters. He treated her with deference and awe. Most of the people in Dun Drumainn had never seen Fiona. To them she must have been like someone out of myth and legend. Fiona thought she might be able to use that fact to her advantage.

AFTER WASHING, she ate a hearty meal of red deer and hard cheese. She was famished after almost a whole day without food. The rations at a military camp were short on delicacies, but warrior-hunters always had a ready supply of fresh game on hand. Though she was absolutely exhausted and desperately wanted to take Bhatair Rhu's advice to get some much-needed rest, her curiosity got the best of her. She had to find out what had motivated Manas to betray her trust and the trust of his people.

Fiona made her way across the compound with dozens of pairs of eyes watching her every move. She took Finnan's counsel and carried herself with the absolute confidence of a creature of the Otherworld. A pair of druid adepts guarded the door of the tower chamber.

"I want to speak to the prisoner," Flora demanded in a tone as tinged with authority as she could muster.

"I'm sorry, Fiona *Taghte*," one of the guards replied. "*Ard-Draoidh* Bhatair Rhu left instructions that no one may enter the cell without his permission."

"Good," Fiona said. "You know who I am. I assume you also know who I am about to become. You risk my displeasure when I take my place in the Otherworld. I want to speak to the prisoner. Alone." She glared at the guard with a silent stare.

The two druids glanced nervously at each other and finally capitulated. "Yes, *Taghte*. Please forgive our reluctance. Surely the Arch Druid would not object to *your* presence here." With that, they stepped aside and ushered her through the door.

The cell was dark and dank. It had no windows, and an acrid smell wafted through the air. Manas sat against the far wall with his head bowed as if in prayer. He looked up as she entered the room.

"Good day to you, *Thaghadh*," he said without rising. "I'm glad to see you."

"Quit calling me that. I have no choice to make. I've been chosen by the gods, and my destiny is set."

"I see," he replied. "Well then, it appears you have made your choice already."

"I'm not here to talk about my choice. I'm here to talk about yours. Why?" she spat, throwing her hands in the air. "Why did you do it? Why did you betray your own people? Why did you betray *me*?"

"I was disloyal neither to our people nor to you, *Thaghadh*. I did what I did for the sake of our people."

"By turning me over to the Romans?" Fiona fumed. "How exactly is that in the best interests of our people?"

Manas flicked a small pebble across the room, and it skidded over the floor.

"You've seen the people gathered at this fortress, yes? Do you know who they are and why they are here?"

"They're here to plan an assault on the wall. They're here to drive our Roman oppressors out of this land forever."

"Yes, but they are planning an assault which has no chance to succeed. Oh they might break through the defenses at the wall. They may even penetrate deep into the lands of the south. But we have no capability to occupy and hold those lands. Our people are raiders, not conquerors. We might possibly push the Romans to the sea, but I assure you, the tide would eventually turn, and the might of Rome would wash back over this land, destroying everything in its path. Our people are about to kick a sleeping bear. If they proceed with these plans, they will only succeed in provoking its wrath."

"Where is your heart? Where is the passion of a highlander? Does the hunger for freedom not burn in your gut? You forget, I saw what the Romans would do to our land. I experienced the horror of their rule in my visions from the gods. I know what they would do if we stopped fighting and yielded to the yoke of bondage they would place on our necks. They would utterly destroy us. The gods showed me what would happen if I allowed them to reign here."

"You saw what Bhatair Rhu wanted you to see."

Fiona was about to unleash another torrent of vitriol when Manas' words penetrated her rage. "What do you mean?"

"The visions you saw. Bhatair Rhu and Eliavres planted those thoughts in your mind. They told you what to see."

"What are you talking about?"

"They drugged you with the milk of the poppy and then planted suggestions in your mind."

Fiona pressed her palms to her temples in frustration and then ran her fingers through her hair, gripping her scalp so hard it almost hurt. "You lie. You're a traitor to your people, and now you're trying to turn me against them as well."

"Believe what you may. But I challenge you to search your heart. You know it's true, deep down inside."

"No! No, I don't. I saw things they could never have known about —thoughts they could never have planted in my mind, potions or not."

"That," Manas replied, "is the magic of the poppy. It opens the mind to suggestions, but then those thoughts get mixed together with your own memories to produce experiences which seem as real as the ground beneath your feet. And when you respond to those images in your mind, you move and react as if they were true. You run, and you fall, and you lash out. You strike the air, thinking you have punched a man or fended off a savage beast. I am an expert in the healing arts. I have spent my life studying the effects of elixirs on the body and mind. I know of what I speak."

"What about Fedelma? She saw my vision. She saw the owl and the eagle. She saw the great ceremony in the glen before the sacred yew tree in *Cridhalbane*." Fiona paused and a chill ran down her spine. It was the first time she, herself, had uttered the powerful word, and she spoke it now with trembling and awe.

"Fedelma is also a creature of the Arch Druid. She sees what Bhatair Rhu tells her to see."

Fiona barely even heard what he said. Lost in her own memory of the vision, she went on. "It's where the whole druid community bowed down—all but one." And then the realization hit her like a hammer blow. "It was you, wasn't it? You were the one who didn't bow down. You were the one standing with the crooked staff lifted high."

Manas was momentarily shaken by this revelation. "How did you know that?"

Fiona paced back and forth in front of the Master Healer sitting idly on the stone floor. "But even if that was true, why would you turn me over to a Roman patrol? You say you did it to serve our people. What good would that possibly do?"

"Why are you here, at this fort? Why did Bhatair Rhu bring you here?"

"I don't know. We came straight here after being rescued from your abduction squad. You tell me. Why am I here?"

"You're here to seal the deal with the other tribes. No one really thinks our people can prevail against the Romans, at least not in an attack against the wall. Even with all our forces united, we still can't counter the might of Rome. But Bhatair Rhu promised them help from the gods. More than that, he promised them help from the one god they all believe defeated the Romans once before—the one *goddess* who annihilated an entire Roman legion and took its golden eagle captive. He promised them the aid of Brigid. He promised them *you*."

"You lie," Fiona shouted. "You're a traitor and a liar."

"So I planned to take away the Arch Druid's secret weapon. I planned to abduct his goddess. Without you, there was a good chance his fragile coalition would fall apart. Without the aid of the goddess Brigid, the other tribes would withdraw their forces, and the whole war effort would crumble. If I kept Bhatair Rhu and Kynwal from kicking the sleeping bear, maybe, just maybe, the bear wouldn't rise and devour our people and our land."

"But what if...?" Fiona muttered. Then she completed the thought with more confidence, "What if Brigid *could* defeat the nailed god and lead our people to victory."

"It's not possible."

"What makes you so sure?"

Manas frowned, gravely. "I know it, because the gods aren't real—at least, not how you imagine them to be. Don't you see, Flora, when you walk into the waters of the sacred spring, you won't be transforming into a goddess. You won't be transported through the surface of the pool into the Otherworld. You will be a sacrifice—an offering to gods who aren't truly gods at all. You'll just die a needless death that serves no purpose."

Manas finally stood and grasped Fiona by the arms. "I did not betray you. I didn't capture you to cause you any harm. I abducted you to save your life."

Fiona could see the sincerity in his eyes. He honestly believed his words were true. But, in that moment, she also realized what had taken hold of his mind and stolen away his loyalties. He had been deceived by the nailed god.

"You're a Christian, aren't you? You've abandoned our gods to worship the nailed god of the Romans. That's what made you do all of this."

Manas held her eyes, steady and firm. "I am a follower of the one true god. I have pledged my life and allegiance to him. I face my imminent death with confidence and without fear, knowing I have obtained eternal life through trust in him. My only desire is for my people, and for *you*, to know the truth of his infinite love."

Fiona's heart ached. She could see it now. Finnan was right, after all. Manas was, indeed, a man of convictions. He truly believed what he was doing was right. "Manas, my friend, you've been seduced by a lie into denying the gods of your youth, the gods of your people. Now you bow down before a foreign god. No wonder you don't want me to become a goddess. No wonder you don't want me to become Brigid. You fear for your nailed god. You're afraid I will defeat him in battle. I thought you had betrayed me, but I see you're actually trying to be loyal in your own way. Manas, please, it's not too late. You've been deceived. Please let me explain all of this to Bhatair Rhu. If he understands what happened to you and what they did to you, I know he'll show you mercy. Come back. Come back to the old gods of our people, and I'm sure he'll pardon you."

Fiona looked deeply into Manas' eyes and saw the hope and confidence fade to sorrow. He dropped his gaze, grasped her hands and pressed them to his lips. When he finally released them, he sat back down on the ground and hung his head. "I will pray for you," he said softly. "I am so sorry for how I have failed you. You are very dear to me."

Bhatair Rhu came to Fiona's room. He knocked and then leaned against the door frame.

"I hear you had a visit with Manas. How did that go?"

"He's a Christian. He worships the nailed god. That's why he betrayed us."

Bhatair Rhu nodded. "I suspected as much. He spent a great deal of time with the Greek physicians south of the Wall. I know he respected their skill at the healing arts. It doesn't surprise me he was similarly influenced by their spiritual beliefs."

Flora's head shot up in surprise. "You knew? Then why did you let him manage my preparations?"

The Arch Druid reflected a moment before responding, as if measuring his words. "I thought it might guide him back to the old gods. Such positions of responsibility test a man's inner convictions. They force him to make a definitive choice, one way or the other. I had hoped Manas would choose wisely. Apparently, I was wrong. I had not expected him to go to such extremes. I didn't think he would collaborate with the Romans to abduct you. I must apologize for that miscalculation."

"He thinks the Romans will destroy us if we attack the wall."

"Of course," Bhatair Rhu replied, "It's because he doesn't believe Brigid will defeat the nailed god. But we know the truth. We're placing our trust in you. And I have every confidence you will prevail on behalf of our people. We *will* drive the Romans from our land."

"How can you be so certain? What if I fail?"

"Come. We are about to perform a special ceremony. It is an ancient rite. It was used ages ago to determine the will of the gods with respect to upcoming battles. Our people have not performed this rite in a very long time. But the ancient lore has been passed down through the line of druid diviners. The last time it was conducted, the gods showed our fore fathers their victory over the Ninth Roman Legion. The golden eagle in *An Dun Gael* attests to the validity of the oracle."

"Here," he handed her a deep green woolen cloak. "You'll need this. It's starting to rain."

As Fiona draped the garment over her shoulders and pulled the hood up over her head, she noticed the purple thistle embroidered on the front. Apparently, she would wear the Arch Druid's own symbol over her heart. A calming warmth settled through her body and quelled her anxiety about appearing before a large group of foreign warriors. She would be seen as part of Bhatair Rhu's own inner circle —part of the group that would lead their combined forces to victory.

Out in the fort's courtyard, everyone had assembled in a loose square formation, save only the warriors standing lookout on the ramparts. A tight circle of druids surrounded a single Roman prisoner in the very center of the crowd. He was stripped to the waist and his hands were bound. Fiona recognized him as the commander of the Roman patrol that had seized her the previous evening.

Men gave way to allow Fiona and Bhatair Rhu to pass. Fiona noticed unlit pyres placed between the onlooking warriors and the circle of druids. Seven of the druids were cloaked with feathers and crowned with elaborate headpieces in the likeness of eagles. They must be there to represent the power of Rome. It was very similar to the great convocation she had seen in her vision, when the eagle attacked the owl, and lost.

Eliavres stood in the center of the circle with the captive. He held the silver-tipped staff high over his head, and flames leapt to each of the pyres, instantly igniting them, despite the dampness of the rain. The warriors gasped in amazement. They all knew about the power of a Master Druid's magic, but most had never actually seen it in person. With the bonfires lit and burning high, the eagle dancers began moving and gyrating in time to the chanting from the ring of druids.

Suddenly, Fiona was back in her ordeals, back in the nightmare of her visions. She recognized this place. She recognized this ceremony with blazing infernos and eagle-dancers leaping and spinning in the air. Except in that torrid memory, she, herself, was in the center, not a Roman prisoner. And she was lashed to an altar as a sacrifice to the gods.

A gasp escaped Fiona's throat at the images playing themselves out in her mind. Bhatair Rhu apparently mistook her reaction as an expression of wonder at the spectacle happening within the circle in front of them. He gently grabbed her arm to steady her. His touch instantly caused the apparition to vanish, and Fiona was in the present once again, surrounded by foreign warriors and watching a sacred rite playing itself out. But a cold chill filled her heart as she pondered the fleeting memory. Had it actually been a memory after all? Or had it been a phantom, rippling out from the experience of her ordeals—a ghastly specter haunting the dark place in her mind where she still feared to look?

As the chanting rose to a fevered pitch and the eagles appeared as if they might actually take flight, Eliavres pulled a long-bladed dagger from his belt, and in one swift motion, stabbed the Roman prisoner in the small of his back. The knife sliced into the man's left kidney before ripping out once again. Blood spurted from the gaping wound, which would soon be fatal, but not instantly so. The Roman shrieked in pain. Eliavres stepped back and watched closely as the man jerked and stumbled his way around the ring, splashing gouts of blood in seemingly random patterns on the ground.

The crowd looked on in stunned expectation. The druids chanted. The dancers leapt and swayed. Some of the warriors cheered at the agonized howls of their hated foe. Others watched silently, with stony expressions, apparently taking no pleasure in a gruesome, if necessary, act.

It seemed like the man took forever to fall to the ground. The sun was well below the horizon, and a cloudy, rainy night settled over the captive's funeral pyres before he jerked and spasmed one final time, and breathed his last. Fiona didn't know if the Roman officer worshipped the old gods or the new Christian deity. Would she see him in the feasting hall of the Otherworld? Probably not, since he died a death of shame without a weapon in his hand.

She assumed the rite was over and expected the crowd to dissipate into the night. But the chanting of the druids droned on, and the eagles kept up their dance, so the warriors stood fast. Eliavres once again lifted his staff into the air and it blazed forth with a bright, white flame. Then he used the butt end of the snarled shaft to trace the dying man's spurts of blood soaking into the ground. An old, stooped figure stepped forward from the circle of druids and fell to his knees. He swept his hands across the blood, along the lines marked out by Eliavres' staff.

After a long time, the old man slowly pushed himself up, turning to face the Arch Druid and the fledgling goddess at his side. The chanting stopped and the dancing ceased. The whole crowd grew silent to hear the proclamation.

The ancient one cried out in a raspy voice, "The gods have smiled on us. Our victory is assured. It is written on the earth beneath our feet in our enemy's own blood."

A cheer erupted from the throng. Men clapped each other on the back and lifted their arms in praise to the gods. Then, slowly at first, but with a surging force that grew stronger with every beat, a shout broke out, chanting in cadence to the beating of her heart. "Fiona. *Taghte.* Fiona. *Taghte."* Then, almost imperceptibly, and of its own volition, the chanting morphed into something new, something bold, something powerful. "Brig-id. Brig-id. Brig-id."

Amid the rising tenor of the chant, Bhatair Rhu placed his hand on her shoulder and slowly turned her around. She lifted her head high and looked hard at the faces staring back at her. In that moment, any insecurity she ever felt, any uncertainty about her calling, burned up in the flames and rose as smoke into the sky. She *was* Fiona *Taghte.* She *was* Brigid. And she would set her people free.

CHAPTER TWENTY-THREE

N o one rode on a horse this time. The place they were going was too sacred, too holy. Fiona stood next to Bhatair Rhu, Eliavres, and Kynwal, facing a raging river. Swollen with power from last night's rain, the current of the Tatha rushed and surged.

A select group from among the chieftains and warlords at the fort had left just after mid-day in a procession that zig-zagged down the slope of Drumainn Hill into the Tatha Valley. They were accompanied by the Roman prisoners and a contingent of Bhatair Rhu's personal guards. The group was now assembled on the banks of the roaring river, assessing how they would get across to the other side. Fiona had wondered if Bhatair Rhu might command Eliavres to raise his staff and part the waters so they could pass. But *Incheskadyne*, the village of the Great Chief, was not far upstream, so they sent several druid adepts to fetch men with boats.

When the boatmen finally arrived, they were not paddling their long canoes down the river as she had expected. Instead, they guided their craft from the shores using long ropes. In fact, several teams came down each of the waterway's two shores. Flora watched in amazement as the men worked with purpose and efficiency. They began tying the boats off and lashing them together, side by side, across the river. Once they met in the middle, they secured the two sections and laid flat, wooden planks down across the centers. In what seemed like no time, they had created a bridge, from shore to shore, wide enough for two people to cross abreast. Fiona was impressed at the ingenuity of her people. She had never seen such a feat accomplished before, and she swelled with pride at the capabilities of the men of her tribe.

Bhatair Rhu turned to Fiona. "Walk with me," he prompted her. "It is appropriate for us to be the first ones across. We shall soon lead our people against greater challenges than this."

Fiona took his arm and they placed their feet on the first row of planks. The bridge was much less sturdy than it appeared. It rocked and swayed with every step. Fiona clutched tightly to the Arch Druid to keep from falling. But Bhatair Rhu was as steady as a rock. He never faltered or stumbled. Once they were across, the others followed in files of two. The sun was just half-way to the horizon by the time everyone had traversed the once formidable impediment.

On the far shore, Bhatair Rhu and Eliavres took time to organize the company of warriors. The Arch Druid called them into a tight crowd where everyone could hear his voice.

"The place we are going is very sacred. It was formed ages ago by ancestors we can scarce remember. Normally, only druids are permitted to enter the holy grove in front of you. When other men or women passed beyond this border, they caused great offense to the gods. Cernunos would send a deluding influence upon them, and they would become so disoriented they would never find their way back out. But we have obtained special permission from the gods to bring you here for this sacred ritual—a ceremony that has not been performed for many ages among our people. However, it is absolutely critical that no one strays from the path. To guard against this eventuality, a druid will walk before and behind every warrior. Be certain to always keep your guide in sight. Anyone who loses his way will never be seen again."

A hushed murmur arose among the assembled warlords. Several muttered aloud that the Arch Druid had planned some devious trick to lure them to their deaths. Many seemed on the verge of turning back. There had always been a great deal of mistrust between the tribes and clans of Caledonia. These chieftains were more accustomed to raiding each other's cattle, women, and stores of grain than cooperating together in an effort this large and significant. Keeping the armies focused and working together would be Bhatair Rhu's greatest challenge. And that process began here, with the tribal leaders.

Some unforeseen urge overcame Fiona which she could not control. She understood she was the critical tie which bound these disparate people together. She, or rather the goddess she would become, was the one important thing they all shared in common. If she was going to bind them together in war, she might as well start now.

Without saying a single word, she stepped up on a rock beside Bhatair Rhu. The whole crowd grew hushed before her. She cast her gaze across the breadth of expectant faces. Then she turned around and walked boldly into the forest. Though she didn't look back, she could hear the rustle of footsteps following her. A few heartbeats later, Bhatair Rhu appeared at her side.

"Well done," he murmured. "I was beginning to wonder if we would lose them to their suspicions and petty rivalries. But you have an unmatched capability to inspire these men." The Arch Druid took her arm and gently nudged her to the left. "Now allow me to guide you, so we really don't get everyone lost in this maze."

As they traversed a gentle slope up from the bank of the river, Bhatair Rhu led her on a circuitous path which had no apparent order. Fiona noticed subtle changes in the nature of the forest as they progressed. The trees seemed to have been layered in bands. The ones closest to the water were a typical mix of pine, birch, hawthorn and willow—a collection that would have drawn no special attention from travelers on the river or its shores. But the farther they moved inland, the trees appeared to have been intentionally cultivated in spiral groves according to their order of sacredness—first elder trees, then alder, hazel, ash, and yew.

Mid-way along their twisting path, Fiona suddenly found herself among a cluster of the tallest trees she had ever seen. They were some kind of evergreen that grew almost totally straight. The trunks were so large it would take six or seven people with arms outstretched to reach around their girth. Fiona felt as if she were a tiny mouse wandering in an enchanted forest of giant conifers, cultivated by the gods.

The sunlight filtering through the canopy above dipped toward the western horizon, and Fiona wondered if they would ever reach their destination, or if Cernunos had confounded their sense of direction after all. Would they tramp around in aimless spirals until they died of starvation or thirst, or was Bhatair Rhu true in his knowledge of the path which led to their goal? Fiona wondered if he had purposely taken an overly circuitous route to ensure their guests could not find the holy place again on other occasions in the future.

Eventually, they broke out into a broad clearing which was ringed with mighty oaks, the holiest of all trees. These stood majestically silhouetted against the setting sun, like ancient sentinels of wisdom and lore. Fiona marveled at how their massive trunks and gnarled limbs wove together in a perfect symmetry that spoke of dignity and primal power.

Bhatair Rhu pointed to a small hill in the center of the clearing and drew Fiona's attention to a stone circle which appeared to be as ancient as time itself. "Its name is *Moraig*. It means the Great Sun. It is a very holy place which few outsiders have ever seen."

"What will we do here? What is the *Oblation*?"

"This circle," he continued, "was erected over a thousand generations ago. It originally consisted of eight small boulders and a marker, all oriented toward the rising of the sun at the time of the summer solstice. It was consecrated to Lugh, to honor the great god of the sky for giving us warmth and causing our crops to grow."

"Is that what the *Oblation* is all about? Will we offer a sacrifice to Lugh at sunrise tomorrow?"

"A second, larger circle, was erected perhaps a hundred generations later, made of nine larger stones and two markers oriented toward the setting of the sun at winter solstice."

Fiona, annoyed that he had ignored her question, was nonetheless puzzled by his description. "Why the change? Did the people lose favor with Lugh? Were they begging him not to leave? Did they fear he would not return?"

"No," Bhatair Rhu replied. "Actually, the outer circle really honors Cerridwen. Together the two concentric circles trace out the couple's dance throughout the heavens, from the rising of the sun, when it rules the day, to its setting, when it yields the night to the moon." He stopped and looked down into Fiona's face. "We chose this place for the *Oblation* to honor Cerridwen and Lugh. But the sacrifice, itself, is dedicated to Tyrannis."

"Tyrannis!" Fiona exclaimed. "Why Tyrannis? I thought he and the Cailleach had conspired against the other gods—Cerridwen and Lugh in particular—to eliminate Brigid so spring would end and winter would rule the land. Why would we honor Tyrannis with a sacrifice at an ancient and holy place dedicated to Lugh?"

"It might seem like a contradiction. But for us to achieve our goals —to defeat the nailed god and drive the Romans from the land—we need all the gods to be united on our side. We need to fill the gap in the cycle created by Brigid's absence. We need to restore the normal balance *and* to reconcile the gods. Instead of fighting each other, we need them to unite against the nailed god and unify behind our cause. So a tribute to Tyrannis, the god of war and chaos, at this place which is sacred to Lugh, will help to reconcile the gods, restore the balance, and repair the breach. Brigid is the key. *You* are the key. Does that make sense?"

Fiona was awestruck at the multi-dimensional nature of the Arch Druid's plan and unnerved at the role which she was to play. So much seemed to hinge on her. But then she remembered the eagle and the vision of its attack on the owl, and she was reassured. She had seen her victory against the Romans. The gods had given her the experience of her ordeals to strengthen her will and motivate her spirit. She would prevail.

When they drew nearer to the stone circle, Fiona could see a huge figure, like a giant basket, lying down in its center. It seemed to be an enormous effigy of a man woven out of interlaced hazel rods.

"What is it?" she asked Bhatair Rhu.

"It is the heart of an ancient ritual and will be the central component of the *Oblation*. It is the *Fear Slatach*—the Wicker Man."

"Will it be the sacrifice to Tyrannis?"

"In a way," the Arch Druid replied. "All will be revealed in time."

Fiona bristled at his words. She was sick and tired of people treating her like a child. She was the central player in a drama so bold it boggled the mind, and yet everyone seemed to believe she couldn't comprehend what was going on. They kept feeding her information bits and pieces at a time. She was about to voice her consternation when Bhatair Rhu cut her short.

"I need to make certain the preparations are complete. Please wait over there with Finnan. The ceremony will proceed at sunset, and you will play a critical role."

"What role? What will I need to do?" Fiona called to his retreating back.

"You'll know when it is time," he replied without turning.

Frustrated at this response, Fiona threw up her hands and then frantically searched the crowd to locate Finnan. Maybe he would be able to answer her questions. She found him among a stalk of druids dressed in ceremonial white robes. Manas was in the center of the group, hands bound behind his back. Fiona had not realized he was with the entourage, and she avoided his gaze. Finnan caught her eye and broke away from the group to come join her.

"Greetings, mistress. It seems your display of courage emboldened our disconcerted chieftains. How could they cower in fear at the edge of the woods in the face of your fine example of fortitude? My compliments to you." He bowed his head.

"Do you know what is going on here? And don't you dare tell me that 'all things will be revealed at their proper time.'"

"Well, I don't know for certain, but I do have my speculations. However, I'm not sure it would be appropriate for me to share them if the Arch Druid has chosen to keep the matter concealed."

Fiona pursed her lips and glared at him. "Don't you start in with me too. If I'm such an important part of this whole plan, I think I deserve to know what's going on."

"Even so," Finnan concurred. "But I'm not sure it's my place to say, especially since my own knowledge is mere conjecture."

"Bhatair Rhu said the figure in the center of the circle is a Wicker Man. What is that? I've never heard of one before."

"No. I expect not. It is something out of myth and legend—a rite which our people have not practiced for ages past. It is, perhaps, something which should have disappeared in the mists of time. But, alas, it is being resurrected for this present effort."

"Will it be a sacrifice? A sacrifice to Tyrannis?"

"Indeed, it will."

Then a thought hit Fiona and she changed the subject slightly. "What kinds of sacrifices do the Christians offer to their nailed god?"

"None, really. At least not in the way you mean."

Fiona looked past Finnan and saw a group of druids assembling around the circle. It looked as if the ceremony would begin soon.

"I don't understand. Do they offer sacrifices or not?"

"The offer themselves as living sacrifices to their lord and king."

Fiona's attention snapped back to Finnan as she digested his comment. "You mean they drown themselves in bogs like our own zealots?"

"No," he replied with a shake of the head. "No, they do not commit suicide to appease their god. They offer their lives in service to him. They become willing servants for him to command."

"Then he doesn't sound much different than our gods after all—expecting acts of service and obedience to appease his wrath."

"Except," Finnan replied, "the motivation is different. The Christians claim to serve their god out of love, not out of fear—love for what he has already done for them."

"And what is that?" Fiona asked with an edge of skepticism in her voice. "What has this nailed god done for them?"

"According to their lore, *he* became a sacrifice for *them*. He gave up his own life to reconcile them with the father god. He bore the sickness caused by rebellion and strife in his own soul, so those who trust in him might be freed from its power."

Fiona was confused by the very notion of what Finnan described. It went against everything she had ever been taught about the gods. Gods did not give themselves in sacrifice for mere mortals. Gods held ultimate power over the world of men. They demanded sacrifices to appease their wrath and to earn their favor. This Christian god apparently had no understanding of his own role in the game of gods and men.

"What kind of god would do something like that?" Fiona hissed in disgust.

"What kind of god indeed?" Finnan replied with an introspective air. Then something over her shoulder caught his attention. "I believe the ritual is about to commence."

"I still don't know what I am supposed to do," Fiona interjected with a note of frustration in her voice.

"Unfortunately, neither do I. But I expect the Arch Druid will guide you through the ceremony. He is coming this way, even now."

Bhatair Rhu strode up beside them with a look of satisfaction on his face. "Good day to you, Master Bard. I expect the ceremony this evening will be prime material for legend and lore. I have no doubt you will leverage your skills to give it an appropriate air of mystery and power."

"I will endeavor to be worthy of the task you have set before me. Your apprentice, here, never ceases to amaze and intrigue."

Fiona wondered at his odd turn of phrase and use of the word, 'apprentice,' but let it pass.

"Indeed," Bhatair Rhu replied. Then he said to Fiona, "You and I will need to stand at *Moraig's* entrance, near the two large pillar stones, as the procession commences. Shall we?" He gestured for her to walk with him to their designated spot, while Finnan remained behind.

BHATAIR RHU GUIDED Fiona to a position next to the left of the two great boulders which marked the entrance to the circle, and then he stepped across to the other. The sun was just dipping below the horizon and a brilliant orange glow lit the clouds overhead. Druids stationed between the taller stones of the outer circle lit torches mounted atop wooden poles. The flames flickered and spat. The atmosphere was at once somber and serene. Unlike the ceremony at Dun Drumainn the day before, there were no drums, no dancers, and no chanting. Everything was perfectly still, save the howling of the wind.

Eliavres led an entourage of druids in white ceremonial robes into the space between the two circles. Then warriors, clad in the blue spirals and whirls of their spirit armor prodded eight Roman prisoners into the perimeter of the original sphere. They forced the captives to their knees in front of the eight boulders of the inner circle and held them there. Three of the Romans writhed and seethed with curses and threats, but the others maintained a stoic dignity in the face of their imminent fate.

A long moment of stillness settled over the hilltop. The actors, all assembled on the stage, appeared to be frozen in time as the sun disappeared behind the mountains to the west, and its waning light faded from the sky. Fiona listened to her own steady breathing, in and out, in and out, synchronized with the rhythm of her pulse.

When the last rays of sunlight disappeared from the sky, and the

clouds overhead went completely dark, a shuffle of movement pulled
Fiona's attention back to the ceremony. One final group of druids and
warriors marched past her into the center of the great stone
monument. Manas was in the front, his hands bound, followed by
four Roman prisoners under the control of highland warriors. A
druid forced Manas to his knees and then pushed him inside the
wicker effigy. The priest poked and prodded until Manas was at the
very head. Then two other druids quickly lashed him securely to the
infrastructure of the hollow, woven statue.

A chill ran up Fiona's spine as she realized what was happening.
When the remaining four Roman prisoners were forced inside the
Fear Slatach, Fiona understood *they* were the true sacrifices. The
Wicker Man, itself, was merely a death cage. These men,
representatives of the enemy in the war to come, would be the real
offerings to Tyrannis. The god of war and chaos was a cruel god. He
required blood—human blood—to gain his favor and avert his wrath.

After the men were positioned inside their woven coffin and
bound in place so they could not break free, a band of warriors
emerged from between the rocks and began hoisting the enormous
statue upright with hemp tethers and flaxen ropes. The captive men
wrestled with their bonds and struggled to break free, causing the
huge beast to teeter and writhe—all except the Master Healer,
secured inside the statue's head, his eyes peering out from the
creature's expressionless face. Once the colossus was secured in
place, its lines firmly staked out to the ground, another group of
druids advanced between the entrance stones with bundles of birch
which they heaped in a circle at the Wicker Man's feet. Then Fiona
knew the truth of it. This would not be a blood sacrifice after all, but
an offering made by fire.

The druids finished placing their tinder and filed back out past
Fiona and Bhatair Rhu. Then a line of eight warriors marched in
behind them. They processed slowly and deliberately around the
circle, each one stopping beside a Roman prisoner. The warrior
positioned behind the nearest stone looked up at Fiona, eyes gazing

out from a mask of painted lines, and she recognized the face of her lover. Domhnull was part of this execution squad. Fiona's heart wrenched. She knew Domhnull was a mighty warrior, fierce and fearless in battle. She understood he had killed men in hand-to-hand combat. But she could not imagine him in this role—viciously stealing the life of a helpless victim, enemy or not. He grinned at her, and she couldn't hold his eyes. She feared what she would see inside, and she forced herself to look away.

All the sacred rites had occurred in silence, save for the curses and epithets hurled by the captives. Suddenly a rapid series of drumbeats broke the stillness, and Fiona jumped at the sound. Her heart leapt and she drew a sharp breath. As if in response to this call of men, thunder roared throughout the heavens, drowning out the meager rumblings of the mortals on the ground. Just then, the eight warriors raised their mighty axes, and each one brought a blade down on the bowed neck of a Roman sacrifice.

Apparently, it was not so easy to sever a man's head from his shoulders in a single blow. So the warriors hacked and slashed, again and again, at sinew and bone, until the dirty deed was done, and the eight bodies fell to the ground. Fiona couldn't watch the gruesome scene and turned her face away. She had the heart of a healer, not a butcher, and she could not watch as men were slaughtered like sheep, even if they were Roman scum. Fiona kept her eyes averted as the eight warriors, with Domhnull in the lead, secured the severed heads and withdrew past her to the field beyond. The skulls of these men would, no doubt, be used as powerful totems in the war to come.

Fiona wrestled with her own internal demons, uncertainties filling her thoughts. She felt as if she had fallen from horror to horror in her journey to aid her people. The doubts returned and tugged at her mind. How had she come to this point? All she had ever wanted was to marry Domhnull, raise a family, and be a healer in her village. Whatever made her think she could become a goddess?

Then images of her uncle's rape raced through her mind, and she staggered. She was not pure. She was not holy and undefiled.

She could not be the Maiden Bride. She could not become Brigid. Surely the gods had made a terrible mistake. She teetered and swayed, overwhelmed by a bout of nausea that nearly made her retch, when Bhatair Rhu appeared at her side and thrust a blazing torch into her hand. She looked up at him, perplexed by what was happening.

"We know," he said with a deep look of concern on his face. "The gods have always known about your uncle and what he did to you."

"How?" Fiona muttered under her breath, but Bhatair Rhu ignored the question that wafted away in the breeze. He looked deep into her eyes, his own sparkling in the firelight.

"And still they chose you. They chose you to become the spotless Bride. They chose you to become the goddess Brigid. *You* are Fiona *Taghte*, and you will set your people free."

Fiona scanned the crowd assembled around the sacred stone circle—warrior chiefs from every tribe, druid masters from the Black Glen of the Crooked Stones, highland warriors from her own clan, the greatest bard in all the land, and the lover to whom she was betrothed. They all stared at her, watching to see her consummate the sacrifice. What else could she do? What choice did she really have?

Understanding exactly what they expected of her now, she steeled her nerve and grasped the torch from the Arch Druid's hand. She walked slowly and purposefully through the gateway stones and toward the *Fear Slatach*. The men inside, having watched the slaughter of their comrades and seen the torch in Fiona's hand, must have guessed what their fate would be. They began hurling obscenities and curses at her and at the crowd. They wrenched at their bonds and struggled to break free.

But the man at the top—the white-robed figure staring out of the effigy's lifeless eyes—made no sound at all. Instead, he looked down at Fiona with an expression she could not quite understand. It was an expression not of hatred, nor of fear, but of something she could only interpret as pity—a look of deep sadness, not because of his imminent death, but because of the choices being made by someone he considered to be a friend.

Fiona held her head high, but allowed her eyes to fall. She focused all her attention on the bundled branches at the statue's feet. She ignored the shouts of the Roman prisoners. She ignored the hushed anticipation of the assembled crowd. But most of all, she ignored the silent plea from the Master Healer—the plea for her to think about who she had become.

Fiona took her last step and came to a halt before the Wicker Man. She reached the torch high into the air for all to see. For just an instant, for the space of time between two heartbeats, she faltered. How could she, a healer, do this awful deed? How could she, who had dedicated herself to saving life, now cause these men to be consumed in a fire lit by her own hand? The moment of doubt washed over her, but then ebbed and flowed away. The words of the Arch Druid rang in her ears. She was chosen by the gods. She was destined to become a goddess. She was Fiona *Taghte*, and she would set her people free.

With one fluid movement, Fiona cast the torch onto the pyre, then turned her back and walked away. She heard a collective gasp as the assembled crowd exhaled. She heard the screams of terror and agony as the Roman captives succumbed to the blaze. But she did not hear a cry of fear or a scream of anguish from the voice of a Master Healer she had come to know so well—and his silent courage in the face of a cruel death made her heart weep.

"TELL ME HOW IT FELT," Finnan said, "to offer the sacrifice to Tyrannis."

They were back in the crannog, back in a place that was at once familiar, and yet very strange to her. It was not Flora's old home in Bunrannoch, but it had become Fiona's home, and she was Fiona *Taghte* now. Two days had passed since the offering at

Moraig. The woman who was once her mother had done the morning chores and then left. Her attendants had completed the morning rituals. Now, Finnan was here to question her about her experiences—events she would rather forget. Nandag, as usual, hovered in the shadows, just within earshot, to protect Fiona's reputation of virtue.

"Do we really need to go over this again?" Fiona asked, not wanting to relive the horror of those moments.

"This tale will go down in history. Your situation gives our people a rare opportunity to see into the mind of a goddess. Knowing your thoughts at such a critical moment will shape how men and women of the highlands and islands worship Brigid for all eternity."

"Perhaps there is a reason the gods keep their thoughts private. I know you are a keen observer of motive and character. I'm confident you can craft the appropriate words to reflect my sentiments at the time. And you can, no doubt, portray it with a flair of creativity I could never muster."

"Hmm," Finnan mused. "I could, I'm certain, concoct a phrase or two that would tickle the fancy of eager ears. But I would much rather plumb the wellspring of the very heart which laid the torch at the Wicker Man's feet."

"I'm sure you would. But not today." Fiona cast about for a way to change the topic. "Did you know he was a Christian?"

"Who would that be, dear lady?"

"You know exactly who I mean," she replied, indignantly. "Manas."

"I had my suspicions, to be sure. But one can never be too certain about such things."

The two sat on a single bench, side by side, instead of facing each other as would be typical for such an interview. Fiona was glad she didn't have to look the Master Bard in the face.

"I spoke with him in the tower cell at Dun Drumainn. He said I could not become a goddess, because there was no such thing. He said the Christian god is the only true god. What is that supposed to mean? What about all the other gods? What about the Daghda, and Cerridwen, and Lugh? If they aren't gods, what are they?"

"Well," Finnan replied, "if Manas *was* a Christian, as you say, then he would be speaking from the Christian perspective. According to them, there is only one god."

"Or apparently, just three, right? The father, son, and spirit. That's what you told me before."

"True. But together, in perfect unity, existing as one god—like I said before." Finnan winked at her to take the edge off the jibe.

"So what about all the other gods? Our people have worshipped them for ages past. We've offered sacrifices to them. We've honored them with feasts and festivals. They have given us oracles about the future and performed miracles in the sight of the whole tribe. I have personally seen visions from our gods. More than visions, actually. I have experienced what a future without them would mean to our people." Fiona shuddered as images from her ordeals passed through her mind. "What about all of that?"

Finnan sighed. "The Christians would say those are deceptions from the enemy—the fallen angels I told you about."

"But you described those beings as evil. You said they deceived people and made them suffer in order to attack their god. Our gods give us blessings."

"Do they, now? And just what blessings might those be?"

"They make our crops grow. They help barren women have children. They cause the rains to come and shorten harsh winters. They even do little things, like summon the wind to blow away black flies on the trail to Dun Drumainn. You said it yourself."

Finnan looked thoughtful. He took some time before responding. "The Christians would say all those good things actually come from their god—that he is the one who brings the rains and makes the crops to grow. But they might also contend that the best lie contains the most truth."

"What do you mean?"

"The goal of the fallen angels is to get people to worship anything except the one true god. So, from the perspective of one theory, they took all the Christian god's positive gifts and turned them into objects of worship, in and of themselves."

Fiona shook her head. "I don't understand you."

"According to the Christians, their god created everything—the earth, the sky, the waters and springs, the animals, and people, of course. Those are all real things with real blessings contained in them. So, the enemy just breaks all of creation down into bits and pieces and gets people to worship each part. That way, they lose sight of the one god who really created them all."

"I still don't follow what you are trying to say."

"The fallen angels get people to worship the sun, for example, as if it were an entity in and of itself, instead of being just one part of everything the true god created. It's the same with the moon, the stars, the mountains, sacred trees, holy springs, birds, bears, and everything else. If people worship the elements of creation, then they lose sight of the creator."

Fiona heard Nandag rustling around in the background and wondered how she would perceive this conversation. The ideas Finnan was describing would be considered blasphemous to the druids, and would surely bring down the wrath of the gods. To make sure her intentions were clear, Fiona reiterated her reasons for asking the questions.

"You know I'm asking all of this so I can find a weakness to exploit, when I fight the Roman god in the Otherworld."

"So you have reminded me on several occasions."

"I just wanted to make sure that was clear, so you could help me identify his vulnerabilities."

"Even so," Finnan replied.

"So what you're saying is that Tyrannis is not really the god of thunder, and the Daghda is not the father god of blessings."

"It is what the Christians would say."

Fiona shook her head in exasperation. These ideas were

absolutely ridiculous. "And so Cerridwen is not the moon goddess? Lugh is not lord of the sun?"

"It is as you say, according to the Christians." Finnan touched his finger to his lips in a thoughtful pose, and then added, "Interesting thing about Lugh, though."

"What's that?" Fiona prompted.

"Well, the angel who started this rebellion in the first place—his name was Lucifer."

"Okay, so what?"

"'Lucifer' means 'light bearer' or 'the shining one.'"

Fiona drew a sharp breath. Finnan was treading on very dangerous ground, for Lugh's name also meant 'the bright shining one.'

He went on. "Christians would say that Lucifer actually wanted to do more than merely distract people from worshipping the creator god. He actually wanted people to worship him instead. So he made himself out to be the god of the sun, the greatest of all the gods."

At these words, Fiona stood and began pacing around the room. This conversation was becoming perilous in more ways than one.

"What about the miracles? What about the visions and the oracles?"

"Remember," Finnan replied, "these angels are still spiritual beings, even though they rebelled against the Christian god. They have powers that would seem quite miraculous to you and me. And their primary weapon is deception. Lucifer's first tool was a lie, and it remains his favorite means of attack."

Fiona paused before asking the true question which nagged at her conscience and filled her heart with trepidation. "What about Brigid? If the rest of the gods are really fallen angels, then what is Brigid? Has she truly gone missing? Has the eternal cycle really been broken?" The rest of the questions she left unspoken, but they echoed in her mind. *If Brigid doesn't exist, then what about me? What am I to become?*

"According to the Christians, Brigid is just like all the rest. She's an imposter whose aim is to take our eyes off the creator and cause us to worship the creation instead."

"But I *saw* her, in my visions. She looked back at me from the tiny spring that saved my life. She was there when I passed through the waters. She guided me to the sacred yew. When I saw her face looking back at me, it was just as if I were seeing myself through her eyes. She has given my life hope and meaning. How could I ever deny her?"

Finnan stood and reached out a hand to clasp Fiona's shoulder. "This is what the Christians say about their god. You must choose what *you* believe."

"And you, Finnan? What is the truth in your eyes?"

The question lingered in the air for a long moment. Finally, Finnan replied. "I believe each one of us has a purpose in life—one that reaches far beyond the confines of this world and echoes into eternity. We must each decide what path we will follow and then walk that road with determination and conviction. You must choose your own way. No one else can decide on your behalf. As for me, I am a bard—a singer of songs and a teller of tales. My greatest hope is that my words will far outlast the end of my days."

He gave her shoulder a gentle press of reassurance, then turned to leave.

Her mind racing with tormented thoughts, Fiona rushed across the crannog and fell into her old mentor's arms. "Oh, Nandag. Nandag, what have I done?"

"Shh. Hush, now." The older woman cradled her young apprentice in her embrace, for that is what they were once again in this moment—not servant and goddess, but mentor and student.

"You should have seen his face, staring out of the eyes of that hideous abomination. I thought he would hate me. He should have hated me. But I think he actually pitied me instead."

"To tell you the truth, I'm glad I wasn't there. It's not a sight I'd want to see."

Fiona still clung tightly to Nandag, her face buried in the older woman's hair. "I know he was a traitor. I know he turned me over to the Romans. But he was also my friend." Her sobs momentarily choked back her words. After a few deep breaths, she continued. "I think he truly believed he was doing the right thing."

"There's no doubt Manas was always a man of principle."

"He would have never let them harm me. And yet I lit the fire that took his life. Nandag, he was a healer, just like you and me. He spent his life saving the lives of others. And I killed him with my own hand." She was again overcome with a bout of tears.

"Shh. Hush now. Given the circumstances, what else could you have done?"

"Oh, Nandag, who am I? What kind of person have I become? All I wanted to do was serve my people—my village and my clan. And now I've become some kind of monster who takes the lives of my dearest friends."

"That's not what I see. I see a young woman with a kind heart and a gentle spirit who bears a heavy burden that few could carry."

Fiona pushed herself back and stepped out of Nandag's embrace, daubing the tears from her eyes with the palms of her hands. She sniffled a few times before she spoke. "Nandag, you've always been my teacher. Tell me what I should do now."

"Manas was right about one thing. This life confronts each of us with hard choices. But in the end, we must all make our own decisions. It's not about what others tell us to do or expect us to be. They can't make those choices for us." Nandag reached out and cupped Fiona's face in her hands. The tears still streamed down Fiona's cheeks. Nandag smiled at her. "And if I know you, you'll do what you feel is right, no matter what the cost. You were never one to fear being different or going your own way. Trust your heart."

She pulled Fiona back into a hug and held her close. Outside, the rain began to fall.

CHAPTER TWENTY-FOUR

F iona felt someone shaking her shoulder and whispering her
name. "Flora. Flora, wake up. It's me, Domhnull."

She peeled her eyes open and then blinked several times. The
lamps had been extinguished, but the light of the Eternal Flame cast
an eerie glow around the room. She slowly pushed herself up to a
seated position. Domhnull still dripped with water from his
nighttime swim and clandestine entrance through the crannog's
secret trap door.

"Domhnull. What are you doing here?"

He reached over and gave her a big hug. "Everything's ready. I
made all the arrangements, just like we talked about. But we have to
go tonight. It's our only chance."

"What?" Fiona eased herself out of his embrace and wiped the
sleep from her eyes. "What are you talking about?"

Domhnull crouched near her and shrugged with confusion. "Our
plan. Remember? To escape to Eire. I have a boat ready just up the
shoreline. I stocked it with everything we'll need. Lughnasadh is just
a few days away. If we don't go now, it will be too late."

The fog of sleep was just wearing off, and things were happening way too fast. She needed time to think. This was what she wanted, right? To be with Domhnull. To be free of the snare the gods had trapped her in.

"I..." She rubbed her eyes again, trying to clear her head. "I need to gather some things," she whispered.

"There's no time. I have everything we'll need in the boat. And you won't be able to make the swim up the current if you're trying to carry a bunch of stuff."

They spoke in hushed tones, but it sounded to Fiona like their voices echoed in the darkness. Surely the guards would hear.

Fiona fumbled around for her little leather bag of treasures. If she ran away to Eire, they would be her only reminders of the life she had left behind.

Domhnull tugged at her sleeve. "Hurry. Let's go." Then he paused and shrugged his shoulders. "You'll have to take off your *leine*. It will slow you down in the water. I have another one for you in the canoe."

Domhnull, himself, wore only a thin loincloth to cover his groin. Fiona grabbed a small swatch of cloth she could use for a similar purpose. She quickly wrapped it around her legs and tied it off at her waist. She slipped out of her *leine* and let it drop to the floor.

She glanced down at the intricate designs of her spirit armor. Even in the dim light, she could see they had almost entirely faded away. Even so, she felt completely naked, as if she had stripped herself not only of her clothes, but of every vestige of her present life. She was leaving behind family and friends. She was walking away from her village and her home. She was forsaking the call of the gods to rescue her people. In one sense, she felt free and relieved—the weight of responsibility falling from her shoulders, like the woolen dress lying on the floor. But in another way, she felt like she was abandoning everything of value in her life to venture into an uncertain future.

"Ready?" Domhnull asked as he took her hand. He paused to admire her body in the dim light. She wondered if he was appraising the lines and swirls of the adepts' design or the contour of her own curves. By the hunger in his eyes, she suspected it was the latter.

"Okay," she whispered, tentatively, feeling a bit uncomfortable under his gaze.

As they made their way across the crannog, past the fire pit where the Eternal Flame burned, past the Pool of Brigid's tears, Fiona hesitated. She saw her little flint knife hanging from its leather thong on a crook in one of the timbers, and turned aside to snatch it up and slip it over her head.

Just then, the front door creaked open and a druidess poked her head in to look around. Fiona slipped behind the timber and glanced over to see Domhnull drop to the ground behind a wooden bench shaped from the trunk of a tree. She held her breath and watched the guard step through the doorway and scan around the room. Fiona peered over at her bed, straining to discern its outline in the darkness. She was relieved to see a pile of furs bunched up in a way that made it look like she was still sleeping there. The guard apparently came to the same conclusion and, after glancing once more around the inside of the crannog, retreated out the entrance and closed the door behind her.

Fiona exhaled a long, slow breath and inched her way over to Domhnull's side.

"Let's go," he whispered, and she nodded in reply.

Domhnull lifted the trap door in the floor and shimmied through the opening. Then he waited for Fiona to scramble onto his back. Like the last time, he would carry her down to the water. Fiona wrapped her arms around his neck and sensed the warm sensation of their bare skin pressed together. Her body flushed with heat as the thought of making love to this man shot through her mind. Soon, very soon, they would be husband and wife, and she could forever enjoy the tenderness of his touch.

Domhnull descended with the stealth of a wildcat and they eased themselves into the chilly water of the loch.

"Follow me," he whispered, and put his finger to his lips to remind her of the need for absolute silence.

It was harder to swim against the tide toward the eastern shoreline than it had been to float with the current downstream on the previous occasion. They had to swim a fair distance to get beyond the far edge of the little village. Fiona struggled to make progress without causing a splash that could alert the guards. Fortunately, the skies were overcast, and the perpetual drizzle that pervaded the highlands helped to mask their escape. Fiona kept an eye on Domhnull's head bobbing in the water ahead of her. Eventually, after what seemed like an eternity of fighting the waves, they struggled to shore beside a long canoe.

Domhnull stepped up onto dry land and scraped the excess water from his limbs. He reached into the boat and tossed a cloth to Fiona.

"Here, dry yourself with this. I have a fresh *leine* and cloak to keep you warm."

A short while later they were gliding across the waves in the little boat, heading west. Everything seemed to be going perfectly. They had effected their escape without raising an alarm. The little boat was packed to the rim with supplies. The night was young, and they had plenty of time to get a head start on the search party that would eventually come looking for them. It was all working out just like they had planned.

Fiona listened to the water lap against the hull of the boat and felt the cool drizzle on her face. While Domhnull rowed the little craft steadily forward, she dreamed about the new life they would have together. They would find a small village on Eire, hopefully on the shore of a great lake, like her old home on Loch Rannoch. She would continue to develop her skills as a healer and help cure their new neighbors from all manner of hurts and maladies. Domhnull would prove himself to the village chief as a hunter and a warrior. With his ambition and his bravery, he might one day become a warlord within one of their tribes. They would have children—maybe three boys and one or two girls. Fiona hoped to pass her knowledge of the healing arts on to her daughters, just as Nandag had taught her. She wondered if they had roundhouses of stone and thatch on Eire, like the ones in the highlands. In any case, she knew their home would be a happy place of warmth and love.

But even while these sweet dreams played themselves out in her mind, her gut twisted itself into knots. A deep sense of unease welled up inside her heart. Then the words of her mentors began ringing in her ears—dimly, almost imperceptibly at first. But they eventually grew in fervor and pitch to a raging cacophony she could not ignore or shove aside.

Nandag's voice separated itself from the cries, begging for her attention. "This life confronts each one of us with hard choices. But in the end, we must all make our own decisions. It's not about what others tell us to do or expect us to be. They can't make those choices for us."

Nandag's plea was replaced by the sing-song banter of the Master Bard. "I believe each one of us has a purpose in life—one that reaches far beyond the confines of this world and echoes into eternity. We must each decide what path we will follow and then walk that road with determination and conviction. You must choose your own way. No one else can decide on your behalf."

The misty rain formed drops on her eyelashes that blurred her vision like tears from heaven. And through the bleary fog of night, Manas' face appeared in her mind's eye, shrouded in the Wicker Man's expressionless mask. He didn't shout or cry out, but his words rang forth like the clarion call of a ram's horn. "The path of life is treacherous, *Thaghadh,* fraught with unexpected dangers. Some, we can control. Others we cannot. Eventually, we all confront that critical instance which ushers us from this world into the next. At that moment, the most important thing is for us to be certain about who we are. All we take with us into the realm beyond is our identity."

Now tears streamed down Fiona's cheeks—not the dew collecting on her lashes from the falling rain, but salty rivulets that overflowed from the corners of her own eyes. Manas' voice echoed in her mind. "*Thaghadh. Thaghadh.* The One Who Must Choose."

And Fiona knew deep down inside her heart this was wrong. She still wasn't certain of who she was or who she would become, but this was not it. She might, in the end, truly become a goddess and set her people free. Or she might just be a young girl from Bunrannoch with tainted Roman blood, endeavoring to become a healer. But either way, *she* would have to choose. And this... this was not a choice. This was just running away.

She turned her face to Domhnull—true, stalwart Domhnull—a man who was willing to give up all he had worked for to help her escape from her dreadful fate. Her heart ached for him and for all he would lose as the words slipped off of her lips and into the air. "We have to go back. I can't do this. This is not the way. I have to go back."

He must have seen it in her eyes—that settled resolution which cannot be broken or changed. He stopped paddling for several long heartbeats, and the boat continued to glide across the face of the loch toward Killin. Then he nodded in resignation, dipped the oar back into the water, and turned the boat around.

FIONA TOSSED ANXIOUSLY in her bed. Domhnull had rowed the boat back to its mooring on the shore in silence, and they had floated with the current underneath the towering lake house. He could not carry Fiona up the huge stilts on his back like he had brought her down earlier. So he helped her make the ascent, one precarious step at a time. He had not complained or argued with her even once. Apparently, he had acquiesced to her decision as if it were an unchangeable fact. Or perhaps he, himself, felt relieved they had abandoned the plan. He left her with a long, passionate kiss, as if it was their last, and she clung desperately to his embrace. When they finally parted, Fiona watched her lover descend to the water and drift away in the tide. Then she slipped into a fitful, restless sleep and dreamed.

Flames licked up to the sky from the thatched roofs in her nightmares. She heard the screams of terror, just as she had that night in her ordeals, as women were raped, old men were slaughtered, and children were rounded up as slaves. Her village was being ravaged, and she could do nothing to stop it. The fire crackled and popped as it consumed the huts, roundhouses, and sheep pens. And there was something about the smell—that dank stench of smoke which destroys, so unlike the soothing aroma that emanates from hearths.

Fiona's eyes shot open, and the horror of the destruction in her dreams surrounded her on every side. She was no longer outside of the village, observing Bunrannoch's destruction from atop Badger Hill. Instead, she was in the midst of the dreadful scene, trapped inside a roundhouse as fire from the thatch roof rained down on her head. She screamed in terror and suddenly realized it was not a dream. This was not a vision from the gods, and she was not trapped in one of Bunrannoch's homes as part of some fanciful hallucination. This was real. It was here and now. She was in the crannog, and it was ablaze on every side.

Fiona froze in panicked fear. The flames danced in a ghoulish rhythm all around her. She could see no way out. Though the high-pitched roof of the lake house normally allowed the smoke of the fireplace to ascend out of reach, leaving fresh air below, the present conflagration produced volumes of brackish fumes that filled every open space. Fiona choked and gasped. She fell to her knees in an effort to get below the noxious gas.

Then, perhaps in a flash of inspiration sent by the gods, Fiona had an idea. She crawled over to the Pool of Brigid's Tears. She snatched up a hooded cloak that had not been completely consumed in the blaze and soaked it in the holy waters. Then she wrapped the cloak around her shoulders and held a cloth over her face. If she could only make it to the door, she could get free.

Sparks and cinders rained down from above. Even the huge

upright timbers supporting the structure had started to burn. Fiona ran for the front door, stumbling over random objects on the floor and dodging pockets of flames where benches, furs, or bins of grain blazed with the fury of Gofannon's forge in the Otherworld. She hacked and coughed as billows of smoke filled her lungs. With one final lunge, she leapt to the door and shoved it hard with her shoulder. But the door did not budge. It was jammed shut, as if barred from the outside.

Fiona screamed for help and beat against the door. Surely the guards could see the flames and the billowing smoke. Why hadn't they come to rescue her? She grabbed a small stool and tried to smash through the wall. From inside, it looked like it was made of hazel rods woven around shafts of alder and tucked full of bracken and wool for insulation. She was sure she could break a hole through and escape. But she slammed the stool against the wall again and again and couldn't get through.

"Help!" she cried in desperation. "Help me!"

Her shouts were cut short by a hacking cough as she gasped for air. It seemed as if her pleas had wafted into the night sky on plumes of smoke, without being heard. She stopped screaming and tried to listen past the roaring of the holocaust for evidence that someone was coming to her aid. But all she could hear was the rumbling thunder of timbers being consumed by the raging inferno.

Images leapt to her mind of the maelstrom that had consumed the land in her visions. Suddenly, she was back in the little cavern in the rocky crag, alone in a world stripped bare by locusts and scorched by fire. Was it coming true, just as she had foreseen? Had the eternal cycle finally teetered out of balance so far it could not be brought back under control? Had the nailed god of the Romans won the battle just days before she was to ascend to the Otherworld and engage him in mortal combat over the fate of her people?

She beat the stool against the door with the dwindling strength of waning hope. After all she had been through, the drama would finally end just like it had begun—disappearing like ash wafting up into a stormy sky. She mused that she should have gone with Domhnull after all. Such a short time ago, she had been sitting in the front of a little canoe on the way to a simple life in Eire, free from the schemes of druids and the vagaries of the gods. She could have escaped this prison of death and never been trapped by a searing conflagration that would devour her very soul.

Wait. Domhnull. The boat. The trap door in the floor! Suddenly hope rekindled in her heart. Maybe there was a way out of this hell after all. Fiona dropped to her knees and scampered madly across the floor. The smoke stung her eyes and blurred her vision, but she knew her cage well enough to find her way around by touch alone. She groped her way across the room, allowing her hands and intuition to guide her. A burning roof joist fell across her path, barely missing her head. But she would not be deterred. She rolled to the left, out of harm's way, and shimmied below another blazing beam.

Fiona saw her goal, just a few body-lengths away. The little door was wedged slightly open from where Domhnull had left it when he descended a short time ago. Fiona scrambled in that direction, when another giant, burning beam thundered to the floor, right across the top of the door. This wasn't another ceiling joist. It was one of the thick logs that supported the roof and the walls. There was no way she could move it. Fiona's heart sank, and she collapsed on the carpet of bracken and wool that blazed up around her. The little glowing specks drifting down from above seemed surreal, like stars falling from heaven. Under different circumstances, they would have been enchantingly beautiful.

Fiona lay there, beaten and forlorn. The image of Manas' face drifted into her vision amid the flames. The silent plea in his eyes stabbed at her heart. Was this the work of the Morrigan, weaving the threads of her fate into a fitting punishment for her cruel deed— poetic justice for her brutal murder of the Master Healer who had once been her friend? She longed for absolution from her guilt, but the river of tears that came to her eyes would never be sufficient to quench the fire in her soul.

As Fiona's cheek pressed against the ground, she felt the coarse, woven texture of one of the decorative rugs. Such beauty, such elegant craftsmanship, all destined to burn. At least she would go to her death among the fineries of a palace, rather than pressed together with Roman prisoners in a wicker effigy as a sacrifice to the gods. Or was that, indeed what was happening now? Had she, in the end, been found wanting? Had she, at last, been given up as a burnt offering rather than being transformed into a goddess?

Suddenly, Fiona's eyes shot open. She lifted herself up and groped around for the edge of the rug. It stretched past the edge of the trap door and under the far end of the burning timber. Maybe, just maybe, she could use it to move the blazing log. She grasped the carpet with both hands, took a deep breath, closed her eyes, and stood. Then she jerked up on the rug with all the strength she had left. And slowly, very slowly, the huge timber began to roll. A handbreadth, then two. Fiona grunted and gave one last heave, and finally, her pathway to escape was clear. She collapsed again to the floor, took a deep breath, and burst into a fit of coughing. Choking and gasping for air, she crawled over to the portal and hoisted the door open.

She peered into the darkness of night and saw the water of the loch churning below. It was a long way down. More flaming debris fell all around her, and Fiona knew she didn't have time to hone her climbing skills. She needed to get out and away before the whole structure came crashing down. She took a deep breath, steeled her nerve, and rolled through the opening—into the abyss.

For a moment, she was the great owl from her dream, her wings wrapped around the eagle with its talons gripping her heart, falling faster and faster toward the millpond. And then the water of the loch slammed against her body, knocking the air from her lungs and smacking her face like a blow from the hand of an angry god. A huge splash erupted from the surface of the loch, and she began to sink into its icy depths. She opened her eyes and watched a stream of bubbles trickle from the corners of her mouth and float upward. Then reality broke across her consciousness, like a wave crashing against a sea stack, and she stroked upward, following the bubbles to the surface.

She broke through the flat, glassy plane that marked the border between water and sky, and filled her lungs with fresh, cool air. She took a moment to look around and orient herself, and then began swimming frantically toward the safety of the shore. After an agonizing struggle which seemed to stretch into eternity, she dragged herself up on the beach. She expected to see swarms of druids and warriors clustered along the bridge that reached across the water to the lake house, but the village seemed to be resting peacefully as the crannog burned.

Fiona stood, shivering more from fear than form the cold, and ran toward the nearest little hut. She burst through the door screaming, "Help! Fire!"

The sight before her stopped her in her tracks. Domhnull and Searlaid lay together on a sleeping mat, their naked bodies wrapped in an intimate embrace. They woke at the sound of her entrance and blinked away the sleep in their eyes. When Searlaid recognized the face of their unexpected visitor, she broke into a cruel, mischievous grin.

"Hey there, little sister. How's our budding goddess? It looks like you passed the test after all."

"Test? What are you talking about? Is that what this fire is? A test?"

"Fire?" Serlaid looked confused. "I don't know anything about a fire, but apparently you didn't take the bait and run away with my man."

As her sister's words registered on her mind, the blazing crannog became a lost phantom in the night. "What do you mean, 'didn't take the bait?' What are you talking about? Domhnull, what's she saying?"

Domhnull looked like a sheep cornered by wolves. "Hey, it's not my fault. I was just following orders."

"Orders? What orders?"

"From Eliavres and the Arch Druid. They needed to know you

were fully committed to your calling. They kept saying, 'the Bride must be willing.' They told me to get close to you and to try and lure you away."

Fiona felt like she had been kicked in the gut by a horse. The eagle grasped her heart in its talons and ripped it to shreds. "You mean this whole time you were deceiving me? It was all just a lie? You never really love me?" Her voice trailed off into the night.

"Look, Flora, I like you and all. You're a nice girl. But Serlaid has always been the woman for me. Everyone knows that. You even know it's true. You told me so at the very start."

Fiona stood dumbstruck in the doorway. Light from the burning crannog flickered past her and danced across the couple lying in the bed. A wave of nausea washed over her, and she swayed in the darkness.

Serlaid cocked her head to one side and grinned. "See, little sister, he chose me after all. He chose *me*."

Fiona wanted to scream. She wanted to grab a stone and hurl it at the man she thought was her lover. She wanted to wrap her hands around her sister's throat and choke her until there was no breath left. Instead, she teetered from side to side, and almost fell. At the last moment, she caught herself, turned around, and walked dumbly into the night. Twenty paces out the door, she fell to her knees and wept.

FIONA WASN'T sure how long she had been curled into a ball on the ground when she heard the alarm finally sound. Suddenly, there was a flurry of activity all around her, but she just ignored it. She didn't care anymore. She didn't care about the blazing fire. She didn't care about gods and wars. She didn't even care about what might happen to her people if she didn't become Brigid. Her heart ached from abandonment and betrayal. She had no one left. She no longer belonged anywhere. She had no family. She had no village. She had no husband and no hope. They had robbed her of everything—even her identity. She felt more alone now than in the deepest despair of her ordeals. She had nothing left, and she just wanted to disappear.

Through the misty fog in her mind, she heard a voice calling out to her. It sounded distant and faint. Then, gradually, it was louder and closer and much more insistent. "Fiona, are you okay? Fiona."

She felt a hand touch her shoulder, and she looked up into the face of Bhatair Rhu. She could barely even make out his form through the tears, but he spoke to her in a voice of gentleness and compassion. "Thank the gods you're okay. How did you ever get out? We thought you were lost in that horrible fire."

"Why? Why did you do it?"

The Arch Druid reached out to lift her up from the ground, but she refused to be moved. She just lay in the dirt looking up at him.

"Do what? I don't understand."

"I saw Domhnull and Searlaid together. Why did you do it? Why did you lie to me?"

"Oh, that. We had to know for sure. It was the only way to measure your level of commitment to your calling."

His tone was cold and matter-of-fact, and his lack of compassion galled her.

"It was *cruel*."

"Was it? Was it really? Do you understand what's at stake here? Do you truly comprehend the enormity of the circumstances facing us? *You* are the cornerstone upon which our whole strategy is built. Your preparation, and your dedication to this effort is of critical importance. Without you, the alliance crumbles. Without you, the eternal cycle falls out of balance and spirals out of control. The gods chose *you*. But we, and they, must be absolutely certain of your commitment. When you become a goddess—when you ascend to Brigid's throne—the impacts will ripple throughout time. This is not a casual act that can be taken lightly. This is the most important decision any human has made in a thousand years. So, if we had to hurt your feelings a little to make sure you were committed to the task, it was a small price to pay."

He grasped her arm more firmly and hoisted her up to her feet. "Now, stand up and focus. Quit acting like a sniveling little girl. Look at that fire," he said with a sternness she had never before heard in his voice. "We thought we had lost you tonight. The nailed god is not playing games. He is serious about preventing you from fulfilling your destiny. *You* must be equally determined to defeat him and his followers. The Romans will not leave this land without a fight. You've seen the consequences to our people if we lose. So *be* who you have been called to become. *You* are Fiona *Taghte*, and you will set your people free."

CHAPTER TWENTY-FIVE

Fiona sat in the ceremonial chamber at *An Dun Gael*. Drib and Drab scurried about, preparing her for the ritual. Eliavres had called it the *Ordination*. It was the eve of Lughnasadh, the day before her transition to the Otherworld, and they were getting her ready for the largest gathering of her people anyone could remember. In fact, it was larger than any gathering the bards sang about in legend or lore. Virtually everyone from her tribe, the *Tuath Vuin,* was present, along with large contingents from the other tribes across all of Caledonia. They were joined by scores of chiefs and warlords from Eire to the lands across the Great Sea. Everyone wanted to see the woman who would become a goddess and lead them to victory over the Romans.

Nandag and Fedelma oversaw her preparations. They guided Drib and Drab as the two attendants dressed Fiona in an exquisite dress made of heavy wool, dyed in Brigid's colors of deep red and green. Light streaks of pale yellow and orange licked up from the bottom hem, making the garment look like the soft flame of a hearth fire. They placed the serpent-headed silver torc around her neck, and draped an elaborate necklace below it, fashioned from over a hundred jet beads, as black as the night sky. A green badge embroidered with

Bhatair Rhu's purple thistle sat over her heart. She suspected he was trying to highlight his association with her, rather than the other way around. Her status as a goddess would lend a great deal of legitimacy to his role as architect of the strategy to drive the Romans out of Britannia.

Fedelma pointed to one of the apprentices. "Don't put her hair up. Let it hang loose. Just make one thin braid from the center of her forehead around each side. She needs to look like one of the villagers, but she also needs to look like a goddess. We want people to identify with her, but to be held in awe. It's a difficult effect to achieve."

She directed the next comments at Fiona. "The biggest burden will be on you. You'll want them to like you and admire you, and at the same time reverence you as sacred and holy. This will be the only time most of these people will ever see a goddess in person. You will want to come across as aloof, but approachable."

"And why is that?" Fiona asked. She still felt sullen and didn't try to hide her frustration. "Tomorrow, I will either become a goddess or I won't. What difference does it make what this mob thinks about me?"

Fedelma turned the triple sight on her in full force, but the three overlapping pupils no longer sent a chill up Fiona's spine. The awe and respect she had once felt for the druid class was waning, like a fading moon at the end of a month. In just one day, she would either become a goddess and these people would all worship her, or she would be a living sacrifice to the gods and no longer care what anyone in this world thought of her. Either way, she had nothing left to fear from them.

Fedelma undoubtedly sensed her petulance, but the triple sight never wavered. "You still don't know who you are. I thought it was settled once and for all when you beheld the eagle and heard its tale, but I was wrong. You still wrestle with your identity. The war still wages within."

Fiona found she could no longer hold the woman's gaze, and dropped her eyes to the ground. No, she did not fear the seer. But the observation struck way too close to the mark, and Fiona did not want Fedelma to see too deeply into the truth of her struggle.

Fedelma went on. "Your understanding of the relationship between gods and men is very immature. There is still much you must learn. Yes, the gods hold a great deal of power over us and our land, but they draw that power from our worship. Without our reverence—our sacrifices, rituals, and offerings—the power of the gods in this land will wither and fade. No, they won't cease to exist, for they are not subject to death. But if we cease to honor the gods, our link to the Otherworld will be severed, and they will slip into the mists of time."

"So, you're saying I need to court the favor of the people, or I will lose my place in their pantheon of gods?"

"Not just you. The gods reign over our land together, or not at all. We need them, and they need us. If we turn our worship to other gods, like the nailed god of the Romans, then the power of our old gods will be broken, and their authority will be gone."

"Is that such a bad thing? Wouldn't our people truly be free in that case?"

Fedelma grasped Fiona's chin and lifted her head so she could not avoid her gaze. "Look into my eyes, child. Look into my eyes and tremble at what you see. The gods hold the cycles of the seasons together. They cause spring to follow winter, and summer to follow spring. The cycle has been thrown out of balance for over seven years, and you can even now see the devastation it has brought to our people in that time. If the cycle is broken permanently, winter will come and chaos will rule."

Fiona was not to be cowed or deterred. Something had changed inside her, but it was not what Fedelma suspected. "And what about the nailed god? Could he not rule the land as well as the old gods?"

"Hssss," Fedelma spat. "Look at what Rome has become, and answer that for yourself. When Rome worshipped the old gods, they were masters of the world. Once they switched their allegiance to the nailed god, the whole empire started to rot from within. Rome is a corpse, just waiting to die. It is a hollow shell of what it once was, and it will crumble to dust within another generation. Our little rebellion is just the first salvo in a much larger war."

"Well then," Fiona replied, and this time her eyes never wavered, "I guess you better make me look likable and powerful, so I can curry favor with my people."

"A pretty dress," Fedelma retorted, "will only get you so far. *You* must carry yourself like a goddess, but humble yourself as a daughter of the clans. If you do it well, you can become the link that binds our people to the gods for a thousand generations to come."

"And if I fail?"

"*You* have seen it in your visions, and *I* watched it unfold through your eyes. We both know what the consequences will be if you fail."

Fiona held the seer's gaze for another long moment, and an understanding passed between them which could not be put into words. Fiona knew for certain she would choose her own fate, and Fedelma now knew it too.

Nandag broke the tense moment. "There, now. We'll just finish your makeup, and our part will be done. The rest is up to you. I know you will do well."

Drib and Drab highlighted her cheeks with a red powder made from madder and brushed a green paste around her eyes which had come from dyer's broom mixed with indigo. Finally, they traced her eyes with thin black lines using a charcoal-based compound. The overall effect was one of subdued dignity. It made her look older and wiser, without robbing her of the natural innocence of youth.

Nandag took in the sight and smiled with motherly affection. "You are truly a Bride of the Springs," she said, quoting a line from the Ballad of Brigid. "Your father will be proud."

The comment caught Fiona off guard, and she wondered which father that would be—the man who raised her or the Roman bastard whose blood flowed in her veins. But she kept these thoughts to herself. Nandag didn't deserve to be the target of her scorn.

As if on cue, the exterior door opened and sunlight flooded into the chamber. Bhatair Rhu strode in, silhouetted in a way that made him look like he had stepped out of a painting. His blonde hair gleamed, his eyes shone bright, and his face beamed with a broad smile. The work of his lifetime was coming to fruition, and he basked in the glory of the moment.

"You look absolutely stunning. It's perfect. Our people will, no doubt, be pleased with their goddess. You will become the patroness of this land for ages to come."

"And what will all this mean for you?" Fiona asked, her voice tinged with sarcasm. "I suppose you will finally achieve your dream and return to the Otherworld."

The Arch Druid paused for a moment, and his face took on a slightly harder edge. "I *will* fulfill my vow to my father and to the gods, but there is still much to be done. There is a war to fight and battles to be won. Rome is a formidable foe, and the outcome is by no means certain. But if the gods are on our side—if *you* fight the nailed god on our behalf—I am confident we will prevail in the end. And, yes, then I can return with my mother to the Otherworld, where we both belong."

A breeze swept through the chamber, causing the lamps to flicker and rustling Bhatair Rhu's hair. The smile returned to his lips. "Now, my lady, your escort awaits."

He nodded to Fiona's attendants. "Well done. You have seen Fiona *Taghte* through her preparations. You are worthy of her affections and any blessings she may choose to bestow upon you in the future."

The Arch Druid gestured toward the door. Fiona stepped out of the chamber and into a light drizzle. It was still the highlands after all, and rain would accompany even the most important ceremonies of men. Fiona wondered if the dew from heaven would ruin all of her attendants' hard work by soaking her dress, wetting her hair, and causing her makeup to run. But then she decided she didn't really care.

Eliavres and Kynwal were waiting outside, mounted on their

steeds. Bhatair Rhu's mother, the goddess who had trapped herself in this world as a majestic sorrel mare, waited beside a fine, white stallion. Fiona wondered if she could handle the spirited beast since she didn't really know how to ride. But the Arch Druid surprised her by leading her over to his own mount.

"Today, you will ride with a goddess. You should get accustomed to keeping such company." He beamed with pride, and Fiona could see that nothing would spoil this occasion he had worked so hard to coordinate. He was enjoying the fruits of his labors.

They rode across the top of the ridgeline in the direction of *Feart Choille*. Fiona had never actually seen inside the Forest Stronghold, and wondered what those live timber walls concealed. Perhaps she would never know.

When they emerged from the tree line and glimpsed the glen below, Fiona's breath caught in her throat. She knew a large gathering had been called, but the sight before her almost stopped her heart. The entire valley, as far as the eye could see, was filled with tents and huts and all manner of temporary shelters. An enormous sea of people surged and thronged in a giant arc centered around *Cridhmathairnaomh*, the sacred yew. Streams of people circulated around the tents. It looked like a vast array of vessels, streaming lifeblood to the land, with the yew tree at its core.

Then, all of a sudden, Fiona knew the truth of it. *This* was *Cridhalbane*. This was the Heart of Alban—not the glen, or the stone circles, or even the holy tree, but the people gathered here. The sacred yew might be a portal between this world and the Otherworld. It might provide a conduit for power to flow from the gods to the tribes. But the people were the true lifeblood of this country. The people—her people—were the ones that brought strength and vitality to the land. They were the ones that tilled its fields and harvested its crops. They were the ones who raised its cattle and shepherded its flocks. They were the ones who bore its children and built its homes. They pulsed and flowed to every corner of the highlands and the islands, and without them it would be a desolate waste, like the scorched and barren wilderness she had seen in her visions. Her heart went out to them, the faceless masses that filled the valley below, and she vowed to honor their courage.

They processed down the trail to the valley floor with the Arch Druid leading the way and the Pendragon guarding the rear, as the goddess-to-be rode in majesty on a divine steed. Fiona saw enormous burning pyres and eagle dancers that leapt and gyrated to the chants and intonations of their peers. But the entire ceremony came to a halt as the object of their devotion rode into view. It was as if a huge, live, writhing beast had been frozen in time. Every single person stood in silent stillness—thousands of eyes, transfixed by the sight of a human goddess.

Bhatair Rhu came to a stop. He helped her dismount, and escorted her to an elaborate chair, carved from oak in the form of intertwined serpents rising up out of a sacred well and trimmed with silver flames. It was the seat of a goddess. It was Brigid's throne. And when she came to rest in its consecrated arms, thousands upon thousands of people dropped to their knees and bowed down.

Fiona was dumbstruck. Most of these people had never met her and had no idea who she really was, deep down inside. How could they possibly know, for she was not even certain herself. All they knew was what their druids had told them and what the bards sang about her in their songs. She had ceased to be a real person at all. Now she existed almost solely as an idea, a concept people had been taught to worship during Imbolc their whole lives. She had become the goddess of the eternal flame and the sacred well, patroness of smiths and bards, bringer of spring, and healer of the land. And she would fight against the nailed god of the Romans to bring them the freedom they desired.

The idea had been conceived in the mind of the gods and had taken shape through the machinations of Bhatair Rhu. It had spread to every corner of the land, to every clan and every tribe. And now it sat before them on a majestic throne in the form of young woman, who on the morrow would become the bride of a god. It was a powerful idea. It gave the people hope—hope for a future without the tyranny of Rome—hope for a time when spring would return and drive away the storms of winter. But in the very day that idea had been born, a young apprentice healer, a daughter of the highlands with the blood of Rome in her veins, had ceased to be. Flora was gone and only Fiona *Taghte* remained.

The Arch Druid stood and raised his arms high into the air. "People of Caledonia, of Germania and Eire, your goddess has come before you. She is here to accept your offerings and your worship, your adoration and your praise. As we win her favor this day, she will multiply her blessings to us when she takes her throne in the Otherworld tomorrow. She will bless our flocks and our herds. She will inspire our poets and bards. She will strengthen the hands of our smiths, and share with them the secret magic of fire. She will make the wombs of barren women fertile, and cause dried up springs to flow with living water. She will usher in the springtime and drive the chill of winter away. From this day forward, we shall be known as the people of Brigid. Now bring your sacrifices and votive offerings to our goddess, knowing that whatever you give up today, you will receive a hundredfold in return during the years to come."

The people, as one, rose to their feet, and a great shout erupted from the crowd. "Fiona! *Taghte*! Fiona! *Taghte*!" And then gradually it morphed and transformed. "Brig-id! Brig-id! Brig-id!"

Bhatair Rhu allowed them to revel in their praise for a while. Finally he raised his arms again and hushed the surging throng. "Bring your offerings. Bring your sacrifices. Bring your ewes and lambs and present them before the Bride of the Springs."

Fiona became uneasy at his remarks. This was the eve of Lughnasadh, a day when the people celebrated the victory of Lugh over Balor, who planned to hoard the grain produced by the land and keep it from the people. There was usually a ceremonial dance which portrayed on earth the battle being fought by the two gods in the Otherworld. After Lugh wins the contest and releases the harvest to his people, they honor him by sacrificing a bull and offering the first fruits of the bilberry crop. Then they hold a great feast in honor of Lugh and his exploits on behalf of men. But no one ever made offerings of lambs and goats on Lughnasadh.

Fiona's concern grew as a hundred men brought their youngest and choicest lambs to a great ditch dug out in front of her dais. Each one knelt down, placed a restraining hand on his animal's head, then quickly drew a knife and, in one swift stroke, slit its throat.

The men called out in unison, "This is our offering to Brigid, goddess of our flocks. May the sacrifice be acceptable in your sight, Oh Holy One."

Fiona watched in horror while the herdsmen held the writhing beasts still with firm hands and allowed the blood to pulse out of severed arteries and splash into the great earthen trough. Bile rose up in her throat, and a wave of nausea almost made her retch. Images flashed into her mind of Caora, the little lamb she had brought into the world with her own two hands. She had watched a highland wolf savagely tear her lamb apart. It was a sacrifice which had saved her life at the time. Now, she saw Caora's plight being played out afresh before her very eyes, multiplied a hundred times over, and tears pricked at the corners of her eyes.

The men wiped their knives on the woolen fleeces of the dead sheep, then stood and bowed. A hundred druid apprentices stepped forward to retrieve the carcasses and remove them to where the slaughter could be completed—the entrails cut out and burned on flaming altars, the flesh roasted for consumption at the great feast. And then a hundred more men dragged a hundred more sheep up in a row before her. They knelt down, placed their hands on the animals' heads, and reached for their knives.

Fiona's blood boiled, and her temper flared. She would not sit idly by and watch innocent lambs be slaughtered in her honor. She would not allow this barbaric ritual to continue even one more round. Before she knew what she was doing, she stood up from her throne and cried out at the top of her lungs, "Stop!"

The shepherds arrayed in front of her dropped their blades and glanced up nervously. They looked terrified that they had somehow evoked the rage of their new patron goddess. They knelt in place, dumbstruck, with a mixture of confusion and fear playing itself out across their faces.

Eliavres approached the platform and called out to her in a voice loud enough to be heard by the closest ranks of people in the crowd. "Fiona *Taghte*, these lambs are sacrifices on behalf of the people to Brigid, goddess of the flocks. Their blood is poured out as an offering to honor her. It is a tradition as old as the tribes' most ancient lore. It is a sacred rite."

Fiona looked him straight in the eye with a passion and conviction she had never felt before. Then she raised her voice to the assembled throng. "*I* am Brigid. These lambs are mine. They belong to me, and *I* decide what lives and what dies."

A hushed stillness hovered over the crowd. For a hundred heartbeats not a sound could be heard, save the patter of the rain and the whisper of the wind. Then, slowly, but with growing intensity, a low murmur spread from mouth to mouth up and down the glen. The crowd rumbled and droned in indistinct tones as word of Fiona's statement washed from hillside to hillside throughout the valley. Men thumped their staves on the ground. Women and children stamped their feet. A great roar of thunder rumbled up from beneath and rose into the air.

Fiona feared that she had kicked a hornets' nest and moved this mob to rage. She was certain she had rejected their offerings and offended their pride. If what Fedelma said was true, all of Brigid's power came from the sacrifices and worship of men. She guessed she had just undermined her own authority. Before she even took up her role in the Otherworld, this great multitude would rush the platform and pull her down from her lofty throne. *She* would become the sacrifice this day.

But then the rumblings became more distinct, taking on substance and form. Fiona heard the cry ring out across the glen and ascend to the heavens above in a great shout and a mighty roar.

"Brigid! Brigid! Brigid! Brigid!" The call went out, over and over again, as if it would never cease, echoing into the night and beyond, past the setting sun.

A wave of relief washed over Fiona and she let out her breath. These were her people. She had honored them, and they would devote themselves to her.

She glanced down at Eliavres in triumph, and a sudden chill ran up her spine. To her surprise, she saw a grin spread across his face, and it made her blood go cold. In that instant, she knew terrible truth. She knew they had won. She had become exactly what they wanted her to be.

"You KNOW," Finnan said, "the Christians refer to their Christ as 'the lamb of god that takes away the sin of the world.'"

They sat together in Fedelma's quarters on the second floor of *An Dun Gael*, with Nandag lingering in the shadows to chaperone their conversation. Finnan insisted on hearing her reflections on the day's events so he could capture the moment in verse.

"I don't care," Fiona retorted. "I don't want to hear anything else about the Roman god."

"So be it, my lady. What might you like to hear about then?"

"Tell me about our gods—the highland gods."

"There are a good many highland gods. I doubt we've the time to discuss them all."

"Okay," Fiona replied. "Then tell me about the Cailleach. She is the one I will have to confront in the Otherworld. She is the one who orchestrated this mess."

"Very well. I shall tell you about *Gleann Dubh nan Garbh Clac*, the Black Glen of the Crooked Stones, and the footprints the Cailleach has left behind in that place."

Finnan leaned back and pulled out his pipe.

"I'm not sure Fedelma would want the smoke of your tobacco

mixing with her incense. It might disrupt her visions or her communion with the gods."

"It might indeed. But my concern is not for that. I only worry about whether it will bother you, mistress?"

Fiona just shook her head.

"Very well. I shall fret about Fedelma at another time." He wiped a small twig in the flame of an oil lamp and used it to light his pipe. He puffed twice and blew out a plume of smoke.

"What do you know about the Black Glen?" he asked.

"I've always known it as *Gleann-Linne,* the Valley of Lakes and Pools. I thought it was holy to Brigid, not the Cailleach. Other than that, I don't know much, except that its entrance is guarded by *Feart Choille* and the sacred yew, and only druids can go there."

Finnan nodded. "I see. Is this really what you want to hear about on the eve of your, uh, transformation? I'd have thought other things might occupy your mind."

"That's just it. I have an unending string of thoughts racing around in my head, and I really just want them all to go away. So can you please distract me with some tales of the highlanders and our gods? That's what bards do best, right?"

"As you will," he replied. "The Cailleach used to rule *Gleann Dubh nan Garbh Clac.* It was her original home after she finished creating the land. She placed the mighty Schiehallion beside Loch Rannoch as the jewel in her crown, and then retired to the Black Glen of the Crooked Stones to admire her handiwork. It was, in fact, the place her act of creation began. The navel of the world, where its umbilical cord was attached to her womb before its birth, remains at the heart of the glen to this day. It is a sacred place to the highlanders —a place where the veil between this world and the Otherworld is very thin. It is called *An Toiseach,* the Place of Beginnings."

Fiona leaned forward, soaking in his words. "Have you been there? Have you seen it for yourself?"

"Aye, lass. It is a small rounded hill, much like many others you have seen. But just across the way, two enormous boulders reach to the sky in an unmistakable gesture of prayer. They face the navel hill and mark it out as a place of veneration from ancient times."

"So the Cailleach really did create the world? It wasn't the Roman's nailed god after all."

"I'm afraid you'd have to take that issue up with a diviner or a judge. You see, we bards only concern ourselves with what our people say and think and believe. We are keepers of lore. We needn't worry ourselves with determining the truth of it."

"Well, our people say the Cailleach created the land, and we have a navel hill and ancient stones to prove our claim—and Schiehallion, the greatest of all mountains. What do the Romans have?"

"The *Christians* would say they have the empty tomb of their risen lord." Finnan took another draw on his pipe before continuing. "In any event, while the Cailleach inhabited the Black Glen, she kept the winters mild and the people of the glen prospered. Their crops grew tall and their cattle grew fat until the day the goddess decided to leave."

"Leave?" Fiona asked. "Why would she leave? Where would she go? Didn't the people honor her as they should with sacrifices and festivals?"

"Oh, aye. They were grateful for the blessings she bestowed. But the gods will do what the gods will do. Yet, before she left, she made a promise to the people of the glen. If they would always remember her by tending her shrine, then she would keep their winters short and their summers long."

"Did they do it? Do they still tend her shrine?"

"Aye, lass. So they do. I, myself, have met the caretaker of *Tigh nam Bodach*, and watched him perform his tasks. The shrine is a small turf-covered *shieling* with eight stone figurines. The three largest represent the Cailleach, her husband Bodach, and their first daughter, Nighean. The others stand in place of their wee bairns. Each year at Samhain, this man puts the holy family inside the *shieling*, where they spend the winter indoors. He then treks back up the glen at Beltain to bring them out for the summer months. The tradition has been in place for a hundred generations or more."

"You said the school of the druids was relocated to the Black Glen after the Romans attacked the community on Ynys Mon, right?"

"Indeed. Your memory serves you well."

"Okay, now I'm really confused."

"How so?"

Fiona got up from her stool and paced back and forth in front of the Master Bard. "The Cailleach promised the people of the glen to keep their winters short and mild if they honored her memory by tending the shrine."

"Aye. Just so."

"And the druids who keep the worship of our gods alive, and who maintain the sacred rites have re-established the school of their arts in this same glen."

"It is as you say."

"And this glen is the very heart of Alban, the most remote and protected place in all of Britain. Not only is it surrounded by mountains on every side, but the clans of my tribe are positioned to guard every avenue of approach."

"Indeed. This is all quite true."

"Then why would the Cailleach go back on her promise? Why would she displace Brigid and break the eternal cycle of the seasons? Why would she bring everlasting winter and drive the summer away? Wouldn't this betray the very people who honor her memory and who keep her worship alive?"

"It would appear to do just that."

Fiona threw up her hands in exasperation. "Then why? I don't understand. It doesn't make any sense."

"Ah, lass. Don't you see? The gods are not so different from we ourselves. They, too, suffer the same kind of fear, insecurity, greed, and pride that plague mankind. They just have more power to exert their will. The gods are forever quarreling amongst each other and trying to gain the upper hand. It's simply the lust for power that drives the Cailleach to disrupt the balance and undermine her own position. Because she created the land, she thinks she can rule it according to her whims and desires. But she feels like her authority is being challenged by the rising power of the Daghda, and Cerridwen, and Lugh."

Fiona shook her head. "That seems so childish and short sighted when so much is at stake."

Finnan blew out a big puff of smoke. "Nay, my lady. Children squabble over toys and treats. Men quarrel over the things of this world. But the gods fight over issues that ripple throughout eternity, with consequences that impact their world and our own."

Fiona grew silent for a long while. When she finally spoke, her voice was weak and withdrawn. "Finnan, what is the Otherworld really like?"

"Oh, mistress. Are you fearin' for what the morrow might bring?"

Fiona nodded her head, pensively, and then rushed to embrace him. The intensity of her reaction apparently surprised Finnan, and he was slow to return the hug. Fiona felt him pat her on the back gently. He whispered in her ear, "Hush now. Shh. Shh. Everything will be alright."

"Will it?" she choked through her sobs. "Will it really?"

Finnan exhaled a long breath. "To be tellin' you the truth, I don't honestly know. I've never been to the Otherworld. I can recite all the stories and the lore, of course. But I'm only a bard..." His voice trailed off.

"'...and you needn't worry yourself with determining the truth of it,'" she quoted his own words back to him. "I'm scared, Finnan. I'm really scared."

She pulled him tight one more time, then dropped the embrace and sank to the floor at his feet. She curled up into a ball and hugged her knees.

"What frightens you the most, mistress? Perhaps I can offer some solace after all."

She looked up into his face, while tears streamed down her cheeks.

"Everyone else calls me Fiona *Taghte*, Finnan. Everyone but you. You call me 'mistress' or 'my lady' or even 'lass,' but never the other. Why is that?"

Finnan knelt down and sat beside her. "Well, I suppose I'm of the same mind as Manas. I think, perhaps, *Thaghadh* might be a more fitting title. It seems to me that you're the one with a choice to make."

"Am I? Am I really? Do I actually get to decide anything at all? I don't honestly know what will happen tomorrow. Will I become a goddess and ascend into the Otherworld? Or will I be a sacrifice to placate Tyrannis and the Cailleach? Tell me, Finnan. Is that choice even up to me?"

"No," Finnan replied, shaking his head. "No, that's not the choice you'll be havin' to make. That decision is out of your hands. But you..." He reached over and took her hand. "You must choose who *you* will be in the face of it."

Fiona gripped his hand tightly in both of hers. "*That* is what I fear the most. Who am I, really? And what will I become? Everyone else seems to be very certain." Her voice cracked and the words came out in a whisper, "But I don't really know."

"Oh, lass. That's not an easy question for any of us to answer. But I'm certain of this one thing. If you follow your heart and remain true to yourself, you'll have no regrets, now or in the life to come."

Finnan wrapped his arm around her and pulled her to his side. He held her there for a long time—long enough for the tears to stop and for her to know she was not alone.

CHAPTER TWENTY-SIX

F innan was gone and Nandag had followed soon after, leaving
Fiona alone with her thoughts. They warred inside her mind—a
fierce battle raging between her reason and her heart. When sleep
finally came, it was no more settled than the stormy emotions that
plagued her waking thoughts. Her dreams would give her no peace
this night.

She drifted into a hazy fantasy, and the vision folded her into its
arms. It was a bright, sunny summer's day, and she wandered into a
field filled with bluebells. It looked like a huge flutter of azure
butterflies on a blanket of green bracken, their wings flickering in the
sunlight as they danced in the gentle breeze. She thought she might
pick a bunch for her mother to set in a jar on the sill. But first, she
would just lie down in the bed of flowers and enjoy the rare spot of
summer sunshine.

A shadowy figure emerged from the woodline and descended
upon her, causing silent tears to flow and a dark blackness to settle
over her heart. It grew inside her—a malignant rot that fouled her
mind and blighted her soul.

She pushed herself up and looked around. The sunshine was

gone, masked by dark thunderclouds that swept across the sky, casting an eerie pall across the gentle meadow. The bluebells had disappeared, and foxgloves grew up in their place, their delicate lavender blossoms concealing the venomous poison that seethed through the roots and stems. She could do it. She had the knowledge to extract the toxins and use them to destroy the vile creature who had spoiled her purity and robbed her of innocence. But if she succumbed to the temptation, she would become just like that deceptive flower—a fanciful healer on the outside with deadly venom coursing through her veins. Or had she, indeed, become that very thing already?

She walked through the field of lovely, lethal flowers, and the blossoms transformed in her wake, like waves breaking across the bow of a boat. The pinks and purples of the foxgloves morphed and surged until she was floating in a sea of bright red blooms, each one with a cluster of black seeds at its center. The field stretched as far as she could see in every direction.

She began to run through the tide of scarlet blossoms, laughing and dancing. She felt light as air, as if she could fly away. She reached down, picked one of the flowers, and breathed deeply, expecting to savor a fragrant aroma. But the bright crimson petals gave off no odor at all. Disappointed, she dropped the blossom to the ground and the whole world began to spin out of control. She teetered with dizziness and fell to the ground. The flowers engulfed her, growing in a rapid frenzy to bury her body beneath a flood of blood-red waves.

Images from her ordeals flashed through her mind. A burning village. A locust swarm. A fiery inferno. A hungry wolf. A raging stream. She stood in the midst of death and destruction in a charred, desolate land crying out in pain.

Then, ever so faintly, she heard it whisper in her ear. The voice. The sage advisor. The harbinger of doubts. It called to her now, as it had in her visions. "Trust me," it breathed. And the resemblance to Finnan's brogue was unmistakable.

Trust? She scarcely even knew what that meant. Trust implied relationship, and she had no one. She was all alone in the world. Even so, she lay back and closed her eyes, just like she had done when struggling in the roaring river and when drowning in the broiling loch. If she was to perish beneath a surging tide of red poppies, so be it.

But then the voice echoed in her mind once more. Just a single word. "Look."

She opened her eyes and all around her, radiating in every direction, the red petals of the flowers turned to a brilliant white, their once black centers now shimmering as gold. The blossoms glowed in the warmth of the returning sun. It was as if every wrong thing had suddenly become right again, and peace washed over her heart. With a renewed sense of hope in her soul, she settled into a deep, restful sleep, and a tear trickled out the corner of her eye.

THE *TRANSFORMATION*. That's what Bhatair Rhu had called this day.

It was, in fact, Lughnasadh, but without the traditional rites that usually accompanied the day. No bull had been slaughtered. No parody acted out of Lugh's battle against Balor to rescue the grain from his hoards on behalf of mankind. No one feasted on bilberries and new wine. Instead, everyone from across the whole land, representatives of every tribe and tongue, had gathered to this place for a wedding.

Fiona *Taghte* would walk into the sacred pool and emerge in the Otherworld as a goddess—as Brigid, patroness of healers, bards, and smiths, sovereign of the hearth fire and of holy springs and wells, queen of serpents and of lambs, daughter of the Daghda, divine sister of the Morrigan and the Cailleach, and virgin bride of Bres. She would restore the breach in the eternal cycle, end perpetual winter, and return springtime to the land. She would engage the nailed god in immortal combat and set her people free from the scourge of Roman tyranny.

Fiona stood on a small hill that sloped gently down to the water's edge below. Her bridal dress was a simple woolen *leine,* dyed in Brigid's color of deep red. She insisted on wearing her old deerskin *brogen* because they were comfortable and she liked them. Her thin, silver, serpent-headed torc had been recast in a much thicker and heavier black iron, because Brigid was the patron goddess of smiths. Though the Romans prized gold for its shiny luster, the pragmatic highlanders found iron to be of much more practical value. Chains of jet beads, black as midnight, hung around her neck and she wore black iron snakes coiled around her upper arms. Her hair was pulled up and interlaced with sprigs of heather and mistletoe. But she wore no makeup at all, and her attendants had scrubbed her skin free of the fading lines and swirls of the spirit armor, leaving it pale and pure.

When Nandag had examined her earlier that morning, tears had come to her old mentor's eyes. "You look radiant, as if you were a goddess already. I'm so proud of who you've become."

Fiona had let the comment go. She knew it was offered in genuine affection, and she didn't wish to trouble Nandag with the doubts that plagued her own mind. Instead, she smiled with all the warmth and tenderness she felt for the woman who had been more of a mother to her than her own flesh and blood. But the smile alone wasn't enough, and she pulled Nandag into a tender embrace.

"You are more dear to me than you could ever know. You have been my *bean-teagaisg.* But you are also much more. You are the truest friend I have ever known."

Fiona hoped she would get one last glimpse of her mentor and friend amid the thronging crowd before she stepped through the watery portal into the Otherworld.

Unlike the rituals of the *Ordination* ceremony on the previous day, the activities of the *Transformation* were solemn and subdued. There were no bonfires, no eagle dancers, and absolutely no sacrificial lambs. Instead, Bhatair Rhu had given a grand speech about Fiona's virtue, her courage, and her sacred honor, before leading a long procession from the ancient yew tree across the glen to the hill where she now stood.

The crowd filled the entire valley from side to side—an unprecedented mass of people gathered to see the girl who would become a goddess. They would tell the stories to their children and grandchildren about how there were there on that glorious day.

A column of warriors, regaled in spirit armor and wielding spears, held back the surging human tide, forming a clear path from where she stood to the pier's head at the water's edge. Druid masters of every discipline lined the borders of the bridleway. Instead of the traditional white ceremonial robes, they all wore green cloaks with purple thistles on the breasts, indicating their allegiance to Bhatair Rhu and his cause.

Fiona began her walk down the hill, and the crowd cheered her on. Her father was not at her side, escorting her down the aisle to give her away, and she scanned the multitude to see if she could catch a glimpse of his face. To her amazement, she was able to pick him out, even though he had been given no special place of honor and was just buried among the masses. Her mother stood at his side, eyes downcast. Flora wished she would look up. In her last moments, she longed to offer some kind of forgiveness, if only with her eyes. Her mother was not to blame for what had happened. In a way, her mother's decision to run away with the blacksmith and her subsequent rape had made this moment possible. But her mother kept her gaze to the ground, and the opportunity for reconciliation passed them by, like the fading rays of the sun disappearing into the dusk of night.

Her father, on the other hand, caught her eye and beamed with pride. He whispered to her across the gulf, "I love you, my daughter," and tears pricked at the corners of her eyes.

She recalled his words to her on the night when Finnan had arranged their clandestine meeting. "Oh, my girl, my precious girl.

It's not the blood running through your veins that makes you my daughter. It's a father's love that makes you mine. And you've had that since the day you were born. You are my very heart."

The memory made her stumble in her stride. Her eyes dropped to the path ahead, and when she next looked up, his face was gone, having disappeared within the multitude of the faceless throng. She realized it was the last time she would ever see her parents again, and a wave of despair washed over her, bringing with it a flood of other memories. With each step, another dear friend came to mind.

Manas was the first. Though he had betrayed her to the Romans, she understood his intentions, and whispered her forgiveness to him now. Perhaps he was in the Otherworld after all, or whatever place the Christians called their eternal home, and he could hear her words of reconciliation. Deep down inside, she knew he had been her friend. His words of counsel, offered in sincerity and truth, returned to her thoughts.

"The path of life is treacherous, *Thaghadh,* fraught with unexpected dangers. Some, we can control. Others we cannot. Eventually, we all confront that critical instance which ushers us from this world into the next. At that moment, the most important thing is for us to be certain about who we are. All we take with us into the realm beyond is our identity."

Those words became more auspicious now, in this very moment, than the Master Healer could possibly have imagined. Or, perhaps, he had known her fate all along.

Finnan had echoed those same sentiments just the night before. Fiona searched the crowd for the Master Bard. He had to be somewhere nearby, if he was to capture the final moments of her story and transpose them into verse. But the Legend Weaver was nowhere to be found. Yet, Fiona could never forget his voice—the same voice that had haunted her visions and dreams. Could they actually have been one and the same? No. That voice was distant and ethereal. Finnan's was genuine and true. Sould she never forget his own sage words of wisdom, offered to her in sincere friendship.

"I believe each one of us has a purpose in life—one that reaches far beyond the confines of this world and echoes into eternity. We must each decide what path we will follow and then walk that road with determination and conviction. You must choose your own way. No one else can decide on your behalf. It's not an easy question for any of us to answer. But I'm certain of this one thing. If you follow your heart and remain true to yourself, you'll have no regrets, now or in the life to come."

As Fiona walked, step by step, closer to her rendezvous with fate, her hand instinctively fumbled for the little leather pouch that had hung on her belt for as long as she could remember. Yet it was missing. The one thing she longed to have at her side, her little bag of treasures, had been consumed by flames in the crannog, taking her memories up into the heavens as a burnt offering to the gods.

Eliavres would have chastised her for these childish sentiments. He was, no doubt, pleased the trinkets were gone. She remembered his words from the day he threw her treasures into the loch.

"These are mementos from a life that is gone. They can serve no purpose but to dredge up memories that are best forgotten. You are no longer that young woman. You are Fiona *Taghte*, the Chosen One. You shall be the goddess Brigid, the Bride of Bres. Your place is in the Otherworld. You *must* leave your former life behind."

Fiona *Taghte*. That's what people called her now. The Chosen One. She took two more steps and continued to scan the crowd for family and friends. The two faces she finally recognized were ones she would just as soon forget. Serlaid and Domhnull stood, arm in arm, just beyond the retinue of warrior guards. Her sister's last words flashed through her mind and cut her to the quick.

"See, little sister, he chose me after all. He chose *me.*"

Who indeed, then, had truly been the Chosen One? She looked at Domhnull now and wept inside for a love that had never been.

Fiona didn't allow her eyes to linger on the hurtful scene. Dwelling on unrequited love would do nothing but break her heart all over again. She turned her attention to the green carpet beneath her feet, and continued her march to the water's edge. She had to concentrate on something else, something stable, something she could rely on without question or doubt. She stole a furtive glance behind her back, and Bhatair Rhu caught her eye. He beamed with satisfaction and joy, and motioned her forward with a gesture of his hand.

The Arch Druid was the wisest man in all the land, and, no doubt, the most ancient. Surely he was someone she could count on. His advice and counsel had never changed, from the very moment they had met. He was the steersman whose steady hand was guiding her people to freedom. He was, unquestionably, one person on whom she could rely. His own words of challenge and encouragement echoed in her mind and urged her to continue down the path to her destiny.

"Do you understand what's at stake here? Do you truly comprehend the enormity of the circumstances facing us? *You* are the cornerstone upon which our whole strategy is built. Your preparation, and your dedication to this effort is of critical importance. Without you, the alliance crumbles. Without you, the eternal cycle falls out of balance and spirals out of control. The gods chose *you*. When you become a goddess—when you ascend to Brigid's throne—the impacts will ripple throughout time. This is not a casual act that can be taken lightly. This is the most important decision any human has made in a thousand years. The nailed god is not playing games. He is serious about preventing you from fulfilling your destiny. *You* must be equally determined to defeat him and his followers. The Romans will not leave this land without a fight. You've seen the consequences to our people if we lose. So *be* who you have been called to become. *You* are Fiona *Taghte*, and you will set your people free."

The memory filled Fiona with a renewed sense of purpose and restored her courage. She would follow the path laid before her. She would become who she was chosen to be. She mouthed the words to herself, "I am Fiona *Taghte*, and I will set my people free."

She approached the pier, a special bridge built for this occasion. It stretched out into the water and then just stopped. She was to proceed to its end and then continue on into the Otherworld. As she contemplated that final stride, she suddenly realized why she had been adorned with so many lavish ornaments. Once she took that last step, there would be no turning back. The weight of the iron would ensure she didn't change her mind and try to swim back to shore. And so the decision drew nearer with her every footfall. Within moments, she would have to be absolutely certain of her choice—to have the issue settled once and for all in her own mind. That's ultimately what mattered most.

Isn't that what Nandag had said? Nandag, whose affection for her was beyond any doubt. Her teacher's words came back to her with renewed force.

"Manas was right about one thing. This life confronts each of us with hard choices. But in the end, we must all make our own decisions. It's not about what others tell us to do or expect us to be. They can't make those choices for us. And if I know you, you'll do what you feel is right, no matter what the cost. You were never one to fear being different or going your own way. Trust your heart."

Suddenly, Fiona's thoughts were drawn back even farther, back to the very beginning, back to the day Nandag had consecrated her in the sacred pool as a healer in her clan. The words sounded almost prophetic, given all that had transpired since then. Every footstep down the pier gave her mentor's prescient observations an ever more ominous tone.

"Though your touch brings healing, your methods will frighten many. Some would call you *bana-bhuidseach* and claim your powers come from the darkness. I know this is not true. Some will claim your abilities are a curse and will fear you, but I believe they are a gift. I can see that you are touched by the gods, but I cannot discern your path."

Nandag had paused before continuing, and Fiona remembered the moment with absolute clarity now. "We dare not conduct this holy consecration before your family and friends, as is our custom. Yet I cannot withhold from you what Brigid, herself, has bestowed. You are a healer of your clan. I charge you to bring your skill to all those in need, to deny no one out of hatred or scorn, to seek only good, and to do no harm." Then Nandag's final words sent a chill up Fiona's spine and raised goose bumps on her flesh. "You hold the lives of your people in your hands, from newborn *bairne* to warrior chief. It is a sacred trust."

Fiona reached the last plank in her walk down the pier and came to a stop. A hush fell over the assembled crowd, but none of that mattered anymore. They all faded from her consciousness and vanished from her thoughts. She stood alone at the precipice of eternity, and not another soul existed in all of space or time.

Fiona gazed across the pond at the mill house as if she were in a trance. The steady turning water wheel was the only moving thing in her view. The clear blue sky, the lush green trees, and even the mill itself reflected off the surface of the pond, giving her two different pictures of the world around her. The sun shone down, not in the intense, oppressive strength of mid-summer, but with a gentler warmth that soothed her soul. A slight breeze in the air caused small ripples on the surface of the pond, transforming the reflected image in subtle ways that made the whole scene less surreal, less abstract— more tangible and present for her.

Fiona focused on the turning water wheel. Its steady, rhythmic chant helped buoy her spirits ever so slightly. Inside, the millstone turned just as steadily to grind kernels of grain into the fine powder she had so often used to make oatcakes or bread or chowder broth. There was certainty in the connection between the turning wheel and the stone and the grain that nourished. They were real, tangible things that linked together in a real, tangible world. She gazed at the water wheel. Swoosh. Swoosh. Lap. Lap. Steady. Certain. True.

Then a realization struck Fiona that resonated in her soul. She had been in this very spot before, peering across the same mirror-smooth pond at the very same mill house. It was the exact image she had experienced in her ordeals. The memory came rushing back in upon her like a flood. But this time, there was absolutely no doubt about whether the scene was real.

Then another thought swept through her mind, causing her limbs to shiver. This *was* the scene she had seen in her ordeals. It hadn't been real then, but it was real now. She had somehow peered into the future and glimpsed this very moment in time. Everything that had happened since then had occurred in order to make this vision come true. And so the question became even more compelling. Was she still Flora now? Or had she actually been Fiona all along?

She gazed down into the water beneath her feet and saw her own image staring back. Small strands of light brown hair leaked out from beneath the heather and mistletoe, and trickled down around the edges of her face. A faint flush colored her cheeks, even without the help of rouge. And her crystal blue eyes stared back into her own, as if they peered into her very soul. But something was different in the watercolor picture she saw below. All the black accoutrements shimmered as pure gold, and the dress in the image was changed. The one she wore was a deep red hue. But the one reflecting back in the water was pure white—as white as snow—as white as the petals of the flowers in a dream.

Fiona's breath caught in her throat and her father's last words came rushing back into her mind. "You're my girl, my wee *fauth*, and nothin' can ever change that. I love you, lass, not because of where you come from, but because of who you are."

Tears streamed down her cheeks, and a peace settled over her soul. In that moment, all the doubts and fears that had tormented her mind and ravaged her soul were gone. For the first time, perhaps in all her life, she was absolutely sure of who she was.

She stood tall, straightened her back, and stepped off the end of the pier. For a moment, she was the great owl from her dream, her wings wrapped around the eagle with its talons gripping her heart, falling faster and faster toward the millpond. And then the water of the pond reached out its silken hands and drew her body into its gentle embrace. She sank into its icy depths, her wedding ornaments pulling her relentlessly toward the bottom. But she didn't struggle or fight against the yawning blackness that lured her into its lair, for this was her destiny.

She opened her eyes and watched a stream of bubbles trickle from the corners of her mouth and float upward. It was like a surreal wonderland, and she savored the moments as if they were her last. All the worries of the world above were left behind and only the beauty remained. There was no longer any pain or sorrow or tears. The former things had passed away, and all that endured was purity and truth. She still did not know what the future would bring, or even if there would be a future for her at all. But for once, at last, she was certain of who she was.

With the final bit of air that remained in her lungs, she opened her mouth and spoke the words into the empty void of eternity, for no one's ears but her own.

"I - am - Flora."

I hope you have enjoyed reading *Daughter of the Gods*. Please leave a review on Amazon.com. Your feedback really matters.

FREE OFFER

What's true and what's fiction?

Get a free fact sheet that describes which elements of the story were true and which were created by the author.

Visit this link: https://BookHip.com/PXGNDCM

or scan this QR code with your phone:

EXPLORE FLORA'S WORLD

Find out more about the history, mythology, and geography of Flora's world by visiting bryanEcanter.com/florasworld.

Made in the USA
Las Vegas, NV
20 July 2024